PRAISE FOR THE OF SIMONE ST. JAMES

The Other Side of Midnight

"No one mixes romance, mystery, and that faint, spine-tingling sense of the supernatural, that curtain lifting in a breeze that isn't there, the hair prickling on the back of your neck, like Simone St. James. Her novels are the perfect combination of classic ghost story, historical fiction, and romantic suspense."
—Lauren Willig, author of the Pink Carnation series and *The Other Daughter*

"St. James stages a thoroughly gripping murder mystery. . . . St. James's intense story drips with atmosphere and emotion. Set in the time between world wars when spiritualist belief ran high, this briskly paced mystery offers action, romance, and a puzzle that proves talking to the dead isn't a game—and can be deadly."
—*Publishers Weekly*

"Simone St. James has once again crafted a headily atmospheric and suspenseful mystery that kept me reading until the wee hours."
—Jennifer Robson, author of *Somewhere in France* and *After the War Is Over*

"Lyrical writing, chilling ghost stories, complicated characters, and gripping mysteries are all contained in the wonderful books of Simone St. James."
—*RT Book Reviews* (top pick, 4½ stars)

"Simone St. James has created her own genre—historical gothic mystery romance, with more than a dash of the creepy."
—Susan Elia MacNeal, *New York Times* bestselling author of the Maggie Hope Mysteries

Silence for the Dead

"Kudos for Simone St. James. I was swept away by this atmospheric and truly spine-chilling page-turner. . . . If you love a good ghost story, you will be entranced."
—Mary Sharratt, author of *The Real Minerva* and *Daughters of the Witching Hill*

continued . . .

"A twenty-first-century version of Mary Stewart. . . . St. James layers the atmosphere with the requisite dread, and one can't help but read on. . . . Just the right mix of suspense, creepiness, and empathy." —*National Post* (Canada)

"Vivid, eerie, and atmospheric. St. James's latest will simultaneously tug at your heartstrings and send chills down your spine. Absolutely riveting."
—Anna Lee Huber, author of the Lady Darby Mysteries

"Aficionados of the classic gothic style in the tradition of Victoria Holt won't want to miss this atmospheric tale of romantic suspense." —*Library Journal*

An Inquiry into Love and Death

"At once an intriguing mystery and an eerie ghost story, it had more than enough spine-tingling moments to keep me gripped. The perfect book to curl up with by the fire on a stormy night . . . although perhaps not by yourself in an empty house!" —Katherine Webb, author of *The Unseen*

"Another chilling story. . . . St. James delivers a quickly paced read that will satisfy both new and old fans." —*Publishers Weekly*

"This is a perfectly balanced combination of mystery, romance, ghost story, and history." —*RT Book Reviews* (top pick, 4½ stars)

The Haunting of Maddy Clare

"Downright scary and atmospheric. I flew through the pages of this romantic and suspenseful period piece."
—Lisa Gardner, #1 *New York Times* bestselling author of *Crash & Burn*

"An inventively dark gothic ghost story. Read it with the lights on. Simply spellbinding."
—Susanna Kearsley, *New York Times* bestselling author of *A Desperate Fortune*

"A compelling read. With a strong setting, vivid supporting characters, and sympathetic protagonists. . . . Simone St. James is a talent to watch."

—Anne Stuart, *New York Times* bestselling author of *Consumed by Fire*

"A compelling and beautifully written debut full of mystery, emotion, and romance. . . . Great story, believable characters, wonderful writing—I couldn't put this down."

—Madeline Hunter, *New York Times* bestselling author of *His Wicked Reputation*

Other Books by Simone St. James

LOST AMONG
the LIVING

SIMONE
ST. JAMES

BERKLEY
New York

BERKLEY
An imprint of Penguin Random House LLC
penguinrandomhouse.com

The Library of Congress has catalogued the New American Library trade paperback edition of this book
as follows:

Names: St. James, Simone, author.
Title: Lost among the living/Simone St. James.
Description: New York, New York: New American Library, [2016]
Identifiers: LCCN 2015039480 I ISBN 9780451476197 (softcover)
Subjects: LCSH: Families—England—Fiction. I Family secrets—Fiction. I
BISAC: FICTION/Historical. I FICTION/Ghost. I FICTION/Romance/Gothic. I
GSAFD: Gothic fiction. I Mystery fiction. I Ghost stories.
Classification: LCC PR9199.4.S726 L67 2016 I DDC 813/.6—dc23
LC record available at http://lccn.loc.gov/2015039480

New American Library trade paperback edition / April 2016
Berkley trade paperback edition / September 2020

Printed in the United States of America

For Adam

ACKNOWLEDGMENTS

Many thanks to both of my editors on this book. To Ellen Edwards: Five books with you has been nothing short of an honor and a privilege. To Danielle Perez: I hope this will be the start of many great books together. Thanks as always to my agent, Pam Hopkins, for advising me in this crazy business. I give gratitude every day for my wonderful mother, brother, and sister—I love you all. Molly, Maureen, Tiffany, Sinead, Stephanie—you cannot know how you save my sanity on a regular basis. My extended family has been supportive from the very first. And, as always, Adam, this is not possible without you.

LOST AMONG
the LIVING

CHAPTER ONE

ENGLAND, 1921

By the time we left Calais, I thought perhaps I hated Dottie Forsyth. To the observer, I had no reason for it, since by employing me as her companion Dottie had saved me from both poverty and a life robbed of color in my rented flat, the life I was trying to live without Alex. However, the observer would not have had to spend the past three months criss-crossing Europe in her company, watching her scavenge for art as cheaply as possible while smoking her cigarettes in their long black holder.

"Manders," she said to me—though my name was Jo, one of her charms was the habit of calling me by my last name, as if I were the upstairs maid—"Mrs. Carter-Hayes wishes to see my photographs. Fetch my photograph book from my luggage, won't you? And do ask the porter if they serve sherry."

This as if we were on a luxurious transatlantic ocean liner, and not on a simple steamer over the Channel for the next three hours. Still, I rose to find the luggage, the photograph book, and the porter, my stomach turning in uneasy loops as I traveled the deck. The Channel wasn't entirely calm today, and the misty gray in the distance gave a hint of oncoming rain. The other passengers on the deck gave me only brief glances as I passed them. A girl in a wool skirt and a knitted cardigan is an unremarkable English sight, even if she's passably pretty.

I found the luggage compartment with the help of the porter, whose look of surprise turned to one of pity when I asked about the sherry, and from there I rummaged through Dottie's many bags and boxes, looking for the slender little photograph book with its yellowed pages. I didn't think Mrs. Carter-Hayes, who had been acquainted with Dottie for all of twenty minutes, had any real desire to see the photographs, but perhaps because of the pointlessness of the mission, I found myself lingering over it, taking longer than I needed to in the quiet and privacy of the luggage compartment. I tucked a lock of hair behind my ear and let out a breath, sitting on the floor with my back to one of Dottie's trunks. We were going back to England.

Without Alex, I had nothing there. I had nothing anywhere. I had given up my flat when I'd left with Dottie, taken the last of my belongings with me. There wasn't much. A few clothes, a few packets of beloved books I couldn't live without. I'd sold off all our furniture by then, and I'd even sold most of Alex's clothes, a wrench that still made me sick to my stomach. I wasn't afraid of poverty; before Alex had swept me into the grand adventure of our marriage, poverty had been all I knew, and it was as familiar to me now as the old cardigan I wore. There was no room for sentiment when you were poor.

The only fanciful thing I'd kept was Alex's camera, which I could have gotten a few pounds for but hadn't been able to part with. The camera had come with me on all of my travels, on every boat and train, though I hadn't even opened the case. If Dottie had noticed, she had made no comment.

And so my life in England now sat before me as a perfect blank. We were to go to Dottie's home in Sussex, a place I had never seen. I was to stay on in Dottie's pay, even though she was no longer traveling and my duties had not been explained. When she had first written me, declaring starkly that she was Alex's aunt, that she'd heard I was in London, and that she was in need of a female companion for her travels to the Continent, I'd imagined playing kindly nursemaid to an undemanding old lady, serving her tea and reading Dickens and Collins aloud as she nodded off. Dottie, with her scraped-back hair, harsh judgments, and grasping pursuit of money, had been something of a shock.

I tried to picture primroses, hedgerows, and soft, chilled rain. No more hotels, smoke-filled dining cars, resentful waiters, or searches through unfamiliar cities for just the right tonic water or stomach remedy. No more sweltering days at the Colosseum or the Eiffel Tower, watching tourists blithely lead their children and snap photographs as if we'd never had a war. No more seeing the names of battlefields on train departure boards and wondering if that one—or that one, or that one—held Alex's body forgotten somewhere beneath its newly grown grass.

I would have to visit Mother once I was back; there was no escaping it. And I did not relish living on another woman's charity, something I had never done. But at least at Dottie's home I would be able to avoid London, and all of the places Alex and I had been. Everything about London since he'd gone to war the last time had stabbed me. I never wished to see it again.

Eventually I gave up the musty silence of the luggage compartment and returned to the deck, photograph book in hand. "What took so long?" Dottie demanded as I approached. She was sitting in a wooden folding chair, her cloche hat pulled down against the wind and her feet in their practical oxfords crossed at the ankles. She looked up at me, frowning, and though the cloudy light softened the edges of her features, I was not fooled.

"They don't serve sherry here," I said in reply, handing her the book.

Dottie's eyes narrowed perceptibly. I thought she often convinced herself that I was lying to her, though she could not quite figure out exactly when or why. "Sherry would have been most *convenient*," she said.

"Yes," I agreed. "I know."

She turned to her companion, a fortyish woman with a wide-brimmed hat, sitting on the folding chair next to hers and already looking as if she wished to escape. "This is my companion," she said, and I knew from her tone that she intended to direct some derision at me. "She's the widow of my dear nephew Alex, poor thing. He died in the war and left her without children."

Mrs. Carter-Hayes swallowed. "Oh, dear." She looked at me and flashed a sympathetic smile, an expression that was so genuine and kind that I almost pitied her for the next three hours she'd have to suffer in Dottie's company. When Dottie was in a mood like this, she took no prisoners—and she'd been in this mood more and more often the closer we came to England.

"Can you imagine?" Dottie exclaimed. "It was a terrible loss to our family. He was a wonderful young man, our Alex, as I know well, since I helped raise him. He spent several years of his childhood living with me at Wych Elm House."

Her glance cut to me, and in its gleam of triumph I knew that my shock showed on my face. Dottie smiled sweetly. "Didn't he tell you, Manders? Goodness, men are so forgetful. But then, you weren't together all that long." She turned back to the bewildered Mrs. Carter-Hayes. "Children are life's greatest joy, don't you agree?"

It would go on like this, I knew, until we docked: Dottie speaking in innuendoes and double meanings, cloaked in polite small talk. I moved away and stood by the rail—there was no folding chair for me—and let the noise of the wind blow the words away. I hadn't bothered with a hat, and I felt my curls come loose from their knot and touch my face, my hair tangling and my cheeks chapping as I watched the water sightlessly.

This wasn't her only mood; it was just one of them, though it was the most vicious and unhappy. Over the last three months I had learned to navigate the maze of Dottie's ups and downs, a task I'd learned naturally, as I was well versed in unhappiness myself. She was fiftyish, her body narrow and strangely muscular, her face with its gray-brown frame of meticulously pinned-back hair naturally sleek, with a pointed chin. She looked nothing like Alex, though she was his mother's sister. She was not vain and never resorted to powders or lipsticks, which would have looked absurd on her tanned skin and narrow line of a mouth. She ate little, walked often, and kept her hair tidy and her clothes mysteriously immaculate, even when traveling. All the better for chasing and devouring her prey.

I glanced back at her and found that she was now displaying the photographs to Mrs. Carter-Hayes. She kept six or seven of them in the slender photograph book, on hand for occasions in which she had cornered a stranger and wished to show off. From the softening of Dottie's features I could tell that she was looking at the picture of her son, Martin, in his officer's uniform. I had seen the photograph many times, and I had heard the accompanying narrative just as often. *He is coming home to be married. He is such a dear boy, my son.* The listeners were always too polite, or too bored, to question the fact that the war had ended three years ago, yet Dottie Forsyth's son was only now coming home. That she still showed the photograph of Martin in uniform, as if she hadn't seen him since it was taken.

There had been a daughter, too—I knew that much from Alex. *My queer cousin Fran,* he had said, in one of the few times he had referred to this side of the family at all. Queer cousin Fran had died in 1917, though Alex's letter from the Front had not said how or why. *She has died, poor thing,* he wrote. *Are the rations as bad back home as I hear?* He never spoke of her again, and in the months I'd worked for her, Dottie had never mentioned her queer daughter Fran at all. Her photograph was certainly not in the book.

I turned back to the water. I should quit. I should have done it long ago. The position was unpleasant and demeaning. I had been a typist before I married Alex, before my life had been blown upward like a feather, then come down again. My skills were now rusty, but it was 1921, and girls found jobs all the time. I could try Newcastle, Manchester, Leeds. They must need typists there. It wouldn't be much of a life, but I would be fed and clothed, with Mother's fees paid for, and I could stay pleasantly numb.

But I would not quit. I knew it and, I believed, so did Dottie. It wasn't the pay she gave me, which was small and sporadic. It wasn't the travel, which had simply seemed like a nightmare to me, as if I were taking the train across a vast wartime graveyard, the bombed buildings just losing their char, the bodies buried just beneath the surface of the still-shattered fields. I would not quit because Dottie, viperish as she was, was my last link to Alex. And though it hurt me even to think of him, I could not let him go.

I had last seen him in early 1918, home on leave before he went back to France to fly more RAF missions, the final one from which he did not return. His plane was found four days later, crashed behind enemy lines. There was no body. The pack containing his parachute was missing. He had not appeared on any German prisoner-of-war rosters, any burial details, any death lists. He had not been a patient in any known hospital. The Red Cross, in the chaos after Armistice, did not have him on any prisoner or refugee lists. In three years there had been no telegram, no cry for help, no sighting of him. He had vanished. My life had vanished with him.

He died in the war, Dottie had said, but it was just another sting of hers. According to the official record, my husband had not died in the war. When there is a body, a grave, then a person has died. But no one ever tells you: When you have nothing but thin air, what happens then? Are you a widow, when there is nothing but a gaping hole in what used to be your life? Who are you, exactly? For three years I had been trapped in amber—first in my fear and uncertainty, and then in a slow, chilling exhale of eventual, inexorable grief.

As long as I was with Dottie, part of me was Alex's wife. He still existed, even if only in the form of Dottie's innuendoes and recriminations. Just hearing someone—anyone—say his name aloud was a balm I could not let go of. I had followed her across Europe for it, and now I would follow her to Wych Elm House, her family home. Where Alex had lived part of his childhood, something he had never thought to tell me.

I stared out to sea, uneasy, as England loomed on the horizon.

CHAPTER TWO

When she'd hired me, I had assumed Dottie's trip to the Continent was a pleasure jaunt, the sort of thing rich middle-aged women did for no reason. By the time we arrived in Rome, I understood that my employer's aim was entirely different: Though she was already richer than I could ever be, Dottie was in business to make money.

The war, Dottie explained to me as we sat in a train carriage and she inserted a cigarette into its holder, had created a great many ruined and cash-starved denizens of the upper class. The smart ones had invested in arms factories and army supplies when war broke out. The foolish ones, the ones who had sat on their ancient piles of property and waited for the old world to right itself, had lost, and Dottie meant to take advantage of it.

Her currency, her Great White Whale, was art. Paintings, sculptures, sketches, from shards of ancient Greek masterpieces to rolled-up canvases by the geniuses of the last century—all of it could be found on the Continent, owned by someone who was desperate for money. And money was something Dottie had. She offered them low prices for the contents of their galleries, paid in cash, and was slowly building a stockpile of art that would be priceless once the postwar depression lost its hold, as she believed it would.

"But you already have money," I said that day in the train car. "You're going to a lot of trouble."

"Pay attention, Manders," she said, gesturing for me to light a match for her cigarette. "Look around you at these people. Look at what's become of them when I come to call. Rich old families—centuries old, some of them. My family is younger than theirs, and so is my money. The lesson is that we have money now, but we have no idea what will happen to us in ten years, or twenty." She took a puff of the cigarette as I shook out the match. "I have no intention of letting anything of the sort happen to my son, or to his children. You can never have too much money. Perhaps that makes me avaricious; I suppose it does." She took another drag and regarded me. "If my sister had had a little more avarice when she married and had Alex, you wouldn't be in the situation you're in now."

Another of her stings, but it was true. I thought of her words now as I sat on a different train months later, this one traveling from London to Hertford. Alex's mother had gone against her parents' wishes and married an unsuitable man—she'd lived in a state of happiness and limited funds as her husband had begun to see success, until both had died unexpectedly when Alex was young, leaving him orphaned. The subsequent years had drained the little money they had left, and now it was gone.

I stared out the window of the third-class car, unseeing. I was back in England, just as I'd dreaded. I'd been given two days off, enough time to travel up to see Mother in Hertford, stay the night, and return to London, where Dottie was spending the time arranging for the delivery of her looted pieces and seeing them on to Wych Elm House.

Dottie must know all about Mother; I assumed it, though we had never spoken of it. She would make it a point to know everything about me. She could not possibly have approved of someone like me marrying into her precious family—someone who did not even know who her father was, whose mother was committed to a hospital for the insane. And yet, for all her poking and prying at me in her moods, she never threw those particular flaws in my face. She was strangely tolerant of the fact that my mother was incurably mad, that I needed days off to visit her in the hospital whose fees I paid from my salary. I asked no questions and took the reprieve of silence, since Mother was a topic I had no wish to dissect under Dottie's blunt lens.

"She's doing well today," the nurse said to me as she led me to the visiting room. "We're being ordered around like a set of ladies' maids." She gave me a smile.

I smiled politely back. So it was to be Mother's Lady of the Manor mood, as I called it. I'd seen it many times. It was puzzling and some-times irritating, but at least it was one of her calmer phases.

Mother sat in a wicker chair in the visiting room, staring out the window at the garden. She wore a gingham dress and soft slippers, her long hair tied in a loose braid down her back. She'd been given a robe, presumably because she'd complained of cold at some now-forgotten moment, and she'd left it crumpled on the floor at her feet. She was forty-six by my last count, but her skin looked younger, and her slumped shoulders and her narrow, fidgeting hands looked older. She turned her large brown eyes to me as I came in the room.

"Here's your visitor," the nurse said to her as I put down my hand-bag and lowered myself into the chair across from her.

"How lovely," Mother said.

The hospital was situated in a former private estate, on a green hill in the countryside. It had pretty grounds and rustic shutters on the windows. The view was of the rolling countryside falling away, dotted with trees, hedgerows, and fences. The nurses spoke softly and did not shout. There were no locks, restraints, or cold-water baths. I could have put her somewhere cheaper, but instead I used most of my money to keep her here, where she'd been since I was eighteen.

She gave me a smile now, polite and frozen. Her skin was flawless, translucent in the light coming through the window. As so often happened, she did not recognize me.

"I'm your daughter," I said gently to her as the nurse left the room.

Something flickered briefly across her face, tightened the skin between her eyes, and was gone again. "Please have some tea," she said graciously. "I've asked the maids to bring it."

I did not need to look around the visiting room to see there was no tea and there were no maids. "That's very kind," I said. "I'm sorry I've been away for a while."

"Have you?" said Mother. "How very interesting."

Even in a madhouse, my mother's beauty was a sight to see. She had deep cocoa brown eyes, a pointed chin, and a nose that was small and feminine. I had not inherited her looks—my own eyes were set straight beneath dark arched brows, my nose was unapologetically normal, and under bright light I had a faint patter of freckles on my upper cheekbones, which I did not cover with powder. My hair was dark and wild where hers was honey-colored and soft as cashmere. I must have received my looks from my father, though I would never know. Mother had never told me who my father was; if she knew the answer anymore, she was not saying.

It had been just the two of us, my mother and me, for all of my childhood, moving from place to place in the shabbier parts of London. Mother worked whatever sporadic jobs she could to support us: waitress, artist's model, bit player at the theater, ticket girl at the cinema when the first one opened near our shared flat. I kept house, did the cooking, took care of the practicalities, and tried to go to school. We'd cobbled together food and shelter, somehow, for the first eighteen years of my life. When she was lucid, it was hard, but it was manageable. When she wasn't—which was more and more frequently as time went on—I existed in a sort of blind panic, unable to think or breathe, pulling myself from one minute to the next, one hour to the next, waiting for some inevitable, terrible outcome, yet fighting it.

I never knew when she'd vanish in the middle of the night. I never knew when I'd come home to find her crumpled on the floor, sobbing that she didn't want to live anymore. I never knew when a strange man would come knocking on the door, claiming that Mother had been bothering him and she had to stop before he called the police, or when she'd spend days in bed, unable to get up, even to go to her paying job before she was dismissed. I never knew when she was lying to me—she'd find a photograph of a stranger and tell me it was my father, or she'd tell me of the days she'd traveled with the circus, dancing for the audiences in tights and a pretty tiara.

The police actually had come to the door a handful of times, always after one of Mother's spells. Vagrancy was one of her sins, wandering the streets and laughing quietly to herself. Petty theft was another—once she was in a state, she could not tell the difference between what was hers and what was not, and would pick up items and walk away with them, certain they belonged to her. And sometimes she fixated on a man, followed him and looked in his windows, convinced he was her imaginary lover or the man who would take her away.

She was always sorry, so sorry, when her mind returned. *I'm not fit for you,* she'd say, stroking my hair and holding me. *I'll do better, my good, sweet girl.* And she would, for a time—she'd work industriously, help with the cooking and the cleaning, encourage me to study, laugh with me over the day's absurdities. And then I'd wake in the night to find her gone, and it was happening all over again. And again.

At eighteen, I'd scraped up the money to take a typing course. I worked hard at it, and I excelled. Soon I'd be earning my own money, and things would get better. But I came home from class one day to find the police in our flat once again. Mother had been caught trying to take a fur stole from a ladies' garment store, claiming she needed it for a trip to Russia. The stole was worth a lot of money, and the store wanted to press charges. She had to go away, the policeman explained to me, not without pity in his eyes, or face prosecution.

It was the thing I had feared all these years, the outcome that had stolen my breath and my sleep over countless nights. Exhausted and numb, I gave in—but still, I fought for her. I got a job and used the money to give her the best care I could. Always, always, I fought.

And now she sat across from me, years later, the blank look on her face saying that she did not recognize me at all.

"Did you finish *Ivanhoe*?" I asked her. "They were reading it to you when I visited last."

Mother looked back out the window, where a gardener was working on the grounds. As she turned her head, I could see the red marks of scratches on her neck, just above her collar. "I have told him repeatedly that the roses are too dry," she complained. "He never listens. I may have to dismiss him. It's so hard to find good help, don't you think?"

"Mother, have you been scratching yourself?"

Her voice turned icy, and still she looked out the window. "I have no idea what you mean."

I sighed and leaned back in my seat, checked my watch. I'd have to ask the staff about the scratches—they were supposed to be watching her more closely. Had she made them herself, or had she been in an altercation with another patient? I pondered for a moment over which was most likely, but I couldn't decide.

I looked up again to find Mother staring at me, her gaze wide and clear.

"Joanna," she said.

I froze in surprise. It had been years since she'd said my name.

"Hello, Mother," I replied cautiously. "It's me."

"I worry about you," Mother said, pressing her fingertips to her porcelain temple and frowning. "All the time, all the time, I worry."

I frowned. Did she mean now, or was she remembering some worry in the past? "You needn't. I'm quite all right."

"Where is that man you married?"

This was another surprise. I could not follow the quicksilver paths of Mother's mind, her rapid drops down the rabbit hole. Alex had come with me twice to visit her, and though Mother had given him the same blank reaction she gave me, he'd made such an impression on her that the memory of him still bubbled up from time to time.

"He's waiting in the motorcar," I answered her. They'd told me it wasn't a good idea to shock her, especially with talk of death, so when she asked me about Alex I always pretended he was alive.

"He should come in," Mother said. "It's impolite to leave a guest outside."

"He has a cold," I replied. "He doesn't want you to catch it. He'll come in next time, I promise."

"Is he very sick?"

I shrugged. "You know how men are. There's a big drama about it, but in a few days he'll be well again." I said it as though I were any other wife, who had her husband home every day to get underfoot.

Mother blinked at me; she had never had a husband and had no idea what I meant. "He's very good-looking," she said. "The man you married. Isn't he?"

"Yes." I forced the words from my throat. "He is."

She opened her mouth as if to say something else, then closed it and looked out the window again, the scratches visible on her neck.

I waited. The mention of Alex, the pretense that he was outside in the motorcar and not dead these three years, hit me with a stab of pain. I wondered if that pain was my destiny, if it would ever ease. In a sharp slice of self-hatred I wished I could change places with Mother, who did not know there had been a war, did not know Alex had jumped from his airplane and disappeared. Even though she groped for the line between fact and fiction like a blind man gropes through a room, still she thought that if I said Alex waited in the motorcar, then he must be there: alive and vibrant, the brim of his hat pulled down over his handsome forehead as he leaned back in the seat, wearing an overcoat and a pair of leather driving gloves I'd bought him for Christmas, dabbing his nose with a handkerchief pulled from his pocket. For Mother, it could be real.

"That skirt," Mother said, turning back to me again. "It's plaid. So unbecoming. And that cardigan. You should dress more nicely for him."

Reflexively, my hand smoothed my skirt in my lap. For three years, I hadn't cared how I dressed. "Alex likes how I look."

"No man likes that," Mother said, and for a single moment the Lady of the Manor was gone and Nell Christopher stared at me. "It isn't enough just to *marry* the man, Joanna. You have to *keep* him."

"I *did* keep him," I protested, the words out of my mouth before I could remember I was arguing with a madwoman. "He loved me. He was mine." Until he wasn't. Not ever again.

"You're not listening," she said. If she noticed that I had used the past tense when talking of Alex, she did not let on. "No man is ever yours, not entirely. You must make an *effort*." She glanced around the room. "Goodness. What time is it?"

I looked at my watch again, my heart sinking at her absent tone. "Four o'clock."

"Oh, dear. I'm terribly sorry, but I must cut our visit just a little short. The viscount is coming, you see."

"Today?" I said in dismay. "Now?"

"Yes. He'll be here any minute." Her eyes had gone blank again, just like that, looking at something I couldn't see. "He's taking me to Egypt. It's going to be a grand adventure!"

The viscount—he'd never been given a name that I'd heard—was one of Mother's favorite fictions, a wealthy man who was always on the verge of arriving and taking her away. He usually made an appearance when Mother was stressed or confused, or when she simply wished to exit a conversation. Once he was fixed in her mind, she would talk of nothing else for hours, sometimes days. It was a trip to Russia with the viscount that caused Mother to steal the fur stole from the ladies' shop when I was eighteen.

The brief glimpse of Nell Christopher was gone, and I wasn't sure I would see it again. The thought was painful and almost a relief at the same time.

"Mother," I said, knowing she would not hear me, "the viscount is not coming."

"He is!" When she was happy, she glowed with beauty. "He will be here soon. I'm not dressed properly. Where are my maids? I have to get ready." She pulled back her sleeve and, right there before my eyes, she dug her nails into the soft skin of her arm just below the wrist and dragged them, putting red grooves into the white flesh as her gaze stayed far away.

I jerked out of my seat, shocked. I called for the nurse; she took Mother away, letting her believe she was going off to prepare for the viscount's arrival, giving me an apologetic look. "This has just started," she said quietly to me. "It's been reported to the doctors. A spell of rest seems to help."

I stared at Mother's retreating back in its faded gingham dress. "I'll come back . . ." I meant to say *soon*, but I realized that I was traveling to Wych Elm House tomorrow and had no idea when I'd be back again. "I'll come back." Mother did not acknowledge me.

Outside, I turned my steps toward the small hotel where I always stayed during my visits to Mother, erasing the hospital smells with the brisk outside air and listening to the birds chatter their end-of-day conversation. I had gone several blocks when a wave of sweaty, nauseated feeling came over me, so fierce it made me dizzy, my eyes burning with tears. I stopped and sat on a bench, sagging like a wilting plant. I was twenty-six, and in that suffocating cloud of sadness I felt that I had no fight left in me. I felt like an old woman.

Surprisingly, it was Dottie's face that came into my mind, her eyes narrowed, her mouth expressing disgust with only the slightest movement of her thin lips. *Pay attention, Manders. Look sharp. No girl ever got anywhere by sitting and moping on a public bench.* I made a low sound of self-pity, but I straightened and leaned against the back of my seat, watching the few passersby and taking a deep breath. What was there to do, after all? Quit being Jo Manders, *nee* Christopher, of no fixed address? There was no way to resign. One's mother went mad, and one's husband leaped from a plane into thin air, and one simply got on with it.

I went back to my hotel, where I drank a cup of tea, lay on the narrow bed in my underwear, and read D. H. Lawrence by lamplight until I fell asleep. The next morning, I took the train to London.

Dottie met me at the station, wearing a new suit—an olive green skirt and matching coat with gold buttons, like a military uniform. She gave me one of her hard, appraising glances, taking in my gray wool skirt, my cream blouse with its wide collar, the light gray cardigan trimmed with satin that I'd tossed over it. Her gaze narrowed on my dark curls, which escaped from their knot no matter how hard I tried, my scrubbed-clean face, my impassive expression. She nearly dismissed me as usual without comment, but almost grudgingly, something made her say, "She is well?"

I hid my shock and shrugged. "As well as can be expected."

Something thoughtful flickered across Dottie's gaze, but she shut it down quickly and looked away, snatching up her handbag as if I'd made to steal it. "Come along, Manders," she said. "The car is waiting."

CHAPTER THREE

Dottie had a car and driver to take us to Sussex. I must have been more exhausted than I thought, because I fell asleep almost instantly, the warmth and the hum of the motor sending me into oblivion. I awoke slouched into the corner of my seat, my arms crossed, hugging my cardigan to my body. Dottie was sitting upright, a leather notebook across her lap, going through a stack of papers with a pen in her hand.

"We will be at Wych Elm House in just under thirty minutes," she said to me as my eyes opened, though she had not looked at me. She checked the watch on her narrow wrist and reconfirmed to herself. "My husband, Robert, will be there. He has come home for Martin's return."

I sat up in silent surprise. In the months I had traveled with Dottie, she had never mentioned a husband. Logic dictated she must have one, of course, since she had children, but he had never once figured in the conversation, even in passing. I had assumed him long dead.

Dottie stared at the seat back in front of her, searching in her brain for something. Her jaw flexed and her hand twitched on the pages. "I cannot emphasize enough, Manders," she said slowly, "that you must behave properly at Wych Elm House."

I rubbed a hand over my eyes, wondering what in the world she was getting at. "I always behave properly," I replied. "I've never given you cause to complain."

"Don't be a fool, Manders," she snapped. "We are not in Europe anymore."

I stared at her, trying to parse her meaning. Was she implying I had loose morals? People sometimes did, because of Mother. I opened my mouth to protest, offended, but stopped, watching her.

She dropped her gaze to the papers again, signed one of them with a flourish. "He will tell you that his behavior does not matter. Do not believe him." The page disappeared with a flick of the wrist, and another replaced it. "It does not matter that you were Alex's wife. If you give Robert even the slightest encouragement, I will dismiss you and you will no longer be connected to this family."

It was absurd, insulting—that she thought I would somehow misbehave with her husband under her roof. But I could see the misery carefully disguised in the lines of Dottie's face. It pained her, humiliated her, to speak of this at all. She had become more tense and unhappy the closer we traveled to her home. This homecoming, I realized, was not exactly going to be the joyous one she'd likely described to Mrs. Carter-Hayes as we crossed the Channel. It gave me a jolt to think that hers might be a family even unhappier than my own.

"I understand," I said.

She signed another paper, flipped the page again. "Martin arrives tomorrow morning." Again, her voice was grim, so unlike the cloying tone she'd used when she'd shown her son's photograph on the boat from Calais. "He had a health problem that affected his nerves after the war and has been in a spa in Switzerland."

So the husband was a lech, and the son was a madman fresh from the asylum. No wonder Dottie had been sparse with details until now, when she had me captive in the motorcar, unable to run screaming.

And I still knew nothing about queer cousin Fran. "It's nice that he's coming home," I managed.

"I do not want any distressing subjects raised in the presence of my son," she said as if I hadn't spoken. "The war is not to be mentioned. Alex is not to be mentioned—Martin liked Alex a great deal and found his death upsetting. If he asks you about it, I expect you to deflect him and change the subject."

"All right," I replied, unable to think of anything more repellent than discussing my husband with a man who had lost his senses. The conversation with Mother had been more than enough. I studied my thumbnail, scraping a fingernail along it and rethinking my decision not to live in poverty in London. "What exactly will my duties be?"

She glanced at me for the first time, then directed her gaze back down to her papers. "You are to accompany me throughout the day and assist me. I expect you to report to me at eight o'clock every morning, at breakfast. I will be meeting with artwork buyers and negotiating with them. You are not expected to make conversation—in fact, the less you speak, the happier I will be. Your job will be to serve tea and help me manage my correspondence. I understand you have typing skills."

"Yes," I replied. "I can type. But I have never served tea."

She gave me a glare that plainly said I was stupid. "It isn't hard, Manders. Just try not to spill it." She leaned back in her seat. "Aside from selling the pieces I've bought, I will also be busy planning Martin's engagement and wedding."

I frowned, confused. "Who is Martin engaged to, if he's been in a spa?" If she wanted to call it a spa, I would go along with it.

"He is not yet engaged. I believe I have mentioned that he is coming home to marry."

"Yes," I said slowly. The sequence seemed backward to me. "I thought you needed a fiancée in order to have an engagement."

Dottie dismissed this detail with a flick of her hand. "I will take care of it," she said, and as I sat gaping at her, she picked up her pen and continued. "There will be some afternoons when I will not require you, and you will be released for free time. After six o'clock, unless I have a special requirement, your evenings are your own."

I looked out the window at the woodland passing by, thinking about long evenings alone as the autumn stretched into winter. "It seems isolated."

"There is a town less than an hour's walk away," Dottie replied. "It's possible you can use the car and driver, if they are free. There is a lending library, I understand."

It was a generous offer, most unlike Dottie. I turned to her, ready for once to be friendly, but she wasn't looking at me. She was staring ahead, her papers forgotten. She pulled out her long cigarette holder, attached a cigarette to it, and lit it, right there in the motorcar, creating a foul fug of smoke. She had forgotten me, and she had certainly forgotten the driver, who had never registered to her at all. Her gaze clouded, and something about the look on her face chilled me.

The Dottie I had spent three months with in Europe had been disagreeable, but she had been energetic and edgy, unable to sit still. I now saw that that woman had actually been the happier version of herself— marshaling her luggage from train platform to train platform, negotiating with hotel clerks, clipping briskly down cobblestoned streets with a map in her hand and a cigarette between her lips, haggling for hours over works of art. In her way, she had seemed to thrive. This still moodiness, this introspective unhappiness, was new, and it made me uneasy, because clearly something at Wych Elm House was the cause of it.

In silence I followed her gaze, tearing my own gaze away from her profile. She was staring past the driver and through the front windshield, where, as the thick trees parted and we juddered along the unpaved drive, a house was coming into view.

Dottie took a long, slow drag of her cigarette, exhaling smoke like a dragon. She blinked slowly, the lines of her face settling into tension, and when she opened her eyes again, they were shuttered, impenetrable, whatever had been on the surface sinking back into the depths again.

"Well, then," she said to no one in particular. "There it is. Home."

CHAPTER FOUR

It just looked like a house to me. Big, with buttery yellow brick and gables and large, double front doors at the head of a circular drive. The center of the building, above the entrance, was crowned with a high gable, thrusting upward through the canopy of trees. It was not one of those rolling, manicured estates you saw in newsreels of the royal family, the kind of place that had been there for centuries, attended by throngs of gardeners. Instead it was an expensive house built in a tangle of woods, dappled by the encroaching trees that tapped the roof, surrounded by browning thickets of brush adorned with dying flowers. It had a forlorn air of emptiness to it. The house itself worked to impress with its rich blood, but if a gardener had been here, it wasn't for a very long time.

The driver helped me from the motorcar, and as I straightened, a full breath of brisk country September air hit my nose. It smelled like dead leaves and brisk sap, and it was strangely cold. I was used to the woolly heat of a European summer mixed with the stale air of travel and the eternal stink of London. I took another breath and fancied I caught a whiff of the sea.

Dottie, papers clutched under her arm, discarded her cigarette and marched up the steps to the house. She vanished inside without a backward look at me. I followed her, hurrying to keep up, and came through the front door with an ungraceful clatter. I had nothing but my handbag with me, as our luggage was following in a separate van.

The front hall was dim, the only light coming indirectly from the high windows in the adjacent room, to which glass doors were thrown open. I glimpsed an umbrella stand, a sideboard, floors of dark wood covered with clean, matched rugs, a few mediocre paintings of landscapes on the walls. It was dusted and tidy, the air smelling close, with the pungent edge of cleaning vinegar. There were no coats thrown carelessly over hooks, or hats hung by the door, or any other signs of people coming and going. I realized that with Dottie in Europe, her husband God knew where, and her son in a hospital, no one had actually lived here for some time.

I followed the sound of Dottie's clunking oxfords down the corridor, past a sitting room and a study, a small parlor with uncomfortable antique chairs squeezed into an awkward arrangement, where a maid, bent over with a dusting cloth, looked up surprised as I passed. The furniture everywhere looked immaculate and new, even the pieces in antique style, and each room seemed filled with expensive bric-a-brac— lamps with glass shades, ornate vases filled with expensive flowers freshly arranged, clocks and shepherdesses and brass lions and painted silk screens placed just so in corners. Dottie's acquisitions, I guessed, accumulated over the years. I had seen her in action, and she was very good at buying expensive things.

There was no time to stop and gape. Dottie would charge full speed wherever she wanted, then expect to turn and find me at her shoulder; she was like clockwork. I hurried faster.

I watched her spindly frame stop at the entrance to a dining room, pausing only a moment before she plunged over the threshold and inside. "I see you made it," I heard her say.

I followed her and found a man sitting alone at the dining table, a plate of beef and a glass of wine before him. He was fiftyish, trim, with light brown hair cut short and curling naturally. He had blue eyes in a face that made a fair attempt at handsome, though there was a tinge of dissipation around the edges of his features, like a piece of paper that has been foxed over time. He wore a suit of tawny brown that had been expertly tailored to his frame and a silk tie that gave a dull gleam in the electric light.

He did not rise, did not even put down his knife and fork, when Dottie came into the room. "Hello, Dottie," he said, his voice melodic and uninflected. He put his knife to the slice of beef. "I arrived barely an hour ago. Had the cook put something together, as I'm completely ravenous. Luckily she already had something nearly ready."

Dottie took another step into the room, so she was no longer standing in front of me. She was not wearing a hat or gloves, having dispensed with them in the car in order to work more comfortably, and now she looked lost, wishing for something convincing to fidget with. Her hands twitched on her papers. Her cigarette holder had already been slid back into her pocket. "I take it your journey was uneventful?" she asked, her gaze fixing on the man before her, then tearing away. "You were in Scotland, I believe."

"Hunting with some fellows, yes. We were having a good time until your wire interrupted it. And the journey was a bloody nuisance." He raised his gaze and saw me. "I beg your pardon," he said, still not lowering his eating utensils or standing. "We have not been introduced."

"This is Manders," Dottie said before I could speak. "My companion."

"Jo Manders," I broke in, just this once not wishing to hear myself spoken of as a last name, as if I had no identity of my own. Dottie gave me A Look, her eyes glaring like a spooked horse's, but I ignored her.

The man seemed to think over the name, going through possibilities in his head. "Alex's wife?" he finally asked.

"Yes," I replied.

His gaze flickered over me, up and down, his eyelids drooping carelessly, and I knew I'd just been categorized. My breasts, my hips, my waist, the length of my legs. I watched him note my unfashionably long hair, my unstylish clothes, until his gaze rested on my face, the blue eyes sharp and thoughtful. "You did not tell me you hired a companion, Dottie," he said. "Mrs. Manders. I'm Robert Forsyth, as my wife has neglected to tell you. It's nice to meet you. A little excitement is welcome, and we've always been curious here about the woman who ran Alex to ground."

"Is the house ready for Martin's return?" Dottie interrupted, her voice sharp, as I fumbled for a shocked reply.

Robert glanced at her and shrugged. "There's a housekeeper somewhere."

"When did she report? I asked her to begin work two days ago."

"I've no idea, do I?" Robert asked. "I've just arrived. Housekeepers are your domain."

"Martin docks tonight and takes the first train tomorrow. I told her which rooms to prepare. And there should be three maids as well."

"Then it's likely done," he replied, turning back to his slice of beef. "If there's a newspaper somewhere in this backwater, please have it brought to me. I'd like to know a little of what goes on in the world."

Dottie stood in strangled silence. Months apart, and her husband already found his plate more palatable than his wife. I could almost feel sorry for her. But then she turned to me, her cheeks flushed, and barked, "Why are you standing here? Go find the housekeeper and make sure everything is done, for God's sake."

I turned on my heel without a word and retreated down the hall, to the room where I'd seen the maid. She was not there. Instead, sitting in one of the chairs was a girl. She had dark blond hair tied up neatly at the back of her head, the pins of which I could see clearly, as she was angled away from me. She wore a dark gray dress and a string of small pearls around her neck. When I approached the doorway, she turned and looked at me through calm blue eyes. Her face was long, her forehead high, but she was strangely attractive. She looked about seventeen.

"Oh," I said in surprise. "I beg your pardon."

"Miss?"

I turned. The maid stood in the corridor behind me, duster in hand.

"Is there something I can assist you with?" the maid asked me, tilting to look over my shoulder.

"Yes, I just—" I turned to the girl in the chair again, confused, but the girl was gone. The chair stood empty, as did the rest of the room.

"Miss?" the maid said again.

"Where did she go?" I asked. "The girl. The one who was just here."

"I'm sorry, miss. I don't know quite what you mean?"

The room was certainly empty. So was the corridor, when I spun on my heel to look. There was no sound of footsteps. But I had *seen* her.

"I don't—" I stuttered. "I—"

"Perhaps you mean me, miss?" the maid asked. "I was dusting in that room not long ago."

I paused. It hadn't been the maid I'd seen—there was no question. I could still see the girl's face, the expression in her blue eyes beneath the high forehead as she regarded me. But to insist on it would make me sound like Mother, talking of her imaginary viscount. So I said, "Perhaps that's it. I'm sorry."

"It's nothing at all," the maid said, and she gave me a smile that was tentative and curious at the same time.

I pushed what I had just seen forcefully from my mind. "I'm Jo Manders, Mrs. Forsyth's companion," I said. "Can you tell me where the housekeeper is?"

Her smile relaxed a little. "Mrs. Bennett is in the kitchen, I believe, dealing with the wine. She was there half an hour ago."

"Are there other maids here besides yourself?" I asked, shakily remembering Dottie's directive.

"Two others, ma'am. All of us arrived the day before yesterday."

So there was no constant staff of loyal servants kept on at Wych Elm House while the family was not in residence. The entire staff seemed to be newly hired. I thanked the maid and found the door that led downstairs to the kitchen, but as I approached it, for some reason I heard the maid's steps behind me. I turned to tell her there was no need to follow me, but I found she was gone, and there was no one there at all.

In the kitchen I came upon two women over sixty, one of them sorting through a box of wine bottles and the other sitting in a chair at the kitchen table. When I entered, they dropped silent in embarrassment, and the seated woman made to rise.

"Please," I said. "I'm only Mrs. Forsyth's paid companion."

The woman promptly sat back down, and the two exchanged a brief look of surprise. It seemed Dottie had not bothered to tell anyone about me. As it was, I was stuck halfway between being a servant and a member of the family, which made everything awkward.

The woman with the wine bottles was Mrs. Bennett, the house-keeper, and the woman sitting down was Mrs. Perry, the cook. Both had tidy hair under caps and strong, rough hands. They were women of England's servant class, brisk and unshakable, who had likely been sweeping and dusting and pounding dough into pie crusts since they were thirteen. A class that was quickly vanishing into a world of tinned suppers and carpet-sweeping machines. They were wary at first, given my uncertain status, but since I had no desire to go back to Dottie after the nasty scene in the dining room, I pulled back a chair and sat at the kitchen table instead.

"I suppose you know Mrs. Forsyth very well, then," Mrs. Bennett said to me. Her tone was casual, but I knew she was fishing for information.

"Yes," I replied, thinking that as of today, I did not know Dottie at all.

"I've heard she can be a difficult mistress," Mrs. Perry said bluntly. "It doesn't frighten me. I've dealt with difficult mistresses before."

"So have I," Mrs. Bennett said. "In my last place, the mistress lost two children, one after the other. Both died at birth. She was never the same after that. It hits them hard, some women harder than others."

"I suppose," I said. She must be referring to queer cousin Fran.

"I'll never believe the things they say." Mrs. Perry lifted her chin disapprovingly. "I don't take to gossip."

Mrs. Bennett closed the box of wine bottles and made a dismissive shushing noise. "Tales to frighten children, that's all it is."

"What tales?" I asked.

Again the two women exchanged a look, but this time their professionalism overruled the need for gossip. "As I said," Mrs. Bennett repeated, "silly tales for children."

"Please," I said, suddenly ravenous to know. "Mrs. Forsyth never speaks of her death, and my husband wouldn't tell me."

It was Mrs. Perry who finally answered me. "The girl was mad," she said, her voice tight with disapproval. "They kept her locked up, out of sight, until one day she escaped her room. Jumped from the roof, she did, from the gable right up at the top of the house. She wasn't but fifteen."

For a long moment, I could not speak. The room receded. I remembered getting out of the motorcar, looking up at the high gable. Walking across the cobblestoned path beneath it. *Dottie,* I thought, *no wonder you were unhappy to come home.*

Mrs. Perry broke in again, her voice grim. "A man died in the woods that same day," she said. "Some said the girl must have done it, though he was ripped to pieces, so I don't see how she could have done such a thing, mad or not. As I say, I don't take to gossip. They shut up the house after it happened, and all of them left. But now they're back, and we're to expect the son, who's been in a hospital. I hope he isn't going to be any trouble."

"If it's shell shock, he might be quiet as a lamb," Mrs. Bennett supplied. "I had one of those two employers ago. Barely said a word, the poor boy."

I pushed my chair back and stood. "I should go," I said. "Mrs. Forsyth will be looking for me."

"Tell her the rooms are prepared, just as she requested," Mrs. Bennett said to my retreating back.

I turned back and looked at her. "How many?" I asked, thinking of the girl I'd seen in the parlor, forcing the question from my throat. "How many bedrooms are prepared?"

Mrs. Bennett frowned, as if I were slow in the head. "Why, four, of course," she said. "For yourself, Mr. Martin, and Mr. and Mrs. Forsyth." Her lips pursed briefly. "They sleep separate."

I had nothing to say to that. I turned in silence and left the room.

CHAPTER FIVE

My bedroom at Wych Elm House was on the second floor, overlooking the front of the house. I could see the circular drive
leading off into the trees, and the overgrown front lawn. It did not
escape me that my window was almost beneath the upper gable and
that my view was of where Frances Forsyth's body would have landed
the day she jumped.

Queer cousin Fran. She has died, poor thing.

That simple sentence of Alex's, one that hid so much. Perhaps he had
hoped to shield me from disturbing family news; perhaps he hadn't
wanted to put the distressing facts in a letter from the Front that would
be read by censors, strangers. Perhaps he'd been ashamed of Frances's
madness, the strain of insanity in his family, and he'd hidden it from me.

But Alex had known about Mother. He had met her. He knew
about the madness in *my* family. And he'd come home on leave in
early 1918, after Frances had died. Why hadn't he told me of it then?

They kept her locked up, out of sight.

I sat in my bedroom's window seat and pulled up my legs, hugging my knees, gazing out at the tangled landscape, a book unopened in my hand, as darkness fell and the house settled into silence. I could not complain about my room, which was nicer than any flat I had lived in—the furnishings were polished and expensive, including the high bed heaped with thick linens and the imposing walnut wardrobe that reached nearly to the ceiling. I almost did not want to touch the gleaming wainscoting or the expensive carpet, so perfect were they. My own modest trunk, lodged against the door of the wardrobe, looked shabby in comparison.

Alex and I had been as intimate, I'd thought, as two people could be. We'd married quickly—I supposed marrying a man two weeks after you'd met him even qualified as hasty—but we'd spent endless hours talking deep into the night, telling each other about our lives. He had been orphaned as a child. He had German relatives on his father's side— foreign blood was part of what made his father so unsuitable, according to his mother's family—and had spent some years with them. He had gone to Eton, then Oxford. He'd told me of his relatives in Sussex, but the family rift meant they were not close.

His was a slightly unusual life, due to his being orphaned, but it was not an overly strange one. A man from a good family, educated, brilliant, handsome, tall, and athletic—granted every privilege, on his way to becoming something breathtaking and splendid until the war had taken him. As it had taken so many others.

A mist had settled, sliding among the trees. I watched it dully, following its dirty gray smear as it moved across the darkness. I scraped a cold knuckle across the glass.

I could not countenance what I had seen today. That girl in the small parlor, the set of her thin shoulders, the way she had turned and looked at me. I wondered with a chill if somewhere in this house there was a photograph of Frances Forsyth. Whether that same face would look out at me if I found it.

No. That is Mother. That is not me. That was never me.

I had been the sane one, the one who saw that the rent was paid, the one who had gotten a job and married a good man. Mother was the one who saw things, not me.

A man was torn to pieces. They kept her locked up, out of sight.

The mist had stopped moving, I realized. It hovered in the woods, blurred among the trunks of the trees, still and cold. It almost seemed to be watching me. I stared out the window and watched back.

When I had packed up Alex's things, getting ready to leave for the Continent with Dottie, I had gone through his personal papers. I had found the usual dry things—bank records, school records, our marriage certificate, all the milestones of his life. But I had not found one memento. No letters, photographs, or journals. No postcards or souvenirs from vacations, no notebooks or letters from schoolmates. Not one.

The man I had married was gone.

I slid into the overweening bed late, and I slept badly. I dreamed of something falling past my window, the ruffle of a skirt and a sleeve, the fabric flashing as I startled awake. And somewhere in the dim place between waking and sleeping, I thought I heard soft footsteps in the corridor, tapping past my door.

I reported to Dottie at eight o'clock the next morning, as instructed. She was in the morning room, located at the back of the house, a warm room with glass French doors that opened out to the back terrace. The windows let in swaths of sunlight, bright and slightly chill. The sideboard was set with a variety of breakfast foods, steaming in large dishes and smelling thickly of sausage. Dottie sat alone at the table, straight as a needle, surrounded by an expensive tea set. Robert was nowhere to be seen.

I filled a plate with eggs and toast. Dottie checked her watch ostentatiously as I pulled out a chair and sat. She did not greet me, but gave me a prying glare. "I trust you have settled properly in your room," she said.

"Yes," I said, picking at my breakfast. "Thank you."

Her gaze raked me up and down. "Now that we are at Wych Elm House, I see that we will have to find you some new clothes. I will be meeting important people, and you will be with me. I cannot have you dressed like a fat schoolgirl."

I looked up at her. I was wearing a skirt and blouse again, with a cardigan. Part of me was offended—I was not in the least fat—and another part admired the deftness of the insult. Besides, she was right. I had looked well enough on European trains, but in the luxury of this house, I was as out of place as chipped china or an unpolished lamp. "My dresses are too old," I said.

"Then go into town and buy new ones. The dressmaker there will be able to send to London for anything she cannot supply. You'll need new stockings, too, and shoes. Tell the shopkeepers to put the items on my account."

"Thank you," I said, though I knew well that the items were not a gift. Dottie would extract repayment from my wages to the penny.

She gave me a nod, then stared at my hair. We had seen each other every day for three months, yet this morning she inspected me anew. "At least you don't wear cosmetics," she commented. "I don't approve of them. You must do your hair more tidily; have a maid assist you if you need it. Also, I warn you that I do not approve of the current fashion for bobbed hair. I think it's fast and horribly unattractive."

I touched the chignon at the back of my neck. Alex had always loved my long hair. "I have no desire to cut my hair."

"That is excellent news," came a voice from the doorway. Robert Forsyth came into the room, freshly bathed and clean-shaven, dressed in another well-cut suit. He gave me a wink. "Good morning, Mrs. Manders. Dottie." He moved to the sideboard and put food on a plate. "I've had a letter from the Dennistons," he said to Dottie before either of us could return his greeting. "They've heard of our return. I believe I'll drop over and pay a visit. Denniston has a first-rate stable, and my riding in Scotland was interrupted. I'll take my own motorcar."

"Robert," Dottie said, her voice low. "Martin comes today."

Robert poured himself a cup of coffee and shrugged at her. "I'll see him later."

"He comes *this morning*."

"I don't see why it matters." His tone had a note of sullenness now. He pulled back his chair with a bang and sat.

"You don't see why it matters?" Dottie's cheeks were growing red. "Don't you want to be here when your son comes home for the first time in three years?"

"For God's sake, the boy isn't going to be expecting me." Robert jammed his fork into a piece of sausage. "Must you ruin everything? Do you expect me to sit here all day while we wait? What did you drag him home for, anyway?"

"You know perfectly well," Dottie said. "He is coming home to be married."

"To whom?" Robert said. "I suppose you're going to choose some milksop girl for him so you can get grandchildren? The boy's just been to war, and already you're trying to suffocate him."

Dottie's jaw flexed, and she blinked her small eyes. For a horrified second, I thought she might cry. "Martin and I have written about this," she said, her voice tight. "He has agreed to take a wife. It is our chance for children in this family. Someone to leave our legacy to."

"Your legacy, you mean," Robert said. "He's always been your child, not mine. Besides, I've nothing to do with weddings. If I want to go riding, I'm going to go riding. You know how I hate this house."

"Yes, you've made it very clear," she sniped, "with all the assistance you give me in the running of it."

"It isn't even mine," Robert said. His brow smoothed and he turned to me. "Did you know that, Mrs. Manders? Wych Elm House came to me as part of the settlement upon marrying my lovely wife. From her side of the family." He smiled sourly, his eyes traveling me as I sat, uncomfortable and horrified, in my chair. "We should start a minstrel show, you and me. The Poor Married-for-Moneys."

I made to push back my chair, but Dottie held a hand up and I froze. "I won't sell this house," she said to Robert, her chin up, her eyes furious. "I won't."

Robert put down his fork. I felt the hideous presence of Frances in the room, the heavy memory of her in all of our minds, as if her name were even now echoing off the walls, and all I wanted was to escape.

"It shouldn't be sold," Robert said. "It should be burned." His gaze flickered to me again, and I saw how grief and dissipation had worn away his long-ago handsomeness into something tired and almost haggard. "You've made me heel so far as to come here for Martin," he said to Dottie, "and I'll do my duty. But you can't make me sit in this fright of a house all day." He stood and left the room without another look at either of us.

A long, painful silence followed. I stared at my hands. Finally I raised my eyes and looked surreptitiously at Dottie. Her expression was blank, impassive. The flush of anger had gone from her face.

"Manders," she said.

"Yes, Dottie."

"I wish you to go into town and run errands for me. Purchase your new clothes at the same time. Use the car and driver."

"Yes, Dottie."

She sat quietly. She made no comment on my use of her first name; she never had. It was one of my small victories. I may be her paid companion, but I was family. I had refused to call her Mrs. Forsyth, and she had never complained.

She turned her head and looked at me, taking me in with her intelligent gaze. "I suppose you think I'm a fool," she said.

"No," I said truthfully. "I do not."

"You were a married woman, so perhaps you have some understanding."

I nodded. Alex and I had never had a row like that—he had never shown me one-tenth the contempt that Robert seemed to think was Dottie's due—and yet I did understand. A marriage is unfathomable to those looking on, running as deep as the strata of rocks in the earth. That, I understood.

I pushed back my chair and stood. "What are the errands you wish done?" I asked.

Dottie followed the change of subject without a flicker of expression. "I have letters to post—they are on the holder by the front door. I do not trust the servants to do it. And you must make a trip to the chemist's for me. You know the stomach remedy I usually use."

"Yes, Dottie."

"Manders, there is one more thing."

I stood by the door and waited.

She raised her impassive gaze to me. "I assume Alex told you about Frances," she said.

I was so surprised that the truth sprang from my lips without thought. "He told me about her existence. But all I had was a letter from the Front saying she had died."

She blinked, and before she shuttered her gaze I saw honest surprise in her eyes. "Is that so? How interesting. However, when you go into town, you will likely hear certain rumors."

I nodded, not wishing to mention that I'd ferreted out those same rumors from the servants' quarters already.

Dottie lit a cigarette, the fumes mixing with the leftover smells of sausage and tea, making my stomach turn. "Frances is buried in the churchyard in town, if you want to see her," she said. "That should tell you everything you need to know. I do not wish to speak of her, for obvious reasons, and I expect you to maintain the family's privacy if you encounter any prurient interest in town. Do you understand?"

"Yes, Dottie."

"I hope so. There is also a letter in the holder to go directly to my solicitor and not into any other hands."

I left the room, collected the letters, and went to the kitchen to ask Mrs. Bennett how to go about ordering the motorcar and driver.

Once in the car, I sat in the back, watching the trees go by on the way to town. *She is buried in the churchyard, if you want to see her.* As with everything with Dottie, it was not a casual suggestion; it was an order, deep with meaning I could not yet discern. And as we came closer to town, I began to wonder what it was she wanted me to see.

CHAPTER SIX

The village was called Anningley, and it was a brisk little place, pretty and polite, cradled in the palm of a cup of land. I had the driver drop me near the edge of town and instructed him to wait; he gave me a succinct nod and sat back in the driver's seat, likely hoping for me to leave so he could light a cigarette. I walked into town on foot, taking in the fresh smell of the air and the scent of the sea, somewhere over the rises to the south.

High Street held a few ladies shopping, servants gossiping at the butcher's as they waited for the day's cuts of meat, nannies from the nearby homes walking with small children. Shopkeepers nodded at me as I passed. I immediately felt like a stranger, dark-haired and wild-eyed after my sleepless night and unpleasant morning at Wych Elm House, lacking a husband or a child or even a pleasant routine of shopping and talk. I already felt painfully visible, so I took Dottie's letters to the post office first and let the postmistress have at me.

The postmistress was a woman of about forty, immensely large, her flesh so soft and ruddy that I briefly wondered if she'd just had a late baby. She looked at the letters, but when she raised her gaze to me, there was no smile. "Wych Elm House," she said. "I'd heard the family was in residence again."

I shifted, remembering Dottie's instructions. "Yes, they are."

She took the letters and tucked them away. "They've been away for a long time."

"They had their reasons," I allowed.

"Perhaps." The postmistress turned back to me. "I'm Mrs. Baines. And who might you be? Are you a member of the family?"

I stared at her. This woman, standing in her tidy rural post office with the sun shining outside, was giving me a sour expression that made me feel like an unwelcome intruder. It was a chilly interrogation, not cheerful gossip. "I was married to Mrs. Forsyth's nephew, Alex Manders."

"I've heard of him," Mrs. Baines said. My husband's existence, it seemed, was now verified by the village authority. "A decent man, as far as the Forsyths go, though I hear he kept to himself. I also hear that Mr. Martin is coming home."

Of course she had. "This morning," I said. "We expect him shortly."

"That's as well, then." Mrs. Baines turned away from me and ran her gaze over the shelves of letters on her left. "I don't know Mr. Martin myself. No one saw him much before he went to war. I hear he's been in a hospital since."

I tapped my fingers on the counter. No wonder Dottie had no desire to come into town herself, but had sent her lackey instead. "You seem to hear quite a few rumors about the Forsyths."

"I do, but rumors are all there is to hear about the Forsyths, you must understand." Mrs. Baines turned to look at me again. "They never come to town, and when it's time to hire servants, they always hire from away. The only local girl who's worked for them is Petra Jennings, and she was dismissed when the girl died. They must have threatened her with something, because she doesn't speak of them."

I understood some of her hostility then. A wealthy family like the

Forsyths would be expected to provide work for the locals, not for people from away. Trust Dottie to be obtuse about something so simple. "I can speak to Mrs. Forsyth about it," I said, "though I can't promise anything."

Mrs. Baines only shook her head. "I don't think you'll find anyone from here willing to work at Wych Elm House. Not now."

"What do you mean?"

"The woods," Mrs. Baines said. She gestured behind her with a beefy arm, in the vague direction of the trees two miles away. Her expression was almost angry. "That mad girl haunts them. None of the children will go in—mine certainly won't. They're too afraid to play in there."

I tapped my fingers on the counter again. "You can't hold the Forsyth family responsible for the fact that your children are afraid to play in the woods."

"I can, and I will. It's easy for them—they closed up the house and left. It's us who have had to live with the ghost these three years. That girl was kept in chains, I hear. She was a beast."

"She wasn't a beast," came a voice from the doorway behind her. "She *had* a beast, my dear. That's a different thing."

The man who had spoken leaned against the doorjamb, his arms crossed. He was a year or two older than she, in shirtsleeves and a waistcoat, a cloth cap on his head. He gave me a brief nod of greeting. "Good afternoon, madam. I'm Mr. Baines."

"Good afternoon," I replied. "What do you mean, she had a beast?"

"Please excuse my wife," Mr. Baines replied, eyeing me levelly. "The topic of the Forsyths upsets her. I only mean that young Miss Frances Forsyth had a dog, that's all."

"They're not good people," Mrs. Baines protested, hurt. "My sister has been in service for ten years, and they wouldn't even talk to her. And that thing was not a dog, not from what I hear."

"Did you ever see it?" Mr. Baines asked his wife. When she was quiet, he turned back to me. "You see how upset she gets. As a stranger you may not know this, Mrs. Manders, but the Forsyths are not popular in this part of the world."

"I see." Dottie had warned me, if obliquely, of the attitude in the village, and she'd been correct. "What do you mean about a dog?"

"Only that Miss Frances had one," Mr. Baines replied. "A big, angry beast. Kept outdoors, in the woods. It's gone wild since she died and the family left the house, I'm afraid. The children say it roams the woods, vicious. That's why they won't go in, especially after the sun has gone down."

I frowned. "Could that be the animal that killed the stranger on the day Frances died?"

"That's the opinion of some," Mr. Baines said. His wife had subsided to a chair, sullen, leaving him to take over the conversation. "No one knows who the dead man was. A vagrant meets a wild dog in the woods—who knows what happened? A simple conclusion, really. However, Mrs. Forsyth herself testified at the inquest that her daughter owned no dog at all."

"She testified at the inquest?"

"Certainly she did. There had to be an inquest, to determine how the man had died—whether it was murder. The man was torn to pieces. Many had the theory that Miss Frances's dog was responsible, but Mrs. Forsyth swore on a Bible that no such animal existed. And it came out that no one had seen the dog with their own eyes; nor could they produce it." He shrugged. His gaze on me was flat, and I realized he did not feel quite as friendly as he was pretending.

"It's her that was the beast," Mrs. Baines said. "It's her that haunts the woods. That's what the children say."

"It's an outlandish story," I said, trying not to think of the girl I'd seen in the small parlor at Wych Elm House.

"It is that," Mr. Baines agreed. "We also have stories of boggarts and wood sprites here, if you care to hear them. Myself, I am a logical man."

I regarded him curiously. He spoke with such confidence, as if well versed in the topic of the Forsyths, his tone not hostile like his wife's but more disdainful. "And what do you think?" I couldn't help but ask.

Mr. Baines straightened from the doorjamb and took a step forward, uncrossing his arms. "Me? Oh, I think that Miss Frances Forsyth was mad," he said. "There's no doubt of that. The children who encountered her in the woods said that she wandered alone, talking to herself, pale and thin. Nothing sets people off like madness, does it? You can imagine any kind of tale." He took another step forward, his eyes still on me. "And yes, despite her mother's lies, I think Miss Frances had a dog. I think the dog killed that man—perhaps the man threatened his mistress somehow, or the dog was bad-tempered, as some dogs are. To avoid responsibility, Mrs. Forsyth did away with the dog, then lied about it. And it worked—because the man in the woods was nobody, and to such as the Forsyths, his death meant nothing. That's what I think."

I stood staring at him, unable to think of what to say.

Mr. Baines nodded toward my hand. "I also think you have another letter there that you did not give to my wife to post."

"This?" I said. I blinked down at the letter in my hand. "I'm to take this to Mrs. Forsyth's man of business. His name is Mr. David Wilde."

The Baineses exchanged a look I could not read.

"Very well, then," said Mr. Baines. "You'll find his offices two streets over, in the white house with the green shutters. If your business is with him, then you've no more business here today."

"What?" I said. "What is it?"

"Don't worry, Mrs. Manders," Mr. Baines said, and though the words were kind, his tone was not. "You'll see for yourself. I wish you good day."

I wasn't very keen to knock at the door of the white house with the green shutters, but I didn't have much choice. Perhaps Mr. David Wilde was a crotchety old man, or perhaps he liked to abuse unsuspecting ladies' companions. In either case, I was to deliver Dottie's note to his hands only, so there was nothing for it. I knocked.

The door was answered by a man of about forty-five, with large gray eyes and premature silver in his hair. He wore a shirt and waistcoat, immaculate and expensive. It would be a challenge to tailor a shirt so well for such a man, I noticed, because his left arm was irregular, withered, the folded hand encased in a gray glove and hooked like a question mark. I blinked at it in surprise.

The man regarded me politely. "Yes?" he asked.

"I beg your pardon," I said. "I'm looking for Mr. David Wilde. I'm—I'm Mrs. Forsyth's paid companion, Jo Manders."

Recognition warmed his eyes, and I knew then that he was not a servant. "Ah," he said. "I'm Mr. Wilde."

I pulled the note from my pocket and held it out. "Then this is for you, Mr. Wilde."

He reached for the envelope with his good hand, while I most determinedly did not look at the other one. "How thoughtful," he said, but when he spoke, his eyes were on my face. "I was just about to have a cup of tea. Would you like to come in?"

"Oh, no," I said. "There's no need."

"But there is," Mr. David Wilde said with gentle persuasiveness. "I may need to send a reply."

Of course. How could I forget I was Dottie's paid letter-delivery girl? "Very well, then," I conceded. "Thank you."

I followed him into the house, which was decorated in dark colors—dark wood floors, dark wainscoting, pale gray wallpaper. Even the electric lamps were of dark metal, their shades dim and obscure. Still, the house smelled of wood polish and the flowered rugs on the floors were clean and tidy. He led me to an office off of the main hall and tossed Dottie's letter to the desk. "Have a seat," he offered, motioning to a chair.

A tea set was laid out on a sideboard. I opened my mouth and came half out of my chair as he walked over to it, but his back was to me, and I could see he planned on pouring the tea himself. "It's nice to meet you, Mrs. Manders," he said, picking up the teapot with his good hand as his other dangled, useless, in its glove. "Mrs. Forsyth was in need of a companion."

"She told you about me?" I asked.

"Of course." Mr. Wilde glanced over his shoulder at me and raised a brow. "I handle the money."

I sorted through my memory. If Dottie had ever mentioned a man of business, I didn't recall it. She gave the impression of being an entire civilization contained in one woman.

Mr. Wilde's hand was deft, and in moments he was handing me a cup of tea on a saucer. "Mrs. Forsyth speaks quite highly of you," he said.

I took the cup. *It isn't hard, Manders,* I heard Dottie say. *Just try not to spill it.* If a one-handed man could pour tea, then I supposed I could as well. Was this what the Baineses had been so suspicious of? A man with a withered hand? "I doubt that very much," I told him.

Mr. Wilde gave a small laugh as he poured his own cup. "She says you're not entirely stupid," he amended. "From her, that's high praise. I know you were the wife of Alex Manders. I must say how sorry I was to hear he died in the war."

"Thank you," I managed. He must know of Alex through Dottie, I thought, since he was her man of business. There was no way he could have known Alex in person.

"I could not fight, myself," Mr. Wilde said. He set his teacup gracefully on the desk and sat in his large desk chair. He raised his withered arm slightly, letting the gloved hand dangle. The upper arm, I saw, was as thick and strong as its mate, but below the elbow the arm seemed to nearly vanish, pinned into the tailored sleeve. He did not take his eyes from me. "A defect from birth. I tried to enlist, of course, but they told me I could not fire a gun. I asked how they could be sure, since I'd never tried, but they would not be convinced."

I held my cup and saucer in my lap and looked back at him. His eyes were kind, his expression intelligent, but there was something about him I did not like, something that resided behind his gaze. "I'm sorry to hear that," I said.

"My wife is not," he replied, lowering the arm. He let the silence stretch out, comfortable in it, seeming in no hurry to open Dottie's note and reply to it. I took a reluctant sip of tea.

He leaned back in his chair, the withered arm resting at his side. "Tell me, Mrs. Manders," he said, "does Mrs. Forsyth have you doing errands for her all day?"

"It's my job, Mr. Wilde," I said, putting my cup down again.

"It seems somewhat beneath your station as Alex's wife."

"I'm his widow. And there are girls with worse jobs than this."

"Quite true," he agreed. He watched my face, and I felt certain he guessed at how desperate I was for money, the exact reason I'd taken the job. He reached out and touched the edge of Dottie's letter on the desk, tracing it slowly with his fingertip, his gaze turning thoughtful. "May I ask you something?"

"Do I have a choice?"

He gave me a smile at that. "I apologize. I'm a lawyer, and we like to ask questions. My days are usually very quiet. You are quite the most exciting thing to cross my threshold all week."

The words hung in the air, suspended. My tea seemed to have congealed to paste in my stomach. I wondered if Dottie would dismiss me if I stood and left.

"You mustn't worry," Mr. Wilde said into the silence. "My questions are not so very personal. I simply wondered if you plan to be a ladies' companion forever."

"Forever?" I could not keep the dismay from my voice.

"Yes." Mr. Wilde picked up the envelope with his good hand, stood it idly on end. "You've never thought of it? You're an intelligent girl. Mrs. Forsyth is in the prime of health, but she will not live forever."

I leaned over and set my teacup on a side table. "Are you asking," I said slowly, "whether I expect Dottie to leave me something in her will?"

He did not answer that. "My job," he said with a lawyer's evasiveness, "is to look after the family. To protect it from harm."

"Is it?" I said. I was being impertinent, I knew, but I was stung and I could not help myself. "It seems to me the harm to the family has already been done."

"Ah," Mr. Wilde said. "I believe you're referring to Frances."

"There are rumors in town."

That made him smile. "Oh, yes. Mad girls in chains, killer hounds, ghosts. It's quite 'The Fall of the House of Usher,' is it not? Such is the imagination of the English countryman. I admire the locals their creativity, but don't believe everything you hear. I'm part of the rumor, myself— I believe I play the role of Mrs. Forsyth's evil accomplice, helping to keep Frances in chains and cover up her murders at the inquest. I don't suppose you heard that part?"

It was the easy superiority, the cold condescension in his tone, that gave me a chill when he spoke to me. "No," I said.

He nodded. "A man with a withered arm is born to play the villain, you see. But since you're attached to the family now, would you like to know the truth?"

"I don't—"

"Frances was a sweet girl," Mr. Wilde said. He looked at my expression and smiled. "Does that surprise you, after what you've heard? She was certainly intelligent, and I believe she never meant harm to anyone."

"Yet she was mad," I said.

He finally took up Dottie's letter and slid his finger under the flap, opening it. "She was . . . afflicted. There is no other way to describe it." His gaze stayed on me and not on the letter in his hand. "The spells started in childhood. That was before my time with the family, but by the time Mrs. Forsyth engaged me as her man of business, Frances's spells had progressed."

"What type of spells?" I asked.

"Hallucinations," he replied. "She saw things that weren't there, spoke to people who weren't present. I witnessed it myself any number of times, and I questioned Frances—when she was capable of it—as well as the doctors Dottie had called in to treat her. Some of the things Frances thought she saw were benign, and some of them were terrible. But by the time she was thirteen, the hallucinations were pervasive and incredibly real to her. She claimed there was a door that the visions came through. She could describe it to the finest detail if you asked." He gave me a small smile that was entirely sad. "It took some questioning before she trusted me enough to explain, but I finally understood that the things she saw coming through that imaginary door were dead."

I gaped at him. My tea had grown cold on the table next to me. I could not think of a thing to say.

"You can imagine," Mr. Wilde continued, "what a torment everyday life must be for someone so afflicted. Frances believed she saw the dead, waking and sleeping. She often had screaming fits that were terrible to behold—her madness sometimes produced particularly gruesome visions. No doctor could help her, and eventually Dottie would not hear of her being examined yet again. So Frances lived at home instead, in privacy, plagued by her waking dreams." He looked at me closely with his chilled gaze. "You have a look of pity in your eyes, Mrs. Manders, but not a look of great shock. According to my information, you are well acquainted with madness, are you not?"

I thought of the long, red scratches on Mother's neck, and the words sprang to my lips, defensive. "It is not the same, Mr. Wilde. Not at all."

"If you say so. In any case, the rumors you hear are nothing but poison. Frances was never locked up or chained. There was no dog. The vagrant dying in the woods on the same day as Frances was a cruel and gruesome coincidence, that is all. Though something did strike me the day she died."

"What was that?" I managed.

"I had known Frances for years by then. For all her torment, she had never been suicidal. She had never attempted to take her own life until that day. In fact, because of her hallucinations, she was terrified of dying. The last place she ever wanted to go was through that terrible door, to be with the things on the other side." He shrugged. "Don't you find that strange?"

"Yes," I said, keeping my voice steady. "I suppose it is."

Mr. Wilde flipped open Dottie's letter at last and read the lines inside. He showed no reaction to whatever they said except for the faint tightening of his jaw. "If you will be so kind as to wait a moment, Mrs. Manders, I will write Mrs. Forsyth a reply."

I sat in silence as he pulled out a creamy piece of paper and scratched on it with his pen, one brief line, two, three. There seemed to be no air in the room. I wondered if David Wilde had ever seen a strange girl in Wych Elm House sitting in a chair and staring at him. But no, he couldn't have. The house had been empty since the Forsyths had left.

When he had finished, he sealed the letter and rose. I followed him to the door. "Mr. Wilde," I said, "I have one question."

"And what may that be?"

"Why do I feel like you have been assessing me for the past hour?"

He gave me his small smile again and placed the letter in my hand. "Don't worry about it, Mrs. Manders," he said. "My duty to the family comes first. Good day to you."

CHAPTER SEVEN

I finished the rest of Dottie's errands in numb silence. I visited the dressmaker's and came away with two ready-made frocks in packages under my arm, as well as an order for two more to come in a week's time. I had barely looked at them, letting the dressmaker select what was best. I also bought new stockings, one pair of new shoes, and a new hat. I had paid for all of it on Dottie's credit; likely I'd have to work for her for years before we were even again.

Next to the dressmaker's was a photographer's studio. It was closed—the sign said the proprietor was in only on Mondays and Thursdays—but I paused and looked at the photographs in the window. One showed Anningley's own High Street, on a misty early morning, looking toward the gentle rise of a hill, which was crowned with a pretty church of old stone, its spire coming out of the mist above the roofs of the village houses. I thought of that same church, rising out of the same mist, two hundred or even three hundred years ago, patiently waiting for Sunday attendance by villagers now long dead, weathering storms long forgotten, just as it would do when I was dead and so was everyone around me. And I thought for the first time in months of Alex's camera in its case in my bedroom at Wych Elm House.

I turned and looked down High Street at the spire from the photograph. A church meant a graveyard. *She is buried in the churchyard, if you want to see her.*

Still, I dawdled on my way to Frances's grave. I stopped at the pharmacist's and the lending library, David Wilde's words turning over in my head. Finally I had no more errands, no more excuses, and I opened the churchyard gate with my gloved hands, listening to it creak in the peaceful stillness of the sunny afternoon.

The church was a snug building of buttery stone. I saw no sign of a vicar or a groundskeeper, though the grounds were immaculate; there were only the starlings crying at one another in the trees over the hill.

From the very first, I knew which monument I was meant to see.

It was a long block of shiny marble, raised and gleaming, overshadowing all of the graves around it—humble stones from the eighteenth and nineteenth centuries, planted by the good people of Anningley. Frances Forsyth's grave was slick and shiny, almost obscene. As I approached I could see the lettering—FRANCES FORSYTH, B. 1902–D. 1917—and an angel etched, weeping, into the marble above it. Beneath the dates was a single sentiment: ANGEL ON EARTH.

I stared at the grave. It made my throat thick, made my heart beat slowly and sickly in my chest. This was Dottie's work, there was no doubt of it—Robert had had nothing to do with this monstrosity. She must have faced some objection to having Frances buried in the churchyard at all, as a suicide and a suspected murderer. She had not only prevailed, but she had raised her daughter's monument above the rest. It was a mother's act of love, of defiant and loyal belief.

But as David Wilde had intimated, I knew something of what it was like, caring for the mad. I knew how it drained you, how it ate at you, how your love for the mad person both fed you and consumed you.

How you felt it was all your fault, or all theirs. I knew of the unspoken moments as you worried in the dark—as your own life sat frozen and forgotten—when you hated the mad person with all your heart, when the black part of you wished they would simply go away, that they would simply die. And I knew of the hideous wash of relief that overcame you when the burden of caring for that person was finally lifted.

Frances Forsyth's monument was an act of love. But I could see what it also was—an act of guilt, the kind that bows a person and alters them forever. This was what Dottie lived with, what no one could understand. No one but me, who had lived with Mother.

The last place she ever wanted to go was through that terrible door, to be with the things on the other side. Some mad people wished for death, but others clung to life, even when that life was filled with pain. Yet Frances had, finally, decided to go through that door she so dreaded. Or had she? Was it possible her mother had helped her? That the final result was this monument to Dottie's own guilt?

I turned away and walked back to the motorcar in silence.

When I arrived in the front hall at Wych Elm House, all was quiet. I removed my hat and stood for a moment. I heard the ticking of the grandfather clock in the next room. I smelled furniture polish and dust. I looked at the sunlight coming interrupted through the glass door from the sitting room, sliced by the lines of a tree branch. At the quiet corridor, its floor gleaming.

This house shouldn't be sold; it should be burned.

A murmur of voices came from one of the rooms down the hall, and reluctantly I walked toward the sound. I found Dottie and Robert in the small parlor where I had seen the girl yesterday, sitting in the chairs in an awkward arrangement. A tray of tea sat on a spindle-legged table, the steam no longer rising from the pot. Dottie's color was high, her posture straight, a teacup all but forgotten in her lap. Robert sat uncomfortably, looking pained. So Dottie had won some part of their argument after all, then.

A third person rose from his chair to greet me.

He was, unmistakably, the boy from the photograph Dottie carried in her book. I could see Dottie in the narrow, clean shape of his jaw, the shoulders that were not wide yet firm of line. I could see Robert in the set of his dark eyes, his long lashes, and the charming ease of his smile, which he flashed me on sight. But there the resemblance to either of his parents, and the photograph of years ago, ended. The man who stood before me had the painful thinness of the long-term patient: his cheeks hollowed, his tidy shirt and jacket hanging as if from a clothes hanger in a shop. He was in his early twenties, but the creases on his forehead and the lines bracketing his mouth aged him past thirty, and the soft shadows under his eyes hinted that the travel he'd just undergone had taken more out of him than he cared to let on.

"Manders." Dottie's voice was tight with excitement, her gaze trained on the man as he turned to me. "This is my son, Martin."

"Cousin!" Martin said, smiling at me. Despite the gauntness of his features, there was something compelling about the forced brightness in his eyes. "Cousin Jo! What a delight to finally meet you. Alex told me everything about you."

I blinked at him, surprised. I glanced briefly at Dottie, remembering her injunction not to talk of Alex with her frail son. "Oh," I said stupidly.

"Martin," Dottie said, changing the subject on cue. "You must eat something. I imagine you are famished."

"Don't harass the boy, Dottie," Robert said.

Martin ignored them both and took one of my gloved hands in his. I still held my packages in the other. Dottie's comment hung in the air; Martin looked like he hadn't eaten in weeks. His gaze was fixed on me, and I returned the look, trying to read his expression. I had interrupted a family conversation on some serious topic—I inferred it from the color in Dottie's cheeks and the way Robert's gaze roved around the room, as if he was waiting for the first chance to escape.

"You are lovely," Martin said to me. His voice was not seductive, or even particularly inviting; the words were spoken more as a message, as if he were telling me something in code. He squeezed my hand once, briefly, reinforcing the feeling. "Just as I heard. I am so glad I came home."

I stared back at him. I should know what he meant; I should know. And yet I racked my brain and came up with nothing. "Thank you," I managed.

Dottie spoke again, something about Martin seeing the artworks she'd bought on the Continent. Robert countered that no young man would want to see such a dull thing, and instead they should go riding at the first opportunity. Martin agreed with both his parents without committing to anything. He seemed adept at navigating the treacherous territory between them, skipping past the many land mines with the agility of an adored son.

But I was only barely paying attention. I had figured out the subtle tension in the room with the sudden understanding of a thunderclap. *My son is coming home to get married.* Her dismissive wave of the hand when I had asked about his fiancée. *I'll take care of it.*

Mr. Wilde's assessment of me, the exchange of notes between them. *Our chance for children, someone to leave our legacy to.*

You are lovely. I am so glad I came home.

Martin must have seen understanding on my face. I stood transfixed as he stepped closer, dropped my hand, and pulled me to him in an embrace. My packages bumped between us awkwardly, but still Martin patted my back, his thin hands touching me coldly through my coat at my shoulder blades.

"Cousin Jo," Martin said, his breath in my ear, his voice dark with understanding. "We are going to have *so much fun.*"

CHAPTER EIGHT

I fell in love with my husband's legs before I fell in love with the rest of him.

It was April 1914, England's declaration of war still four months distant. With Mother living in the hospital, I had found a job in London as a typist for a lawyer named Casparov, who kept an office in the streets near Gray's Inn. Casparov had a thick salt-and-pepper beard and a fondness for checked suits. He saw few clients in his shabby office, but he had a voluminous correspondence, all of which he wrote in nearly inscrutable shorthand. He kept two typists—both women—for the sole purpose of wading through his snowdrifts of notes, which he seemed to write day and night. We sorted them, typed them into understandable form, and posted them.

The salary was low, but it paid the rent at my boardinghouse and Mother's hospital bills, and I was lucky to have the job. I was only a middling typist, but there was almost no other employment for women unless I wanted to be a nurse, a teacher, or a nun. So I put up with Casparov's terrible shorthand and his occasional grasps of my bottom and earned my money as best I could. My fellow typist, a big-boned girl named Helen who was raising her "niece"—quite obviously her daughter, though Casparov never figured it out—did the same.

Helen and I were sitting in the office's dark, unprepossessing antechamber, typing as the clock ticked on the wall, when the door banged open and a man walked in. Neither of us spoke a greeting to him; we were typists, Casparov had made clear, not receptionists. *You do not speak to my clients,* he'd said in his Russian accent. *They are not your business. Your business is the typing only, and the looking respectable.* We were functional decorations, like vases of flowers that managed correspondence. But I raised my eyes just above the level of the page in my typewriter and looked. And watched, transfixed, as the man crossed the room toward Casparov's inner office.

The visitor was tall. He wore a leather jacket, cut to the waist and trimmed with a wool collar—the sort of coat a city fellow wears when he's on a weekend out in the country. A cloth cap with a peaked brim was pulled down low on his head, and he did not bother to remove it. He wore leather gloves against the April chill, and as he approached my desk, I caught the scent of the damp, cold air he'd brought with him, the drip of the icy fog that coated the city. He strode through the antechamber without a word, his heavy-soled shoes thumping purposefully on the worn carpet.

I could see his legs perfectly in the span of my demurely lowered gaze. Clad in well-tailored wool trousers, they were the most spectacular male legs I had ever seen—long, muscled, swinging easily in a graceful, powerful gait. They were Lord of the Manor legs, made expressly for tight buckskin breeches and high, polished riding boots. I felt something inside me as I watched them, something that was lust mixed with stinging joy at seeing something so beautiful yet so utterly unattainable. *You will never have that. Never. He will not even look at you.*

The legs slowed as they neared me, and as they passed right in front of my typewriter page, so close I could see the weave of the wool trousers, they nearly stopped. I swallowed and looked up.

He was looking down at me. The face below the brim of the cap was handsome, well proportioned, with a fine jaw and a firm line of mouth, but there was nothing soft about it. It was obviously a well-bred face, along with the rest of him—class always tells—but the shadow of stubble on his jaw and the narrowness of his cheekbones spoke of a man who had not been raised in a country home. His eyes were dark blue, the lashes short and the irises ringed with black. They were alive with fierce, uncompromising intelligence, and they were focused on me.

I met his gaze and did not look away. I felt cold sweat form on my back, beneath my serviceable office dress with the collar I'd thought so pretty when I'd bought it. I felt my fingers go still and cold on the typewriter keys. I felt something happy and queasy and afraid turn over in my stomach. I did not blush; I did not stammer. But I looked at him, watching him watch me, taking him in as he took me in, as the moment spun on and on.

Behind him, Casparov's door creaked open and his voice came across the room. "Alex."

Alex, I thought.

Without a word, the visitor turned away from me and vanished through Casparov's door, which clicked closed. Only then did I feel my face heat, my breath come short.

I turned to Helen. "Did you see him?"

She stopped typing, and I realized belatedly that she had been clacking away the entire time the visitor—Alex—had been in the room. "See who?" she asked.

"The man who just came in."

She frowned. "No, and neither did you. We're not supposed to notice his clients."

It was true. If Casparov had seen me looking at his client, he could dismiss me. "I didn't *notice* him," I lied outrageously. "I just wondered who he was, that's all."

"Well, stop wondering," Helen said, and went back to work.

I fumbled through my own pile of Casparov's notes, trying to regain the thread that had been interrupted. Casparov had not said anything; nor had he given me a look. It had seemed like a long moment, but the visitor and I had exchanged a glance for likely a few seconds, nothing more. We had not spoken. There was nothing to be dismissed over, not if I resumed my day. I forced my hands to work, pushed my fingers to type word upon word, not thinking about the man on the other side of the office door. He was lovely—more than lovely, really—but I had Mother's fees to pay. I could not lose this job.

Nearly an hour later, Casparov's door opened again. This time I kept typing and did not look up.

"My thanks," Casparov said in his gruff accent.

"It's nothing," came the reply. His voice was low and confident, the two words tossed off even as he walked away.

The legs came back across the room—I was not looking at them, though I could sense them large in my awareness—and passed my desk. Still I did not look up. Still I typed, aware that Casparov was watching us, watching me. I'd never see the visitor again. It was tragic, but *c'est la vie*.

There was the faintest *shush* of sound as a piece of paper landed on my desk atop the others.

And then he was gone, without a pause, the outer door thumping closed, leaving me to wonder if I'd imagined it. From the other direction, Casparov's door closed as well.

Helen kept typing, unmoved. But I stopped and stared at the folded slip of paper that sat accusingly before me. Like a villain in a stage melodrama, I wiped the back of my hand across my forehead, feeling the damp perspiration there. I unfolded the note and read it.

> *Will you meet me in Soho Square, at eight o'clock tonight?*

My mouth dropped open. It was madness, pure madness. I would think I'd imagined it, except for the fact that I held the note in my hand.

I knew the man not at all; we had not exchanged a word. He could be a madman, luring me somewhere alone to murder me. He could be a Lothario, leaving notes for typists all over the city, then meeting them and despoiling them one by one. I did not know what this man was about, but one thing was certain: I would not go. I could not go.

I tucked the note into the bodice of my dress and went back to typing.

And that night I went home to my flat after work was finished. I took off my work dress—one of the three I owned—and put on the nicest dress in my wardrobe, a lavender wool with buttons up the front and a hemline that fell nearly to my ankles, as hemlines did in 1914. I brushed out my hair and repinned it in a different style, topped it with a modest hat, and put on stockings and shoes. Then I sat on the edge of my sorry bed, my hands in my lap, thinking.

At seven thirty I put on my coat and belted it tightly at my waist. I put on my threadbare gloves. If Alex was a murderer, I found I didn't much care. And if he was a despoiler, well—at least I'd be despoiled. I was nearly twenty, with no marriage prospects, and perhaps it was time.

Perhaps, I mused, he'd change his mind. Perhaps he wouldn't even be there. But he was, still in his leather coat and wool trousers, the hat pulled down on his head. He saw me immediately and watched me approach, his blue eyes missing nothing, giving nothing away.

"You changed your hair," he said when I drew close.

I looked up at him. The sodden cold of April was numbing my cheeks and creeping down the neck of my coat, but he seemed unaffected. "I shouldn't be here," I said.

He sighed, as if he knew I was right. "My name is Alex Manders," he said. "Who are you?"

"If you're asking my name," I replied, "it's Jo Christopher."

One eyebrow rose inquisitively beneath the brim of the cap. "Jo?"

I shrugged. "Joanna. Though I never use it." I looked briefly around us, at the evening crowds passing us in the square. "Why am I here?" I asked, though I was unsure whether I asked it of him or of myself.

He turned to face me directly for the first time, looking down at me. I caught the faint whiff of leather, and I knew with perfect certainty that the inside of his leather coat would be warmed by his body, the thought rocking me back on my heels. "You're here because you're being asked out to dinner," he replied.

"With you?" The words burst out of my mouth, incredulous. "Alone?"

He hesitated for the briefest moment, but in that moment I had a glimmer of understanding. Despite his bluntness, he was not telling me; he was asking. The note he'd left me had been a question, not a command. He was asking, and a part of him thought I'd say no.

"I realize I've gone about it the wrong way," he said. "But I had no chance to speak with you. There's an Italian place just across the square here, and I thought—"

"Yes," I said. "Yes, I'll have dinner with you."

He smiled at that, and I found myself smiling back at him, something inside me melting like wax. He lifted his elbow to me.

"Very well, Jo Christopher," he said. "Follow me."

CHAPTER NINE

He knew everything about everything. We talked about politics—I read the news every day, devouring Casparov's many newspapers when I took my luncheon—and we talked about art, and we talked about novels. Without Mother to care for, I'd found myself with time alone for the first time in my life, and I'd spent my leisure hours in galleries, museums, and lending libraries. It was a wealth of riches, but I'd had no one to talk to about the things I'd seen.

The Italian restaurant was small and intimate, with perhaps twenty tables, its light dim against the evening darkness of early spring. The food was delicious, and Alex ordered first one bottle of wine and then another. He knew exactly which wines to choose from the list, of course. He simply knew.

In the absence of the cloth cap, his hair was light brown, burnished in the light, with perhaps a hint of russet—in the candlelight it was hard to tell. He wore it short, combed back from his forehead and his temples. Beneath the jacket he wore a white shirt, tailored perfectly to the lines of his body, the top button open at the throat and the cuffs rolled back to just above the wrists. It was incredibly, unthinkably casual; I had never in my life seen a man dress so. I could have devoured him whole.

He had the same thought about me, I could tell. Even as he talked his gaze wandered my throat, my jaw, the line of my ear, the slope of my nose before he'd come back to his senses and look away. I was completely unused to such close attention, and it both embarrassed me and made my head spin.

"You seem to be a very capable typist," he said when the conversation turned personal.

I took a sip of my wine, which rolled wonderfully past my tongue. "How would you know?" I asked.

He frowned, caught out. "Well, there was a lot of . . . clacking." He saw the amusement on my face and said, "Very well, then. You seem to be a *rapid* typist."

"Thank you," I said politely. I was giddy with the wine and the good food and the tiny little restaurant; the evening seemed otherworldly, as if it belonged to someone else's life. "And you seem to be a very capable . . ." I raised an eyebrow.

"Layabout," Alex Manders supplied. "I've just been traveling, and now I'm at loose ends."

It must be nice to be wealthy enough to be at loose ends, I thought, but I couldn't help saying, "You don't look particularly happy about it."

He shrugged, the movement graceful in the dim light. "I'm happy enough, I suppose. I'm twenty-two, and I have what I want."

The words hung in the air, crackling between us. They seemed to affect even him, because he dropped his gaze to his wineglass and ran a finger around the rim as I watched, hypnotized.

"That must be nice," I said softly.

"Don't you have what you want?" Alex asked, looking up at me again. "An independent woman in London, with a job and her own money, spending her time at museums and in intellectual pursuits. I think there are a lot of girls who would envy you."

I stared at him, caught between feeling aghast and breaking out in laughter. My life was hardly one any woman would envy. But he did not know about Mother, of course—that was why he had such an absurd impression of me. "It isn't quite that simple," I said.

"Why not?" he asked me. "I want to know."

"I don't think it's possible to explain."

He took a drink of his own wine. "You don't think I can understand, do you?" He gave me a half smile that made my toes curl beneath the table and shrugged. "Perhaps you're right. Perhaps we're not meant to see eye to eye, you and I. Perhaps you'll always be a mystery to me."

I had to laugh at that. "I'm not a mystery," I said. "I'm just a typist. And of course there are things you don't know about me. You've only known me an hour."

He did not answer that. Instead, his gaze drifted over me softly this time, taking in my features with an expression I could not read until it came to rest on the center notch of my collar, which rested demurely on my clavicle. I felt my skin flush. "We can talk about Serbia again, if you like," he said.

I cleared my throat. "We talked about Serbia enough, I think. And about arms races with Germany and your strange idea that there will be some kind of war."

He shrugged, his gaze still soft on my clavicle, as if it fascinated him. "It's inevitable."

"It's impossible."

Again he smiled a little, almost to himself. He was trying to impress me, I thought, with his worldly opinions. "Let's talk about something else, then. There's something that makes me curious."

"What is it?"

Alex raised his gaze to me. His expression had eased a little, lost some of its dreamy seriousness. "How is it that you're certain your fellow typist's niece is actually her daughter?"

It took me a moment to follow. I'd told him sometime during the first bottle of wine about Helen and her ruse, barely thinking about what I was saying in the rush of conversation, the pure pleasure of talking to him. But it had snagged in his mind, I could see now.

"It's simple," I said. "Of course I know it."

"You've never spoken to her about it. Did she confess to you?"

"God, no." He still gave me a searching look, so I had to explain. "It's not a new ruse, Alex." I closed my mouth before I could elaborate that my own mother had introduced me as a niece more than once, when she introduced me to people at all. It nearly always worked.

"Perhaps the girl's parents truly did die," he persisted. "Perhaps you've got entirely the wrong idea, and you're slandering the lady in your mind unnecessarily. Do you think that's possible?"

I did not even hesitate. "No," I replied. "Helen has sacrificed everything for that little girl. She has no friends, no family. She'll never marry, because no man will want a single woman who already has a child, niece or not. She never goes anywhere, does anything, and she lives in terror of losing her job. That's the kind of sacrifice you make for a daughter, not a niece." I looked away from him for a moment, trying not to let on how closely I understood Helen's life. "Helen must type or perish," I explained, keeping my voice steady. "Like me. It's why we get on as we do. No questions asked, no secrets told."

Still he watched me, his hand resting around the stem of his glass, the candlelight flickering on his face. There was gentle surprise in his expression, and an effortless intelligence that swiftly put the pieces together behind his eyes. *Good breeding*, I had thought when I'd first seen him. He didn't seem wildly wealthy, and he certainly wasn't titled, but Alex Manders came from a background that let him live at loose ends, that had no concept of *type or perish*. In his world, women had the money to do what they wanted; or they married and kept houses and children while their husbands cared for them, with no thought that to some women, that was good fortune such as they had never seen.

But there was no judgment in that look. He saw me just as I

was—all of me, clearly and in detail, without the preconceptions of class, despite his declaration that I was a mystery. I didn't know how he had come by it, but he had the ability to observe, to understand, with the same stark clarity as a film camera. It was thrilling and terrifying at the same time, to truly be seen.

I took a breath. "My mother," I managed, and then I stopped. My cheeks heated, shame and anger and fear mixing in my veins in a brief flash under Alex Manders's clear, unwavering gaze. "My mother is in an asylum for the insane. The nicest one I could find. The nicest one I could afford." I let the words hang there between us for a moment, like smoke. I did not look at him. "She has been ill all my life, I think, though it has worsened over the years. She will never walk out of there. She will never get well." I blinked hard, fighting everything I felt, always fighting. "That is the truth of it, Alex. The truth of me. I type or I perish."

His extraordinary eyes with their dark-ringed irises never left me. "And your father?" he asked softly.

"I don't know who he is," I confessed. "I used to think that Mother kept the information from me, but now—now I think perhaps she doesn't know. Her memories are . . . precarious. She remembers things that were never real. I think that perhaps, if she ever knew, that knowledge has gone."

There was a pause. "I am sorry," he said at last, with a sincerity that made my breathing nearly stop. "I am so very, very sorry."

It wasn't just sympathy in his voice. It was as if he *knew*. But of course he couldn't know, not really. "Yes, well," I said. I took a gulp of wine, trying to process the fact that he wasn't putting the leather coat back on, putting the cap back on, and walking away. No one had ever said to me that they were sorry and meant it. The sensation was strange, like falling. "I have a question for you," I said to him, deflecting the topic.

"What is it?" He sipped from his own glass.

"Are you an orphan?"

He froze for a moment, the rim of the glass still against his lip, before he lowered the glass again. "How," he said softly, "could you possibly know such a thing?"

"I guessed," I said, pleased despite myself that I'd guessed correctly. "You assumed that Helen's girl really was an orphan. It was something in your tone when you asked."

He leaned back in his chair and regarded me. "I shall never attempt to hide anything from you," he said. "There is no point. My parents died while on holiday without me in Turkey. The train they were on derailed in an accident. They were both killed instantly. I was seven."

"That's terrible," I said. I meant it, but at the same time part of me eased and took a deep breath. He knew. He knew what it was like to be without parents, to fight and fight every day alone. Money didn't matter here; anyone who has lost their parents, or never known them, knows that money doesn't make it better. What matters is that horrible, yawning feeling of facing the world alone.

"It was terrible," Alex agreed, keeping a close shutter on his expression. "And it was unexpected. They left enough money to see me raised and through Oxford, at least. And they left no plan of where I'd go, so I was passed from relative to relative for a time. I spent three years in Germany with my paternal grandparents."

Yes, now that he said it I thought I could see German ancestry in him. "So you speak the language, then?"

"Fluently, and French as well. It's my second home, Germany. But I came back to England for Oxford. And when I finished there, I traveled about for a time." He smiled. "And now you see me, an aimless fellow with a great deal of education and not much to do."

I looked at him, and the yearning in me was painful, like a sickness. The strong line of his wrist against the table, the careless glint of his wristwatch in the light, the line of his chin, the shadow of his Adam's apple on his throat, the soft rise and fall of his chest beneath the white shirt—all of it had infected me like a plague. "I am glad I see you," I managed.

He took one look at my eyes and pushed his chair back, fishing urgently in his pockets for money to pay the bill. "Let's go."

We walked for a time in the April night, our shoes splashing through thin puddles on the London streets, my gloved hand on the arm of his coat. I have no memory of what we talked about—serious things, things that made us laugh. He flirted outrageously with me, and I flirted back. He kissed me on a street corner somewhere, his hands in their leather gloves cradling my face, his lips warm on mine. It was a curious feeling—the leather so impersonal on my skin, as if I had a stranger's hands on me. But his kiss was passionate, his intent unmistakable, and when I leaned into him, my own hands grasping for purchase on the front of his coat, he broke the kiss, hailed a taxi, and put me into it.

He had an apartment somewhere off Chalcot Road, near Regent's Park, in a building that was respectable without being ostentatious. It was dark, tidy, nearly unused, with a front hall, a kitchen, a small parlor on the ground floor, and a flight of stairs leading upward. We toured none of it. By the time he got us through the door, I was dropping my coat and had started frantically unbuttoning my dress, and he was undressing nearly as fast. In the front hall, he kissed me until we were both panting. On the stairs, he debauched me. And in the bedroom— we barely made it past the doorway—he had me for the first time, and it was the best thing that had ever happened to me.

We stopped bothering with niceties. *Your body is made for mine*, he said somewhere during that long, long night, and I could only clutch him harder and agree. I had never thought such a thing could be possible. But from the moment he'd walked past my desk, Alex Manders had entered my life and burned all of it down in a single night, as if with the flick of a match. And I gave in willingly and watched it go.

It wasn't until much later that I thought to wonder why he had been in Casparov's office that day and what exactly Casparov had thanked him for.

CHAPTER TEN

I behaved unconscionably, of course, that night with Alex. Unforgivably. Stupidly. All a girl had in life was her respectability, and I had thrown mine away.

I bathed as well as I could while Alex slept the next morning, and then I put my lavender wool dress back on and went to work at Casparov's office. I had cleaned myself up, so I did not look exactly like I had just engaged in an illicit night of passion, but the dress was too fine for workaday wear. Helen barely looked at me, but Casparov noticed; he seemed to suspect that I was dressing to impress him, and when I sat down to start work he paid me an effusive compliment, badly translated from Russian. He did not touch me, for which I was glad. If he had touched me, I thought I might have screamed.

I kept my face impassive and sorted through the day's pile of notes. Then, my mind scheming furiously behind my calm features, I began to type.

*Pursuant to the previous matter, it is my understanding
that the letter of 20 March outlined all ramifications,*

with the exceptions already noted in the previous Con-
tract (32-C) clause 7B, subsection D, as well as ramifi-
cations previously discussed . . .

There was no way for Casparov to find out that his typist had been deflowered by his own client, of course—unless there was a baby. We had done nothing to prevent it. If there was a baby, I calculated, I had four months—five if I was lucky—before I was dismissed. I could pretend to simply get fat up to that point, but no further. I toyed with the idea of getting rid of the baby, if there was one—there were ways—but dismissed it. My mother had not gotten rid of her unwanted child, and neither would I. A baby would be a disaster, but at least it would love me, and that was something.

I listened to Helen, typing away next to me, and I stole a glance at her round, impassive face, her shoulders in their well-worn blouse squared obediently as she hit the keys. I had always understood her, but today I had a new appreciation for her, and a creeping sense of fear. *I could be you,* I thought. *Even now, I could be you.*

But it would take some planning. I pulled a finished page from my typewriter and scrolled in a new one, thinking as fast as I could and trying not to panic. The main problem was money. After paying Mother's fees and my rent, I didn't have much left from Casparov's pay for savings, and once I was dismissed for being a loose woman I would have no income at all. I would have several months of nothing until the baby was born, when I could pretend once again to be an untouched girl worthy of employment.

If I made it that far without dying of starvation, I would have both a child and Mother to support. I could not marry, not only because no man would marry an unwed woman with a child, but because no married woman could work in an office. Any woman lucky enough to have a job in the first place was let go on the day of her wedding. It was enough to make a woman fantasize about such silly, far-off notions as voting and being the captain of one's own life.

Still, I would find some way to keep fighting. I could not count on Alex to support me, and I certainly could not count on him to marry me. My own birth, and Mother's example, had taught me that men, while wonderful, were completely unreliable, especially when it came to serious things like babies. By his own admission, Alex was aimless, a layabout, a man who already had everything he wanted. I did not want to think about how I felt about Alex. I did not want to think of the look that might come on his face when I told him, of how things would cool, how he would quietly fade from my life and become the faint memory of a wild incident. Men, no matter how honorable their intentions at first, could walk away from such difficult complications, and women could not; to expect anything else was foolish.

> *I do respectfully address your inquiry. However, with*
> *regard to the person or persons mentioned, such issues*
> *would be comprehensively addressed in the matter under*
> *contract, and heretofore referred to under subsection B . . .*

I took only a brief luncheon, perusing Casparov's newspapers unseeing. Perhaps I was lucky, and there was no child. I would not know for weeks. In the meantime, I could make preparations just in case. I ran the numbers through my mind as my eyes traveled the words blurred in newsprint over and over again. I had a small sum put away. I could move to a smaller room in my boardinghouse, save the train fare if I cut every second visit to Mother, skip two meals per week, and just perhaps . . .

At five o'clock I covered my typewriter and put on my coat and hat. I had walked out onto the street and was pulling up my collar futilely against the wet wind when I saw Alex leaning against a lamp-post, waiting for me.

He had changed his clothes. I had not spoken to him when I left his flat that morning; I had left him still sleeping. Now he wore a knee-length black wool coat and black leather gloves, as well as a fedora of deep charcoal that matched his trousers. He was clean-shaven and well rested; he had not been working a job, under a crushing burden of worry, as I had. I saw him instantly—I would have seen him from a mile distant, even though he looked just like every other Londoner heading home in the faltering April light.

Thinking of Casparov, who might follow behind me through the door at any moment, I pulled my collar yet tighter and walked away, moving briskly in the direction of the bus that would take me to my boardinghouse. "Go away, Alex," I said.

I heard him follow me, could picture how his body moved beneath the cover of the wool coat. "I'm worried about you," he said.

"Go away," I told him again. "If he sees us, I'll lose my job." A squeeze of panic jolted through my veins. If I lost my job now, before I had a chance to save any more money . . .

"Are you all right?" Alex asked, his voice coming from just behind my shoulder. "Where are you going?"

"Home, of course."

"I'll come with you."

"You needn't."

He must have read something in my tone, because he said, "Very well, Jo. I'm sorry I approached you like that. It was rather stupid after yesterday's subterfuge. But that doesn't mean I can't accompany you home."

"I'm taking a bus," I said.

Now his voice was just a little amused. "I think perhaps I can manage that. I've done it before."

I reached the stop—there were a handful of other people waiting, men and women on their way home from work—and whirled to face him. In my panic it crossed my mind that he was looking for a repeat of the night before, as if I would be foolish enough to risk everything, to lay myself bare before him, every night of the week at his pleasure. But when I met his gaze, I could not sustain the idea. From beneath the brim of his hat, those unmistakable eyes were looking at me with concern—true, sincere concern. There was no trace of lust in his gaze. Or none that I could see, perhaps. It struck me as possible that I wasn't as good a judge of men as I'd thought.

"Go home, Alex," I tried again.

"No," he replied.

So we took the bus, he and I, crowded in with the other London workers, as rain began to pelt the glass. He said nothing, merely sat next to me, his shoulder brushing mine, as if we did this every day. I thought for certain he'd be noticed, not only as of a higher class but also—to my mind—the best-looking man who had ever existed, but in his ordinary coat and hat no one gave him a second glance, not even the women. It seemed that when he wanted to, Alex could fade into the city background, invisible to everyone but me.

I looked out the window, wondered if I could walk to work instead and save the bus fare, and for the first time felt like weeping.

Still my shadow, he followed me off at my stop and from there to my boardinghouse. I roomed in a house that was cheap, horrid, and female-only, the landlady a termagant about her rules. "You cannot come in," I told Alex. "Men are not allowed."

"I'll explain," he said.

I pinched the bridge of my nose, my thin gloves cold against my skin. Now I would lose my home as well as my employment. Perhaps I could find somewhere cheaper. I'd be turned out if I was pregnant, anyway. In defeat, I turned my back on him and came through the front door, taking the stairs to my flat.

The landlady, who lived in the ground-floor room and watched everything from her front window, came immediately into the front hall, protesting, when Alex followed me. I kept walking and let her words wash over me, followed by Alex's soothing tone. He told her something; I knew not what. I did not listen. I took the second set of stairs and put my key in the door to my rooms.

I left the door open behind me—that Alex would succeed with the landlady was never really in question—and walked immediately to the bedroom, dropping my coat, my hat, and my gloves as I went. "There," I said when I heard him come in. "You've accompanied me home. Well done, Sir Galahad."

I heard him close the door and settle on the single chair in my sitting room, and I imagined him looking around my flat. Taking in its mere two rooms—the kitchen was downstairs and the bathroom was down the hall—and their dim corners, the smell of cabbage cooking from downstairs. I began to unbutton my lavender wool dress, not caring that the door to the bedroom stood half open.

"What is this?" Alex asked. I glanced through the doorway to see him holding a framed photo, one of the few mementos I kept in the flat.

"That is me," I replied, ducking back into the bedroom and continuing to undress. "Mother had work for a time as an artist's model, and she convinced the studio to hire me as well. I didn't last." I had been unable to sit still, or still enough. I had wanted to sketch instead.

He was silent for a moment. The photo showed me in nothing but a simple Greek toga, cut to midthigh, sitting chin in hand on a stool with leaves woven into my hair, the fabric of the toga falling artfully off my shoulder almost to the level of my small breast. "How old were you?" he asked.

"Thirteen." I folded the lavender dress carefully and put it away.

I heard a click as he put down the sketch in its small frame. "Dear God, Jo."

"We had to make a living," I snapped, pulling the pins from my hair.

"I know what you're worried about," Alex said. "I'm not a fool, you know. I'm worried about the same thing."

"It's none of your concern."

"I disagree."

Here we were, then, two people who had had a night of passion, facing each other in the light of day. It was sordid and sad, and it made me angry. I came out of the bedroom, wearing only my chemise, and stood before him. He had removed his hat and gloves, but he still wore the black coat, and he was slouched a little in my uncomfortable chair, his hands in his lap. I ignored the wince of unhappiness on his face.

"Money doesn't make you better than me," I said. "Money doesn't make anyone better than anyone."

He looked at me, and there was nothing predatory in it. His gaze did not travel my chemise, my bare arms, my hair tumbling over my shoulders. But his features smoothed as he looked at my face, the unhappiness draining away, for all the world as if he were looking at something he liked. I admitted to myself in that moment that I was horribly, hopelessly in love with him, and that the pain of it would be something that could be overcome but would never entirely go away.

"I know it," he replied, and he stood and shrugged off his coat.

I took a step back as I watched him remove his charcoal suit jacket as well, leaving him in his waistcoat and shirtsleeves. "What are you doing?" I asked.

He did not reply but strode to my bedroom, and for a moment I wondered if I had read him wrong, if he expected something of me after all. But he only reemerged a moment later, my bathrobe in his hands. "Here," he said, sliding it over my shoulders.

I put my arms in the sleeves and pulled the robe tight, still watching him. He stood close to me now, and I could smell the scent of his skin that I had come to know so well. I could not speak.

"Where is the bathroom?" he asked.

I pointed vaguely. "Down the hall."

He nodded and took my hand in his. He pulled me gently toward the door.

I resisted. "What are you doing?" I asked again.

He did not let go of my hand. "You are exhausted," he explained. "And you are worried. A hot bath will help. Let's go."

"We can't," I protested, thinking of my neighbor down the hall, a middle-aged lady with a pimply neck and pouchy eyes, who watched everything I did with sour disapproval. "I already can't have a man here. We can't go—the both of us—everyone will know."

He raised my hand to his lips and kissed it, for the first time giving me a flirtatious look that melted my knees. "I promise not to get in with you," he said solemnly. "Come with me."

He led me down the hall, and when my neighbor popped out of her doorway to stare at us, as she inevitably did, he only nodded politely at her and bade her good evening.

"She cannot have a man here!" the woman shouted at our retreating backs.

Alex only ushered me into the bathroom and turned back to address her briefly. "My good lady, she already does." Then he closed the door with a soft *click*.

He let the bathtub fill as I stood frozen in place, unable to move. The bathroom was not large, and he seemed to fill the space, even in his shirtsleeves. He tested the water, then untied the bathrobe and slid it from my shoulders, rearranging my long hair. "You will not be evicted," he said softly. "I promise."

I said nothing. I had no words left; I had nothing to say. I stood like a tailor's mannequin as he raised the hem of my chemise and drew it up my body. I lifted my arms as he pulled it over my head. I had nothing to say even as I stood naked before him. All of my anger had drained away, and all of my worry, and all of my terror, and I was left an empty shell. Alex took my shoulders, turned me, and helped me into the bathtub.

The water was hot, and something of a shock, and I drew in a deep intake of breath. As the heat worked through my limbs, I took another and another. Alex pulled up the bathroom's small stool behind me without a word and sat. He found a sponge and washed my back, gently, winding my hair out of the way. His hands were adept, his touch sure. I hugged my knees, staring down at the water. He lifted my hair from the back of my neck and ran the sponge there, too, the sensation filling me with warmth. The silence stretched out, settled like an even blanket, free of awkwardness. We seemed to need no words.

He did not try to touch me beyond that. I felt my mind stop spinning, stop scheming. I made a sound, and I realized I was crying, my tears falling into the water.

Alex put the sponge down and slid his arm around me, across the top of my chest, drawing me gently backward. I could feel him behind me, the silk of his waistcoat against my bare shoulder blades. He had not rolled back his sleeves, and his arm, still clad in its white shirtsleeve, dragged in the water, soaked through.

He pressed his lips to the side of my neck in a single passionate kiss, and I felt his breath against me. "Jo," he said.

And suddenly I stopped fighting. I looked down at his arm, soaked so heedlessly in the water yet still holding me, and something about it cracked me open. The old Jo was gone, and someone new and unknown took her place. Someone who wanted to love Alex Manders more than anything. I lowered my defenses, put down my weapons, and let everything go.

Two weeks later, I married him.

There was no baby; not then and not later. It never mattered. We had each other.

And then he went to war, and he died. And he left me alone to start fighting again.

CHAPTER ELEVEN

That night at Wych Elm House, I dreamed.

I was in the front hall, standing next to the familiar umbrella stand, listening to the clock tick in the sitting room past the glass doors. The air was close, hot; I could not breathe, and I could not turn around. Instead, with the inexorable motion of dreams, I walked forward on silent footsteps.

There was something wrong with the light. It was glaring and harsh, burning like late-summer sunlight, and I blinked hard, trying to see. The corridor had somehow become the corridor at Mother's hospital, the two places overlapping, and I felt my bare feet walking over cool tile instead of warm wood.

I turned a corner to find Mother sitting on a sofa, just as I'd seen her in the hospital visiting room. Her large brown eyes implored me silently from her porcelain face. She wore a shawl that drooped past her bare shoulders, and on the skin of her neck and her collarbones I could trace long lines of scratches, like claw marks, some of them welling with blood. Standing over her, wearing the white coat of a doctor, was David Wilde.

Something flickered past, lost in the glare of light. I raised my hand, trying to shade my eyes, trying to stare into the pitiless white. *Stop,* I wanted to shout at Wilde. *Leave her alone.* Behind me, I heard the *snick* of a door opening.

Forget, Mother said to me as blood trickled down her neck.

Then I was once again in the corridor of Wych Elm House. At the end of the hall I saw the front door hanging open to the steps and the cobblestoned drive beyond. Someone had come in.

Wet footprints were pressed into the floor, coming through the door. In the bright light, they gleamed like fresh paint—feet crowned with toes, leading into the corridor beyond. With rising horror, I realized the prints were made in blood, as if someone had waded barefoot through a bloody puddle.

It's Frances, I thought, unable to stop myself. The prints led around a corner and through a doorway where I could not see. *She got up from the cobblestones outside.* She hadn't stayed where she'd fallen; she'd gotten up and come inside, broken and bloody, and if I followed the trail through the doorway I would see—

I gasped awake, jerking in my sweaty bed, a half-formed sound in my throat. In the darkness I put my hands to my neck, pressing my palms to it as I took one breath, then another.

It was the middle of the night, with nothing but darkness coming through my window, yet my bedroom was suffused with faint, eerie light, grayish white and creeping. I inhaled a breath of cold dampness before I realized it was mist.

The dream fell away. There could not be mist in my room; my window was closed. But I could feel it against my face, and it carried a strange smell, sweet and almost cloying. I threw back my covers and sat up, kneeling on the bed and gripping the sash of my bedroom window. It was stuck; I pushed harder, jamming the heels of my hands against it, as drops of water collected on the ends of my hair. I made a low sobbing sound as my fingers slipped over the damp wood of the sash, and then the smell disappeared and the mist vanished.

I turned and stared into the blackness of the room, my breath rasping loudly in the still air. It was full dark again now, the mist gone as if it had never been. The blood pounded in my temples. *I am not mad,* I thought wildly, thinking about footprints in blood. I touched a finger to a lock of hair that lay plastered to my cheek and curled it around my knuckle, watching the drop of water forming at the end. *I did not imagine it. I am not mad.*

In the morning, when dawn finally came, I found leaves scattered on the floor of my bedroom, brown and curled like the palms of hands in supplication, dry and crumbling beneath the soles of my bare feet.

D ottie was waiting in the morning room, her lips beginning to pinch at my tardiness. "You're wearing one of your new frocks, at least," she said.

I put a few scraps of breakfast on my plate, too tired to answer. The horrible night had left me flushed and hot, my eyes gritty. As so often happened when my spirits were low, I wanted Alex with an almost childlike craving. I could see the fine line of his jaw, the strong beauty of his fingers and the palms of his hands. Some mourners found that they could not recall their loved one's face after a period of time, but I was not one of them. I would be haunted by excruciating memories of every detail of Alex until the day I died.

Forget, Mother's voice said.

"Eat quickly, Manders," Dottie broke in. "We have work to do today."

I glared at her dully, but she wasn't looking at me. I remembered her son, Martin, his hands clumsy on my shoulder blades as he embraced me. Had Dottie planned to marry me to him all along? How had she thought I would go along with it? I was only twenty-six, but I would never marry again. I pushed my plate away and rubbed my gritty eyes.

After breakfast we adjourned to the library, which Dottie used as an office. The impressive shelves along the back wall were stocked with books, but I saw immediately that they were dry old volumes, unread and used as a backdrop, like wallpaper. The large desk was covered with neat stacks of papers. In the room's front corner was a small secretary table, placed near the window. Here she set me with pen and paper, a small moon revolving around her planet, to take dictation of her correspondence in the short-hand I had learned as a secretary. The pen and paper were only a tempo-rary measure, she explained to me, since she had ordered a typewriter for me to use, which would arrive within the next few days.

Though I had not thought of my former job in years, it was uncanny how quickly I fell back into its habits. As I had many a time in my Casparov days, I blinked the tiredness from my eyes and hunched over my desk, settling into the numbing routine of work. Most of Dot-tie's letters were to potential buyers of artwork, listing the pieces she had for possible sale, inviting the recipient to come to Wych Elm House to inspect them in person. There were letters to David Wilde regarding money matters I did not understand, as well as something to another lawyer about taxes on the property. Dottie spoke quickly, moving from one letter to the next as I scratched the words down without time to ponder what I was writing.

We had spent the morning this way when Martin came into the room. He was dressed just as a prosperous young man at home in the country would dress: wool trousers and a collared shirt under a pull-over sweater. The bulk of the sweater filled out some of his hollows, but still there was no mistaking the unhealthy thinness of his body and the waxy pallor of his face. I had seen his prewar photograph so many times that I still felt a jolt when I looked at him, as if I was look-ing at an oddly familiar stranger I could not quite place. I also felt, to my horror, a shiver of embarrassed revulsion at the sight of him. It was uncalled for, and unkind, but I was still affected by last night's dream and I could not help it.

"Good morning, Mother," he said calmly. He turned his deep brown gaze briefly to me. "Cousin Jo."

Dottie glanced at her watch, her expression warring between her habitual disapproval of late sleepers and the impossibility of censuring her beloved son. "It is eleven o'clock," she said, settling for a statement of neutral fact.

"The journey yesterday fatigued me, I'm afraid," Martin said.

"Are you well?" Dottie asked him. "Have you eaten? It is late for breakfast, but the servants—"

"The servants fed me properly, Mother. Please don't worry." He smiled at her, that charming smile that was so like Robert's, and I wondered if Dottie could see he was lying, that he hadn't eaten anything at all. "Do you think I could borrow your delightful companion for a time?"

My stomach twisted. Dottie shot me one of her narrow-eyed looks, this one somehow thoughtful and speculative. "You wish to speak to Manders?"

"I wish to go walking with Cousin Jo and show her the grounds," Martin said easily. "Let me guess—you've kept her locked up in here, working her to death. Really, Mother! Cousin Jo is family, not an Egyptian slave. Has she even had a proper tour of the house?"

Dottie leaned back in her chair, inscrutable thoughts behind her eyes. If my suspicion was right, having Martin and me walk together played into her plans; however, she had not expected Martin to suggest it, and she hated surprises. "Very well," she said at last. She turned to me as I tried to hide my terrified expression. "Manders, go take some air with Martin. Please return by two o'clock, as I'd like those letters finished by the end of the day."

I did not move. My hands gripped the edge of my desk, the knuckles white.

"Jolly good," came Martin's voice. I turned my head, as stiff as if it were on rusty wires, and found him looking at me. He had that meaningful look in his eyes, the one he'd given me yesterday. "Get your coat, Cousin Jo," he said. "There's an autumn chill in the air."

CHAPTER TWELVE

It was indeed chilled outdoors; it was the middle of September, and the sunlight was beginning to thin, the wind losing its warmth. Martin had put on a short wool jacket and wound a scarf of dark burgundy around his neck. His brown hair was longish and carelessly cut—the product, I realized, of months in hospital—and when he swung open the front door, it tousled in the wind like a boy's.

As I tugged on my hat, a maid descended the staircase behind me, carrying an armful of linens. I turned to her as Martin waited for me in the doorway. "I'm sorry about the leaves," I said.

The maid paused. "Pardon, miss?"

"The leaves in my room." I was unused to the idea of a servant cleaning up after me, and I felt the need to explain. "I must have tracked them in somehow. It's a bit of a headache for you, I know. I'll try to watch more closely next time."

But she looked at me blankly. "There were no leaves in your room, miss."

"Oh." I felt myself flush. "Perhaps one of the other maids already cleaned them."

"I'm the only maid who does the bedrooms."

I glanced at Martin, who was looking at me curiously, then looked back at the maid. Panic tried to close my throat. "I, er—I must be think-ing of something else, I suppose."

"Certainly, miss," the maid said, bemused.

I escaped through the open front door and onto the front steps. "Is everything all right?" Martin asked me.

I managed a smile. "Yes, of course. Let's go."

He took me over the grounds, starting behind the house. We walked through the gardens—unkempt and dying now—and to the stables, where no horses resided, and the tennis court, where no one played. The tennis court had not been cleaned in years, and piles of dead leaves stood in drifts, straggles of weeds growing through the hard surface.

"Did you ever play?" I asked, trying to forget my exchange with the maid as I pulled up the collar of my coat and followed him past.

"Hardly," Martin replied. "I had no one to play with. Franny was too young—she tried awfully to please me, but she was easily distracted and could never finish a proper game. Alex played with me a few times when he lived here, but he beat me with so little effort I soon became discouraged. He said he learned the game from his father."

I didn't know Alex played tennis—and he had never told me much about his father. I tried to picture a man resembling Alex but older, teaching a six-year-old to play. Where had they practiced? Had they laughed, or was the air tense between them? Had Alex fondly recalled those sessions, or were they memories he'd rather put away? I'd never know, and I was suddenly jealous that Martin knew something of Alex, of his life before me, that I didn't. "Tell me about Alex living here," I said.

Martin flinched a little, and too late I remembered Dottie's rule not to speak of Alex. But my companion recovered himself quickly, taking me over the path now around the side of the house. "Alex was twelve when he arrived," he answered me, "and I was eight, stuck in the countryside with a baby sister and ripe for a bit of hero worship.

He was good enough to let me stay in his presence, as annoying as I was. He stayed for three years, and they were the best of my life."

We were at the front of the house now, and we followed the path into the trees. I thought briefly of the mist I'd seen from my window— and the mist in my room—but in the crisp sunlight the memory seemed distant. Martin's pace slowed; he was tiring already, but still he glanced at me over his shoulder and motioned to the woods around us. "This land goes all the way to the sea. Mother's father bought it for Mother when she married." He gave me a wry smile. "We're new money all the way, you see. My great-grandfather was one of those nasty old Victorian industrialists. Children working in his factories, paying his workers pennies, all of that sort of thing. Mother is of his blood. She tried to sell the land here for lumber value just before the war—she thought lumber would be valuable with war coming, and tried to parcel the whole thing off. But she had opposition from the neighboring estates as well as the local government. She was stuck in a legal mire over it for years."

I looked around me, feeling the dry hush of old leaves underfoot, listening to the throaty *caw* of a crow somewhere, and I tried to envision owning a piece of the earth and wishing to sell it off. "So she lost," I said.

"She did." Martin gestured off to the left with one thin hand. "Our property ends several miles that way—there's a government installation there, though you can't see it through the trees. I think the installation is the reason she couldn't sell."

"What is it?" I asked.

"Ministry of Fisheries." Martin's breath came deeper now, as if the simple walk through the trees had exhausted him. "An outpost thereof. Lots of boats coming and going, which is rather nice to watch. In the other direction, the border of our land ends nearly in town. The locals will tell you the views are lovely." He dropped his hands in his pockets. "It will all be mine someday, which is why I've come home. That and to continue the family line, of course."

My jaw froze shut. *With me. He means to continue the family line with me.*

But when we stepped into the strong sunlight of a small clearing and he turned to me, I saw only weariness in his face. His skin seemed thin as parchment, his cheekbones prominent beneath. He sat on the fallen trunk of an old tree and put his forearms on his knees, his thin wrists dangling. He looked up at me, squinting a little. "It really is nice to meet you, Cousin Jo," he said quietly. "I've always wanted to meet the girl Alex married. I'm glad you were here when I returned after all this time. Franny died while I was away, you see, and I thought I'd be here alone."

I swallowed past the shards of glass in my throat. *Say it, Jo. Just say it.* "I cannot marry you," I blurted into the still air. "I simply cannot." In the pause that followed, I managed to add, "I'm sorry."

Martin sat very still, looking at me. I could see clearly in the bright light that he was ill—not just a case of postwar nerves, as Dottie would have it, but something much worse. He was a man who had looked death in the face, and recently. He kept his wrists on his knees and regarded me with a pensive expression as a lark flew high overhead, crying.

"Thank God," he said evenly. "I can't marry you, either."

I blinked, and some of my surprise and relief must have shown on my face because he smiled.

"Please don't take it the wrong way, Cousin Jo," he said. "You are very beautiful, as I'm sure you know. And I know you have a good character, because Alex would only marry a right sort. But the fact remains that I cannot marry Alex's wife."

I felt the sudden sting of tears behind my eyes. "I loved him very much," I said.

"So did I." Martin pulled his gaze from me and looked out into the trees. "Or perhaps it's more accurate to say I adored him." He scrubbed a hand over his face, the memory dragging on him. "Worship was so easy with Alex."

"I know," I said.

"I joined the army because of him. Did you know that?" Martin said. "Signed up because he did. Thought I'd be RAF, but I never made it. It didn't matter—I was on the same fighting ground as him, fighting the same war. That was all that mattered to me. I thought we'd both come home war heroes." He shrugged, as if he'd given up trying to figure it out. "And now here we are—I look like this, and he never came home at all. War is a funny thing."

"When did you last see him?" I asked, my throat thick.

"He came to see me in the hospital in 1917. Franny was dead by then, and we talked about it. It put him in a dark mood, I thought."

"He was upset over it?" I recalled the careless words Alex had written to me. *She has died, poor thing.*

"I wasn't well—that's putting it mildly—so perhaps I'm misremembering," Martin replied. "But he didn't seem himself. It was odd—Alex had always treated Franny nicely, but he hadn't seen her in years. Yet he was shaken up. 'I don't understand it,' he said to me, 'and now I don't think I ever will.' Isn't that a strange thing to say?" He shook his head. "I asked him what he was going to do next—you know, he'd flown so many RAF missions, I thought he must be due for a promotion, anything he wanted. But all he said was 'I don't have a bloody clue.' You know Alex—always so ambitious, striving for the highest thing, making the rest of us run to keep up with him. It wasn't like him at all."

I stared at him, numb. Ambitious? Alex had finished Oxford, then traveled, doing nothing. *An aimless fellow with a great deal of education and not much to do,* he'd described himself that first night. He was intelligent, of course, and good at everything—but he'd never shown himself as ambitious to me.

But then, Dottie's voice said, *you weren't together all that long.*

"I'm sorry," Martin said to me, looking at my face. "I've gone on and on. The point is that we can't marry, no matter what Mother may want."

That shook me out of my thoughts. "Do you honestly think your mother means for us to marry?"

"Oh, yes." He smiled a little, the corner of his mouth crooking. A breeze, smelling of leaves and rain, tousled his longish hair. "You caught my little message yesterday, did you? I was trying to warn you, in case you didn't know. I know Mother well. I need a wife, and Alex left one; it would seem practical to her, as long as she approved of you."

"I'm not sure she does," I said.

"Of course she approves of you." Martin patted the pockets of his jacket absently. "If she didn't, she would have dismissed you long ago."

The truth of it computed in my mind. "The trip to the Continent," I said slowly. "Those three months. That was some kind of a trial, wasn't it?" I tilted my head back and looked up at the sky. And to think I had started to feel sympathy for Dottie. "My God."

"You can't hate her," Martin said reasonably. "You have to see things her way. Family comes first. Instead of marrying properly, as was his duty, Alex married an unknown girl of no family. He never introduced you to us. He didn't even invite anyone to the wedding."

"No, he didn't," I said. My legs were suddenly tired, and I took a seat next to him on the old tree, keeping a large space between us so we resembled two strangers waiting for a bus. Alex and I had married in Crete, just the two of us. It had been his suggestion, and I'd asked him why. *Because,* he'd answered, *it isn't anyone's damned business what I do.* Perhaps he hadn't wanted Dottie breathing down his neck. It had been romantic, a whirlwind of sea and sunlight and passion, and I'd had no objection at all.

"Then, you see," Martin continued, "the war came, and took Alex with it. Nothing turned out the way Mother planned it. But you behaved respectably as a widow, and there were no accounts that you were a fool. So she took you on to see for herself if you were suitable for the family."

I put my elbows on my knees and my head in my hands in a most unladylike manner. "It isn't just that I don't want another husband," I told him. "Any husband. It's that I truly can't marry you. The War

Office never sent the official notice of his death, and the paperwork is a mess. So under the law I'm not precisely a widow—I'm still his wife. I can't even get a widow's pension."

"That's beastly," Martin said softly. "I assume Mother doesn't know. I'll be the one to tell her, if you like."

"She'll dismiss me if we don't marry."

"No, she won't. Mother has her faults, but she wouldn't leave a member of the family with no means. Just leave it to me."

I looked up at him. He spoke with the confidence of an only son who knows his mother will listen to his wishes. "And what will you do about a wife?" I asked.

"I'll tell her to find me another, of course."

"That's madness. Don't you want to choose your own wife?"

"My wife for how long?" he asked. He gave me a smile. "I'm not quite healthy, and the war nearly did me in. It's made Mother frantic. If I shuffle off this mortal coil without leaving an heir, all of this will be for nothing." He gave a grand wave at our surroundings, indicating the house and the woods. "I've known my duty since I was a boy—even more so after it became clear that Fran could never marry. Don't worry about me, Cousin Jo. After the trenches, and then the hospital, it doesn't seem like such a bad lot." He pressed his hands to his knees and stood. "Come. I haven't shown you the house yet."

He rose from his seat and started slowly off through the trees. When we emerged, I looked at the house, standing tall and silent in the sunlight. There was something sullen about it, as if it kept its secrets on purpose, buried in the tangled brush that surrounded it. As the sunlight winked off the glass of one of the upper windows, I saw a figure looking out at us, but when I looked again, it was gone.

A servant, I thought. *One of the maids. That's all.* I forced myself not to hesitate at the front door, not to think of the bloody tracks I'd seen in my dream. I couldn't start babbling about nightmares, mists, and leaves. Instead, I stared ahead as Martin led me to the staircase.

Upstairs, Martin showed me Dottie's picture gallery, a massive

open space at the east end of the house in which she displayed her paintings. Two workmen were on ladders, rearranging works of art, moving
the paintings already on the walls to make room for the new pieces
Dottie had just bought. "This room is actually a ballroom," Martin said,
his hushed voice echoing from the walls. "But of course Mother doesn't
use it that way."

I nodded and followed him. As we crossed the room, I thought
footsteps echoed behind us, but it must have been a trick of the acous-
tics, because when I glanced back, no one was there.

On the same floor, at the other end of the house, were the rooms
that included my bedroom. I was the only tenant in this part of the
house, he explained, while himself, his parents, and the servants were
upstairs. He paused on the stair landing, his hand on the rail, looking
up. "Fran's old room is up there," he said, his voice quiet. "I suppose no
one has emptied it out. I haven't gone to look. I don't think—Mother
wouldn't throw away her things."

I looked at the expression on his face and placed a hand on his
wrist. "We don't have to go up there," I said softly.

But his usual easygoing humor was draining out of him, leaving
his gaze cold and bleak. "It's a terrible thing to say," he said, "but it was
hard to love Fran. It was *hard*. You know?"

"I know," I said, the words pricking my skin like needles as I
thought of Mother.

"It was always something." The words seemed to have come loose
in him. "She'd have one of her spells, and the doctors would come.
She'd break valuables, shout nonsense at the servants. And sometimes—
the screaming."

I had come home one day, at fifteen, to find that Mother had pulled
all of our belongings from the closets and cupboards and piled them in
the middle of our tiny flat. She had convinced herself that our landlady
watched us somehow, listened to all of our conversations through secret
telephone wires she'd laced through the walls, and we needed to move.

It had taken days for me to undo the damage and put everything away. I let Martin talk and said nothing.

"She was desperate," Martin said. "It was part of what made it so hard. Beneath it all, she wanted love so badly. Mother's, of course, though Father was her favorite. He didn't speak to her much—Father doesn't like to deal with difficult things—but Fran would have shined his shoes if he'd let her. As for me, she would throw her arms around my neck, and all I'd be able to think about was that she hadn't bathed since the last time the nurse had made her do it. Do you know, when I first heard she'd died while I was in the hospital, the second thing I thought was, *Thank God it's over.*" He glanced at me. "Not very brotherly, is it?"

I remembered the monument Dottie had bought for her daughter, expensive and overweening. "What was the first thing?" I asked. "The first thing you thought when you heard she was dead?"

He swallowed. "Well, I was very ill, and it was a shock. I'm afraid I wept a little more than is considered manly. But the first thing I thought was, *Fran wouldn't do that. I wonder if someone did her in.* I didn't know the circumstances, you see. I thought maybe one of the village children—they hated her. But she died here, at home, so it wasn't possible." He shook his head. "Enough morbid talk. Let me continue the tour." He moved ahead of me and began to climb the stairs.

In the hall behind us, a door slammed.

I was still at the foot of the stairs, Martin several steps up. I felt a chill—as if a hand had touched me—and I took a step back, my feet quiet on the carpet, and looked down the hall. There was no one in sight. *A servant is about*, I told myself, *changing linens or cleaning . . .*

"Martin, did you hear that?" I asked softly.

There was no sound from him. I stood frozen. The air grew thick, hard to breathe.

"Hello?" I called.

Near the end of the hall, my bedroom door swung open in a silent motion. I did not hear the click of the latch. The door hung open like a gaping mouth, dark and somehow obscene, for a long moment before another door in the corridor swung open in exactly the same manner. And another, on the other side of the hall.

A bead of cold sweat ran down between my shoulder blades. I opened my mouth, wanting to call for Martin—for anyone—but I could not make a sound. I forced my feet backward and nearly stumbled onto the staircase, turning and looking up.

Martin had sunk down onto a step, his body sagging. His hands gripped his knees and his head hung down, as if its weight were too much to carry. He was breathing heavily. With the lowered angle of his head, I could not see his face.

I climbed the steps and approached him. "Martin?" I whispered.

He raised his face to me. It was ghastly in the dim light of the stairwell, his eyes sunken, his cheekbones stark. Beads of sweat stood out on his forehead and his temples. His jaw sagged.

"I'm afraid I cannot show you any more of the house," he said to me in a voice that was nothing but a low rasp. "I don't feel quite capable." Behind me, I heard soft footsteps, and one of the doors in the hallway snicked closed.

Martin blinked. "I'm sorry," he said.

I reached out and grasped his arm. It was thin as a matchstick inside his sleeve. "Martin," I said.

But he was already gone, his eyes rolling back in his head, his body falling gracefully on the jagged steps.

CHAPTER THIRTEEN

Wych Elm House fell silent after Martin's collapse. Dottie called it an attack of nerves, as if her son were merely anxious instead of wasting away to nothing, incapable of taking a walk around the house and back. Doctors came and went for a few days, and then Dottie declared that what Martin needed was rest and absolute quiet. Her rule was law, so everyone, servants and family alike, took to tiptoeing silently around the house, speaking only in whispers and low tones.

Robert quickly finagled a steady stream of invitations that took him out of the house in his motorcar, as he had no patience for Dottie's rules. That left Dottie and me alone. I ran her errands, wrote out her correspondence, and made her telephone calls—she had a distaste for the instrument and had me use it in her stead. After a small meal at my desk or a tray in my room, I would continue work in the afternoons until she dismissed me.

There was plenty to do. We sent out a volume of correspondence that rivaled Casparov's, handling the business of the house, inviting potential buyers to view and purchase her art, and receiving replies.

Dottie also took delivery of the art itself, dealing with deliverymen and the display of the works in the upstairs gallery, as well as overseeing the servants and the daily people she used to supplement them, including a woman to help with laundry twice per week and a single hapless gardener she hired to tackle the overgrown grounds.

Despite the nunnery-like rigidity of our routine, Dottie was tense and irritable, impossible to please. As she had throughout our trip home from the Continent, she nitpicked me endlessly, from my messy curls to the dull shine on my new shoes. She acquired a typewriter for me to use for her letters, then stood by like a harpy as I used it, searching for errors and complaining about the noise it made. She had spent much time at Martin's bedside, and the sour disposition that resulted made me wonder if he'd told her about my marriage situation. Perhaps she was hoping I would quit. Or perhaps she was simply miserable, and it had nothing to do with me at all.

I was miserable myself. I was suffering from incurable insomnia, my nights plagued with sleeplessness and my few bouts of slumber weighted with dreams that were complicated and vivid, filled with images like I'd seen on that first night, real and somehow horrible. I sometimes woke weeping, or laughing, or trying not to scream. Twice I woke to find my hair and nightgown soaked with chill water and a sickly sweet smell in my nose as I clutched my sheets in panic. I would spend the rest of the night awake, until it was finally time to rise and dress and sit at my typewriter, gritty-eyed and dull. I found no more leaves in my room. If I had deluded myself into seeing them the first time, I had done it convincingly.

I barely recognized myself. I had never been like this, prone to hallucinations and dreams, even in the awful days after Alex died. My mind kept circling back to the footsteps I'd heard and the doors I'd watched swinging open—including the door of my own bedroom—as I'd stood transfixed in the hallway. No one had witnessed that but me, not even poor Martin. Either I was going mad or something uncanny was happening.

Frances.

In the haze of my exhaustion, her face was clear in my mind. I

could see her that day in the small parlor. I could see her gray dress and
the string of pearls around her neck, the clasp where it sat at the back of
her collar. I could tell myself that I doubted her identity, that I was not
sure, but pure exhaustion lowers your ability to lie to yourself, and I
knew deep down that I'd seen Dottie's lost daughter. I felt at times as if
I could turn a corner or look in a mirror and I'd see her again, glimpse
her image in the shadows of the huge, silent house. I thought I heard her
footsteps in the corridor, ahead of me or behind me, or saw her hand on
the curtain at the window from the corner of my eye. *The things she saw
coming through that imaginary door were dead*, David Wilde had told me.
She lived at home in privacy, plagued by her waking dreams.

As I watched the days grow colder and shorter through the windows, that was beginning to sound familiar.

You are acquainted with madness, are you not?

Frances terrified me—but she drew me, too. Just like Mother did.
Whatever was happening, Frances was the key. Dottie couldn't help
me, and Robert was gone. As day after day dragged on, I realized that
if I wanted to understand Frances, I needed Martin.

Two weeks after Martin's collapse, I left my room one evening
and stepped onto the landing, ready to ascend to the upper floor. I had
just screwed up my courage to broach my cousin in his bedroom when
I realized I was not alone on the stairs.

On the landing below me stood a man I had never seen before—
short, middle-aged, his graying hair combed back neatly from his forehead and temples. He was carrying a case, and he had paused in his
descent, looking up at me. I froze in surprise, and for a moment I wondered if he would disappear, as Frances had. Then he moved, and I realized that he held in his hand a doctor's case.

"Good evening," he said to me.

I nodded. He gave me a polite smile, a little apologetic. Then he
turned and descended the stairs below me, unaccompanied, as if he
had free run of the house. I stared after him, bemused.

"Curious?"

I turned. Martin stood on the landing above me, looking down. In the dim light of the stairwell, his face was smudged and soft. He was slowly rolling one shirtsleeve back down the length of his arm. I realized I was standing nearly where he'd fainted that day after we'd walked in the woods, the last time I'd seen him.

"Martin," I said.

"Hello, Cousin Jo."

His voice was harder than it had been before, some of the kindness in it vanished. "Who was that?" I asked him.

He shrugged, the motion tight and uneasy. "My doctor." He dropped his gaze to the sleeve he was unrolling.

"I thought the doctors had already come," I said.

"Those were Mother's doctors," Martin replied. "Dr. Weller is mine."

I felt my jaw drop open. "Dottie doesn't know," I said. "She doesn't know you're seeing him, that he was here."

Martin raised his gaze to me. "You can tell her, if you like."

I thought it over. I would get in trouble if she found out I knew and didn't tell her, but I realized I didn't care. "Is it helping you?" I asked. "Whatever he does?"

That made Martin smile. The lines on his face were deeper than they'd been two weeks ago, the shadows darkening the sockets of his eyes and the brackets around his mouth. "Would you like to see something?" he said in reply. "Follow me."

I ascended the steps, my hand on the rail. He watched me come toward him, and some indescribable emotion crossed his eyes, fear and pain and a queer sort of excitement. The charming young man who had led me on a tour was not in evidence tonight. When I reached the top of the stairs, he grasped my wrist—his hand was icy and strangely soft, as if made of wax—and led me down the corridor to a room with its door ajar, light spilling from within. His bedroom.

It was messy, the night table and the desk covered in books and papers, empty dishes, empty cups, pens and bottles and jars. He had just blown out a candle, and the tang of smoke was in the air, scenting the room with that curious edge of fire that candles leave. I saw the thin line of smoke on the table next to the bed, twisting toward the ceiling, and wondered why he'd needed a candle when Wych Elm House was fitted with the latest electric light. I was still looking at it when I heard the door click shut behind him.

I turned to him. I was not afraid, even though we were now alone in his bedroom; I'd never felt any prurient interest from him. He leaned his back against the door, and without waiting for any further cue from me, he gripped his shirt just below the breastbone and yanked it upward. The shirt disengaged from the waist of his trousers, and I was suddenly exposed to an expanse of Martin Forsyth's stomach, white and intimate, displayed before me.

"My God," I said softly.

Across his abdomen was a jagged line, pinkish and healed. It rode upward, knotting the skin before tapering off in a jaunty curve that looked like the blade of a scimitar or half of a wicked smile. The wound had not healed cleanly or kindly; the puckers of skin that marked its length stood stark and angry against the smooth flesh below his rib cage, which I noticed was curved inward in pitiful thinness.

"Shrapnel," he said. "Infected before the medics could get to me. After three surgeries, the doctors claim they got it all out, but I've never believed them."

He dropped the shirt, and I raised my gaze to his face. He was watching me avidly, as if looking for something in my reaction. I lowered myself into the hard wooden chair by the desk. "This is why you spent three years in hospital," I said.

"Four," he corrected me. "I acquired this lovely wound in 1917. The first two years were for the surgeries. The next two were to cure me of the morphine habit I'd so conveniently acquired in the meantime."

"Morphine," I said, thinking of the doctor I'd just seen. "Does your mother know?"

"Of course." He began to tuck his shirt back into his trousers. "She paid the hospital bills."

"And your father?" I asked.

"You could say Father knows," Martin replied. "Though he doesn't quite believe it. 'Use your backbone, son,' is his advice. 'It's just a little pain.'"

"That's why you fainted," I said. "I'm so sorry."

"It's me who's sorry, for frightening you," he replied. "The fact is, I'm usually in pain. Eating pains me. Exertion pains me. Sometimes even sleeping pains me. Mother's doctors are useless, so I had to find my own. She has tried to help, but you know—just once I'd like to have a doctor who doesn't report to my mother."

"And morphine?" I asked. "Is that why you send for him? To supply you?"

Martin leaned his head back against the door, his gaze rising to the ceiling for a long moment before lowering back to me. "I have not had morphine in nearly six weeks," he said slowly, as if the words fought him. "Forty-one days, if you wish to be exact. This is the third time I've purged myself of it in two years. Needless to say, the other two tries were failures."

I put my hand to my mouth. I could not imagine it.

"Do you want to know something?" Martin said. "Dr. Weller doesn't even help, not all that much. He gives me vitamin shots—he claims a stronger constitution will help me kick the addiction—and a mild analgesic. But other than that, he listens to me. He sits in silence, in that chair just there, as I go on and on with the candle lit. It's so strangely cathartic." He raised his gaze to the ceiling again. "Perhaps talking helps me forget that I would gladly strangle him if he had a few drops of morphine in his doctor's bag."

"What do you talk about?" I asked softly.

"The war," Martin replied. "My parents. My childhood. My condition, and how ashamed I am. Franny jumping off that goddamned roof." He winced, whether in pain physical or mental, and I stepped forward, took his arm, and pulled him gently toward the bed.

"You should sit," I said.

"Thank you. Awfully sorry about the language."

I shook my head. "I've heard it before." I helped him sit against the pillows, swinging his legs up onto the mattress, then took a seat in the wooden chair.

"So you see," Martin said as he eased back in the bed, "how horrified Mother would be if she knew I was telling the family secrets to a doctor. It's why I haven't told her."

I took his hint. "I won't tell." I remembered why I had come to visit him, the information I needed. It seemed harsh to question a man so sick, but he was relaxed now, and I could tell he did not wish me to leave. *We may as well talk,* I thought.

"There are a lot of rumors," I said, "about the family's secrets. In town."

Martin nodded. "They've never liked us in the village. Mother has never tried to ingratiate herself, I'm afraid, and Father only bothers with his wealthy friends. When Mother hired David Wilde as her man of business, it put the final nail in the coffin."

"David Wilde is disliked so much?" I asked. "Just because he has one hand?"

An expression of discomfort flitted across Martin's face. "Let's just say no one in town approves of Mr. Wilde. What else do our happy neighbors say of us?"

I stared down at my hands in my lap. "That your sister haunts the woods," I replied. "That the children won't play there."

That brought a frown from him. "False," he declared. "Franny wandered the woods, yes, but she was terrified of the town children when she encountered them. They bullied her mercilessly. I can't imagine she'd come back from the grave to seek them out now."

"They say they've seen her," I persisted, embellishing a little so I wouldn't have to admit that the one who had seen her was me. "And they say she has a dog."

Martin turned his head sharply on his pillow and looked at me. "Now, that's interesting," he said. "That they're still talking about Princer."

I blinked at him in surprise. "Princer? There truly was a dog?"

"No," he replied. "There wasn't a dog." He saw the confusion on my face and added, "There was only a dog in Franny's mind, do you see?"

"So it was one of her hallucinations," I said. It made sense, then, why Dottie would deny the dog's existence at the inquest.

"Princer was different," Martin said. "She imagined him, yes. But he was different. He appeared later. He came through the door, like the others, but Franny trusted him. He was her ally. I think she conjured him in an effort to soothe herself, to bring herself comfort." He shook his head. "I'm not explaining it right. It's so hard to make someone understand who didn't live with Franny. Her delusions became so real after a while."

"You'd be surprised," I said, thinking of Mother and her viscount, the illusion she summoned every time she felt helpless or distressed. "So if the dog was a hallucination, it couldn't have killed the man who died in the woods that day."

"I don't know." Martin turned his head back and stared at the ceiling, his expression beginning to close down the same way it had the last time we'd talked of Franny. "I wasn't here."

"David Wilde says he doesn't believe Franny was suicidal," I persisted, thinking of Martin saying the same thing himself just before he fainted.

"Oh, yes." Martin's voice was turning hard. "Wilde always did like to pick at her and inspect the pieces. He wanted to know what made Franny tick."

I watched him carefully, his pain-etched face in the dim light. "And what did you want?" I asked him softly.

"To protect her, of course," he replied. "I may not have been much of a brother—but I was her brother, wasn't I? What a failure I made of that. What a failure we all made of giving her any kind of a life. An imaginary dog gave her more comfort than I did—than any of us did." He turned on his pillow again and looked at me. "I know I said I was glad it's over, Cousin Jo, but really I'm grateful she's done with all of this. That she doesn't have to deal with the sorry lot of us anymore."

"You don't mean that," I said.

"Don't I?" He closed his eyes. "I'm tired, Cousin. I have to wish you good night."

When I left the room, I opened the door to find a scattering of leaves, brown and dry, in the hallway. The air was chilled. I stood for a long moment, listening, my heart pounding, my breath shallow in my chest. Finally I stooped and picked up a leaf, running my thumb over its waxy surface. It began to crumble in my hand, releasing the tangy smell of autumn. I was afraid, but I was excited, too, vindicated. *Real. The leaves are real.* I raised the leaf to my face and inhaled, closing my eyes.

"He didn't mean it," I said to the girl who wasn't there. "He didn't."

There was no answer but silence.

I let my hand fall and dropped the leaf. When I opened my eyes again, the leaves were gone—all of them, the ones on the floor, the one I had held and dropped. I still smelled the tang in my nose, but there were no leaves in the hallway at all.

Her delusions became so real after a while.

Why not, after all? I was surrounded by madness. Why not me? Perhaps madness had its uses.

Because Martin had said many things, some of which he would regret. But he had said something that lodged within me, that fit with what I already knew.

He'd said his sister was not suicidal.

I wonder if someone did her in.

And if someone had killed her, there was only one person to find the truth. Me.

CHAPTER FOURTEEN

The next time Dottie released me early in the afternoon, I remembered the photographer's shop in town and Alex's camera, which I kept packed in its case in my room. I pulled it from the bottom of my trunk and hefted it to the floor, opening the fine leather case and examining the camera inside.

Alex had bought the camera in 1917, while home on leave. It had been, I recalled, a curious purchase. Alex wasn't a spendthrift; nor was he overly fond of gadgets, though he was excellent at handling them. But the camera had arrived by delivery one day at the Chalcot Road flat, which I had moved into when we married. Alex had seemed almost surprised to see it, as if he'd forgotten he'd ordered it. "I thought we might take a trip to the countryside while I'm home," he said when I questioned him, buttoning his collar with his long, nimble fingers and reaching for a tie so he could take me out to dinner. "I like the idea of taking my own photographs."

Our money had been pinched already by then—and I'd been hoping for a child, which would strain it further—but Alex had come home so exhausted, and he bought things so rarely, that I did not argue. I still did not argue when a custom leather case came by delivery the next day; I merely put the two items together and left them where Alex could use them whenever he wished.

I forgot about the camera after that. Having Alex home was intoxicating, and I had room in my mind for little else. His leave was only of two weeks' duration. How exactly we spent that time, I could not later recall. I only remembered the smell of him, the feel of him, the way he would run his fingers gently through my hair, sometimes rubbing the strands between his fingertips as if reassuring himself I was real. War had changed him; I knew he had seen things he did not talk about, and he often seemed as if something unbearably heavy weighed him down. There were bruises, new and old, beneath his skin, which he claimed came from the juddering discomfort of an airplane—he had gone into RAF training almost immediately upon enlisting. Still, he would trace the back of his finger beneath my jaw or the lobe of my ear, or brush his hand over the back of my neck, even as he read the newspaper and sipped his tea, as if his hands wished to touch my skin of their own accord.

The trip to the countryside never happened. Thinking back on it now, I wondered whether Frances Forsyth was dead even then, whether Alex had been to see Martin in the hospital, or whether those events were still in the future. I no longer knew all the pieces of my husband's life.

Sometime after Alex had gone back to France, I found the camera and put it away in a closet, unable to look at it. I filled my time with volunteering, rolling bandages and sending care packages to soldiers with the local ladies' circle as the war rolled on.

Now, four years later at Wych Elm House, I looked closely at the camera for the first time. It was a heavy thing, a thick black box with a handle on the top, a small lens in the front, and an eyepiece in the back. It was encased in dark leather, the texture patterned under my hands, a circled crest with No. 2 BROWNIE stamped into the leather on the back. A latch at the side seemed to release the front mechanism and swing the camera open, but I did not touch it. Beneath the latch was a knob of silver metal—used, presumably, to advance the film through the chamber while taking photographs.

I picked the camera up, studied it, shook it and listened to the insides. I had no idea if it had any film in it; I didn't recall Alex acquiring any and loading it. I put the camera down and picked up the custom leather case, turning it over, running my hands over it. For the first time it struck me as curious that the camera had a case at all, since it seemed to be a self-contained unit, protected by leather and equipped with a handle. I pondered it for a moment. The case looked a little like a valise—perhaps it was easier to carry than the camera itself, and protected the camera from wind and rain.

When I opened the case and looked inside, I noticed lettering stitched into the lining. I tilted it toward the light. HANS FABER.

I frowned. Perhaps Alex had bought the case secondhand. Had both the camera and the case belonged to Hans Faber? Why, then, had they been delivered separately? Where had Alex met Hans Faber, and why had he forgotten about the camera almost as soon as it arrived? And why had he bought a camera from a German in 1917, the middle of the war?

I picked up the camera again, feeling the weight and heft of it. A pulse of excitement went through me. I could use this. I had never considered it before, but if I could buy film and a means of developing it, I could take my own photographs.

The leaves, I thought. *If I could take a picture of the leaves, I could prove they're real.*

The mist that came to me in the night—I could capture it. Or possibly even Frances herself.

I'm not mad. I'm not.

I put Alex's camera back in its case, snapped the latches shut, and left the room to ask if I could borrow the motorcar.

A s it was a Thursday, the photographer's shop in Anningley was open. A bell over the door tinkled as I entered and looked about the empty studio, the camera in its case in one hand. The bare room that made up the front of the shop contained only a few easels displaying portraits and two large worktables scattered with tools, debris, and camera parts.

I heard the click of a door and a man came from the back room, looking at me over the rim of his half-glasses. He was perhaps sixty. His hair had gone a bright, snowy white and was brushed thickly back from his forehead. His skin was florid, his body short and rather heavy-looking, as if secretly made of pewter.

"Good afternoon," he said to me. "You've just caught me, I'm afraid. I'm about to close for the day."

"I'm sorry," I said, fighting my disappointment. "I can come back Monday, I suppose. It's just I've come from Wych Elm House and—"

"Yes, I know who you are," the man said with some amusement. "Mrs. Baines at the post office has told everyone all about you." He glanced at the case in my hand. "I'm Samuel Crablow," he said, holding out a hand for me to shake. "And I don't mind helping out such a lovely young woman at the end of the day."

"Nonsense." I laughed, noticing the interested gleam in his eyes and seeing through him perfectly. "You only want to know what sort of camera I have in this case."

"Perhaps." Crablow removed his reading glasses and tucked them in a front pocket. "Though I'd gladly photograph you—I think it would turn out very well. I don't suppose I could talk you into sitting for a portrait?"

I shook my head. "I came to ask you how to use my camera, not how to sit in front of one."

"Very well. You have a camera you don't know how to use—I'm intrigued. Let me know how I can help you."

I explained briefly how I had come across the camera. Since he already knew of my widowhood from Mrs. Baines, it didn't take much for him to understand.

"And so you'd like to make use of this impulsive purchase of your husband's," he said, taking the case from me and setting it on one of the worktables. "Let's see what we have. I can give you a few instructions, I'm sure."

I stood watching him, realizing that part of me had expected to be turned away, to have to argue that my whim was a serious one. "Thank you," I said.

But he had already forgotten my existence as he pulled the camera from the case and inspected it. "Interesting," he said. "I see your husband bought this in 1916."

"Actually, it was the next year," I said.

"Yes, well. This is the 1916 make. It's in excellent condition. There is no film in it. You open the case here," he said, pressing the lever and peering inside the box when the door swung open. The insides of the camera looked impenetrable to me, but he pulled out his glasses and stared into it, making little sounds.

"It looks perfectly functional," he said at last. "I can teach you to use it in the space of a few minutes. Whether you have any artistry with it is up to you, I'm afraid. I have some film I can sell you, and when you've used the roll, you can come back here and I'll develop the prints. I'll have to charge you for that."

"Of course," I said. I wasn't sure I wanted Mr. Crablow seeing the things I hoped to capture. "Can you teach me to do it myself? The developing?"

He gave me the sort of smile men have given women since time immemorial. "One thing at a time, my dear lady. I don't wish to overwhelm you. Now, the case." He put down the camera and took up the leather valise. "This is an interesting addition. I see a name here. Was your husband Hans Faber? I thought you were the wife of Mrs. Forsyth's Manders nephew."

"I am," I said. "I was. I don't know who Hans Faber is. My only theory is that my husband bought the camera secondhand."

"It's quite possible," Crablow agreed. He turned the case over in his hands. "This is very finely made, and it's custom fitted to the camera, which is not of standard valise dimensions. The leather is of the best quality. Whoever Mr. Faber is, or was, he invested a good penny in the creation of this case."

"I don't understand what it's for," I said. "It seems to me that the camera stands on its own with no case at all."

"It does," Crablow replied. "Mr. Faber went to some trouble for this."

"Does the case keep out the rain?"

"Possibly, but it isn't sealed with waterproof rubber. Besides, if one is using a camera in the rain—which I do not recommend—one can purchase a slick to prop over it, much like a mackintosh." He studied the case again. "If I had to guess, Mrs. Manders, I would say that whoever carries this case is disguising his camera as a simple piece of luggage."

I crossed my arms over my chest and nodded. "So thieves won't recognize it," I said.

"Perhaps. The other thing that strikes me is that there is no tripod included. If one is serious about taking photographs, a tripod is a logical piece of equipment."

My heart sank a little. Alongside paying for film and development, I did not think I could afford a tripod. Photography seemed to be an expensive hobby. "Can the photographer not take pictures by hand?"

"Yes, of course. But the human hand is not as steady as you think. Your husband wasn't an aspiring journalist, by any chance?"

"No."

Crablow shrugged. "Well, it's no matter. I happen to have a spare tripod here. You can borrow it for as long as you like."

I swallowed. "Thank you. You are very kind."

"It's nothing. If you wish to repay me, you can suggest to Mrs. Forsyth that she bring the family in for another portrait."

"Another?" I asked, watching as he walked to his shelves and rifled through the boxes there. "You took a portrait of the Forsyths?"

"Yes, just before the war. Before the girl died." Crablow picked up a box, read the label, and came back to his worktable. "They're not a popular family around here, I know. People still talk about what happened to the daughter and the dead man in the woods. All I know about Frances Forsyth was that I had a difficult time making her sit still. But I was happy with the end result, though Mrs. Forsyth would not let me display it in my front window."

"Do you have a copy of the picture?" I asked him. "May I see it?"

He glanced at me in surprise. "Yes, of course. I have it in my box of samples I show to private clients. Just over here."

He had mounted the photograph on thick pasteboard to make it easier to handle. He pulled it from a box of similar pictures and handed it to me.

The family was posed in the large parlor, Wych Elm House's most formal room, in front of the grand mantel. In the back stood Robert, younger, slimmer, his face blandly handsome and less puffy than it was now. Standing beside him, Dottie looked curiously softer, as if the years between had set the lines of her face in stone. Her hair was tied back as tightly as it always was. Seated in a chair in front of his father, Martin was a young man grown out of childhood, his shoulders thrown back, his eyes soft and staring directly at the camera, a confident smile on his face. This was the same Martin I had seen in Dottie's picture of him in uniform, the Martin who looked almost nothing like the man today.

Frances was placed beside her brother, seated on a chair in front of Dottie. She was perhaps twelve or thirteen, wearing a dress with puffed sleeves and a high lace collar. Her face stared out at me, the same face I'd seen in the small parlor—the high forehead, the clear, calm eyes. She was a few years younger than the girl I'd seen, wearing a different style of dress, her hair down around her shoulders and tied back with a ribbon, but she wore a string of pearls around her neck that I recognized. Her face wore no expression, and there were shadows under her eyes. Her gaze was serious and fathomless and somehow sad.

I stared at her, captured in silver nitrate and printed on paper. I realized with a jolt that I didn't just recognize her face—I *knew* her. I knew something of the fear she suffered, the isolation. I knew it because even though she was dead, she had made me see.

What do you want, Frances? What do you want from me?

"Mrs. Manders?" the photographer asked.

I stuttered an apology and handed the portrait back to him. "Can you show me how to use the camera?" I asked.

He spent an hour teaching me how to set it up, how to load and unspool the film, how to take pictures and advance the film using the lever. He talked about light—I'd need a powerfully strong light to shoot anything indoors, unless I acquired a flash, and outdoor sunlight would work best, especially the less harsh hours of dawn and dusk. Thinking me a hobbyist, he even gave me tips on where to find the best vistas in the area. I tried to take it all in, and then I left, carrying the camera in its valise and my borrowed tripod, my mind spinning.

At Wych Elm House, I had missed dinner. The sky was dark, the late-autumn wind chill now that the sun had gone.

I pulled off my hat and gloves and stopped in the library first, looking for Dottie, the camera and tripod still in my hands. She had dismissed me for the day hours ago, but there were potential art buyers due to arrive tomorrow, and if she were still working I would offer to help. I found the library empty, Dottie's desk tidy. The new typewriter sat on my little writing desk, hunched under its cover.

A single letter in a sealed envelope lay in the middle of the desk. This was Dottie's way of indicating that the letter was for me and had come in with her stack of correspondence. I knew immediately what it was. I received no mail except for the monthly updates from Mother's hospital.

The letters were always written by one of the senior nurses, though rarely the same nurse from month to month. Perhaps they rotated writing letters to keep their distance from the families; perhaps it was simply part of the shift rotation to write letters once per week from a list. I opened the envelope there in the empty library and read the letter.

> *Mrs. Christopher has been quiet and very well behaved. There was an incident in which she became agitated and broke some breakfast dishes, but the doctors have adjusted her dosage and she has been quiet since. We have moved the patients' outdoor time to the solar as the weather is chill and some days inclement, and she is much disappointed in this as she does like to sit outdoors. Her appetite is still thin, though the doctors do monitor her eating habits. She enjoys having her hair brushed of an evening, and when one of the nurses reads a novel to her, it seems to calm her, though she does not always comprehend the story.*
>
> *There have been several instances of night terrors, in which she complains upon waking of having been walking outside in the cold, but the doctors have made note of it and a sleeping powder will be administered if her rest is much disturbed. It pains me to say that she does not ask for her family, for her mind is in much of a fog; but I am certain that deep within her she carries her love and memory of you.*

So dutiful, so kind. It must be easy to write such things when it wasn't your own mother sitting there, staring at you in puzzlement as if you were a stranger she has never seen. Such a simple thing to call her Mrs. Christopher, as if she'd ever had a husband.

And not a word about the scratches on Mother's neck.

I pocketed the letter and carried the camera equipment through the quiet house to the kitchen, where I scavenged a bowl of soup. One of the maids, who was washing the dishes under the kitchen's dim electric light, informed me that Mr. Forsyth was out, Mr. Martin was in his room, and Mrs. Forsyth had just retired early, claiming a headache. I wondered briefly if I should check on Dottie—when we'd traveled the Continent, her infrequent headaches had been my responsibility—but was assured by the maid that she'd already been given a pill and wanted only rest.

I finished my soup and continued upstairs to my room, dragging my feet with exhaustion. Martin was still sick, and the house was too quiet. But I knew that I would not sleep.

I stopped in my bedroom doorway.

I noticed the bed first: The cover had been pulled all the way down and trailed from the end of the bed like a bridal veil. On the table next to the bed, the shade of the lamp had been removed, and placed next to the bald light—which had been switched on—was a figurine I recognized from one of the glass cabinets in the morning room, depicting Salome cradling the head of John the Baptist in her lap, looking rather sorrowful; I could not think where Dottie had acquired it or why she had thought it worth money. The figure now sat under the glaring light of the lamp, John the Baptist's unseeing eyes staring upward.

The wardrobe door stood partly open, and one of my cardigans had been pulled from it, half in and half out. The waist of the cardigan rested inside, and the neck and arms were drawn out the wardrobe door and onto the floor, the sleeves raised pitifully and eerily lifelike, as if someone inside the wardrobe drew the cardigan in against its will. The room's only chair had been placed next to the wardrobe, and a pair of my shoes was set beneath it. A set of my stockings dangled empty from the seat to the shoes, one of my skirts lay on the seat, and one of my blouses hung unbuttoned from the chair's back, the sleeves folded decorously on the lap of the skirt. The entire display, looking oddly like a woman sitting in a chair, was topped with the shade from my bedside lamp, balancing like a misshapen head.

My numb fingers dropped the camera case and the tripod to the floor. There was no thought in my mind that someone in the house had done this—not one of the family or one of the maids. I listened to my breath rasp loud in the still air and stared again at the wardrobe, the pitiful cardigan, its deliberate message, its unmistakable display.

Frances saw a door, David Wilde had said. *The things she saw coming through that imaginary door were dead.* She was showing me. She wanted me to see.

"Frances," I whispered.

I looked again at the figure in the chair. It looked withered and dead, inhuman, the head misshapen and eyeless, and yet it was a woman. Posed in a chair with her hands in her lap. Was she standing sentry over the awful doorway? Or mimicking the pose in the portrait I'd just seen? *You've seen me*, the hideous figure seemed to say. *I see you. We see each other.*

I made a strangled sound. I should run. I should pack my bags, call for the motorcar, and leave this house, never to come back. Find some other way to make a living. I should not stay here, sleep in this bedroom, anymore.

And yet despite its monstrousness, the figure in the chair was pitiful. There was something about the lifeless way the empty sleeves were folded, the weakly dangling stockings. I had taken a step forward again, my hand out to knock the lampshade off the chair, when I remembered the camera.

This was what I had wanted—to be able to take pictures so someone outside my fevered mind could see. I crouched and fumbled with the latches of the camera case, and I had removed the camera before I remembered Mr. Crablow's lecture about light. I'd need powerful artificial light to shoot indoors, he'd said. I did not have a flash.

Still, I raised the camera, balanced it on my crouched knees—I did not bother with the tripod—and snapped a picture of the chair. I rotated the film, then snapped another. I rotated the film again, angled the camera toward the wardrobe, and snapped a third.

"I see you," I said aloud.

It was the best I could do. I could not look at the eerie chair anymore. I put the camera down and stood. I found myself staring at the lampshade as if it were a set of features looking back at me. I quickly turned and left the room, closing the door behind me.

In the corridor, I paused. I looked down at my hands, which were trembling but not shaking. My throat was tight, but I could still breathe. She wanted something—from me. She wanted it so desperately she was willing to come back, to come through the door she had feared in life, to beg it of me. That what I had just seen was a violation of every rational belief, I knew very well. But I also knew an act of desperation when I saw one. I knew what it was to want something that badly. To feel that deeply.

I would not run screaming. Frances had come to me; so I would go to her. I would go to her own places, her private places, as she had been to mine. I would start with the place where she died.

I turned toward the stairs and headed for the roof.

CHAPTER FIFTEEN

To get to the roof, I had to climb to the attic floor, where the main stairwell ended, then cross to the other end, where a small door led to a service staircase winding upward. I didn't know my way, but it wasn't difficult, since the attic floor contained only a single long, musty corridor, with failing light coming through its windows, and the dark, closed door to Frances's room. I followed the corridor, which was empty and silent, until I found the service door, which was unlocked. Then I climbed the smaller, dusty set of stairs.

At the top was a second door, wooden, held shut by a latch. I could hear the low howl of wind from the other side, as if someone were moaning pitifully. I lifted the latch, the damp wood chill against my palm, and pressed the door open.

A gust of wind blew in at me, touching my hair. Outside, all was dark; twilight had given in to full night. The air was cold, stinging, trailing its fingers under the neck of my dress before I'd even left the stairwell, but I felt braced by it after the stifling corridor and the dusty stairs, and I lifted my face.

I stepped out onto the roof. Immediately the wind gusted in my hair again, slapping my skirt against my legs, chilling the fabric of my clothing even as it touched my skin. I was on a landing atop Wych Elm House's highest gable, a space about four feet square enclosed by a black wrought-iron railing at waist height. To my right and left, the roof of Wych Elm House fell away, as if I were the mermaid on the prow of a ship, sailing into the woods. Before me spread the tops of the trees, the closest ones visibly rippling and shimmering in the wind, the farther ones mere ribbons of black and pewter and dusky silver, blending into a mass that spread for miles.

I stepped to the railing and put my hands on it; it was icy, and even under my touch it barely warmed. My eyes watering in the sting of the wind, I gazed out at the view, vast and beautiful and terrifying, as if I were a queen alone in a tower. A handful of lights twinkled far off to the right, all I could see of the town of Anningley. Through the roaring of the wind in my ears, I imagined I could hear the sea. It was cold and beautiful up here, powerful, hypnotic.

And then I looked down.

The drop was sheer, the precipice of the house falling away from the tips of my toes, past the attic room, the window of my own bedroom, and straight to the cobbled circular driveway below, looking from this height like a child's drawing. I felt my hands clench the iron railing, the edges digging into the flesh of my palms, my wrists and forearms aching as my grip wrenched tighter. I blinked the water out of my eyes, unable to look away. This was where it had happened. Frances had stood here, placed her feet here, possibly placed her hands where mine were right now. And then she had bent forward, her weight taking her over the edge of the railing, her grip loosening, letting go as she fell down and down and down . . .

Forget.

So simple. Lean out, lean over, let gravity take you. Let go.

Forget.

The wind howled in my ears. Alex gone, no child to love me, my mother mad. What did it matter? I could simply feel the cold wind in my lungs and the rush of air as I closed my eyes.

In the woods, deep beneath the canopy of the trees, a dog barked. Not a happy bark or an alarmed one, but a low, snarling snap, booming in a deep bass. It sounded once, and then again, closer.

The door behind me swung shut.

Cold shot down my spine, and I pushed away from the railing, shoving myself off with my slick palms. I whirled, but there was no one on the landing with me—just the dark and the scream of the wind. I stepped to the stairwell door and wrenched it, expecting to feel the knob slick in my hand, unyielding, the door latched shut. But it turned, and I swung the door open, the latch on the inside swinging limply as the door hit the wall. I quickly moved onto the stairs, turning briefly to fasten the latch again.

What were you thinking? I berated myself as I descended through the gloom. *What is the matter with you? To stand there like that and contemplate such things . . .*

I dashed the water from my eyes with the heels of my hands as I came through the service door. My hair was tangled, my skin cold. I stepped into the corridor.

Frances's door was ajar. From behind it, I heard a faint creak.

I put my hand to the striped wallpaper, steadying myself. I could see a faint strip of light between the edge of the door and the door-frame. It hadn't been there before; the door had been closed and locked, silent. The creak came again.

I stepped softly on the flowered carpet, holding my breath, as the sound came again, furtive. With a chilled hand, I pushed open the door.

It was a girl's room. A pretty wooden dresser, painted white, against one wall; a matching wardrobe; a bed covered in linens the soft green of new leaves, a canopy above it; a window seat furnished with pillows, much like the window seat in my own room. The curtains on the window were drawn back, tied neatly, showing the blank black square of night outside. A bookshelf, crowded and scuffed, adorned the far wall. A single lamp, barely throwing light past its own circle, was turned on, casting a glow beneath its china shade. In the middle of the room stood a wooden rocking chair, the source of the creaking noise. In the rocking chair sat Dottie.

She was angled away from me, so I could see only the neat twist of her hair on the back of her head, the line of her neck and shoulders, and a glimpse of her ear and jaw, the same way I'd seen the ghost of her dead daughter. She wore the same dress she'd worn all day, of soft, expensive wool, its color drained to gray in the weak light. She did not turn to look at me. As I watched, the image of Frances overlapped with the image of her, her feet in their practical oxfords pressed to the floor, and the chair rocked slowly, back and forward again.

"You have never been in this room, have you?" she said.

I swallowed. "No."

"Do you see any chains?"

I blinked, recalled the rumors in town about how mad Frances Forsyth had been kept under lock and key. "No," I said again.

Dottie nodded. "I couldn't bear to get rid of her things," she said. "Pack them up as if she'd never been. I left the house instead. I haven't been in this room since she died."

I stepped farther inside, circling Dottie until I could see her face. It was half in shadow, her expression subdued, though her lips formed a tight line. Her hands curled over the arms of the rocking chair. She was looking straight ahead, into her own thoughts, and not at me.

"It's a pretty room," I offered.

Dottie was silent for a long moment. Her gaze traveled to the bed, with its untouched cover. "Frances was a difficult girl from the day she was born," she said. "Even as a baby, she fought me. The nannies I hired quit—they said she was unmanageable. I ended up caring for her myself."

I held my breath, listening.

"She had imaginary playmates," Dottie said. "All children do. I'd overhear her, alone in this room, talking quietly. I'd think she was talking to her dolls, but she never was. She never played with her dolls at all. I'd always find her sitting on her bed or in the middle of the floor, alone." Dottie paused for a moment. "When she was six, she began to speak of—things she was seeing. Faces. Voices she heard in her mind. She complained of a face that would appear at that very window, over there." She pointed briefly to the window with its furnished window seat.

"A face?" I asked.

"A man," Dottie said. "With a white face and black, deep-set eyes. He'd appear at night, begging her to let him in. There is no way anyone could stand at that window—it's three stories from the ground—but it didn't matter. She couldn't sleep. And one night we heard a crash and a scream. I found Frances crouched by the wall, just there, her hands cut and running with blood. She'd tried to smash the window, telling the man to go away."

I stood silently, picturing it.

"It got worse," Dottie continued. "I had doctors come, but they were fools. They told me she'd be better off in a hospital, just because she saw faces and heard voices. A *hospital!*" For the first time, Dottie looked at me, and her eyes were like small, hot coals. "Do you have any idea what can happen to a little girl in a place like that?"

A chill went down my spine as I thought of the hospitals I'd toured while looking for somewhere to put Mother. I could guess very well.

"Robert wanted her to go to boarding school," Dottie said. "I fought it, but he said I was being overprotective. Frances wasn't stupid, and given the opportunity, she could learn as well as any other child. And finally I gave in." She took a breath, and I realized she was quietly furious. "It didn't stop the visions—her letters told me there were ghosts. A girl at her bedside, a dead girl in the pond. She didn't fit in, of course—she had no hope to. The other girls showed her no mercy. They smelled blood, as girls will. They teased her, played tricks on her, put terrible things in her bed. I wanted to remove her, but Robert said no. He said she had to wait it out, that the girls would eventually leave her alone."

I walked to the bookshelves and glanced over them, unable to observe Dottie's pain anymore. I saw books of nursery rhymes, fairy tales—the books any girl would own. I ran my fingers gently over the spines. This room looked so much like a normal girl's room, like a living girl's room. I'd never had a room like this one, and if someone had given it to me, I would have thought I was in a dream. "What happened?" I asked.

Dottie's voice was brisk, hard. "They chose a cold night and locked her alone in the school's bell tower. But first they took away all of her clothes."

I exhaled a shocked breath. What that must have done to Frances— already isolated, terrified, and alone. How it must have broken her.

I heard the chair rock. "I brought her home. She wouldn't speak for weeks. When she did speak again, she was worse than ever. She spoke about a dog named Princer. She said he'd come through the doorway to protect her."

I turned back around. "Come from where?"

Dottie shook her head, and then she sighed. "From her dreams."

I stared at her, silent.

"They all came from her dreams," Dottie continued. "The faces, the figures. The dog. She believed they were the spirits of the dead. But Princer was different. He was—a demon of some kind. He did not come to kill her, but to keep her safe." Dottie raised a hand and pinched the bridge of her nose briefly, the only indication she gave of her deep distress. "My own daughter talked of these things. My own daughter. What was I to say?" She dropped the hand and continued. "Things were better for a time, after she began to imagine the dog. Frances still saw things, but she felt that Princer made them go away. It was a sort of self-suggestion, I think, but at least she was less tormented. I hired tutors, and she'd take walks in the woods, sketching and exploring. And then one day I was in the library when I thought I heard a sound on the back terrace. I walked to the morning room and looked out the doors. And then I heard screaming."

I stood, transfixed, thinking of the view I'd just seen from the gable, the sheer drop to the cobblestones. *I saw her,* I wanted to tell Dottie. *I saw your daughter the day we came here, sitting in the parlor. She never left. She's here.* I almost spoke the words aloud, but they would not be a comfort.

"I knew what it was," Dottie said. "In that moment, I knew. But I couldn't make myself believe it. Not when things were going well. Not my Frances." She took a breath, raised her chin, and looked at me. "But it was. It was Alex who stopped me at the front door and told me she was dead."

For a numb moment, the words did not sink in. Then I thought perhaps I'd misheard, the blood pounding in my ears confusing my perception. "I beg your pardon?"

"You didn't know he was here, did you?" Dottie asked. I must have looked bewildered, because she nodded. "I gathered as much. He was here on leave, paying us a visit, the day Frances died."

"No," I said. "Alex had leave in April 1917, and he spent all of it with me." It was during that leave that he had received the camera. "He didn't have another until 1918, which was the last one before he disappeared."

Dottie nodded again, as if she had expected my answer. "Frances died in August 1917," she said. "And Alex was here. On leave."

"I—" My hands had gone cold. I stared at her in shock, the same kind of surprise I would have felt if she had risen from her chair and slapped me. "Alex—Alex came home on leave without telling me? Without seeing me?"

"Yes. He even spent quite some time walking the grounds with Frances the day before she died." Dottie looked at me for a moment. The pain had left her expression, which was now unreadable. She pressed the arms of the rocking chair and stood, the chair moving emptily behind her. When she stepped toward me, the dim lamplight played over her features, putting the sockets of her eyes and the hollows of her cheekbones in shadow. "You met a man, and you married him," she said to me. "I've known you for some time now, and I've come to understand that you loved him. But what did you know about him?"

I tried to think of how it had been with Alex, how it was when we were together. It was so long ago now. "He told me everything," I said.

"He told you nothing." She stepped forward again, and this time the lamplight showed her features to me. Her eyes were fixed on my face, blazing with some emotion I could not name. "Do you understand? He was my nephew, my dead sister's child. I took him in, raised him for nearly four years. Then he went off to live with Germans. Germans! And he looked me in the eye and told me, 'Aunt Dottie, I want to go.'"

"They were his relatives," I stammered. "There wasn't a war then."

"It doesn't matter," Dottie snapped back. "I didn't hear he'd come home to England until he'd been at Oxford for six weeks. When he was finished, he said he was off to travel the Continent, but I never got a letter or a postcard. Where did he go?"

I stood transfixed, her questions cutting me like needles.

"He married you," Dottie continued, "a woman we'd never seen. He didn't invite us to the wedding. Yet for all that time, I still saw him as my nephew. My family. He was always Alex. And then the war came, and suddenly he came to visit me on leave. He told me he was visiting you next, that he was going to London before going back to the Front. And at the same time, he never told you anything."

My stomach turned. I would have done anything—literally anything—to see Alex for a second leave in 1917, and he knew it. I'd been home, worried that every day would bring me the telegram telling me he was dead, and he'd come to England *without telling me*. If I had discovered he had another woman, I could not have felt more empty, more betrayed.

"It makes no sense," I said. "He could have visited me. Why did he lie about it to both of us? Why?"

"That's a very good question," Dottie countered. "I have wondered that myself. Perhaps it was the war that did it—I wouldn't know. But the moment he told me Frances was dead, when I looked into his face, I realized he wasn't the boy I'd known. He was a man, and a stranger to me."

"He wasn't a stranger to me," I replied. "He wasn't."

"Then ask yourself why he was here that day while you were at home worrying about him," Dottie said. "That's what I would do."

Then she was gone, though I did not see her leave, did not hear the door click shut. I stood in the dim lamplight, my mind spinning and my stomach sick, as the clock ticked quietly on the wall.

CHAPTER SIXTEEN

O n our drive from London, Dottie had told me she expected me to serve tea among my other duties. As art buyers began to arrive at Wych Elm House, I put this task into practice.

It wasn't difficult, as Dottie had noted. A potential buyer would arrive for a meeting; a maid would bring in a tray within five minutes, containing a tea service and several dainties; the maid would depart, and I would take over. I would pour the tea and serve it, my job only to be helpful, decorative, and silent. I felt much like I had in Casparov's office, like a brass paperweight with the added bonus of arms. I wore the new frocks Dottie had had me order, and I kept my hair pinned up as neatly as I could. Dottie even loaned me a string of pearls, expensive but understated, to add to the effect. I was the same girl from Casparov's office, but older, wiser, and more elegant.

There were a few advantages. It was easy, for one. And unlike Casparov, Dottie held all of her meetings in front of me, letting me hear every word of conversation while I sat there as if I didn't exist. In this way I learned how she did things, and I also learned how she was going about finding a wife for Martin.

"That last fellow seemed very interested in the Turner," I ventured to comment one day after a buyer had left.

"He talked too much about painters," Dottie scoffed. "As if I wish to talk about *painters*. However, his daughter is pretty, and I hear he's going to settle a good amount on her. If he writes asking for another meeting, say yes."

She did not, in fact, want to talk about painters. Despite months of acquiring it, art for art's sake was not Dottie's goal. Art was simply a means to an end—or, in this case, a means to two ends: to make money and to find a suitable daughter-in-law, now that I was out of the equation.

We did not talk about our conversation in Frances's bedroom. Nor did we discuss her original plans to wed me to her son. Martin told me she'd taken the news of my muddied legal status remarkably well. "I told her to find me somebody else," he reported to me. "Anybody else, really. Though I hope she finds me someone pretty, at least."

"I don't like the sound of it," I told him for the dozenth time. "You should pick your own wife."

"I think of my life in terms of weeks, not years," Martin replied. "I can't imagine I'll be with a wife for any length of time, so I can't say it rightly matters."

We debated this at length, over lunches and walks and the occasional evening drink in the drawing room. He had an easygoing nature—too easygoing, I thought. But he wasn't just being agreeable when he acquiesced to Dottie's plans to marry him off. I sensed true apathy beneath it all, a blankness that was dark and a little frightening. He had grown strong enough to come down from his bedroom again, but his health was dangerously fragile, and he didn't often have the energy to be social. When he did, despite our debates I found myself enjoying his company.

But I often found myself alone in my off hours. I experimented with Alex's camera, wandering about at dusk and—less frequently, for the mornings were increasingly cold—early dawn. The pictures I'd taken of the tableau Frances had left me in my bedroom had not turned out—Mr. Crablow, who developed them for me, showed me that the prints were simply black squares. "Are you quite certain you opened the lens, my dear?" he asked me. I was, but he only shook his head indulgently and encouraged me to try again. So I did.

I had begun using the camera with a specific reason in mind, but to my surprise I discovered I enjoyed using it. When I took photographs, alone in the slowly failing light, huddled inside a sweater and a coat, my feet damp and cold, my pretty dress and borrowed pearls left behind in my room, everything fell away. I did not think about Dottie's family or my own uncertain future. I did not think about the fact that I could not spend the rest of my life as Dottie's handmaiden. I did not think about Frances's mysterious death and who may have pushed her from the roof. And I did not think the thoughts that threatened to consume my mind: that Alex had lied to me. That Alex had come to England without telling me. That he had been seen speaking at length with Frances the day before she died. *You met a man, and you married him. But what did you know about him? He was a man, a stranger to me.*

In the first days after my conversation with Dottie, the thought was like a fist in my gut. I had spent three years with the Alex I had in my mind, the husband I carried in my memories, so certain that the picture I had was accurate. Dottie's words changed all of that. I wavered between shaky denial and cold fear, brought on by my memory of Alex's face, his handsome features and extraordinary blue eyes those of a stranger.

After several days, I could touch the thought of Dottie's conversation tentatively, like a bruise, run my tongue over the thought like a healing tooth. And then I began to grow angry.

"Mrs. Manders." This was one of Dottie's art clients, sitting on the sofa in the parlor, watching me pour tea. I was so lost in my thoughts, so unused to being acknowledged during these meetings, that for a moment I forgot my own name.

"Yes, sir," I managed.

"You are married to Mrs. Forsyth's nephew, I believe?"

I paused, the teapot poised just at the end of a pour, and glanced at Dottie. I had not been given instructions should a client ask me questions. Dottie was frowning but silent.

I turned back to the man. He was sixtyish, distinguished, with upright posture and thick, silver hair. A prominent, well-shaped nose, high in the bridge, made him look especially aristocratic. I searched my memory for his name.

"I was married to him, sir." I choked the words out—had he known I was thinking about Alex? "He died in the war."

"A great shame," the man said. His gaze traveled down my arm to my hands, where they held the teacup and pot, and I wondered if he was looking at my wedding ring, the narrow band of gold Alex had given me one golden day in Crete. "An officer, I presume?"

I gritted my teeth. What did Alex's status matter now that he was dead? "Yes, sir. An officer in the RAF. His plane went down in 1918."

"Indeed." He took his teacup from my hand and sat back on the sofa, regarding me. My spinning brain did its job and supplied his name: Mabry. Colonel Mabry, though he did not wear a uniform. "I knew a great many RAF men. They were brave lads."

I set the teapot down, trying not to bang it. "Yes, sir."

"Colonel," Dottie broke in, gesturing impatiently at me for her own teacup, "perhaps you'd like to come to the gallery and see some of the works you've expressed an interest in."

Colonel Mabry turned to look at her, and for a second I thought I saw faint surprise in his eyes, as if he'd forgotten she was there. "That does sound enjoyable," he agreed, "but there is lots of time."

Dottie raised her thin eyebrows. "I beg your pardon?"

"I am staying in the area," Mabry said. "I have put up in the small hotel in the village. I'm mixing business with pleasure on this particular trip. I spent some time working in the neighboring government installation some years ago, and I am here again at their request, assisting them with a small matter."

"I see," Dottie said. "How fortunate."

"The Ministry of Fisheries?" I asked. "That is a strange assignment for an army colonel."

The air in the room grew as brittle and cold as the ice over a puddle. I did not look at Dottie, but I felt the blast of her disapproval, and I dropped my gaze to the lap of my skirt as I lowered myself to the sofa.

"It was a personal matter," the colonel said. His voice was low and cautious, but not angry. "Not official business, I'm afraid. It was some years before the war."

"Yes, sir," I said. "I apologize."

"It's quite all right. I am flattered you take a personal interest in me, Mrs. Manders."

I looked up at him. He was not flirting with me; his expression gave nothing away. I had an inkling that I was dealing with a man whose words carried a great deal of obscure meaning. "Colonel," I said, ignoring the poisonous look that was no doubt being sent my way from Dottie's direction, "you say you knew many RAF men."

"I did," Colonel Mabry agreed. "I spent most of the war in France and Belgium."

"Did you know my husband?" I asked, keeping my voice calm. "When you served? Alex Manders?"

Mabry regarded me calmly, but a quick spark of interest crossed his gaze, a light that I could not quite read. "It is possible, Mrs. Manders, that I came across him at some time or another. I will give it some thought. My aging brain does not recall names as quickly as it used to."

Of course. I had hoped for honesty, but he was humoring me, as would be expected when an army colonel spoke to a civilian woman. The realization did nothing to bank my anger.

"I would appreciate it if you could recall any memories of him." I tried to sound sweet, though I was not certain I succeeded. "I cherish any memories of him I can find, as you can imagine."

"As any good lady would," he agreed. "Where are your people from, Mrs. Manders?"

"London," I replied, lying blithely, as if I had people. "Though my mother now lives in Hertford. She is retired."

"Well earned and well deserved, I'm sure," Mabry said, and suddenly I knew that he knew I was lying. *A liar knows a liar,* my mother had always said. My mad mother, who had retired to an asylum in Hertford, where she dug her nails into her own neck. "I am certain you do both her and your husband credit. The brave widows of the war are a part of what makes England a great nation."

"Oh, but I am not necessarily a widow." I was not sure what had come over me, but the words would not stop. "You must not count me in that number. My husband disappeared when his plane went down, you see, and his body was never found."

"Manders," Dottie interjected, her voice choked, "Colonel Mabry is not interested in your anecdotes."

"It's quite all right, Mrs. Forsyth," the colonel said. "Mrs. Manders, though I do not recall your husband, you can rest assured that he provided an invaluable service to England. Perhaps more so than you, a lady, can ever quite know. It is his sacrifice that matters. That much I am confident of, sight unseen." He picked up his teacup and turned to Dottie. "Mrs. Forsyth, please continue."

CHAPTER SEVENTEEN

"He was lying," I said to Martin.

We were sitting on the back terrace as night fell. I was perched on the tiled marble slabs of the steps, my coat around my shoulders, my arms hugging my knees. I still had my hair tied back neatly, and I still wore the new, modest heels Dottie had had me buy. I watched darkness creep over the trees, savoring the slap of fresh air that likely reddened my nose.

"That's a tall accusation, Cousin Jo," Martin replied. He sat next to me, a scarf wound around his neck. I hadn't seen him all day, and the pained lines of his face told me why. Still, he seemed to enjoy our moment of peaceful privacy as the dinner preparations went on in the house behind us.

"He knew who Alex was," I insisted. "I'd bet all of my money on it. He fed me a dose of claptrap about brave widows, but it was all a lie. I think he just wanted to watch me swallow it."

"Jolly good," Martin said, watching me with some wariness. "You're a little frightening right now, I don't mind saying. However, if you start shouting at one of Mother's cronies, it'll be the most entertainment I've seen in a year."

"He lied to me," I said. "Alex, I mean. He lied to me about his leave. I've spent three years not asking questions because I was terrified of the answers—it was too hard. But now I think I want to know. I'd like to know what Colonel Mabry could tell me, if only I could convince him to help me."

Martin sighed and gazed off into the trees. "I know what you mean. I tried to find answers myself, you know—to his disappearance. While I was over there. I don't suppose I've told you that."

I stared at his pale profile. "No. You never told me."

"I didn't know you—I wasn't sure you could handle it," he admitted. "However, now you've asked. I was in the hospital when Alex disappeared, barely conscious most of the time. But it haunted me. The thought of him simply gone like that—it's hard to get used to, in a different way than death, which I've seen plenty of. I started thinking about it, specifically about his plane."

"His plane?" I asked.

"Yes. Did anyone see it go down? Who found it? How closely did they go over it? Was there some possibility, some clue that pointed in any direction? Anything at all? I was lying in bed with nothing to think about, nothing to do, and it tormented me. I kept having nightmares about his crashed plane, the cockpit splattered with blood and brains." He stopped himself and stared at me. "Oh, God, Cousin, I'm sorry. I keep forgetting you weren't over there with me, growing accustomed to it all. I'm an idiot."

"It's all right," I said. "I'd rather your honesty than Colonel Mabry's pabulum speeches. Go on."

"When I was well enough, I made inquiries," Martin said. "I had a few contacts, and I begged for favors. Alex was my beloved cousin, a heroic officer. I wanted to find answers for my family—*et cetera, et cetera*. There are certain phrases one can use when asking favors. I wrote letters from my hospital bed and used the hospital telephone a few times. I finally got the ear of someone in the RAF who found the file with the crash report. He had no authorization to send me a copy, but he read it to me over the telephone line from Berne."

"For God's sake, what did it say?"

"Not much," Martin replied. He was looking off at the woods again now, though it had grown nearly too dark to see. The wind was blowing cold down the back of my neck. "It was the most frustrating thing. Alex's flight that day was listed as a reconnaissance mission, though the objective was not recorded. He was not listed to fly with a gunner, which was a strange oversight—a pilot without a gunner can get into combat without being able to shoot back. Even on reconnaissance, a pilot should have been assigned a gunner, since it gave him a better chance to get back in one piece."

"So he flew alone?"

"Yes. Odd, though not unheard of, especially at Alex's level. He'd flown enough missions that I expect he could go without a gunner without question."

I tried to picture Alex flying a plane, as I often had. I pictured him in a pilot's heavy coat and gloves, in the hat and goggles. He'd been good, of course; he was good at everything he did. He'd passed pilot school easily.

Still lost in his own memories, Martin continued. "No one saw his plane shot down, at least no one on record. When he didn't return, a second team, of two reconnaissance planes—this time with gunners—was sent to look for him. They found the plane crashed in the trees just beyond enemy lines, and one of them managed to get aground to look for him. They found his parachute gone, but no other sign of him." He looked at me. "And there was no blood in the cockpit—that was specifically noted."

"So he was shot at, and he parachuted out when his plane started to go down." Though it had been three years, I had never spoken in detail to anyone about Alex's disappearance, and to do it now was a massive relief, as if a pressure around my rib cage had started to ease. "If there was no blood, then he was not injured when he jumped."

"Perhaps," Martin agreed. "There was no one else in the plane to use the parachute. But I have to say, Cousin Jo, that it's possible he was injured without leaving blood in the cockpit. Broken bones, bruises. A head wound can knock a man so hard he's helpless as a baby."

I was quiet, staring into the dark.

Martin continued. "And if he jumped in broad daylight in the middle of the German woods, where the hell did he go? Why didn't he turn up anywhere? He'd be a valuable prisoner for the Huns—an RAF officer like him. His name should have appeared on prisoner lists."

"Alex had German blood," I said. "He knew the language."

"Which just means he could have negotiated better treatment at one of their prisons if he was taken up. I had my contact do a thorough search, Cousin. Alex's name does not appear in the records *anywhere.*"

I pressed my fingers lightly to my forehead. The pressure from my rib cage seemed to have migrated there. "Alex could have been killed in those woods," I said. "The enemy could have found him and shot him, buried him in an unmarked grave. If he had a head wound, he couldn't have defended himself. For all I know, he took the chance to—" I clamped my mouth shut, my cheeks heating.

"Took the chance to what?" Martin asked.

To switch sides and join the German army. The words had been on the tip of my tongue, impulsive—I had almost spoken them aloud. I was shocked that I had even thought them. Stupid words, shameful words. Words I did not mean and could never say, especially to a man who had given his health and nearly given his life fighting for England.

"I'm upset," I said. "I'm sorry."

He looked bemused. "Of course you're upset. You needn't apologize."

I shook my head. I was losing my perspective, letting the dark conversation I'd had with Dottie get to me. *He went off to live with Germans. Germans! And he looked me in the eye and told me he wanted to go.* Alex was fluent in German. He had family there—family he was loyal to. He had never spoken in detail to me about his father's family, but I knew his time with them had been important to him, that he had been grateful they'd taken him in.

He told you nothing.

If he'd joined the enemy's army, his name wouldn't come up on any lists. If he'd even used his own name, that was—

Hans Faber.

I sat still, my head in my hands, my heart stopped in my chest, my breath going still.

"Jo?" Martin asked.

Hans Faber. The name in the camera case. I had nearly forgotten it until this moment.

No. No. It cannot be. Stop thinking this, Jo. Stop it.

"Jo? Are you all right?"

"I'm fine," I said. I raised my head. "I'm just upset. I've been over and over this so many times, and I never get any closer to an answer."

Martin rubbed a hand over his face. "I know. I wish I could be more help. But you see, I did try."

"I'm going to write Colonel Mabry," I said. "If I meet with him, will you come?"

"Of course. What do you plan to ask him?"

"I want Alex's military record—his file at the War Office. I'm certain the colonel has the authority to get it for me."

Martin looked at me thoughtfully. "You can try it, Jo, but I don't think the official record is going to tell you very much."

"It'll tell me more than I know now, which is nothing." A thought occurred to me. "Unless you can pull more favors and get it for me?"

He shook his head. "My influence doesn't reach that high, I'm afraid. But you know, I've heard Mabry's name before. I'm sure of it. I'm just not certain where."

"He seems rather high ranking," I said, "though I don't know much about these things. It isn't strange that you'd have heard his name."

"No, no, it wasn't through the army. I have it now. It was Mabry's son—he was in one of those hospitals, you know, for shell-shocked fellows. Do you remember the hospital in Yorkshire that was in the news a few years ago?"

I dimly recalled it. "The one that was closed due to mismanagement?"

"That's the one. It was supposed to be an exclusive place, but there was an influenza outbreak and some sort of scandal."

"I remember," I said, "though I don't remember Mabry's name."

"I do. The poor chap was one of the patients. That must have been a tough pill for a man like the colonel to swallow, having his son in a place like that. Not that I'm judging anyone—I'm in no position for it."

The terrace door opened behind us, and a set of footsteps sounded across the stone. "It's a little cold out here for telling secrets, isn't it?"

We turned. Robert was coming toward us, the light from the house behind him casting him in silhouette. He was dressed in his usual dapper suit, his hair slicked back from his forehead. I had barely seen him in the weeks I'd been at Wych Elm House.

"Good evening, Papa," Martin said. "Care to join us?"

"No, though I do admit I'm curious as to what you're whispering about. Your heads are bent so close together I'm wondering if we should plan a wedding after all."

The words had a teasing tone to them, but Martin ignored it. "Let me guess," he said to his father. "Mother has spotted us out here and doesn't like what she's seen."

Robert shrugged. I hadn't considered anyone might have seen us from beyond the terrace doors. Now that I wasn't going to marry her son, Dottie wouldn't like the idea of my acting too intimate with him. "Your mother has asked me to call you in to supper," Robert said, "which I have the misfortune to be home for tonight. You're welcome to our table as well, Mrs. Manders."

"That's quite all right." I stood and brushed off my skirt. "I have a headache. I'll find something in the kitchen."

Robert put his hands in his pockets and looked at me. I realized that although the light from behind the terrace doors put him in shadow, it illuminated me perfectly well in his view, and I felt exposed. "Scavenge for scraps in the kitchen? How sad. I don't think we've treated you well since you came here, Mrs. Manders."

"You don't need to treat me any way at all," I retorted. "I am capable of handling myself."

"Such a fiery temper for a lady!" he said with a patronizing grin. "You have spent too much time with my wife. Still, I suppose you must fend for yourself, now that you're not marriageable. Does it bother you, I wonder, to still be legally married to a man who's been dead for three years?"

"Papa." Martin had risen, though more slowly than me, and he now stood at my shoulder. "Enough." He sounded tired.

Robert turned his attention to his son. From the aroma wafting from him, I realized he'd been drinking, though he held it well. "Your mother is in a mood tonight," he said. "Something has excited her. I think perhaps she has her sights on a girl for you, though I haven't asked."

"Good," Martin said. "Let her be excited, then. At least someone will be happy."

"I'm surprised she hasn't had the doctors check that you're capable of giving her grandsons," Robert said. "Though for all I know, perhaps she has."

"Papa, don't start."

Robert gazed closely at his son through the haze of alcohol. "Do you think I didn't worry about you?" he asked with a suppressed tremor of emotion in his voice. "Your mother isn't the only one capable of worrying, you know. I did my share these four years, while the doctors took you to pieces. If you would just gather some gumption and get off the morphine—"

Martin winced, so fleetingly I knew I was the only one who saw it. "Yes, I know."

Swaying faintly, Robert took a step forward, put a hand on the back of Martin's neck, and looked into his son's eyes. "She'll find someone to run over you if you're not careful," he said, his voice low. "Someone who will make you as miserable as she's made me. I thought I didn't care who I married, either, but I was very bloody wrong. Do you understand?"

Martin returned his father's gaze, unwavering. "Yes," he replied. "I understand. But this has nothing to do with Cousin Jo, so please leave her alone."

"I'm trying to give you advice," Robert said. He dropped his hand and stepped back, and I could only dimly see his features in the half-light. "Let's go in and get this over with, shall we?"

Martin watched his father's retreating back, then turned to me. "I beg your pardon for my father's behavior," he said softly. "He can be crude when he's been drinking."

"Martin," I said.

"He's right," Martin said. "Mother is expecting us both to dinner for the first time in weeks. I need to go inside and get it over with."

I took a tray to my room and set it on the small writing desk—bread, cheese, a slice of cold meat, some fruit, and a glass of wine, a treat I didn't usually partake of. I turned on the bedside lamp—I had long ago put the shade back where it belonged, and it had not been moved again—and stood, looking down at the tray and around at the rest of my room.

I could sit here and eat quietly, reading a book. I had done so for many a night. I could sip the wine, hoping it would help me sleep and keep away the dreams. I could think about what was happening downstairs, what the family was talking about at the dinner table, if they were talking at all. I could be alone with my memories and my questions and my traitorous thoughts.

Instead, I left the room and moved quietly into the corridor.

With the family and the servants busy downstairs, the rest of the house was quiet. I had at least another hour before anyone would come upstairs at all.

I climbed the stairs to the second floor, then on upward to the attic floor. This time, I did not open the door to the roof. Instead, I approached Franny's bedroom door, dark and silent, and turned the knob.

The room wasn't locked. It was hushed and still inside, and I noticed a dusty, unlived-in smell that I hadn't registered before. Though kept clean and tidy, a room that isn't lived in announces itself—the clothes that are tucked away in perfect stacks, the bedspread and pillows that lack a single dent. I moved silently across the thick rug and turned on the lamp Dottie had lit when I'd found her here, sitting in the rocking chair. The circle of light bloomed.

If someone had killed Frances, making it appear like she'd jumped, the first place I could think of to find evidence of it was somewhere in this room.

I was brisk and quiet, trying my best not to disturb anything. I searched the bed, including under the pillows and under the bed itself. I searched the wardrobe, running my hands along the insides, brushing the pockets of Frances's few dresses—she'd been tiny and slender at age fifteen—and going through her drawers, lifting neat stacks of her underthings and letting my fingertips trace the bottoms and the sides. I searched the closet, which was nearly empty but for cold-weather coats and a few rows of shoes. I folded back the corner of the rug, got on my knees and peered beneath the dresser, looked carefully into the recessed window seat. My final stop was the bookshelf, where I even removed each book and shook it, looking for a clue to fall out.

Dottie had said that Frances liked to sketch; it was odd that the shelf contained no sketchbook. But when I pulled out a book called *World Atlas for Girls*, a folded packet was revealed on the shelf, tied with a faded ivory ribbon. I held the slim packet in my palm and tugged on the ribbon, revealing a small stack of photographs.

The first photograph was of a baby, dressed in a plush, frilly dress, sitting up and staring with baffled solemnity into the camera. Even in infancy, I recognized Frances. I turned over the photograph to find a single sentence written on the back in a blocky hand, the pencil nearly too faint to read:

Do you love her?

Frowning, I looked at the next picture. It showed Frances again, aged perhaps three, holding the hand of her brother. Martin was

around nine, wearing trousers and a jacket. They were on the front
lawn, Wych Elm House behind them, Martin squinting into the sunlight, Fran staring into the camera, clutching hard on her brother's
hand. It was a picture like any of thousands of others—the impatient
boy, holding his little sister's hand for a portrait in the bright sunlight.
But I turned the picture over and saw words scrawled in the same faint
pencil on the back:

It watches me

I turned the picture over again. Who had written these? It must
have been Frances—but what did she think was watching her?

I was moving the picture aside to look at the one beneath it when
the lamp behind me went out, then turned on again.

I froze. There was a breath of something cold on my back—a draft
of icy air, as if a window were open. To my left, the wardrobe door
creaked shut with a gentle *snick*.

Panic rooted me still for a long moment; I could feel my pulse
pounding in my fingertips where they held the pictures. I swallowed
thickly and turned around. I just had time to see the room was empty
when the lamp went out again, the *click* making me jump as if it were
a gunshot, and it stayed out this time, leaving me in the dark.

I blinked, my eyes watering, and focused on the square of the open
bedroom doorway in front of me. It was just lighter than the blackness
of the bedroom, gray with ambient moonlight in the hallway. I stepped
toward it, my only thought now to leave. I placed one foot cautiously
before me in the dark, then another, hoping not to stumble.

I had come closer to the door, my gaze fixed unwaveringly on its
square of cloudy light, when a figure crossed the doorway from right
to left, swift and silent.

I froze in shock. I knew that figure; I recognized it. The dress, the
pinned-up hair, the high forehead. Frances Forsyth had just walked
past the doorway on her way down the hall.

I could not go back—to stay in the room was unthinkable. What if the bedroom door was the next to close? Panic pushed me forward, propelled me in its icy grip to the doorway, though my mind rebelled at coming any closer to the figure I'd seen. The air grew colder as I advanced, and when I reached the corridor, I saw that the door to the service stairs hung open and the cold wind was blowing down from the entrance to the roof.

She had gone there, then. For a moment I pictured it—Frances, standing on the small landing on the house's top gable, the place where she had died. She would cut a lonely figure, standing stark against the cold dark of the night. Would anyone be able to see her but me?

I fled down the corridor, making my footsteps as soft as I could, as if the dead girl could hear me. I was on the landing leading to my room before I realized I was still holding the photographs. I had turned to the third picture, but I hadn't looked at it. I looked at it now and stopped, a soft sob of agony in my throat.

It was the picture from my London flat—the one Alex had seen when he'd come to my place that fateful day, the one of me posed for Mother's artist friends in nothing but a draped Greek chiton. I had last seen it when I'd packed it in my trunk on my way to the Continent. As far as I knew until this moment, it was in that trunk still.

I turned it over. On the back was a now-familiar lettering in pencil. *Where is your Mother?*

I put the photographs in my pocket quickly, unable to look anymore. That picture had come to this house when I did—and yet I had found it on Frances's bookshelf, tied with a ribbon, inscribed with a message. It was tangible, real.

From downstairs, I heard voices—the Forsyth family had finished dinner and were going their separate ways. I listened as one door closed and then another. When I heard Martin's steps slowly ascending the stairs, heading for his bedroom, I went into my room and closed the door.

But for Frances, I was alone.

CHAPTER EIGHTEEN

Robert was right about one thing: Something had Dottie excited. It wasn't just the fact that she sold two paintings over the next few days—at a considerable profit, as I was in a position to know—though that was part of it. "You see, Manders," she said pointedly as she entered the amounts in her massive, detailed accounts book, "this is the benefit of a little avarice."

She was gleeful about the money, of course, but there was something else she wouldn't tell me. She'd give me her suspicious, narrow-eyed looks and dismiss me early: "We're finished, Manders. Go away." I was no longer allowed to go through her correspondence, and once I even caught her using that most hated instrument, the telephone.

"You can tell me, you know," I said to her, exasperated at last. "I'm quite capable of being rational."

"In good time," Dottie said. "Things are delicate at the moment, and I must handle them myself."

I couldn't help it. "Is she pretty, at least?"

She pressed her lips together, but she considered the question. "Men put far too much importance on beauty," she said at last.

"Oh, no." I groaned. "Please tell me that money isn't the only factor you're considering. Tell me she's kind. He deserves someone kind."

"Then you should have married him yourself," Dottie snapped back. "It would have been perfect. You had every opportunity."

I stood and put the cover over my typewriter, since she had dismissed me for the day. "I'm already married," I said.

"Manders," she said, in a tone that warned me I was going to hate whatever came next. "You are capable of thinking clearly from time to time, but in this matter a more sentimental idiot I have never known. If the War Office never gave you a death certificate, you should have pressed them to give you one. A sensible girl needs a widow's pension and the freedom to marry another husband, or she may as well walk into the Thames."

"Thank you for the insight," I said coldly, "but I'm afraid I'm not capable of avarice when it comes to my husband's disappearance."

"That makes you poor, not morally superior," Dottie replied, "as I'd have told you from the first if you'd asked me."

I left without saying much further, but I wondered—was that what Dottie wanted? For me to ask her advice? I dismissed the idea as preposterous. I was her paid companion and favorite outlet for her disappointments, nothing more.

I wrote Colonel Mabry, care of his hotel in the village, and made my request for Alex's records. I received a brief reply stating that he would do what he could for me, though he feared I would be disappointed in the results. It seemed he thought a lady had no use for a war record. I thanked him and asked him to write me when he had an update.

That night, when I finally slept, I dreamed again, vivid and wild. I was in the woods, in the cold, the frost cracking beneath my feet. My hands and toes ached; my lips would not move. Through the trees, splitting the black, cold air, came a whistle: high, faint yet disturbingly shrill. *She's calling him,* a voice in my mind said. *She's calling him. It's time to run.*

I turned, though I did not know which direction to take. Still, I tried to move, my legs pushing slowly as the whistle died off far behind me. Something would come now, something would move through the trees, large and vicious—her dog, her protector. Princer. I tried and tried to run.

But the footsteps that approached behind me were human.

Look at me, Jo, said Alex.

I put my hands to my ears to block him out, kept my gaze forward. Still I could hear his footsteps, his voice.

Martin was wrong. Alex's voice sliced the frigid air. *There was blood in the cockpit. Blood and brains. Turn around, Jo, and look at me.*

I could not shake him. I tried to run harder, but my motions slowed as if I stood in quicksand. I tried to sob, but only a dry sound came from my throat. And somewhere off in the woods, the trees shook. Something large was coming.

Look at me, Jo, Alex said again and again as the thing came closer. *Look at me. Look at me—*

I jerked awake, gasping for air, my hands over my ears as I lay in bed. I was cold, horribly cold, my fingers and toes numb as they had been in the dream. A clock chimed downstairs, the sound distant and dreary. Far off outside the window a dog was barking in a deep, throaty voice that echoed through the trees.

Gripping my twisted blankets in fingers that could not feel, I turned to my side and drew my knees up. My hair was damp and chill. *I'm tired of this,* I thought dully. *I'm so tired of the fear, of the pain.*

Forget.

Where is your Mother?

I blinked as my eyes discerned something in the darkness. Alex's camera case stood in the middle of the bedroom floor, shrouded in shadow, its lid open. When I had gone to sleep, it had been in its place against the wall next to the wardrobe, closed.

I stared at it for a long time, my eyes aching and dry.

Come back to me, Alex.

He never would. He would haunt me for the rest of my life, tearing me apart by day and stalking after me, bloody and broken, in my dreams.

Come home.

Dawn light began to tinge the room, and I sat up, swinging my stiff legs out of the bed. I needed to move. Anything would be preferable to this.

I dressed quickly, then closed the camera case—the surface of the leather was chilled—and picked it up. I picked up the tripod in my other hand.

In for a penny, in for a pound.

I left the house and walked into the woods.

CHAPTER NINETEEN

Thirty minutes later, I stood on a tree-lined lane to the east of Wych Elm House, adjusting the camera on the tripod. There was frost on the ground and the wind bit my skin, but the sting of the cold had helped dissipate the nightmare and settle my mind.

I had found a pretty view on a back road on the border of the neighboring property, a rustic path beneath a proscenium of thick autumn trees. I had set up the camera on the tripod and was tinkering with it, trying to get the best view before the sun rose too high. It was six thirty in the morning, and I was due to report to Dottie at eight.

I had not forgotten that the children of Anningley were afraid to play in these woods, claiming that Frances and Princer haunted them. I had seen a mist under the trees from my window, and I had sometimes heard the throaty bark that did not sound exactly like a dog. Yet still I was here, alone, as the sun came up and traced an edge on the night's chill. It was an act of desperation, an act of exhaustion, and something of a dare. There was no safety from ghosts in the house, after all, and the woods fascinated me, drew me. When I was outdoors, my stifling thoughts lost some of their stranglehold on my brain.

To my surprise, the faint hum of a motorcar broke the silence, the only man-made sound in the quiet of dawn. I pulled myself away from the camera's viewfinder and turned toward the sound, which came from somewhere near the house. The motor stopped, and after a moment I saw a figure approach me, coming down the lane. I recognized it instantly, and I watched with wariness as it came closer.

"Good morning," Robert said, his long wool coat flapping in the autumn wind. "I saw you from the bend just over there, through a gap in the trees as I drove by."

I did not reply. He wore the same suit as last night, now rumpled. I knew that he'd left shortly after the family finished dinner. So he hadn't been to bed, then—at least not his own bed.

"You look disapproving," Robert said. In the growing light, I could see the harsh lines of dissipation on his face, the pouchy aftereffects of a night of drinking. "Don't act such a prude, Mrs. Manders."

I turned away and looked through my lens again.

He seemed to take this as an invitation, and stood behind my shoulder. I could smell stale smoke on him. "Do you know, Mrs. Manders, that you've been living at the house for weeks, yet this is the first time we've been alone together? When I saw you just now, it occurred to me that this is an excellent opportunity for you and me to talk."

I thought of Dottie's words to me on the drive here. *He will tell you his behavior does not matter. Do not believe him.* I recalled the misery on her face in that moment. Robert had not made advances on me, but we had never been alone together, and his wife knew him better than I did. "I don't see what we have to talk about," I said. "I'm your wife's paid companion."

"Oh, but you're so much more than that. Where did you acquire the camera, by the way?"

I pressed the shutter and captured a photo. "It was Alex's."

"Was it? It's a midwar model, unless I miss my guess. Curious that a man would buy such an expensive hobby item, then take off to fight," he said. "Though it seems Alex had a pattern of acquiring beautiful things and leaving them behind, barely used."

That made me stand and stare at him, color rising to my cheeks.

He laughed a teasing laugh. "You're so easy to rile, you know." He stepped closer, and I stiffened. "Are you worried, Mrs. Manders?" he asked, amused. "You needn't be. I can see you're truly Dottie's creature. So am I, in fact—my nighttime wanderings are just my childish way of asserting my independence. But as you depend on your salary, so do I."

Dottie would tan my hide if I played into his game, and I wouldn't blame her. "Your marriage is none of my business," I said, choosing my words carefully and wishing he would go away.

"Do you think I should divorce her?" he asked. I didn't answer, and he shook his head. "Lots of people do. I admit it's tempting, but she wouldn't give me a penny if I left. It's how she keeps people dancing to her tune." He looked away, and his expression tightened. "There was a time she thought I was the handsomest man on earth. Did you know that? Even Dottie was young and foolish once. Nothing is the same as it used to be."

I opened my mouth to say something, but I stopped as the hair on the back of my neck stood up. The wind shifted in the trees, the sibilant sound overhead suddenly loud in my ears. Behind Robert's shoulders, a handful of leaves on the path flew upward, kicked up by a spiral of wind.

"Here's my advice, Mrs. Manders," Robert said to me, his voice barely carrying against the wind and the rush of the leaves. "You've done well enough by marrying into this family, just as I did. The only difference is that you didn't have to spend the next twenty-five years in misery with Alex for your pay. Now you've latched onto Dottie instead—a wise move. But there's no future in it. Dottie won't keep you past another few weeks. A smart girl like you would think ahead, take her pretty face and find another man to pay her bills—married or not."

It was an outrageous speech, but I barely heard it. I stared over his shoulder at the path behind him, rooted to the spot, my blood gone cold.

Frances stood there, in the spot on the path where the leaves had kicked up. She wore her gray dress, her hair pinned up. The familiar loop of small pearls was around her throat. She watched us from the dark hollows of her eyes, her expression no longer calm, but somehow wretched with anger and despair. Her hands were loose at her sides, her buttoned boots still on the forest floor. Overhead, the wind blew the trees into a frenzy, but her hair and her dress did not move.

"Frances," I said, the word taken from my lips on a cold breath of wind.

"What did you say?" Robert demanded.

I tore my gaze from Frances to answer him, to warn him, and I saw the twisted fury and pain in his expression. And then his hand was on me, his fingers digging into the soft flesh below my jaw. There was sick exhaustion in his eyes, disappointment that ate at him like acid. "Don't you speak her name," he said to me, his face so close to mine I could feel his breath, the soft and pitiful degenerate gone. "That name does not pass your lips. Do you hear me?"

I jerked back, startled. "I'm—I'm sorry—"

He pushed me, his hand shoving me backward in a single motion that snapped my head back and sent me stumbling. I nearly unbalanced into the camera and tripod, my feet seeking purchase on the uneven path. I righted myself with a wrench and felt a stab of pain through my back and up my side.

"That was a warning," Robert said darkly. "I've half a mind to do more, but I'm too tired this morning. If you say her name again, whatever I do is your fault. Remember that."

I put a hand to my face and looked past his shoulder, but Frances was gone. I stood shivering on the path, my breath burning in my throat, as he turned and walked away from me, unseeing, striding directly through the place where his daughter had stood not a minute before.

I stood on the path for a long time, the camera forgotten, until the sun was high overhead. When I stopped shaking, I gathered the camera and put it in its case. The leather felt like cold skin under my fingertips; I barely wanted to touch it, and I thought I might never use the camera again.

I folded the tripod and pressed my hands to my eyes. *Ghosts,* I thought. *I am living with ghosts.*

Eventually, I picked up the equipment and walked on shaking legs back to the house, getting myself together so that Dottie would not see my fear.

CHAPTER TWENTY

"I hope you haven't wasted your time," Colonel Mabry said. "I did warn you that this might be a futile exercise."

We were in the small sitting room at the inn in Anningley, where a serving girl was laying out a tray of tea. It was early in the afternoon, a week after my encounter with Robert, and the taproom of the inn was deserted. Still, the colonel had taken a private room for us, which was furnished with a table, a few overstuffed chairs, and a mismatched cherry sideboard. Colonel Mabry was dressed in a three-piece suit of formal gray, his white shirt crisp, his tie knotted to perfection, and his distinguished hair brushed back from his temples. It was the immaculate appearance of a career military man.

I glanced at Martin, who had accompanied me. "I'm sure it won't be a waste," I said politely. "I appreciate everything you've done."

Colonel Mabry grunted and gestured for me to sit. "I've received a copy of your husband's file from the War Office," he said. "It's very slender, as I suspected it would be. I had them send it to me for you to look at, but I doubt there will be much in it of use."

I sat on one of the chairs, fighting to keep my legs properly crossed as I sank into the cushions, and pulled off my gloves. "May I see it?"

Martin broke in as he claimed the chair beside mine. "Mrs. Manders is rather impatient, as you can imagine, sir," he said. "I'm sure you've dealt with widows before."

The colonel looked at Martin, taking in every detail in a glance. He did not see me bite back a retort to Martin's condescending remark. "You served, Mr. Forsyth." It was not a question.

"Yes, sir." Martin wore a suit today, a jacket of checked wool over a stylish waistcoat, but his painful thinness altered the effect of the clothes. He had slicked down his hair and combed it back from his forehead, which made him look disconcertingly adult, like a man instead of a boy just out of his sickroom. Yet his chair nearly swallowed him, and his knobby hands gripped the arms.

"Air, ground, or sea?" the colonel asked.

"Ground, sir," Martin replied. "Artillery. I spent most of my time on the Marne."

"Difficult fighting there," the colonel commented. He picked up a leather briefcase and opened it, taking his time, my female presence completely forgotten in this male exchange. "I traveled through there in May 1916, and again just before the end of the war. It's still abandoned, or so I hear." He glanced up briefly. "Did you take an injury?"

"Shrapnel, sir."

"I see. To the stomach?"

Martin looked surprised. "Yes, sir."

The colonel shook his head. With what seemed excruciating slowness, he found a particular envelope in his briefcase and began to extract it. "I don't have second sight, Mr. Forsyth. I've just seen the effects of shrapnel wounds to the stomach a number of times. You're lucky you survived. Most of the men I saw with such an injury lived barely a week, and it was a mercy by the end."

"Yes, sir."

I resisted the urge to fidget in my seat. Martin was only doing his part; I had known that military small talk would make the meeting go more smoothly. But still I wished they would get on with it. I looked at the envelope in the colonel's hand—Alex's file—as if I could read through the thick, creamy paper.

"How much do you know of Mr. Manders's death?" the colonel asked Martin.

"Not much, sir," Martin replied quietly. "Though I believe he is officially missing in action, as Mrs. Manders has no official death notice."

Colonel Mabry appeared to think this over, then nodded. He turned to me. "I suppose it's quite frustrating for you, as his wife," he said. "But disappearances like your husband's were unfortunately common. We have some several thousand men still missing in England alone, Mrs. Manders. The recent burial of the Unknown Warrior illustrates this exact point."

I nodded. The Unknown Warrior—the exhumed body of an unidentified soldier from a French battlefield—had been buried with great ceremony at Westminster Abbey the previous year, attended by royalty and thousands of mourners. I had sat in my flat alone that day, trying, like countless others, I was certain, not to imagine that it was my missing husband in that box, its solemn photograph in all the papers.

"You will not understand everything you see in the file," Colonel Mabry said to me, as if I were a child or a recent student of English. "But wherever I can give clarification, I will do so."

I took it from him and set it in my lap. Then I opened the slender file.

The first thing I saw was Alex's face. The photograph was clipped to the inside cover of the file—a small, square shot of him. He was dressed in uniform, his collar just visible in the close-cropped shot, though he was hatless. There were the familiar planes and angles of his features, the eyes that I knew were extraordinary dark blue ringed with black, the familiar, well-bred set of his chin. His lips were closed and set in a serious line and his gaze was carefully blank as he stared into the camera.

"This is the photo from my husband's passport," I said.

"Yes," Colonel Mabry agreed. "It is standard procedure."

My eyes traveled the particulars of my husband on the page: height, six feet three inches; weight, fifteen stone; hair, dark blond; eyes, blue; age, twenty-three years. The file dated from 1915, when Alex enlisted, leaving him frozen in time, permanently twenty-three years old.

I tore my gaze from Alex's face and turned the page. Here was what I had been looking for: his war history. He had enlisted in February of 1915 and had been sent almost immediately into pilot training at the Military Aeronautics School in Reading. After eight months he'd gone to France for advanced training in Reims that seemed to consist of both classroom work and flight practice, both of which he excelled at. A note was written in pencil beneath the Reims record: "Skills very promising. Naturally suited for this kind of work." The signature beneath the note had been blacked over with ink.

After training, Alex was moved to the Western Front, where he spent most of the rest of the war. The record listed relocation to Soissons and Neuve Chapelle in 1916; and an extended period up and down the Somme in 1917, moving every four to five weeks. In every place he was assigned as a pilot, "for purposes of reconnaissance and battle, if engaged." He seemed to have gone wherever the authorities in charge needed photographs or other kinds of intelligence information, his piloting skills reserved for close observation of the enemy rather than head-on battle.

I studied his leave record. He had been given ten days' leave in 1916—I remembered it well; it had been spring, several of the days unseasonably warm, and Alex had seemed intensely happy to be home in a way that had almost confused me. The war was still new to both of us, and we'd bumped through the first days of his leave like strangers until we remembered how to be married. His second leave, in early

1917, was when the camera arrived, and he had seemed more distant by then, more quietly weighed down by the things he'd seen.

There was no leave listed for August of 1917, the month Franny had died. There was, however, a notation in the file.

"What does this mean?" I asked, breaking the silence in the room and looking up at Colonel Mabry. "In August of 1917. There is a note that says 'authorized travel.'"

I turned the file toward the colonel for him to read, but even from several feet away he barely glanced at the writing on the page. "I'm uncertain of the details, Mrs. Manders, but the implication is that your husband's superiors sent him somewhere for official reasons."

"But it wasn't leave," I said.

"If the file doesn't state that it was leave, then no," the colonel replied. "Your husband was sent somewhere for a purpose, which in this case does not seem to have been recorded."

"Would 'authorized travel' have sent him to England?"

"I would be very surprised if it did. Travel to England was strictly monitored during the height of the war, as you can imagine."

Martin was looking at the file over my shoulder. "That's the month my sister died," he said. "Alex was here then. At Wych Elm House."

"Was he?" Colonel Mabry said.

I studied the colonel's face, the even features, the salt-and-pepper eyebrows above impassive eyes. "How could he have been at Wych Elm House when he was not on leave?" I asked.

"There's one way, I suppose," Martin answered before the colonel could speak. "That is, if Alex was sent somewhere on official business— and then came here on his way back. A sort of side trip."

"But it wasn't authorized," I said. "That would mean Alex took unauthorized leave. He would be court-martialed for desertion."

Martin seemed surprised I even knew such a thing. "That may be true, Cousin Jo, but not if he were granted a favor. Off the record, you see."

"Off the record?" I asked.

"It might not be so," Colonel Mabry interjected sternly. "But Mr. Forsyth is correct. It's a possibility that could explain what's in the file."

"It makes sense," Martin said. "By then Alex was an officer with a very high flying record. He could have simply called in a favor." His voice gentled. "So you see, Jo, it wasn't the case that he took leave without telling you."

I stared at the file in my lap, appalled. No, Alex had not been granted leave without telling me. Instead, he had called in a special favor asking to make an off-the-books trip—to Wych Elm House, instead of home to me.

Hans Faber, I thought. *Who is Hans Faber?*

I could feel both men's gazes on me—the colonel's sharp and unwavering, Martin's soft and concerned. I did not want either of them to see the pain on my face, so I kept my gaze in my lap and ran my finger along the page. Alex's final leave had been in early February of 1918, and it had been three weeks long—the longest leave he'd ever been given. Even at the time I had known that it was a longer leave than most men were granted, but I had guessed it was a sop for a man who had been fighting so well for so long. Except for a strained shoulder and an infected hand, Alex had never even been sick enough to be out of the fighting.

The rest of his war history was pitifully short. After his three weeks' leave he had been sent back to Reims, where he had originally trained when first in France, for some kind of retraining. After leaving, he'd been sent to the airfield at Verdun, from which he had left on a mission and never come home. There was a notation in the file regarding his recovered plane, but it contained no details that hadn't already been given to Martin in his inquiries. Alex had been alone. No one had witnessed the plane go down. His parachute was missing. He had not left any identification or indication of where he'd gone. He'd simply vanished as if he'd never been. His status was listed as "Missing in Action."

I closed the file—I did not turn the page to look at Alex's face again—and handed it back to Colonel Mabry. "Thank you, sir," I said, keeping my voice steady. "I appreciate your assistance."

For the first time, the colonel seemed a little unsure. "I realize it must be unsatisfactory," he said. "But I hope it has answered some of your questions."

I nodded. "Yes, thank you." I turned to Martin. "Perhaps it's time to go."

As we took our leave, Martin making more small talk with the colonel and me pulling on my gloves, I could feel the colonel's gaze turn to me. He was no fool, Colonel Mabry. He knew I was holding back. "Would you like me to inquire with the War Office about your widow's status?" he asked as Martin and I walked to the sitting room door.

"Please don't," I said. "It isn't necessary."

He did not argue, only gave me another penetrating look, as if he did not believe my impression of a quiet, cowed widow. But I revealed nothing more as we descended to the street and into the Forsyths' motorcar.

Martin seemed relieved as we pulled away. "I find the higher-ups rather intimidating," he said. "He makes me glad I spent most of my wartime in the mud and not in an office, playing politics. I'm afraid I'd be no good at it. I'm sorry if I bored you horribly, Cousin Jo, but I felt I had to."

"You did just fine," I said absently, watching the town of Anningley disappear from beneath the rim of my cloche hat.

"It's a bit of a disappointment for you, as he said. But I still think it was worth it, don't you?"

I could no longer speak, even to make polite talk. I kept my face angled away from him, my gaze out the window. Perhaps he thought I was grieved; in fact, I was angry. My eyes were burning and dry, and I was angrier than I could remember being.

Alex had lied to me, and not just about his trip in 1917.

The file from the War Office had told me more than I had let on. It said he'd gone to Reims in 1915; he'd told me he'd stayed in Reading that entire time. He'd never mentioned any advanced training in France. He had never told me of authorized travel for official business, or of asking a favor of his superiors to come to Wych Elm House. And after his three weeks' leave in 1918, he had told me he was going back to the fighting, not into retraining at Reims. What had he been training for, and why?

Why had he gone to great lengths to be at Wych Elm House? He hadn't seen Dottie or the rest of the family for years by then, and Martin wasn't even home. What had made him ask a special favor to come? How could it possibly be a coincidence that Alex had been at the house on the day that his cousin was flung from the roof?

She has died, poor thing.

What motivation could Alex possibly have had to murder his own cousin? Was it even possible the man I loved could have done such a thing?

Could you? Did you? Was it you?

And what about the other man who had died that day? Had Alex somehow been involved in that, too?

I closed my eyes, shutting out the woods as they passed the window. Alex had lied to me; I was more than certain that Colonel Mabry had, too. It was not standard procedure to put a man's passport photograph in his War Office file. And the note made next to Alex's training record—*skills very promising, naturally suited for this kind of work*—had been signed by his commanding officer, the name blacked out. Except that even as a simple, foolish woman, I could see that the ink was fresh. Colonel Mabry himself had inked it over.

Lies, lies, lies.

"Jo." Martin laid a gentle hand on my arm. "I know the past years have been very traumatic for you. But I think this meeting today can be useful. I think perhaps it may help you to finally let go."

I felt the muscles tense up my back, across my shoulders; felt my neck tighten and my jaw begin to grind. He was being kind and considerate, and in that moment he had no idea that I could have slapped him.

"I have been living with my own grief for him," Martin continued. "I loved Alex. But today has made me see that perhaps there are no answers. We may have to accept things, just as all the other families of missing soldiers have had to do." He paused, and from the deepening of his breathing I knew that the day had exhausted his few resources. "Do you know, I found Franny's death easier, ultimately, than Alex's. Franny was sick, and she chose to take her own life. There is a sort of finality to that. Alex's death just never felt final. Until today."

My eyes were like hot coals in their sockets, my temples pounding. I made myself open my eyes, made myself breathe. I should tell him. About Alex's lies, about my suspicions that Frances had been murdered. About the photographs, the leaves, and the open door to the roof. I should tell him all of it. But Martin was already sick, exhausted, shouldering the burden of incessant pain and his addiction. I couldn't open my mouth to form the words. And what if Martin knew more than he was telling me? This was my problem alone.

My thoughts were halted when we pulled up the drive to Wych Elm House. Another car was here already—an expensive Daimler, sleek and black. I felt Martin tense at my shoulder.

"Who is it?" I asked him.

He did not speak. The gentle, concerned expression had gone from his face. He looked pale and stiff, his skin pallid, thin as tissue paper.

I followed him as he got out of the car and entered the house. I did not remove my hat or my coat—I could barely keep up with him and forgot I was wearing them.

We had walked into an occasion, like the day I had come home to find Martin waiting to be introduced to me in the small parlor—but today's occasion was much grander than that. This one was in the large parlor, the formal room used by Dottie for meetings with her rich art clients. I had been in this room only as an invisible tea pourer, and I had never seen the rest of the family use it at all.

The tableau in the large parlor now could have been a painting itself. On one side of the room, nearest the window, sat Dottie and Robert, Dottie in a fine suit over a formal blouse with a high lace collar, Robert in one of the more expensive pieces in his well-heeled wardrobe, his hair slicked back and his expression blank and obedient. I hardly recognized either of them—Dottie looked like she'd borrowed the Gibson Girl's wardrobe, and her face was gentled, her posture subdued. Robert did not even look at me, and instead of sprawling on his chair, he sat like a well-trained dog, his hands in his lap.

Aligned along the other side of the room were a man and a woman I had never seen before. She was middle-aged, pale, her ash blond hair mixed liberally with gray and worked into a formal knot on the back of her head. The man was obviously her husband, seated next to her in the chair mirroring Robert's, mustached, with thinning hair and a paunch that strained his waistcoat. He, too, sat with his feet and knees together, only the reddish tinge of his neck betraying how uncomfortable he was.

The center of this awkward tableau—and the focus of everyone's discomfort—sat on the small sofa in the middle of the room, like the Queen of Sheba among her attendants. In this case the Queen of Sheba was a girl of approximately twenty-three, with a birdlike figure and wide gray eyes, wearing a blue-and-white shepherd's-check suit and black Mary Janes, her golden-brown hair bobbed, its soft curls feathering her neck.

I held back in the corridor, outside the door, watching. Martin barely paused, but strode into the room, still wearing his overcoat, folding his hat under his arm.

"Good afternoon," he said. I wondered if anyone else recognized the vibration of strain in his voice.

"Martin." Dottie rose from her seat, a warm smile on her face like no expression I'd ever seen on her before. "Here you are. We were just

about to have some tea." She turned to her guests. "I'd like you to
meet Mr. and Mrs. Staffron. And this is their daughter, Cora."

I watched, invisible and forgotten, from the hall.

Martin stepped into the room, and over his shoulder I could see
the face of the blue-and-white shepherd's-check girl, Cora Staffron. She
raised her gray gaze to his and gave him a wide smile. She wasn't a particularly beautiful girl—she had a thin and bony physique, a slightly
blotchy complexion, and a long neck like a baby bird's—but she had
nice upturned eyes, and the smile she gave him was brassy and bold,
yet somehow genuine, like that of a girl who could not be trusted not to
break Dottie's china.

"This is my son, Martin," Dottie said.

"Well," said the girl in a trumpeting voice that ricocheted through
the room. "Aren't you handsome!"

I could not see Martin's face from where I was standing. But I saw
him take a brief, formal bow just before a maid brushed past me with
a tea tray and closed the parlor doors behind her.

CHAPTER TWENTY-ONE

Events moved quickly after the Staffrons arrived. They were acquaintances of Dottie's through one of her art connections; he was a banker, the kind of new rich that was Dottie's exact kin. Some of the wealthy aspired to marry their children to old titles, but not Dottie. All she wanted was more wealth to pile atop her own.

They were on an indefinite visit, and they were installed in my corridor, Cora's bedroom across the hall from mine and her parents' at the end. Though we passed one another regularly, I spoke to the Staffrons but little. Mr. and Mrs. Staffron were polite and well bred; Cora was noisy and exuberant, her laugh too loud, her jokes just a shade too racy, her clothes too fast, her lipstick not quite the right color. She was friendly enough to me, but treated me like a schoolteacher she had to behave herself in front of. Considering she was only three years younger, it made me feel positively ancient. What Dottie thought of Cora's dreaded modern bob or her pert ways—or of her social duties entertaining Cora's parents—she did not say.

I reported to Dottie every morning as usual, but after briskly assign-

ing me a day's worth of tasks, she would disappear with the Staffrons. I
was left alone to type her correspondence and send it, as well as open the
incoming mail—she had given me back this responsibility, now that she
was no longer conspiring with the Staffrons in secret—and sorting it for
her. I dealt with her telephone calls and made copies of her records, all
in the library, my typewriter keys clacking into the silence.

I slipped easily into my role as Wych Elm House's forgotten inhab-
itant. My nights were as sleepless as ever, and it was a relief to be free of
the responsibility to be friendly to Dottie's art buyers. I was soured on
the task since my meeting with Colonel Mabry. I brooded over the lies
Alex had told me, the hopelessness of my situation, the memory of
Robert's hand on my face. I had not told anyone of that encounter—
what purpose could it serve, except to muddy the family's courtship of
the Staffrons? I had already sunk Martin's marriage prospects once; I
could not do it again by making a complaint about his father while the
Staffrons were here.

The weather cooperated with my mood, the days dark and chill,
rain coming down in angry fits. Whether I was waking or sleeping,
Frances Forsyth was never far from my mind. I remembered the anguish
in her expression that last time. I believed she had appeared to me in the
woods for a reason, that she had sought me out. I found myself looking
for her—in the corridors, the parlors, the kitchen. Everywhere I went, I
thought I caught the chill of mist and a sickly sweet scent.

It was not healthy, spending my time alone, searching for a ghost.
But I could not stop myself; I had no desire to. Frances felt close to
me, as if she were around the next corner. I had no one else.

I looked up from my typing one afternoon to find Dottie standing
in the middle of the library staring at me, smoking a cigarette. I'd had
no idea she was there.

"Manders," she said. Her feet in their oxfords were placed apart,
her body braced on its short, narrow legs beneath the practical suit she
wore. "You sold one of my paintings."

"Yes," I said dully. "Two days ago. Mr. Bergeron wished to purchase it, and you were not at home. His men will be here tomorrow to remove it."

She puffed her cigarette forcefully, pinching the holder and removing it from her lips. "*Dutch House,* or so I hear," she said, naming the painting.

"I left you a note," I said. "It's on your desk."

She grunted; we both knew perfectly well she'd read it already. "How much did you get for it?" she asked.

If she didn't already know the answer to this, I'd eat my hat, but still I answered. "Six hundred."

"Hm." She puffed the cigarette again. "Acceptable, I suppose."

"It was more than you discussed when you met with him."

"Not *much* more. I'd have negotiated harder."

"You would, if you'd been here," I said. "As it is, I employed as much avarice as I could muster."

To my surprise, that seemed to amuse her. "You're not a completely lost cause," she commented. "I suppose I've been busy of late. However, your work is not at an end. Martin and Cora are becoming acquainted, and I will need you on chaperone duty."

"You can't be serious," I said. "They are both over twenty, and her parents are staying here." The last thing I wanted to do was play chaperone, like a spinster from the last century. I may as well begin planning my own dusty grave.

"I agree that it's stupid," Dottie said in her usual blunt way. "Martin is hardly going to debauch the girl. However, her parents want the proprieties observed, and I am determined that the thing should be done right. And you will help me."

"I suppose I'll do it if I have to," I said. "I'm the nearest dried-up old widow in the vicinity."

Dottie walked to the ashtray on her desk and doused her cigarette. "Manders, you are glum. It does not suit you. Please don't tell me what's bothering you, because I have no interest, as you may have guessed. Just accompany the young lovers whenever I tell you to. Is that clear?"

I had to admit that it was.

I awoke that night from another dream, the sheets twisted around me, my face flushed and hot. My heart raced in my chest, thudding in my ears, and my hair was damp with sweat.

When cold air trickled over my face, I forgot to be afraid. I closed my eyes and inhaled it, savoring the harsh surprise of cold on the back of my throat, breathing it deeply into my lungs. My sweat went cold and gooseflesh rose on my arms and down my stomach beneath my nightgown.

"Frances?" I said.

The wind blew against the panes of the window. My nose and cheeks grew cold, and even my closed eyelids felt chilled. When I rolled over on the damp mattress, my hand touched something under the blanket next to me.

I jerked upward, coming awake. Whatever it was had been tucked into the bed with me, resting almost against my body. The bedroom door was closed; nothing else in the room had been disturbed. I swallowed and pulled back the cover.

It was a book. A large, flat book, the hard cover gleaming in the moonlight through the window. I touched it tentatively, found the texture of the paper rough. The pages inside were thick, some of them warped, so the top cover did not sit exactly level. I scooted over on the bed, turned on the bedside lamp, and opened it.

From the first page, I knew it was a girl's sketchbook. The subjects were domestic: a vase of flowers, leaves on a checked tablecloth, a cat in the old stables behind the house. There was a profile of Dottie, her head bent over her work at the library desk, and another of Martin in his war uniform. All of them were detailed and clearly rendered, as if the artist had taken the time to catch every detail.

I turned the pages. There was a portrait of Wych Elm House, taken from the woods. Another of the vista that rolled down from the edge of the woods to the village, where I could see the spire of the church and smoke rising from some of the chimneys. I pictured Frances—for this was most certainly her work—sitting on the stile in the lane I'd passed only that day, perched for hours, drawing and drawing until her hands cramped and her feet lost all feeling. I could see it so clearly in that moment, it was as if I'd seen her again.

I tilted the page with the sketch of the village toward the light, looking more closely. From behind the hedgerow leading to the village she'd drawn a shadow, stretching long and dark, that did not fit with the rest of the scene. A man, perhaps? Or something else? I turned back the page to the picture of the house again and looked at it, too, under the light. There was a shadow breaking away from the main shadow of the house, difficult to see at first glance. And in an upper window, on the third floor, was the shadow of a face in the smudges of pencil, two deep-set black holes of eyes in a white oval.

She complained of a face that would appear at that very window. A man begging her to let him in.

It watches me.

Was it a man? It was impossible to tell. Was this the face Frances had seen in her nightmares, one of the many faces she claimed wouldn't leave her alone?

Strangely excited, I leafed through all the pages of the sketchbook. Some of the pictures had shadows in them; some did not. The drawing of Wych Elm House was the only one that featured a face. Some of the book's pages had been torn out, the jagged edges visible in the spine of the bound book. From outside my window, the dog with the low, throaty voice barked until the sound trailed off in a whining growl.

I slid my feet over the edge of the bed and opened the drawer in the nightstand, where I'd put the photographs I'd taken from Frances's room. I picked the photo of Fran and Martin standing in front of Wych Elm House. Then I turned the sketchbook to the drawing of the house and placed it side by side with the photograph under the light.

It was there, in the photograph—the same shadow in the upper window, behind the children. Two pinpoints of black in a larger shape. I hadn't seen it before, or perhaps I'd assumed it a natural shadow in the window glass. But now, putting the sketch next to the photograph, I could see what it was.

It watches me.

"Frances," I said softly into the darkness, "is this what you want me to see?"

There was no answer.

I gently closed the book, placed it reverently on the table with the photograph inside, and turned out the light again.

CHAPTER TWENTY-TWO

"Are you all right?"

It was February 1918, and I was standing in Victoria Station, seeing my husband off after his final leave. He had been home for three weeks—longer than I had expected, longer than he'd ever been home before. And now he was leaving again.

I gripped his sleeve with my gloved hand. "I'll be just fine," I said.

"You look frozen solid."

"No, no."

It had snowed the night before, and London was deep in slush, the rims of it icy on the pavements and in the gutters. Filthy half-frozen snow had been tracked through Victoria Station by thousands of hurried feet and continued to be tracked in by thousands more. I wore my thickest shoes, my heaviest coat and gloves, but still I could not get warm. I felt the muscles between my shoulder blades contract in a convulsive shiver, but I fought it down. A headache was making its way up the back of my neck and over the top of my skull.

"Look," Alex said, "you needn't come farther. We can say our fare-wells here."

I gripped his sleeve harder and looked up into his face. "No."

He looked down at me, and those extraordinary eyes softened beneath the brim of his handsome, sharp cap. "The train leaves in fif-teen minutes, Jo."

"Fifteen minutes, then. We should keep moving. You're going to be late."

He looked into my face a moment longer; then he turned away and led me through the crowd. I followed with my arm entwined with his, staring at the line of his shoulder, the weave of his wool coat. I had done this before, seen him off on leave. This was always the worst, these last moments, in the middle of a crowd, wanting to say everything and nothing at once. It was an experience so painful one's mind suppressed it, like the death of a loved one or the agony of childbirth. Yet there was no avoiding it. I would not say good-bye at home and let him walk away without me any more than I could detach my own limbs from my body and let them walk out the door.

Still, this was worse than any of the others. I wasn't well, though I was trying to hide it. I was shaking with cold sweat beneath my heavy coat, my feet clammy and frozen, a fog in my head that shrouded my vision. My stomach roiled, threatening to give up the little breakfast I'd eaten. Fifteen minutes. I just had to get through them one by one.

Before this leave, he'd been gone nine months. I could recall not a single one of the days of those nine months, not one meal, not one night or morning. I could not tell you what I had done, what clothes I had worn, whether it had rained or been hot or cold. I had kept myself occupied, volunteering for soldiers' charities, but at the moment I could not recall a single person I had met, not a name or a face.

I had tried. One must get on with things, after all, and not sit around making a cake of oneself over a man, even if that man was one's husband. One must not live only for his letters, coming alive briefly when the thin envelopes arrived, not caring that the thick, clumsy fingers of the censor had already handled the page before I did, that a stranger's eyes had already read my husband's words. *Not much to report from here, my Jo. We are grounded due to fog. The men are playing cards. I can hear the shelling in the distance at the Front. I am picturing you, sitting at the table in our kitchen, reading this, wearing the dress with blue and white flowers you wear so often, your hair tied back, the curls coming loose . . .*

We had come to the entrance to the platform now, and there was a gray-haired man in a crisp uniform and a thick mustache looking at Alex, taking in his uniform and his ticket and giving him a respectful nod. He gave me a nod as well as we passed him, but I barely noticed it, and he was gone, swirling into the crowds behind us before I could think to turn and return the gesture. I could not have turned anyway—my neck seemed to have been soldered into my shoulders in a straight line. I touched my gloved fingers discreetly to my face and sponged the sweat from my temples.

The platform was crowded, the cold air mixing with the warmth of hundreds of bodies in a horrible miasma. I tried to cover my nose. My feet were numb with cold while sweat dripped under my arms and down my back. Someone bumped into me and I stumbled.

Alex caught me, his arm coming around my waist as naturally as breathing. "Jo?" he said.

"I'm all right."

He turned away, kept his arm around me. "Pardon me," he said as he arrowed through the crowd. "Make way, please. My wife is not well. Make way."

People made way, of course—Alex never had to raise his voice to be obeyed. It was something in the tone that made you do what he asked almost before he'd finished the sentence. But people looked past him to me, alarm on their faces. A woman pulled her child away by the hand, and two girls, arm in arm, stepped back. Influenza had begun its deadly sweep, leaving piles of bodies in its wake. I tried to look normal, to meet people's eyes and give them a nod. *Not influenza, no, no.* I had the presence of mind to catch one woman's eye and discreetly pat my stomach. Immediately I saw the relief on her face.

"Make way, please. My wife is unwell." Alex maneuvered me to a bench on the platform, that someone—whoever it was, I never saw—immediately vacated, and sat me down. He crouched in front of me, balanced on those long legs of his. "You shouldn't have come," he said.

Now that I was sitting and I could see all of him, I felt a little better. I had a clear view of the long, lean shape of him, the dark wool trousers I'd watched him put on that morning, his heavy boots. The hem of his winter wool coat rested on his thighs, and he'd partially unbuttoned it, so I could see the uniform he wore beneath. He set down the rucksack he'd been carrying over one shoulder and leaned in toward me, his eyes never leaving my face.

"What is it, Jo?" he asked. "Tell me."

"I don't know," I confessed. "I didn't feel like this until this morning. I know I haven't been getting enough sleep."

He spoke nearly in a whisper, to avoid alarming anyone who could overhear. "If it's influenza, for God's sake . . ."

"No, no." I smiled at him. "I really do feel better now that I'm sitting down. It's nothing like that at all."

I hadn't convinced him, I could tell, but his train was leaving in minutes. He glanced behind him at the track, then turned back to me. "Can you get home?"

"Yes, of course." I blinked as pain shot up the back of my head as if I'd been speared with a knitting needle. "This is stupid. I'm here to say good-bye to you, not to make you worry. Please don't."

He glanced back at the train again. In one motion, he pulled off one of his heavy leather gloves and touched his fingers to my face. His skin against mine felt icy, and I realized it was because my own was burning hot. The touch was almost painful, as if my skin was swollen and thin as rice paper, but still I leaned into him as the world tilted a little.

"I can't miss this train," he said.

"I know," I replied, my eyes drifting half closed. "The war awaits."

"I want to tell the war to fuck itself," he said, his coarseness shock-
ing me into a smile, as he'd intended. "I do. There's part of me that
would do it in an instant. But, Jo . . ."

I nodded and put my gloved hand over his. "I hate the war," I said. I
felt strange, disconnected, as if I were listening to someone else. My spine
ached.

"Jesus." Alex pulled off his other glove and put both hands to my
face, the effect like icy blades on my skin. "Promise me you'll see a doctor. Today."

"I promise." Again someone else was speaking through my lips,
making words I barely understood.

There was a high, shrill whistle, a warning that the train was about
to leave, that threatened to split my head in two. I focused on staying
still and not throwing up from the pain and the dizziness, still smiling
at Alex as if nothing were wrong. He was leaving. I mustn't worry him.

He glanced at the train one last time, then picked up his rucksack
and put it over his shoulder. He took my face in his hands again and
leaned close to me, his clean-shaven cheek against mine, his breath on
my ear. "I have done everything wrong," he said to me, "everything,
and you will never forgive me. But stay alive and I will come back to
you. I will come back to you. Do you understand?"

"Yes," I said. *No*, my mind screamed, as high and shrill as the train
whistle, though my tongue could not form the words. *No, no, don't leave,
I love you, don't leave.*

Then he kissed my lips and let me go.

I gasped. My mind scrambled through its fog. I tried to stand, but
my legs wouldn't obey me. Alex vanished into the crowd—gone, gone.
Had he looked back at me? Already I couldn't remember. It had all
been so fast. What sort of kiss had it been? I knew all of Alex's kisses,
what every one of them meant. Had it been one of his passionate ones,
or one of his sweeter, gentler ones? I didn't know.

I finally levered myself from the bench and pushed myself through the crowd. Now I was just a flushed, red-eyed girl like dozens of others on the platform, stumbling about in grief. I tried to get to the train—I had no idea how long I'd been trying when the train gave a whistle and pulled away. I was pummeled on all sides, pushed and pulled by the crowd, by women waving handkerchiefs, crying children. My cheeks were wet with tears.

Had he looked back at me?

I had no recollection of how I got home that day—there were gaps of time that were utterly blank, as if I were asleep. I did not go to a doctor. I could recall sitting on the stairs of the Chalcot Road apartment, pulling off my shoes and sobbing as I rubbed my icy feet. I remembered crying out in pain as I pulled my clothes off my aching skin. I remembered thinking that it was influenza after all, and that I would die, and that Alex would be disappointed because he had told me not to.

I was sick for a week, sweating and shivering in bed. I did, in fact, have influenza—though I got away with a milder strain that was not deadly, like the Spanish flu. After a week I was as wrung out as a dishrag, the act of merely feeding myself so exhausting I could barely perform it. I stayed in our dim apartment, one day after another. I had no friends or family, in London or anywhere. No one came.

I lay in bed one night as I was recovering, listening to the rain out the window and watching the wall. The signs had come that day that once again I was not pregnant. I would not have Alex's child. I was alone.

Someone should write a poem, I thought, about the women. Not just about the men marching bravely to war and dying, but about their wives, their girls, their mothers and sisters and daughters, sitting in silence and screaming into the darkness. Unable to fight, unable to stop it, unable to tell the war to fuck itself. We fought our war, too, it seemed to me, and if it was a war of a different kind, the pain of it was no more bearable. Someone should write a poem about the women.

But I already knew that no one ever would.

CHAPTER TWENTY-THREE

We were approaching All Hallows' Eve, the tail end of autumn, when the last drifts of wet, loamy scent left the air and the world began to lose color.

"I'm sorry you got dragged into this, Cousin Jo," Martin said. He tugged his scarf tighter around his neck. "You must know it wasn't my idea."

"I know," I replied. We were standing outside, waiting for Cora. Martin and Cora were to go walking, and I was to accompany them, the awkward old stick of a chaperone. It wasn't the first time.

"She's rather nice, you know." Martin turned and looked back toward the house, where the front door opened and the figure of Cora, swathed in a wool coat that looked expensive even from a distance, emerged. "I think I may ask her today."

I hadn't thought I would be surprised, but I was. "Are you certain?" I asked.

"Mother has a schedule," he said with a hint of humor. "In any case, I think we'll get on well enough, for as long as I'm alive."

168

I raised my eyebrows. "Please don't tell me you've been saying that to her," I said. "It's hardly the ideal way to court a woman."

That made him smile. "I haven't, I promise. Though I hardly know the ideal way to court a woman, do I? I've never done it."

"I'm sure you're doing fine."

He gave me a curious look. "How did Alex court you?" he asked.

The memory gripped me heavily for a moment, fraught with emotion, then let me go. "He took me to dinner," I replied.

"That was all?"

"That was all."

Martin gave a low whistle.

"Good afternoon, Mrs. Manders." This was Cora, approaching us with her hands in the pockets of her expensive coat, a perfectly matched cloche hat on her head. Despite the sophisticated clothes, her gait was awkward, the coat hanging heavy on her gawky frame. She looked almost pretty, the cold air flushing her thin cheeks beneath her tilted eyes. She gave me a smile of even, white teeth.

"Good afternoon, Cora," I said. If she insisted on addressing me like an ancient matron, I might as well act like one.

Martin glanced back at the house, where undoubtedly at least one parent was watching us from a window. "Let's head off and figure out today's route."

He offered Cora his arm, and she took it, squeezing it a little and turning the smile on him. Martin said something to her as they walked, and Cora laughed, the sound honking over the trees. "You're a funny one," she said, her voice drifting back to me where I followed behind them. Then she leaned in toward him and said something I couldn't hear.

I sighed. Chaperoning was positively the worst job in the world, worse than taking Dottie's abuse in the library or listening to Casparov's innuendoes. So far, I'd had to sit out of earshot as the two of them strolled among the abandoned stables and the overgrown tennis courts.

I'd brought a book with me the second time, when it became clear I didn't particularly need to stare at the courting couple as they sat side by side, talking quietly, Cora occasionally laughing at Martin's jokes. Today they'd decided to walk in the woods. I swallowed my dread and tried to appear calm about it. It wouldn't do for the dried-up chaperone to go raving about mists and dogs barking and Martin's dead sister at the crucial point of the courtship.

When we were well into the trees, Martin stopped and Cora dropped her hand from his arm.

"Where d'you want to go?" Martin asked her.

Cora snapped her sleeve smartly and checked her watch. "I don't know. How long will satisfy them?"

"Forty-five minutes or so," Martin said. He turned to me. "What do you think, Cousin Jo?"

I shrugged. "Forty-five minutes sounds good to me."

"All right," Martin said. The wind blew through the trees, and the tips of his ears were already growing red with cold. He turned to Cora. "That gives me enough time to take you over the rise toward the village before we have to turn back. It's a bit steep in places, though. What do you think?"

She bit her lip, her eyes on Martin's face. "I'm dressed nice and I didn't eat much breakfast," she said. "Can we do something easier?"

In that moment, I began to like Cora Staffron. Despite her thin frame and no doubt knobby knees, she was hardy and could have done the walk—or even a longer one—without losing her breath. It was Martin who would struggle. I silently applauded her.

"Easier? Yes, I suppose." Martin thought it over, oblivious to the subtext. "We'll go toward the village. Then I'll bring you around the back way by the path through the woods. No rocks that way. Sound good?"

"Well, sure," Cora said.

Martin turned back to me. "Right back here in forty-five minutes, then. Do you have somewhere to go, Cousin?"

I paused in surprise, and his cheeks flushed. It had been demeaning enough to follow them about before, but now I was to be overtly abandoned. I recovered myself. "Yes, of course," I said.

Cora looked at me brightly. "You should have brought some birding binoculars. You could have smuggled them under your coat and no one watching would know."

I stared at her. She really did see me as ancient. "Or perhaps I should have brought a flask."

She only laughed. "Wouldn't that be funny!"

I agreed it would be, and we went our separate ways. It was a relief of sorts—I realized as I stepped into the shadowed silence that I had been straining even to make the most meaningless small talk. But I did not want to be alone in the woods, even on a sunny day. When they were out of sight, I paused on the path, and my gloved hand slipped into my pocket and touched the piece of paper there.

Keep it together, Jo.

The fear closed around me for a full moment as I listened to the soft sounds of the forest, the wind rushing through the trees, the far-off calls of birds. I could not go back to the house, or everyone would know that Martin and Cora were alone. And I could not follow them and intrude.

So I kept walking. Martin had told me once of a particularly nice vista over the sea, in the other direction from the village, so I took the path away from my charges. I made my way over the treacherous ground on numb feet, stepping over ruts and puddles, sweating beneath my coat and hat as I climbed a rise, the wind chilling the thin perspiration on my forehead.

When I finally reached the place, I stopped in silent wonder. I was at the very western edge of the woods, on the side facing away from the house and the village, at the place where the trees ended. Just past my feet was a clearing that fell off and sloped sharply down, and beyond it the rocky terrain wound along the coast toward the horizon. The ocean was gray and cold below me, the shore sharp and forbidding, but still the view was breathtaking. I let the wind buffet the brim of my hat and the collar of my coat, taking in the vast expanse.

Just visible several miles down the shore was a low and blocky set of buildings, clustered within a fenced-in square of land. It sat quiet and dull in the sunshine, placed right on the edge of the water, where several small boats were moored. This must be the Ministry of Fisheries, where Colonel Mabry claimed to be assisting somehow. It looked sleepy and silent, and I saw not a whisper of movement.

I turned back to look at the water. There were no pleasure boats, no sloops or neat little sails. This was choppy water, deep and cold. Far on the horizon was the silhouette of a large ship, its smokestacks belting into the sky. Seabirds crisscrossed the shoreline, calling to one another in high, shrill voices. I saw not one other human figure.

I am alone, I thought.

The wind stung my eyes, but the tears on my cheeks were not from the cold. Here, in this remote place where no one could see me, I did not wipe them away, but let them dry, salty, on my skin.

Keep it together, Jo.

I pulled the letter I'd received this morning from my pocket, unfolded it, and looked at it for the hundredth time. The wind flapped the page sharply, but I held on, watching the words blur.

> *We are very sorry to inform you that Mrs. Christopher passed away last night in her sleep. There was no warning, and she spent yesterday as usual, so the doctors have declared that her heart stopped as she was sleeping. Though this news must grieve you, please accept our assurances that Mrs. Christopher went to her Maker peacefully, without struggle or pain, and that she rests now in the arms of Heaven as innocent as a child, as all of our patients do.*
>
> *There are certain arrangements to be made . . .*

I lifted the letter higher, watched it flap in the wind. I thought of my mother, her beautiful hair, her porcelain skin, the fine bones of her wrists, the dark half circles under her eyes like bruises. All of those years with the refrain in the back of my mind—*Where is Mother? What is she doing? Is she all right?*—were over. She had been a mystery, a labyrinth of rooms I could not know, and now she was gone, unknowable forever, and I had no one left to worry about. Had she remembered me, even as she died? Had there been any memory of me at all?

I doubted it. Mother and I were strangers; last night I had been in my bedroom at Wych Elm House, reading a book by lamplight, as she had been dying. But without Alex she was all I had, the only thing mooring me to the earth. With Mother gone, I suddenly felt as insubstantial as the leaves in Wych Elm House, as transient as Frances Forsyth's face printed in nitrate on a piece of paper. Someday I would vanish, and no one would ever know I'd been.

Where is your Mother?

The wind tried to snatch the letter from my hand, but I would not let it go. Eventually I folded it again and put it back in my pocket. Then I wiped my eyes.

I turned my steps away and walked back toward the path, to meet Martin and Cora as they came my way.

CHAPTER TWENTY-FOUR

It was a surprise to no one that Cora and Martin emerged from their walk in the woods engaged. In the jubilation that followed among both sets of parents, I kept the news of Mother's death quiet, privately asking Dottie for time off to travel to Hertford for her funeral and to sign the papers from the hospital.

Dottie had been distracted as I spoke, but when I came to my reason for the time, she turned her gimlet eyes on me with perfect focus. "That is a shame, Manders," she said. "You may have the day. Take the motorcar and driver."

"I will, thank you."

"Are there any financial concerns?"

It took me a moment to realize she was asking if I was capable of paying for Mother's funeral. "The hospital is burying her in their chapel yard," I said. "It's where many of their patients go. The expense is modest."

"They'll bury her properly, then," Dottie said. "Make sure they do. If any of the arrangements are unsatisfactory, have them telephone me."

She was awful—she had granted me only a single day off, and in a moment she would forget about me altogether as she planned Martin and Cora's engagement party—but my eyes stung with embarrassing tears. She had buried Frances properly and had likely had to fight to do it. She was willing to fight the same fight on my behalf for Mother. Why Dottie made it so hard to befriend her, I would never know.

"Thank you," I managed.

"Eight o'clock Thursday morning, Manders," she said in reply. "Look sharp, as we'll be busy. I detest maudlin emotions."

"Yes, Dottie."

As it happened, the hospital did bury Mother properly. Their chapel yard was calm and green, well tended, with a view over the rolling hills. They gave her a small stone, with her name and dates, and the simple word BELOVED. Aside from the hospital's chaplain and one nurse on behalf of the staff, I was the only one in attendance.

It was on the ride back in the motorcar, as I half dozed beneath a headache of grief, that I suddenly realized I would no longer be paying Mother's hospital bills. The expense that had burdened me for so many years—that had driven me to work for Casparov, and therefore meet Alex and change my life; that had driven me to work for Dottie, and to change my life again—was gone. I would still have to support myself, but I now earned enough to put a few pounds into savings. The relief was so hideous that I wept in horror at myself, with no witness but the silent driver. By the time we arrived back at Wych Elm House, I was myself again.

The engagement party was to be grand, the first social affair Wych Elm House had seen since Dottie's father had bought it for her. The bride's parents had offered to host it, as was custom, but Dottie had insisted; she used the excuse that Martin's health prevented him from traveling, which was accurate, but the truth was she wanted badly to show off.

The arrangements were many: flowers, china, additional servants, champagne, music, food. Dottie and I were kept busy morning and night, and though it was dull work, it was a blessing, because there was no room to think of anything else.

Though Martin and Cora were the feted couple, they had nothing to do with the arrangements. I rarely saw them. Martin had taken a turn for the worse again, as if the effort of courtship and proposing had taxed him, and Cora took to reading to him in the back study as he lay on the sofa with a blanket over him. Her voice was grating, her pronunciation terrible, and her reading hardly expert, but still he lay there hour after hour, his eyes closed, as she read on.

Though I was no longer on chaperone duty, I had been tasked with occasionally satisfying propriety and checking on them. The first time I did so, Martin saw the look on my face and took my hand. He gave it a brief squeeze and shook his head once in silent communication. He was not back on morphine, then. I squeezed his hand in return.

Robert, now freed from the work of courting the Staffrons, fled the house in his motorcar. He spent evenings at the neighbors' again, though he sometimes stayed home for dinner and curbed his all-night assignations. He never looked at me or spoke to me, for which I was grateful. As soon as the ink was on the marriage certificate, we might never see him again.

Life went on. I slept as little as ever; my nightmares were vivid and horrible. I watched the pageant before me, made lists of linens and silverware, flowers to be ordered and invitations sent and responded to, and at night I paged through Frances's sketchbook, looking at the shadows she'd drawn over the town I visited and the house I lived in, staring at the face she'd drawn in the window of my bedroom. Twice I ventured to the upper gable again, standing and waiting, hoping Frances would tell me how it had happened, who had done it. I lived separate from the family, alone in my visions and dreams. I wondered if I was suffering from what Mother's doctors had politely called "nervous exhaustion." I vaguely realized I had begun to let go of my life, to let it march without me.

And then the morning of the party dawned, and I decided to take out my camera again.

I hadn't planned to do it. After the encounter with Robert—I could still remember the shock of seeing the figure of Frances past his shoulder—I had packed the camera away and left it. But I lay awake as dawn broke one morning and remembered that Frances had placed the camera on the floor of my room that day. And when I had taken the camera out, she had appeared. It was the last time I had seen her.

I could feel her somewhere close to me, watching, waiting. Perhaps the camera was the key.

I rose and dressed quickly, putting on layers to keep warm. Thick stockings, the plaid skirt Dottie had forbidden me to wear, and both a blouse and a sweater over my chemise. I twisted my hair back in an unkempt bun. Then I took Alex's camera from its case and, shoeless, crept out my door into the hall.

The corridor was silent; there was no sound behind Cora's closed door, or from her parents' room down the hall. The servants would be up soon, so I moved quickly.

Downstairs, I padded through the kitchen to the back door. In the vestibule there, I pressed the small button for the electric light and looked at the array of outerwear hanging from hooks and lined in rows along the floor. I did not own shoes that were warm or thick enough for November in the countryside. Setting down the camera, I rifled through the belongings of the Forsyth family, looking for something that fit. I ended up with a slick black mackintosh that was tight in the shoulders—Dottie's, perhaps?—and a pair of large, ungainly rubber boots that fit my feet perfectly and came halfway up my calves. I contemplated the boots as I wiggled my toes in their chilly interiors. I could not imagine Dottie wearing rubber boots even at knifepoint, and they were too small to be Robert's. It was quite likely that they had been Frances's.

I found a mismatched green woolen scarf, tucked it around my neck, and set out.

It seemed that morning that I had the world to myself. The air was pungent with cold, frosted leaves, and my breath plumed in the air. Dawn had lightened the sky just enough so I could see the knobbed trunks of the trees and the path as it wound into the early-morning mist before me. The night's chill fog still shrouded the woods, so that the trees seemed to vanish upward into unseen eternity, and cries came from invisible birds. The few leaves left on the trees dripped water with a persistent wet sound, and the loamy path sponged frostily beneath the soles of Frances's rubber boots.

I had not brought the tripod with me. I carried only the camera as I traveled the path, my boots sliding in the mud. Thick, cold water trickled down my mackintosh, the droplets catching the light. I could feel my own damp breath on the edge of the scarf that touched my lips. I headed for the lookout where I'd read Mother's letter the last time, settling into a strange state of meditation as I walked, watching and listening. On some level I was afraid, but on another I was excited, alive with almost painful anticipation.

At the lookout, the fog blurred the edges of the view. The sea was a deep, hollow roar, its churning faintly visible through a layer of mist; the Ministry of Fisheries was a ghostly outline of walls and right angles. I stood for a moment, drinking the salty air, feeling the wind brush my damp cheeks, and then I fumbled with the camera.

I sank to one knee on the rocky ground and placed the camera on my other knee to steady it. I took off the cap, advanced the film, and bent to the eyepiece, framing the misty ocean in my view. I snapped a photograph, then moved back to get a wider shot, knelt again, and took another.

"Where are you?" I shouted into the wind.

I changed my angle as the wind rose in the trees behind me. The dawn light was just perfect, making the edges of everything soft, the mist diffusing the rising sun. A single boat on the ocean drifted into my line of vision, and I bent to the eyepiece again, watching the dark speck move on the lonely expanse of ocean, placing my finger over the button.

Something moved on the path behind me.

I straightened, the hair on the back of my neck prickling. "Frances?" I called.

There was no answer. Slowly, my clenched muscles protesting, I twisted my body and looked back over my shoulder at the path into the woods.

There was nothing there.

As I gripped the camera and stood, pain stung my knee where it had been pressed into the hard ground. I turned and faced the path, my back to the water now. Still there was no sound, no movement, but I *sensed* her watching me. I took a few cautious steps, my breath held in my chest, my boots quiet against the damp ground.

She was not on the path. I had nearly reached the first bend when it occurred to me to raise the camera to my eye and look through it.

I held the camera unsteadily to my face and squinted through the eyepiece. I saw the path, the woods around it, the tatters of mist. Nothing else appeared. Slowly, I pivoted on my heel, my damp, icy hands gripping the leather of the camera, my arms shaking as I held it in place at my eye. My breath was loud in my ears as I swiveled carefully, my lens taking in the pattern of tree trunks, turning back to look at the clearing and the water. The wind kicked up, and I heard the rustle of dead leaves.

She was there. Standing where I had just been, her skin the color of parchment, her eyes watching me from their dark recesses, staring, the hem of her dress unnaturally still in the rising wind.

I made a strangled sound in my throat and jerked my face back from the camera, my slick hands nearly letting go. I blinked and stared at the space I'd just seen through the lens, my vision clearing. There was nothing there.

"Frances?" I whispered.

Before I could lower my eye to the camera again, the leaves in the clearing kicked up in the wind, swirling. I stood hypnotized as dead leaves funneled up from the ground and down from the branches overhead, moving like motes of light. It was beautiful and terrible, unnatural. The icy wind howled.

High over the trees, shrill and imperious, came a long, unearthly whistle.

I turned on the path and ran.

I pounded over the muddy path, my clumsy boots slipping. I still carried the camera, held close to my chest in both hands. My fingers struggled to keep their grip and my breath came in gasps as the camera banged clumsily against my body.

The whistle sounded again—it split my brain, like a long-ago train whistle had on the worst day of my life—and a bolt of panic shot down my spine. *She is calling him,* I thought. I changed direction and left the path, scrambling down an incline tangled with brush, no longer aware of my direction or which way led back to Wych Elm House. I hit the bottom of the incline, the thorns of something in the underbrush tearing my stockings above the top of my boot, and kept running.

Far behind me in the woods, the birds went silent, as if they sensed something coming.

I staggered down another incline and found myself on a dirt path, wide and flat, bordered by thick brush. I could see no distance either up or down it—the fog was too heavy. In the spin of my panic I realized this was the same path I had stood on the morning I had met Robert. I was at the other end of it, far on the opposite side of the woods that spanned the Forsyths' property.

I jogged along its easy length for a moment, feeling the jagged pinch inside my rubber boots and a trickle of blood warm on my calf. Cold rain had begun, dripping in the trees and spattering my mackintosh. My breath was sawing in my lungs, and cold sweat slicked down my back beneath my layers, but I did not stop. If I could take the road far enough to get back toward the house, to familiar ground—

Something moved in the trees far behind me. Without thinking, I ducked off the road, struggling through sticky underbrush again. My hands slipped on the camera, but I did not let it go. I slid down an incline into a valley of dead leaves, then scrambled up the other side.

From the road came a heavy scrabbling sound of claws in the dirt. There was a rushing overhead—the birds, this time, still silent, flying upward en masse. The entire woods denuded of birds in a single, soundless exodus. Over the roar of my own pounding heart in my ears, I heard something breathe—the harsh rasp of panting, deep and throaty.

My foot in its clumsy boot slipped, and I fell, bumping and careening into a low, wet ditch, the mackintosh acting like a slick toboggan. I came to rest on my back in a puddle of cold water, staring up into the rainy trees.

There was no time to escape, not now. I froze by instinct, going still, my breath stopping, like a mouse or a shrew when it feels an owl fly overhead. My legs clenched; my mind went white. All thought stopped, all motion, as I lay and waited.

The smell came first. An overpowering rotten stench, damp and greasy. The bushes shifted and tore as something large came through them, up the rise, the heavy grind of paws gaining purchase in the loamy earth. There was a gasp and a growl, and the thing hit the top of the rise and launched itself over me.

I could not scream. A whistle of air squeezed through the back of my throat, its sound lost.

I could not see all of the creature in the fog. I glimpsed long, sprawled legs, muscled almost like a human's, and vicious paws like hands. A chest thick as a barrel, covered in a ruff of long, filthy fur. And a long body, leaping over me in my icy ditch in a single, soundless move, the belly passing within arm's reach of my face. Its head was lost in the white mist, though a vicious, drawled growl came from its unseen throat and trailed after it in the air.

I pressed myself into the puddle of water and watched in terrorized silence as Princer's stomach, matted and foul with a coppery stench like blood, passed before my eyes. Of their own accord, my hands gripped the camera pressed to my chest, and my finger clicked the shutter.

Then he landed on the ridge of land at the other side of the ditch, I glimpsed a heavy curl of tail, and he was gone.

I lay shivering as my hands went numb on the camera and the water in the ditch soaked my hair. The fog swirled past my unseeing eyes. It was a long time before I realized that the birds were singing again.

CHAPTER TWENTY-FIVE

"My goodness, Mrs. Manders—what happened?" Mrs. Perry dropped her chopping knife on the counter and came toward me as I stood in the kitchen doorway.

"I'm all right," I told her. I had pulled off Frances's rubber boots, caked with mud, and left them on the floor of the vestibule alongside the filthy black mackintosh. "I just need a towel, if you please, so I don't track water all through your tidy kitchen."

She picked a towel from a cupboard and snapped it open. "I didn't even know you were out of the house. Did you have an accident?"

"Yes." I rubbed the towel over my soaked feet in their torn stockings and avoided the curious gaze of the maid staring over the cook's shoulder. "I was taking pictures in the woods, and I'm afraid I fell. I'm a mess, but I'm not hurt."

Mrs. Bennett came into the kitchen, spotted me, and joined Mrs. Perry as I explained. "You'll catch a fever," she proclaimed, her hands on her hips. "You need tea and a hot bath."

After walking home, soaked, through the foggy forest, I would have married Jack the Ripper for access to either. "Yes, thank you. I'll just go up the back stairs and—"

"Tildy, go with her," Mrs. Bennett barked at the maid.

"No, please." I straightened, the dripping towel in one hand, and pushed my hair back from my face with the other. I gave both of them a beseeching look. "I'd rather Mrs. Forsyth not know. She didn't know I was out at all, and with the engagement party today . . . It was just an accident. More embarrassing than anything, really."

Mrs. Bennett and Mrs. Perry exchanged understanding looks. "Take the servants' stairs, then," Mrs. Perry agreed. "I'll put the coat and boots away. Tildy will bring up tea in a few minutes."

But as I picked up my camera and crossed the kitchen to the servants' stairs, Cora Staffron walked in. "Do I smell tea biscuits?" She looked at me, and her eyes widened at my disastrous appearance. "Oh. Mrs. Manders."

I sighed. "It was an accident," I said.

She bit her lip. She was wearing a thick, quilted dressing gown decorated top to bottom with twines of flowers that strongly resembled wallpaper. Her blond bob was carelessly combed, her neck protruding gawky and thin from her collar. I realized that she was just as embarrassed as I was.

Mrs. Bennett came to our rescue, since we were both frozen in humiliation. "The tea biscuits will be ready any minute, Miss Staffron," she said. "I'll have some sent up to you, along with tea for Mrs. Manders. Will that be acceptable?"

Cora snapped out of her freeze, probably at the mention of biscuits, and gave Mrs. Bennett one of her smiles. "You bet!" she said, and turned to me. "Let's go, Mrs. Manders."

She was surprisingly sisterly when we got upstairs, drawing me a bath and fetching extra towels from the linen closet. Our corridor was temporarily deserted, and no one saw me hobble to the bathroom, damp and muddy, wrapped in a bathrobe. When I had lowered myself into the water, blessing Wych Elm House's modern, immaculate plumbing, I realized Cora was still in the hallway, on the other side of the closed door.

"I hope your camera can be repaired," she said. "It looked rather wet."

"Wet?" It had been out in the rain with me, but I had thought it came through all right.

"Sure it is!" Cora replied. "There's water coming out of it and everything! It looks a mess to me, and I think your photographs will be ruined. It's a shame, isn't it?"

There had not been water running out of it when I carried it. The word came to me unbidden: *Frances*. There would be no photograph of her dog, not if she could help it. The pictures of the ocean would be ruined as well. I pressed my hands to my eyes and tried to calm down.

"Mama wants a Christmas wedding." Cora chattered nervously through the door. "But that's barely six weeks away. What do you think, Mrs. Manders?"

I dropped my hands and doused my muddy hair in the water. *Keep it together, Jo.* "I hear Christmas weddings are nice," I replied in a shaky voice.

"Was your own wedding very large?"

The words were automatic. "We married by ourselves in Crete."

"An elopement!" I heard her clap her hands. "That's so scandalous, like something a movie actress would do." There was a thumping, shifting sound, and I realized she had sat down on the floor of the corridor, her back against the door. I wondered how nervous she must be, or how badly she wanted to avoid starting her day, to sit on the floor in her dressing gown and talk to me. "Mama says my dress should be satin, but I look so terrible in satin! It never sits right on me. I wonder if Mama will let me wear rouge."

I looked down at my hands, which were still shaking. Her prattle was actually soothing me, bringing me back from the nightmare I had just experienced and was only beginning to understand. "Will your other relatives be here tonight?" I asked.

"I don't have many," Cora replied. "I'm an only child. I wish I had cousins my own age, but I don't, just an older cousin who's a doctor on Harley Street. He said he'd come."

"That's very nice," I said, using the sponge on my face and neck.

"He is nice," Cora said. "Mama asked him if the madness in Martin's sister could run in the family, but he said he didn't think it could."

I sank down in the water, soaping my hair and rinsing it again. *Oh, Frances, Frances. What do you want?* But already I knew. Even through the fog of my terror, I knew. *She wanted me to see. That's why Princer didn't harm me. She wanted me to see.* "Cora," I said, "don't listen to any rumors about Frances. And Martin is not mad."

"Oh, I know!" she said with an awkward laugh. "He's a gentleman, isn't he?"

"Yes." I closed my eyes, trying not to see Princer's hideous stomach leaping over me. I prayed she wasn't going to ask for a lesson about wedding nights. "He is."

"He's kind to me, and he makes me laugh. Everything is going to go swimmingly, I just know it! I just wish he could eat something and rest more. It makes him moody—have you noticed that? He's a little frightening sometimes. Last night I found him in his room, burning his sister's letters in the fire."

I was wringing out my hair, but I stopped. "What do you mean, burning his sister's letters?"

"From the war," Cora said. "All the letters she wrote him at the Front. I don't know what they said, because he wouldn't tell me."

"Why did he burn them?"

"I don't know." The brassy confidence had left her voice, and for the first time since I'd met her, she sounded unsure. "He never talks about the war, at least not to me. He won't talk about his health, either, and he won't let the doctors answer my questions. He just goes quiet and tells me everything will be fine."

I stood from the bath and pulled a towel around myself. *Damn you, Martin. Just tell her about the morphine.* "Men don't talk about the war," I said.

"I just want to help," she said. "We're going to be married by Christmas. Mrs. Manders, you've been married before. How do you get your husband to tell you everything?"

"You don't," I said, and I reached into the tub and pulled the plug, watching the water spiral down the drain.

CHAPTER TWENTY-SIX

Dottie had chosen the upstairs gallery for the engagement party. Tables had been lined along one side of the room, laid with delicacies and flutes of champagne. A string quartet played in a corner, and a raised dais had been set up at the head of the room for announcements. The floral arrangements arrived by luncheon, profusions of gardenias and roses and chrysanthemums, lilies in tall sprays. Workmen had lined the walls with small portable electric lamps that would give off elegant light when the room was dark.

I entered after the first guests had arrived. There were some two dozen people drinking and circulating beneath the canvases we had collected so assiduously on the Continent—Dottie's art and business acquaintances, local gentry who were likely Robert's cronies, the Staffrons, and the members of the Staffrons' circles who had made the journey from London. Every bedroom in Wych Elm House was occupied tonight, as well as several rooms in the area's surrounding inns.

I spotted Cora and Martin near the center of the room, nodding and greeting guests as they approached. Martin wore immaculate black tie and tails, his hair slicked back and gleaming in the soft light. His eyes were bright and his smile was genuine. I breathed a sigh of relief that tonight seemed to be a good one.

Cora was in a dress of striking blue shot with white, puffed at the sleeves and beaded on the bodice. It was almost absurd—she looked a little like Anne Boleyn crossed with a respectable modern matron— yet somehow Cora looked born to it, her hair swept up and her tilted eyes aglow with demure pleasure. She turned to me with her familiar wide smile.

"Cousin Jo!" Martin said as I approached. "You look a vision."

"What an elegant dress!" Cora cried.

I smiled at them. My dress had arrived from London the day before; the dressmaker in Anningley had ordered it special for me. It was a simple sleeveless sheath that fell in a straight line from my shoulders to my hips, then down to a jaunty hemline at the knee. It was of deep, rich jewel blue, and peacock feathers adorned the skirt, their soft fronds waving as I moved. The final adornment was a single flower of pink satin sewn to the left hip. A maid had helped me pin my hair up with just a few curls loose over my temples, and I wore black high- heeled shoes. Since I did not own any expensive jewelry, I wore only my wedding ring.

"Thank you," I said to Cora. "Dottie is going to think it fast, but it's a party, is it not?"

"Mother thinks that anything other than a mannish suit is fast," Martin commented. "She's hardly the first word in fashion. Do get some champagne, Cousin Jo, since I believe you're the one who had it ordered especially."

I was. Ordering champagne had been one of my duties. I was just sipping my first glass—the stuff was divine—when a man approached my shoulder. "Mrs. Manders."

I turned in surprise. "Colonel Mabry."

He gave me a quick, formal bow, elegant in his dark suit. "Mrs.

Forsyth was kind enough to invite me, though I've shamefully put off deciding on one of her artworks." His gaze moved up the walls, taking in the various canvases. "I believe I'll have to make a decision soon."

"Yes," I said, my voice perhaps sharper than I intended. "You should. It isn't polite to prevaricate."

The look he gave me from beneath his salt-and-pepper eyebrows was unreadable. He clasped his hands behind his back and gave no answer.

"Tell me, Colonel," I said, "how long have you been a lover of art?"

"Mrs. Manders, are you quite all right?"

"Yes, thank you," I said. He began to stroll around the room, and I followed at his side. My exhaustion and nerves had amplified the effects of the champagne, I realized. "I don't think I thanked you, Colonel, for letting me see my husband's file."

He looked at me sideways, a glance that was speculative and, inexplicably, had a note of dread in it. "It was nothing, I assure you."

"So much interesting information," I said. "Even a silly woman like me could learn so much."

"And what exactly did you learn, Mrs. Manders?" he asked.

I thought it over. The champagne had made me dizzy, my tongue loose in my head. "Do you know, I don't think I am going to tell you."

"Mrs. Manders." He stopped walking and faced me. Looking at him was like looking into a shallow pool and realizing that you couldn't see the bottom, could not fathom where it was. "You are upset, and I believe we both understand why. But I feel obliged to give you a warning. Things have been very difficult for you—but they are going to get even more difficult, I'm afraid."

"What does that mean?" My voice dropped to nearly a whisper. "Tell me."

He did not reply, and I would have said more, but a hand reached out and grasped me.

"Mrs. Manders!" Robert leaned in and put a heavy arm around

my shoulders. "You really must put a sack on your head, my dear, so you don't outshine the bride. How are you, sir?"

I froze. Robert—who had been drinking since before the party started, by the smell of him—pumped the colonel's hand, then led me away, his beefy hand still on my bare shoulder. I swallowed bile. "It's a party," he hissed at me through gin-soaked breath. "Act like it, if you please."

I circulated around the room under Robert's clammy grip, being introduced to strangers, until he stopped us by a pillar, took two drinks from a passing waiter, and handed me one.

"I don't want this," I said.

"Drink it," he commanded, taking a long swig of his own.

I sipped the champagne, its sweetness on my tongue now making me gag.

"You must loosen up, Jo," Robert said, his bleary eyes watching me. "Take my advice. You may be the best-looking woman in the room, but your expression is positively sour. Mrs. Mandel's cousin-in-law is a baronet, and Staffron brought some of his richer banking friends. You'll never catch any of the eligible men here unless you flirt."

I stepped out of his reach and took another sip of my drink. "What do you care, anyway? You should go paw one of the neighbors' wives."

"Careful, now." Robert raised his glass and gestured to the room around us. "I gave you a warning to watch your tongue. I spotted you right away, you know. Making nice with that old stick of a colonel—he could be your father, my dear. Did you know that Wilde, the lawyer, was observing you two?"

"What are you talking about?" I looked around the room, but didn't see Dottie's man of business.

"Quite interested, he was," Robert said. "Though you could do better, even as a mistress."

Before I could escape him, the band switched to a jaunty march, and Dottie stepped up on the raised dais, waving her arms to get the attention of everyone in the room. She wore, unbelievably, a jacket and skirt—though these were of curious yellow-green and sewn with glass beads that reflected the light in shards. The suit jacket was buttoned down the front and sported an Oriental collar that sat neatly in a ribbon around her narrow neck. She wore the same hairstyle as ever.

"My lovely wife," Robert hissed drunkenly in my ear.

"Shut up," I said to him, and he laughed.

There were speeches—lots of speeches. Dottie said a few words, clipped yet heartfelt. Mr. Staffron, who I'd barely spoken to since he came to stay, spoke sonorously; then his wife, Cora's mother, came to the stage, babbling and dabbing her tears with a handkerchief. Robert left my side, mounted the stage, and made a few jokes that had the room laughing uncomfortably. I stood and listened, my feet pinching, and instead of the twinkling lights of the party, I saw the leaves swirling upward; instead of the wash of words from the dais, I heard the shrill whistle; and as Cora and Martin climbed the steps, I watched Princer's stomach, clotted and stinking of blood, soaring over me again and again. As I hovered alone and unnoticed, my glass in my hand, for a moment the terrors of the woods were more real to me than the pleasant civilization of this room.

I blinked and tried to focus on Cora and Martin. Martin spoke first, declaring how lucky he was to have found such a beautiful woman. Cora followed, uncharacteristically shy, her few sentences stilted and rehearsed, her thin face frozen in stage fright as she thanked everyone for coming and declared how happy she was. They stood a foot apart and did not touch.

There was dancing afterward; the four-piece orchestra began again, more champagne flowed, and couples began to rotate demurely around the dance floor. I was asked to dance by one of Dottie's art buyers and then Cora's cousin, the doctor from Harley Street. I accepted numbly and moved around the dance floor with each man in a daze, making mechanical conversation. Mabry's words went through my head in time with the music. *Things are going to get even more difficult, I'm afraid.*

I took another glass of champagne, wishing I had a watch so I could decide when to leave. The champagne was making me even more tired, and a pulse in my temples was beginning to pound. The practiced tones of the orchestra sounded like screeching. Something was wrong. It wasn't just my feeling out of sorts—there was a thick tension in the air, as of a coming thunderstorm. I looked around the room and realized that Dottie, Robert, and Martin were gone.

The din of voices and music in the room seemed to grow louder. The backs of my eyes throbbed. Where had the family disappeared to? Why had they left their own party? I spied Cora in the corner of the room, nodding and smiling at someone, the corners of her eyes tired now, her smile clenched and tense. I started toward her, but someone intercepted me—David Wilde, clad in a formal black suit. "Mrs. Manders," he said. "Please do me the honor of a dance."

"Mr. Wilde," I said.

Mr. Wilde smiled at me. He looked handsome and distinguished, with the silver in his hair and his matching silver eyes. He crooked his right elbow in my direction. "I promise I'm adept," he said.

It was a strangely unbalanced feeling, dancing with a one-armed man. But he maneuvered me expertly around the room, his right hand firm on my waist, as if he danced with women all the time. Beneath my hand, the shoulder of his wasted arm felt bulky and strong beneath his jacket.

"Did you not bring your wife tonight?" I managed to ask him.

"Mrs. Wilde dislikes social functions," he replied. "Mrs. Manders, I'm afraid I should apologize for the circumstances of our first meeting."

"You needn't," I said. "You were tasked with giving your opinion of me as Martin's possible wife, and you gave it."

"Did Mrs. Forsyth tell you that?" he asked in surprise.

"She never had to. I figured it out from the first minute I got back to Wych Elm House." My tongue was running away with me, I realized vaguely, and I could not control it. "Since we are at Martin's engagement party, Mr. Wilde, it no longer figures. I understand what it means to be obliged to do something as part of your employment."

He was quiet for a moment as the room spun around us. I blinked, trying not to topple, and realized I was clinging to him a little tighter in order to stay upright. He responded by angling his body and placing his hand even more firmly on my waist—not like one of Casparov's nasty old gropes, but a gentlemanly effort to keep me discreetly vertical. "Do you ever wonder, Mrs. Manders," he said, "whether my assessment of you was positive or negative?"

"No," I said to him. "No."

"Perhaps I won't tell you, then."

"You told her I was respectable," I said, my loose tongue moving again. "You questioned me about my prospects and concluded that I wasn't after money, so I was probably trustworthy. You told me in detail about Frances to see if I would be shocked or horrified, and I passed that test, too." I waited for him to protest, but he did not. "But you knew about Mother," I continued. "You'd already researched my background. I suppose you wondered if the madness in my family would mix with the madness in Martin's, if we had children."

The silence he gave me after that was appalled—but not, I knew, at me. "It must be difficult," Mr. Wilde said quietly, "to be such a perceptive woman."

The dance was winding to a close, and we slowed. "Perceptive or mad," I said. "Do you ever wonder if they're the same thing?"

The music stopped, and he stepped back from me. "What do you mean?" he asked me.

"I just wonder sometimes," I said. I swayed a little, and he reached out and gripped my arm with his good hand. "I'm well acquainted with madness, as you pointed out. My mother died. Sometimes I wonder if it's only the mad people who see the truth, or who say it out loud." I pulled my arm slowly from his grip. "Thank you for the dance."

A new dance started, and I returned to the sidelines. I drank more champagne. David Wilde danced with a different woman and did not look my way. *Well done, Jo,* I thought. *Now he thinks you're insane.*

I looked around and saw that the family was still gone, and Cora had gone, too. My head pounded. Something was wrong, terribly, terribly wrong. The orchestra was playing a lively tune, trying to keep the dancers going, but people were beginning to notice. This was not how the party was supposed to go. I was getting curious looks, as I was the only family member—such as I was—left. I shrank back into the corner, hoping no one would approach me and ask. *I don't know; I'm not really family.* Perhaps the champagne had run out, or there had been an emergency in the kitchen.

I turned and saw Frances Forsyth's face, beneath an arch of flowers across the room. She was wearing her gray dress and her pearls, and for a second she watched me before someone passed in front of her and she disappeared. Had I imagined her? I didn't know. I moved across the room toward the empty space where I'd seen her.

I narrowly avoided colliding with a dancing couple—the woman had her head angled back, her neck showing, as she laughed at something her partner said—and wobbled in as straight a line as I could muster. My heart pounded. I stood in the spot where I'd seen Frances, but she was not there. There was not even a breath of cold where she'd been.

There was no emergency in the kitchen, no minor incident that would take the family out of the room for this long. Something was happening. The idea that someone had died lodged in my mind, and I could not get rid of it. Someone was dead—someone must be dead. Had Martin collapsed?

I had another glass of champagne in my hand—I had no idea where it had come from. If Martin were dead, it would all be over. It would ruin Dottie, break her. She'd leave this house and never come back, and so would Robert. But Martin was still fighting, I told myself. He hadn't given in. He had a doctor, and he was trying so hard . . .

I edged around the room and slid out the door. I had to face it. If Martin were dead, if the family was finished and my future erased, I had to know. I had faced worse. I felt panicked and curiously detached, as I had that day in the train station when Alex left, though I was not ill. I walked down the dim corridor in my peacock dress, the empty glass of champagne dangling from my fingers, my heels clicking softly on the floor.

A waiter—one of the staff Dottie had hired for the evening—passed me and gave me a curious look, but did not stop. I reached the staircase and started to descend, my hand gripping the banister. The terrible thing would be happening downstairs, away from the party and the guests. It would be sealed in one of the private rooms, the way terrible things always were.

A maid appeared at the bottom of the stairs. I recognized her—Tildy, her name was, one of Mrs. Bennett's staff. She looked up at me, and the expression on her blanched face was one of such sheer terror I almost stopped in surprise.

"Don't tell me," I said. "Don't." Whatever it was, I didn't want to hear it from the maid.

"Mrs. Manders—"

"Please don't," I said. "You won't get in trouble. We never saw each other." I reached the bottom of the stairs and got my footing. My legs felt too long, too unbalanced. My dress was too short. My heart was beating so hard my breath came shallow. I just wanted it to be over.

Tildy bolted past me and ran up the stairs. I continued down the corridor, which was dark and quiet. Not even the echo of the orchestra could be heard here.

Voices. Low, urgent, unhappy. Dottie's voice—rising, then coming back under control. Robert's voice, low and angry. Voices overlapping. I followed them, placing one foot after the other.

They were in the large parlor. The doors were open, and there was Dottie, standing in the middle of the room in her fancy beaded suit. She looked as distressed as I'd ever seen her. Robert stood several feet away, his hands in his pockets, his face pale and angry. Martin sat in a chair near his father's elbow, leaning heavily on one arm, his face slack and his eyes aglow with painful ecstasy. Cora stood behind him, biting the lipstick off her lips, her hands clenched together.

Martin was not dead. My mind fixed on that fact as my gaze fixed on him and I came toward the doorway. Then I realized what Martin was looking at with such an expression of complex wonderment in his eyes.

There was another figure in the room. A man sat in a chair with his back to me, his features in shadow. The family all stared at him, transfixed.

They did not hear the click of my heels on the floor until I was in the doorway. The air was so dense I could hardly breathe, but I put a hand on the doorframe and kept upright. "What is going on?" I said into the silence.

Dottie's look of horror mirrored the maid's. Her gaze caught mine, pierced it. Her narrow shoulders shook as she took a breath. "We were going to prepare you," she said.

In one motion, the man unwound from his chair and stood, turning to face me. I saw long legs, the familiar set of shoulders. The breath left me. I could not speak.

Alex came forward into the light. Just that small movement pierced me, stabbed me as if someone had thrust an elbow into my gut. His face came out of the shadows and I shattered.

"Jo," he said.

A low moan came out of me. I gripped the doorframe, my fingers numb. I felt my legs buckling, saw spots dance in front of my eyes. The room spun away. "No," I said, my voice hoarse to my own ears. I heard a *click* and saw the empty champagne glass land softly on the floor.

He took another step toward me.

I revulsed in horror, all of my brain and my body rebelling. I stumbled back, wobbling on my heels. "No," I said again. I backed out of the room and ran down the corridor, a sob in my throat. Voices sounded behind me.

I pulled open the door to the morning room and crossed to the glass terrace doors. There were footsteps behind me now—I knew that long, sure stride, had heard it in my feverish dreams. I kicked off my heels and ran out onto the terrace, my feet shocked against the cold tile.

He was coming after me. Alone. I hurried across the terrace and descended the steps to the garden. When my feet hit the earth, I began to run, ignoring the cold and the hard earth on my soles, ignoring the rustle of my dress and the chilled night air in my throat. I ran through the garden toward the shadows of the trees.

Alex's stride came behind me. "Jo," he said, his voice urgent but unhurried. He was catching up with me easily, and he wasn't even running. "Jo, look at me."

I sobbed. This was my dream, my nightmare. *Jo, look at me.* I knew what would happen next. He would say, *They were wrong; there was blood in the cockpit after all,* and I would turn, and I would see his face, his head—

"Jo, look at me!"

I ran faster, my feet numb on the path now, but I was no match for him. Just as in the dream, he came up behind me, closer and closer. I could only hope that I would wake in my lonely bedroom and—

His hand grabbed my arm. I jumped as if his touch burned me and tried to pull away, but he held me fast. He jerked me backward and turned me to face him.

"It isn't you," I said. "It can't be."

"For God's sake, Jo." He yanked me closer, his hand hard on my arm. He was wearing a wool coat, and the motion unbalanced me toward him, made me put my hands on the lapels. It was unfamiliar beneath my fingertips. I had never seen it before.

"Look at me," my husband said.

I raised my gaze. It was Alex—his high cheekbones, his mouth, his blue eyes. His dark blond hair, grown slightly long now and tousling in the cold breeze. He stared down into my face, his hand on my arm, his chest beneath my fingers, and finally I knew him. It was Alex.

He was alive.

I took a breath and regained my footing. He felt my body go still, and his grip relaxed on me, but still he looked at me, searching my expression. I took a small step back.

Three years. Alive for three years, and I hadn't known.

All of the family, sitting in the large parlor, circled around him. *We wanted to prepare you.*

Colonel Mabry, looking at me with concern in his eyes. *Things are about to become more difficult for you.*

As always, Alex read my expression, even in the dark, even after three years away. "I can explain," he said.

"You can't," I said to this stranger, and my voice was sad, almost a sigh. "You can't possibly explain."

He stepped forward and put his hands on my face. His touch was gentle, familiar. I was suddenly warm and suddenly sharply, painfully aware.

"Sweetheart," said Alex Manders. "Yes, I can. I promise. Come inside and I'll tell you everything."

CHAPTER TWENTY-SEVEN

It was him.

But it wasn't.

His face had changed—his features grown harder, perhaps. Yet it was Alex's unmistakable face, the face I had first seen looking down at me when I sat at my typewriter. It was his body, but the clothes were unfamiliar. His hair was longer. And the expression in his eyes when he looked at me—I could not read it. I could not read my husband's eyes.

He took me back to the house. I was dazed and cold, and he led me easily over the terrace. In the corridor, he stooped and picked up my high-heeled shoes, holding them out to me.

"Put these on," he said.

I took them. "I don't—"

"They're waiting for us in the parlor," Alex said. "We have to go. They have questions."

I slid the shoes on, blindly following orders. "What questions?" I asked. "Everyone knew but me."

Alex's blue eyes were bemused for a moment, and then they cleared. "I suppose we looked cozy when you walked in, didn't we? No one knew, Jo. I just arrived thirty minutes ago. We were debating how to bring you out of the party to tell you when you came through the door." He paused. "I didn't know about the party. It looks like I picked a terrible night to come home."

To come home. The words hit me again and left me speechless, and when Alex took my arm, I followed him unresisting. He still had his hand on me when we walked back into the parlor.

The tableau had changed. Cora was gone; Martin had pulled his chair closer to his parents, and the three of them were speaking in low tones. They went silent when they saw us.

"Alex," Dottie said.

Alex steered me to a sofa and lowered me to it, then sat next to me. And that was that; after three years of mourning him, I was sitting next to my husband. He was so close that our legs almost touched and the thick wool of his coat scratched my bare shoulder. Warmth radiated from his body, heat that I knew well. I wanted to shift away, but I was suddenly aware of everyone's attention on me—Dottie's keen gaze, Martin's amazed stare, Robert's hooded eyes. I stayed in place, feeling raw and exposed.

"So," Robert said. "A romantic reunion."

"I know I owe some explanations," Alex said.

"Where have you been?" Martin broke in. And then, as if he couldn't believe it, "Where have you *been*?"

"Where is Cora?" I asked.

There was a second of silence as everyone stared at me. "I sent her back to the party," Dottie said. "She's to tell the guests there was an emergency in the kitchen. Her parents will help her see everyone out. I think they'll be forgiving, since this is a family emergency."

Next to me, Alex shifted, and I clenched my knees together, dropping my gaze.

"It's all my fault," Alex said. "I'm sorry again." He took a breath. "Since the war I've been a prisoner of the Germans. They took me almost the minute I parachuted from my airplane."

"All this time?" Robert asked, his eyebrows rising. "You look well fed for a prisoner."

"Don't interrupt," Dottie snapped at him. "Alex is explaining."

Alex turned his gaze to his uncle. "It was rough at first," he said, "but I come from a good family, and I was valuable to them."

"It makes sense, Papa," Martin said. "Alex has German relatives, and he knows the language."

"Yes," Robert said, calculations moving swiftly behind his eyes. Despite how much he'd doubtless had to drink, he looked as sober right now as I felt. "I'm sure that was most useful."

"It was best to wait it out," Alex said. "There was no use trying to get home until after the war was over. There was a bureaucratic mix-up, and I wasn't on any of the lists." I felt him glance at me. He must know, then—he must know how I had begged the War Office and the Red Cross for any word. I sat numb, staring at my hands in my lap, unable to meet his eyes. Alex paused only briefly, and then continued. "After the Armistice, I got sick."

"What happened?" Dottie asked.

"Influenza," Alex replied. "I nearly died. They transported me to a hospital near the Polish border while I was feverish. En route, I was somehow stripped of my papers and my identity disks—I was unconscious at the time, and I have no idea what happened. But I woke up in a hospital east of Breslau, half delirious, with no identity. Eventually, as I slept, it was determined that I was a German, and they began the paperwork to keep me there."

Influenza. I remembered lying alone in our bed in the Chalcot Road flat, my throat scraped raw, my every nerve and muscle alive with pain.

"My God, Alex," Martin said softly. "What a mess. I'm amazed you lived through it."

"When I started to recover," Alex said, "I was told only that I was going to be sent home. It gave me great comfort for a while, until I realized I was to be kept in the wrong country. I had no papers, no proof of identity, and my German relatives fled the country at the beginning of the war. I had somehow been identified as a German airman who had gone missing three months before—they thought I had been taken captive by mistake. My RAF uniform was long gone by then, and I was in hospital clothes. I had to convince them that I wasn't who they thought I was."

"They didn't notice when you told them they were wrong?" Robert asked.

"Of course they noticed." If Alex was irked by Robert's skepticism, he showed no sign. "I told them I was English. But I was speaking to them in fluent German, so how could they know I was telling the truth? The paperwork they had said otherwise. I was far from the consulate, which was already overwhelmed, and I had no money. You have no idea of the chaos in that part of the Continent in the aftermath of war. I eventually spoke to the right people and convinced them, but it took time."

"Three years of time," Robert said.

"Papa," Martin chided.

"You're home now," Dottie said. "You're back with family, where you belong. That's what matters. I assume you were eventually taken up by the proper channels?"

"Yes," Alex said. "It was the War Office that finally got me home. I traveled to London, but found that Jo was gone from our flat with no forwarding address. So I found myself a motorcar and came straight here. I didn't wish to write first, or even to telephone. I thought you might know where Jo could be found, and I couldn't wait." He put a hand on mine, where it sat lifeless in my lap.

It was all I could do not to pull away. I made myself sit still, and if he noticed that my hand was cold beneath his warm one, he gave no sign. I stayed silent. In that moment, wild horses could not have dragged the first word from my lips.

It was lies. Alex's own words confirmed it. *The War Office sent me home.* I had seen the file only weeks ago; there was no mention of influenza or lost papers. That fact made every word that had just come from my husband's mouth untrue.

I risked a glance at Martin to see if he showed any sign that he knew. But Martin was sitting rapt, his elbows on his knees, watching Alex. Dottie had a gleam of admiration in her eye, and even Robert had subsided, propping an elbow on the back of Martin's chair and listening with a half smile on his lips.

My heart was pounding in my chest. Alex, the Alex I had known and loved, was lying—to his family, to me. That was terrifying enough. But what stole the breath from me was the fact that still *I did not know* where my husband had been for three years. What kind of secret would he bury so deeply he would lie to everyone he loved? Had he worked for the enemy? Had he found another woman? The thought made me sick.

Alex had secrets—years of them. What if somehow Frances had found out? If she had innocently learned something he needed buried, what would he do about it? Would he beg special permission to visit Wych Elm House in private, then push his cousin from the roof? How far, exactly, would he go?

The family was still speaking—Dottie was saying something about limiting gossip about Alex in the village—but suddenly I couldn't stand any more. I shook Alex's hand from mine and stood. "I'm very tired," I said. "I'm going to bed."

"Are you all right, Cousin Jo?" Martin asked. "You've had quite a shock."

My lips were numb and I could barely force myself to speak. "I'm tired," I said again. "Good night."

From his seat on the sofa, Alex took my hand where it dangled limply at my side and squeezed it as he looked up at me. "I'll be up in a moment," he said.

I had no time to see the reaction of the others as I pulled my hand from his and stumbled from the room.

In my bedroom, I pulled the pins from my hair. I took off my shoes again and tossed them next to the wardrobe. Then I stood in the middle of the room and wondered what to do.

I glanced at the bed. Part of me wanted to sleep, or at least make the pretense of it—to lie down and pretend that today, which seemed to have begun a year ago, when I got out of bed to take pictures, had never happened. But another part of me was more awake than it had been in years—perhaps ever. The fog I'd felt over my mind, over my existence, had broken up, been blown away by the reappearance of Alex Manders in my life.

I'll be up in a moment.

He would. My husband may be a different man from the one who left me in the train station in 1918, but I knew as certainly as I knew my own name that he would very shortly come upstairs to my bedroom. And he would know exactly which room it was.

I could lock the door. There was that. It would keep him out for tonight at least. But how long, exactly, did I think I could avoid him? Did I want to?

I walked to the basin, poured water into it from the pitcher, and washed my face, scrubbing vigorously. Alex was a liar, and perhaps even a murderer, but he was also the smartest man I knew. He wasn't just the man who had loved me and married me seven years ago. If he was my enemy now—and I had to admit that I had no idea exactly what he was—then I needed my wits about me. I needed a plan.

He didn't give me the option of locking the door. As I was drying my face, he knocked quietly. "Jo," he said.

I dropped the towel and opened the door, blocking his way. "I don't suppose there is any way I could make you leave me alone?"

Something flashed across his expression—hurt, I thought—but he covered it quickly. "That's a little harsh after three years," he said.

I stared at the column of his neck where it disappeared into his collar. I knew exactly how that warm patch of skin tasted. "I said I was tired."

"I can make a scene in the corridor if you like. There are guests in all the rooms, and I hear Miss Staffron lodges across the hall." He paused. "Jo, I have to talk to you."

I stepped back and he brushed past me, closing the door softly behind him. I was still wearing the peacock dress, and I felt the feathers waft against my legs. "Sit down," he said.

"You needn't explain," I said as I remained standing. "I heard all of it. Influenza, hospitals, missing papers. It was very heroic."

Alex sighed. "Goddamn you, Jo."

I made myself look up at his face, the face that still, after all this time, was the handsomest face in the world to me. The shadows of my bedroom made it look familiar and unfamiliar at the same time. I toyed with the idea that I was being hard on him—that I was wrong, and he'd been telling the truth—but then I remembered his file.

Things are about to become more difficult for you. Colonel Mabry had known.

"If I find a hospital east of Breslau," I said, "and I write them about you, what do you think I'll find?"

"You'll find a record that I was there, suffering from influenza, and that I was mistakenly identified as a German." The words were flat; he sounded tired. But when he stepped out of the shadows, I saw something almost sad in his eyes, something that changed and softened when he looked at me. "It was very carefully done," he said quietly.

I felt my shoulders sag at the admission. I blinked and put my hand to my mouth. "Oh, God."

"It's important," Alex said, "that they believe the story. I convinced them, though Robert still has a few doubts. But I can't convince you, can I? I think I knew that from the first. Now, sit down, dear wife, and I'll tell you what actually happened."

I backed away from him. Without thinking, I sat on the bed and scooted to the farthest corner, my stockinged feet on the coverlet, my knees pulled up. Then I realized what I had done.

"No," I said to him as he came toward me. "Oh, no. This is not a reunion. Don't even think it."

Alex went still for a moment, and then he pulled the room's wooden chair out into the middle of the floor, facing the bed, and sat on it. I heard the breath sigh out of him.

It was too dark, so I leaned over and switched on the bedside lamp. The light from beneath the china shade dimly illuminated his face. "Talk," I said.

"May I take off my jacket?"

"Yes," I said, leaning back and hugging my knees again.

He rose from the chair and shrugged the wool coat off; then he unknotted his tie. "Don't worry," he said, glancing at me. "I heard you. I'm just uncomfortable, that's all."

When he had finished—he wore a white shirt beneath the jacket, his movements as crisp and elegant as I remembered—he draped the jacket and tie over the back of his chair and sat again. He crossed one ankle over the other knee and regarded me, his hands folded neatly over his stomach. He looked tense and controlled, aware of his every movement. Deliberately, he went very still.

"You," he said slowly to me, "are more beautiful than ever. I have spent three years imagining you with your hair down."

Something twisted inside me, hard, but I mirrored him and kept still. I did not speak.

He looked at me for another long moment, simply looking, and then he spoke. "I'll start at the beginning," he said.

"Please do," I snapped, the tension getting to me.

He seemed to think it over, choosing his words. "I lived here for a time. You know that, right?" He saw my expression and nodded. "I know I never told you. My favorite hobby was to sit on a spot near the cliffs of the shoreline and watch the boats. The Ministry of Fisheries is just down the coast. Have you seen it?"

I nodded. He leaned back, and his gaze traveled up the wall, looking into the past as he continued to speak. "I suppose I dreamed of being a brave sea captain, as boys do. But I spent so much time in my observation spot that I began to notice something among the boats. A pattern. There were vessels coming and going regularly—simple boats manned by researchers, mapmakers, other civilians. And then one day a boat entered the harbor that had guns."

"Guns?"

Alex nodded. "This was 1907, remember. We were not at war. The Ministry of Fisheries isn't a Royal Navy installation. But gunboats began to enter the Ministry's harbor, stay a few days, and leave again. In a regular pattern." He thought back again, lost in memory. "I was fifteen and impetuous, and I thought gunboats were romantic. So one day I made the three-mile trek to the Ministry itself, intent on seeing one of them up close.

"The Ministry is gated and guarded. I walked right up the drive to the gate, but before I could say anything to the guard, a motorcar pulled up. I was dazzled, because a motorcar was a wonderful thing in those days. A man leaned out and asked me my business. I told him I wanted to know what the gunboats were for. He looked at me for a long moment, and then he told me to come with him. Then he told me his name."

My mind had already worked ahead. "Colonel Mabry," I said.

Alex paused, surprised. "You were always quick, Jo," he said. "Yes, that's who it was, though he wasn't a colonel then. I take it you've met him. He isn't supposed to be here, but I suppose he's decided to continue as the curse of my bloody life."

I blinked at the hostility in his voice. My own anger at Colonel Mabry paled next to that chilled fury.

"Mabry told me nothing, of course," Alex continued. "He didn't take me to see the boats, which disappointed me. Instead, he sat me down in an office and questioned me extensively. I told him everything I had seen, the patterns of the gunboats' movements, their shapes and sizes, the days and times I had seen them come and go. He asked if I had made notes of what I'd seen, which of course I hadn't. He questioned me about my family and my background. I was bursting with my own questions, but he was as forthcoming as a marble slab. He finally told me that I was an intelligent, observant boy, and that when I got older he'd likely have a job for me."

I blinked. "A job?" I said.

Alex nodded. "I didn't know what he meant at the time—it only became clear to me later. He meant a job in intelligence. Specifically, military intelligence."

"In 1907?" I asked, incredulous. "The war was seven years away."

"In certain circles of government, Jo, the war was a long time coming. For some of them, the question wasn't whether we'd have a war, but when. To this day, Mabry hasn't told me exactly what was going on at the Ministry during those months, but I now believe they were using the harbor as part of a program to test gunboats in the open sea. The Kaiser was already of interest to our government, you see, as was his armament campaign, but Germany was not yet a dangerous concern. Yet Mabry was filing me away for future use, which is what he does."

"You were fifteen."

"I was fifteen, of good family, fluent in German, painfully observant, and keen. Men like Mabry rise to be colonels by using whoever they find, however and whenever they can use them. All he did that day was tell me to write him if I wanted work when I finished my education, and he'd find me a position. Off I went, an orphan boy very proud of myself, thinking I'd assured my own future."

I dropped my arms from my knees and straightened my legs out on the bed, stretching them. "And had you?"

His eyes followed my legs, his gaze resting on them for a long

moment. I went still. The hem of my dress covered my knees, but still
he stared at my calves, my stockinged feet.

"Alex," I said.

He did not raise his gaze. "You are quite certain about your earlier
resolution?"

"Stop it," I said. "You haven't told me *anything.*"

Slowly, his eyes came up to mine. He hesitated for a long moment,
then said, "You're going to hate me."

I held his gaze. "Am I?"

He let out a slow breath. "I wrote Mabry during my last year at
Oxford. There were rumblings of war by then. He hadn't forgotten.
He said he had work for me."

Oxford—before I met him, then. "What work?"

"Germany was building warships, submarines. Tensions were rising. There was speculation in intelligence circles that a possible invasion was being planned."

"An invasion—Germany invading England?"

"Yes. It was believed that the Germans were investigating where an
invasion might land. North? South? What route would it take? We
suspected they had agents here, pretending to be tourists and business-
men, sending back maps and drawings. We needed to track them and
intercept their messages to get an accurate idea of the German network. My job was to locate German contacts in England and report on
them—names, addresses, occupations, descriptions. It all went into the
files. I collected information, and I passed it on. It paid very well."

"And these men you—reported on. Were they arrested?"

"Not at all. Most of them weren't agents, so the information gathered dust. A few of them, however, had agreed to send communications
back to Germany, in much the same way I had agreed to inform my
own government. Those fellows had their letters intercepted, and the
local police kept tabs on their movements. An active agent, you see, can
lead you to even more active agents, whereas an agent under arrest or

executed can lead you to no one. That is the game." Alex uncrossed his legs and leaned forward in his chair, resting his elbows on his knees. His hair gleamed in the lamplight. "As for me, when I had information I passed it to Colonel Mabry's London representative. A solicitor near Gray's Inn."

Ice shot up my spine. I sat straighter on the bed. "You can't mean it," I said. "Casparov?"

"He was acting as an intermediary, yes. He'd take my information and send it along the proper channels."

My mind spun. Proper channels. "Those letters we typed. All those letters—stacks of them."

"Some of them were legitimate," Alex said softly. "Casparov was actually practicing law. But others were most likely code."

I put a hand to my forehead. Helen and me, typing all those snow-drifts of shorthand. *Your business is the typing only, and the looking respectable.* Day after day in that tiny office. And Alex, walking in from the wet cold, and Casparov telling him, *My thanks.*

"Oh, God," I said. "That was why you were there. I typed all those letters with no clue they were code. I never had any idea, and I worked for him for months. You must have thought me so incredibly stupid."

"Stupid?" He sounded surprised and a little angry. "You're missing the point."

"The point?" I dropped my hand and looked at him. "The *point* is that you sat across from me at the dinner table that night and told me absolutely *nothing* about yourself."

"I told you everything that mattered," Alex shot back. "What I was doing didn't matter anymore, because I quit."

"You what?"

"I resigned when I met you," he said. "I did it the next morning, after we'd been together. You weren't stupid, for God's sake; you were *Jo.* I knew what I wanted from the first minute I saw you, and it wasn't ferreting out Mabry's useless Germans. It was you."

I took a breath, my cheeks flushing hot.

He continued, his voice gentling a little. "I knew before we'd finished our first glass of wine that night that I had to do it. I was forbidden to speak about what I was doing. If I kept it up, and kept it from you, you would figure it out eventually. You were too sharp. And once you knew I'd been hiding things from you, you'd walk away without a look back. Of that much, I was sure. So it was easy, really. I had no choice." His eyes watched me in the dim light. "Mabry argued with me, of course, but it was no use. By the time I met you coming out of Casparov's office the next day, it was over."

This was going to kill me. If he kept talking he was going to kill me, but still I spoke—still I pushed him on. "But it wasn't over. Was it?"

He didn't answer for a long moment. Around us, the house was still. For the first time I wondered how late it was, what had happened to the party, whether all of the guests had gone to bed. It all seemed so far away.

When Alex spoke, his voice was a rasp. "It was over for a time," he said. "And then the war came. And it wasn't over anymore."

The war. Me sitting on the bench in Victoria Station that last time, sick and feverish and desperate, his kiss on my lips. The pain had been so awful I had thought I would die.

I closed my eyes, which were burning and dry, and steeled myself. "Tell me," I said. "Tell me."

CHAPTER TWENTY-EIGHT

Alex uncrossed his legs and stood, restless. He paced across the room, his long legs taking it in three strides, and turned. "Mabry contacted me again when the war started," he said. "He had more work for me. I told him no. My reasons were the same as ever—I would not lie to my wife. I would fight for my country, but I would do it as everyone else did—as a soldier."

Bitterness rose in my throat. *I would not lie to my wife.* "Go on," I said.

"Mabry told me I was insane," Alex said. "The war was in its early days, but he already knew how it was. He told me I'd be bloody mulch in a Belgian battlefield in six weeks, when instead I could be doing actual good for my country. With my skills I could be ferreting out agents, decoding messages, even traveling Germany undercover and reporting. He said I had no right to commit suicide." Alex glanced at me. "But I was a foolish optimist, like everyone else in 1914. I didn't know any better. I chose the RAF, because it seemed more challenging and more glamorous than ground fighting. I wanted to do something hard." He shrugged, the gesture almost a flinch of pain. "I got my wish, in that at least."

"I suppose you gave in," I said, not wanting to hear him say any more, not wanting to hear another lie come from his lips. "Because you went to Reims, when you told me you trained at Reading. I read your file."

He stopped pacing. He had turned away from the lamp, and I watched his shadow go still. "Mabry?" he asked, his voice strangled.

"He showed me the file," I said. "I know that you trained at Reims and that you came here to Wych Elm House on authorized travel without telling me. That you were here the day Frances died. That you went back to Reims when you left me at the train station in 1918." The words poured out of me, unstoppable. They did not feel good, only burned me and made me sicker. "I know, Alex."

"That's how you knew," he said softly. "That's why you didn't believe my story. You've seen the file. Mabry plays a dirty game."

"Martin saw the file, too." I tried to keep the bitterness from my voice. "He must know it's a lie, the same way I do."

But Alex shook his head. "Martin will believe me. He was over there. He knows that what makes it into the War Office file usually has nothing to do with the truth."

"Are you certain of that?"

"He'll believe me," Alex said again.

I wanted to argue, but I couldn't. I thought of the rapt expression on Martin's face, the way his gaze had fixed worshipfully on Alex, and I knew that Alex could make Martin believe anything. The thought only made me angrier.

"Are you going to tell me what Reims was about?" I asked. "Or am I not allowed to know?"

Alex rasped a hand slowly over his face. "Reims was training," he said. "In all my self-important posturing, I'd forgotten one pertinent fact: A man in the army is no longer his own master. I went to Reims because I was sent there, and I didn't tell you because I was instructed not to in case my letters were intercepted. I was furious at first, but once I got there it seemed like a small thing, an overreaction on the part of the army. It *was* RAF training. It was just advanced. We were given access to the newer airplane models, sent to learn and test-fly them. We were given instruction in additional skills, like hand-to-hand combat and laying telegraph wires. We were given maps that some of the other pilots weren't allowed to see. We were going to do advanced reconnaissance." He shook his head. "I knew you'd hate me, damn it. I knew it. This is what I was trying to bloody avoid."

"Fine," I said. I wanted to get off the bed and stand, but the room was too small and I'd be too close to him. "You trained, and then you fought. Continue."

"Mabry kept coming to me," Alex ground out, "offering me assignments. He promised to take me out of active combat and give me other things to do, feeding British intelligence. I kept saying no. I had dug in, and I wouldn't change my mind, even when he contacted me while I was home on leave. With you."

The memory clicked into place. Alex, home on leave. A package arriving at our door. "The camera," I said.

"Yes, my perceptive wife. The camera."

I sat up straighter. "Who is Hans Faber?"

His voice was bitter now. "You've figured it out this far, Jo. Puzzle it out a little further." He turned to look at me, his face still shrouded in shadow. "Hans Faber is me. He was to be my German identity when I was sent there by my own government as a spy." He came forward and sank into his chair again. "Hans Faber has been me for three years."

The room was silent. I ached everywhere, my legs and my back and behind my eyes. My head throbbed. Three years. I'd thought him dead for three years, had nearly been driven mad by it, and he'd been living as Hans Faber, a letter or a telegram away.

"Jo," he said.

"I think you should leave now." My eyes burned with unshed tears.

"Jo."

"I'd like you to leave."

He reached out and put a hand lightly on my foot, running his thumb along the bottom of the arch, looking inexpressibly sad. I felt his touch like a bolt of lightning. "Your stockings are torn," he said.

I jerked my foot away. "Alex."

"I don't want to talk about myself anymore," he said. "I'm sick of myself."

I swallowed. "And they're finished with you now? After all this time? That's why you're here?"

"Not quite." His hand reached across the bed again, almost as if he couldn't stop it, and touched my foot. This time I did not pull away. "I'm here because I quit again. At first they wouldn't let me go, but I persisted and they finally gave in." His thumb traced the arch of my foot again. "Mabry is angry over it. He doesn't like to lose."

"He came here pretending to be interested in buying art from Dottie."

"That doesn't surprise me." His gaze was fixed on my foot, and his hand slid up my ankle. "He knew I'd come to you as soon as I was able."

"Alex," I said.

"Hush," he replied. "I heard you. I just want to take your stockings off."

I squirmed. "You agreed."

"Nothing will happen," he said, and I went still, believing him. Always, always, my body believed him, even after three years of devastation and lies. My body quieted as he pulled closer to the edge of the bed and his hands moved up my leg, beneath the hem of my peacock skirt.

Heat roared through me in a terrifying wave. "You shouldn't have told me any of this," I said, trying desperately to hold on to logic. "If it's all so secret, you shouldn't have told me."

"I don't want to talk about it." His voice was a soft, bitter rasp, a tone I didn't recognize. His hands reached halfway up my thigh, his clever fingers finding the top of my stocking and unclasping it from my garter. "I'm sick to death of all of it. I want to talk about you. Tell me, Jo. Tell me everything."

"There's nothing to say," I said helplessly as he undid the second clasp on my garter. "I floated for a while, and then I ran out of money. Dottie offered me a job as her companion, and I took it."

His hands had begun to roll my stocking down my leg, but they stopped, his fingers cradling the back of my thigh. "You ran out of money?" he asked, his voice sharpening.

I felt my own anger answering, taking it as an accusation. "What did you expect?" I shot at him, looking into his blue eyes. "There wasn't much there in the first place, and there was no pension because, according to the War Office, I wasn't a widow."

He was still for a long moment as heat pounded through me from the back of my thigh. When he spoke, his voice was low and dangerous. "They told me you would be taken care of," he said with icy anger I had never heard from him before. "Someone is going to pay very, very dearly for that."

His darkness was frightening me, so I plunged onward. "Yes, well. Dottie has actually been rather nice to me, in her queer way. She pays me—sporadically, I admit—and I have room and board. Though I shouldn't have bought this dress." I looked down at the peacock feathers, which now seemed purchased by some other long-ago woman. "I'll be working for her until I'm sixty to pay it off."

Slowly, his hands began unrolling the stocking again. "I'm going to make things right, Jo," he said.

I nearly laughed as I shook my head. "You can't. Dottie and Robert hate each other. Martin is sick. He's marrying a girl he hardly knows because Dottie wants an heir and he thinks he won't live long. I don't think he'll even make it to the wedding."

"The girl in the parlor?" Alex asked. The torn stocking was rolled down to my ankle now, and he pulled it off my foot. "She seemed polite enough, if not very bright. I think I scared her."

"She was a better choice than I would have been, for certain."

"You?"

"Dottie wasn't about to let me go to waste. She had the idea to marry me to Martin, but we didn't want to do it. Besides, there was a mix-up somewhere in the War Office, and I had no widow's papers. I wasn't free."

Alex started on my other leg. He slid his hands beneath my skirt in one motion, to the top of my stocking, and unsnapped a garter, his features hard. "Dottie shouldn't have meddled. You were most certainly not free."

I stared at him. "You knew," I said softly, watching his face. "You knew about my papers. There was no mix-up at all, was there? You *knew*."

"Jo, be logical," he said. "What were they to do, let you be free to marry? Then you'd be legally married to two different men."

I gripped his hand through my skirt and stilled it. "This isn't about that at all," I said. "It has nothing to do with legalities. It's about the fact that even though I believed you dead, you wouldn't let me go."

"Are you mad?" Alex's voice rose as his gaze pierced me. "I married you. I would rather die than let you go."

"And what about me?" I cried. "It's all very well for you. Without a husband or a widowhood, I'm nothing. I've been invisible for three years. I'm not even a proper figure of pity. I'm just a woman a man might consider a few tosses with, that's all." *You could do better, even as a mistress,* Robert Forsyth had said.

Alex's hand flinched hard on my leg. His face blanched as the words hit him. Then he fought for control, and his eyes searched mine. As always, he saw everything inside me. His hand softened against my skin. "They were supposed to come up with something," he said. "Make

up an interim payment of some kind that you were entitled to. Whatever it was, if it came directly from the War Office, you wouldn't question it. That way you wouldn't have to struggle until I was free to come
home. They promised me, and they lied." His voice cracked just a
little—I had never known Alex's voice to crack. "I am asking you, Jo, to
consider what my options were. If I contacted you, I'd blow the entire
operation, as well as getting myself executed for treason. Or I could go
back to the Front and be killed. I did the only thing I could think of—
paid the only price I could—so that I had a chance of coming home."

A chance of coming home. And there it was again, after three years.
I wanted him—so badly it was an ache pressing through every part of
me. I wanted my husband, his body that I knew almost as well as my
own. I had dulled and suppressed it in my grief, but I had *missed* him.
Yet at the same time I wondered whether Frances had known he was a
spy, whether Alex had had to silence her. Whether there had been
other women in those years, women he had kissed and put his hands
on and taken to bed. I flinched beneath him again.

His gaze shuttered. He pressed my leg casually still and began to
unroll my stocking again. I couldn't breathe. *I could kick him from this
position,* I thought wildly. *I could kick him hard in the chest.* I nearly
did it. "Alex," I said.

"What is it?"

"You need to leave."

He pulled the stocking from my foot. We were silent for a long
moment. I could hear the soft sound of his breathing.

"You mean it, don't you?" he said in a whisper.

"I'm sorry," I said, trying not to notice that my hands were cold
with fear. "I'm exhausted. I can't even think straight."

Still he sat looking at me, his fingers curled around the back of my
bare ankle. He did not take his eyes from my face. He had such a gift
for stillness, my husband did, such utter control of every nerve and
muscle. He watched me for a long moment, his expression impossible

to read. It was this stillness, I saw now, this ability to be silent and the endless patience to wait, that had made him such a good spy.

Without a word, he set my foot down on the coverlet and rose from his chair.

"Get some sleep," he said. A moment later, the door clicked softly shut behind him.

I was trembling. The skin of my legs still burned where he'd touched me. I reached out and switched off the lamp, then lay on top of the coverlet, still in my dress. I wondered briefly if the maids had made up another room for him. If they'd talk of us the way they talked of Dottie and Robert belowstairs. *They sleep separate.*

But he had only told me to get some sleep. He had not said *good night*. And Alex never said anything without meaning.

I curled into a ball and closed my eyes.

CHAPTER TWENTY-NINE

It was dark when I awoke, and I was in bed with Alex, and I had been dreaming.

I blinked against the blackness, and at first, as the dream vanished from my memory like cobwebs, I did not fully grasp that Alex was against my back, his arm slung around my waist. I jerked and rolled over in surprise.

I was still wearing the silk peacock dress, still lying on top of the coverlet. Alex, too, was lying on the coverlet, fully dressed in his white shirt and trousers; he must have been sleeping, though now he was awake, his head lifted from the pillow, his body tense. His hand squeezed my hip, and I realized he'd awoken me. He whispered my name.

"What is it?" I whispered back.

"I heard something," he said. "I thought—there it is again."

From the woods outside, far off in the trees, came the lonely sound of a howl. It rose, echoing, spiraling upward, and then it subsided again. The tone was so eerie, so despairing, it could have come from a human throat.

"What the devil," Alex hissed as it growled into silence.

I was afraid—there was no way not to be when that howl pierced the air—but exhilaration pulsed through me at the same time. "It's Princer," I said. "You can hear him?"

Alex looked down at me. "What did you just say?"

"She calls him," I said. "She whistles when she wants him to come. But I thought I was the only one. You mean you actually heard it?"

He frowned at me, but all I could feel was a wild whoop of triumph. Perhaps I wasn't the only one who could hear these things, see them. If I could show him the leaves—if he could see—

"Jo," Alex said softly, "what are you talking about? Who calls him?"

"Frances," I replied. "She doesn't do it often—I've only seen it the once. The other times, it's just Frances, watching me."

The mention of Frances's name seemed to shock him, and I watched his expression flicker as he got it under control. *Perhaps,* I thought, *he can hear Princer because he killed Princer's mistress.* But that didn't explain why I could hear him, too.

"You're saying that Frances is—" Alex's tone turned from shocked to incredulous. "You're saying she *haunts* this place?"

"She's lonely," I said. I had to make him understand. "She wants to communicate. I thought it was just me—it's only me who has seen her. But you just heard her dog."

Alex frowned and focused on the window again. I watched him closely in the moonlight, his flawless profile, the perfect fearlessness of his posture. I studied him for signs of guilt, but I realized I didn't know what guilt looked like on Alex, not anymore.

"It seems to have stopped," he said after a moment. He turned, the moonlight no longer tracing his profile. Then he blinked, and seemed to see me, my shoulders bare, my hair lying across the pillow. "Come closer," he said. "It's cold."

I felt myself go stiff as the triumph left me and I remembered where I was. "What are you doing?" I asked him.

"What do you mean?"

"I didn't invite you into bed with me. In fact, I asked you to leave. There are plenty of bedrooms in this house, you know. A dozen of them."

"They're all full because of the party."

"Then you should be sleeping on a sofa."

His gaze narrowed on me. "I'll abide by your rule," he said, "but if you think I'm sleeping anywhere else, think again."

"And that's it?" I asked, exasperated. "You're just going to sleep in your clothes every night for the rest of your life?"

He raised an eyebrow, and in the dark I felt my cheeks flush hot. "And if I find myself another bed?" I asked.

"Then I'll follow you to it. I know every room in this house, Jo."

"You agreed to leave."

"I didn't," he pointed out, as I knew he would. "I told you to get some sleep."

I sighed and rolled over again, my dress rustling. Behind me, he put his head to the pillow. We had lain like this for many a night during our marriage, and our bodies fit together; Alex was adept at taking up little space with his long, lean body and leaving me most of the bed.

"Where did you go, then?" I asked. "When you left earlier?"

"Martin was still up," he replied. "I talked to him for a while."

"Getting your story just right," I said.

"I told you, it's important."

Such an accomplished liar he'd become. "You can't sleep here every night."

"Yes, I can. You've been free of my attentions for three years," he said in a light murmur that held a shiver of deadly seriousness. "You may have enjoyed your little vacation, but it's at an end."

"You didn't come back here for me," I said.

"Yes, I did."

"Are you denying that you had other reasons as well?"

He was silent. I was right. I had picked it up without thinking, in watching and listening to him, hidden in the silent code of communication between man and wife. It told me he was thinking of something besides me, that there was something else going on. He had telegraphed it to me unawares. It didn't even hurt—it was sort of a relief, in a way, an easy exit from my painful confusion and back into numbness. I closed my eyes.

"I have my reasons," Alex said, "for not telling you my reasons."

"Then I suppose we're at a standstill," I replied. "Go to sleep."

I did not sleep for a long time, and I didn't think he did, either. My head throbbed. My eyes ached. And still I lay in the silence, feeling his chest against my back and listening to him breathe.

CHAPTER THIRTY

He was gone when I awoke the next morning. The bedroom was deserted, as were the bathroom and the corridor. It was mid-morning, and most of last night's guests had left as I was still in bed, sleeping. The Staffrons were gone as well, their bedrooms empty.

I took my time washing, running hot water from Dottie's expensive modern taps, the peacock dress hanging over the rail above me, the steam making headway on the wrinkles in the silk. I sponged myself thoroughly, then returned to the bedroom and dressed in one of my new dresses, a pair of my new stockings, and my new shoes. I wound my hair neatly and tied it into a chignon, fixing it with pins. Something about the slow routine felt strengthening. I wanted to be ready to go downstairs and see what awaited me.

Breakfast had finished—I was quite late—and the dishes were already cleared from the morning room. The only person there was Dottie, standing at the French doors and looking over the terrace. She turned to me.

"It's about time, Manders," she said. "There's no time for breakfast;

you'll have to eat later. Take a cup of tea with you to the library. We're having a family meeting."

The very normalcy of her rudeness soothed me. I took a cup of tea and followed her narrow wool-clad back down the corridor to the library.

The family was already in the library. Robert lounged against a bookshelf; Martin sat alone on a sofa, looking pale. Alex sat in the chair opposite Dottie's desk, as if he were a visitor, wearing a tweed jacket, caramel trousers, and expensive leather oxfords, one long leg crossed over the other and one elbow flung behind him over the back of his chair. He watched me as I came through the door.

Other than Dottie's, there were no chairs left except the one behind my little typewriter, which had been pulled up next to Alex. I sat in it, my hands in my lap, and waited.

"Well," Dottie said to the room. She walked briskly to her desk and stood behind it. "Now that the guests are gone, we can have a discussion. Last night was unexpected, but I believe the scandal has temporarily been contained."

"We're glad to have you back, old chap," Robert said.

"Thank you, Uncle," Alex replied.

"My concern now is the family's privacy," Dottie said. "We kept the news from the party guests, but the servants have undoubtedly already begun talking. Stories will spread, and as stories spread they become wilder and more untrue."

There was no argument from anyone in the room. I thought of Frances, the tales that she had been kept in chains. I wondered if Mrs. Baines, the village postmistress, had heard about Alex already.

"I think gossip is the least of my worries, Aunt Dottie," Alex said. "I intend to ignore it."

"That would be foolish of you," Dottie said. "It's best if you keep away from the village, at least for now. I don't want any talk to harm Martin's engagement."

"Oh, please, Mother," Martin protested tiredly. "What does it matter? Alex is alive, and he's home. What does it matter what anyone thinks?"

"It matters," Dottie replied. "It always matters what people think."

"I'll make the rounds of the neighbors," Robert said. "Tell them the story. That way we'll have the truth circulating among the better class of people in these parts, at least. I'll start this afternoon."

Dottie looked like she'd swallowed a lemon. She hated Robert's social activities and refused to participate in them, but even she could see that in this instance they'd be useful. "I suppose," she managed ungraciously.

"Besides," Robert said, "I'll get good mileage out of it. My nephew coming home a hero, just now, after all this time." His smile, aimed at Alex, was almost wolfish. "If that isn't worth a few drinks, I don't know what is."

"Very well," Dottie said with sour finality. "But it does leave the question of Manders."

"Yes." Alex's voice was distinctly cool. "It leaves the question of my wife."

Everyone looked at me. My cheeks heated. Robert looked from me to Alex, a knowing smirk on his face. I felt as transparent as glass, as if everything that had happened—and hadn't happened—last night was obvious. "The work Dottie needs done doesn't stop just because Alex has come home," I said.

Next to me, I caught the subtle vibration of Alex's shock. He hadn't thought I'd want to stay on as Dottie's companion. Well, he wasn't the only one with surprises. Besides, at the moment Dottie was more familiar to me than he was.

Dottie didn't even blink. "I have a full schedule," she agreed. "However, Manders, I do not expect you to be productive today, so I am granting you the day off. You may do as you wish and report to me tomorrow."

"Thank you," I said.

"You can hardly think to keep my wife in your employ, Aunt," Alex said, his tone dipping dangerously low.

"She can if I wish it," I returned.

Robert's smirk widened. I stayed anchored to my seat, holding his gaze. *I have reasons for not telling you my reasons.* Alex had his own purpose here—let him follow it, then, and I'd follow mine.

Frances and her murderer were my purpose. I would find out what had happened, husband or no husband. Staying on as Dottie's companion was the best way.

Dottie adjourned the meeting. I needed escape; the air of Wych Elm House was too close, the corridors too dark and musty. Though it was raining, I found the driver and asked him to bring around the car. I walked to the kitchen vestibule and took the black mackintosh from its hook. There was mud on the back from when I'd lain in the ditch, looking up at Princer. I found a brush and quickly got rid of the dried dirt. Then I found my hat and my gloves.

When I returned to the hall, just as the motorcar was brought around, I found Alex standing by the front door in hat and coat, an umbrella tucked under his arm.

"Where are we going?" he asked me.

I stopped. I wanted to escape, but I'd also planned to try to question David Wilde in town. "Shopping," I said.

"I see." His gaze was steady on me from beneath the brim of his hat. Behind him, the rain splashed against the thick panes of decorative glass in the door.

"Alex," I said, "you just promised Dottie you'd stay in the house."

"No, I didn't," he said with unassailable logic, "though that was a good try. In fact, I object to letting you leave unaccompanied."

"We just talked about this," I protested. I took a step toward him, thinking to brush past him, but he would not let me by. "You'll stir gossip if you go to the village."

"And I've already said I don't give a damn," Alex said. He bent down to me, the shadows in the dim hall inky black beneath the brim of his hat. He put two fingers beneath my chin and lifted it. "You are stuck with me, Jo," he said. "For better or for worse. We are married. You are stuck with me forever."

I swallowed. I could feel my pulse in my throat. "Then I'll stay home," I rasped.

"If you prefer," Alex said. "It's a rainy day, and we have nothing to do. We can certainly spend the day in bed."

I tore myself from his grip and wrenched the front door open, striding out into the rain. He followed me easily, taking my arm as I stepped into the motorcar. For a long moment, as the driver started the car and we began to move down the drive, I could not look at him. My own husband. We had spent long, sensuous afternoons together once, listening to the rain against our bedroom window as we lay in bed. I forced myself to turn and look at him. "That was uncalled for," I said.

Alex sat back in the seat cushions, his umbrella between his well-formed knees. "What's uncalled for," he complained mildly, "is that my wife won't spend the afternoon in bed with me after three years away."

I gaped at him. "Can you blame me?"

"Certain parts of me blame you a great deal, yes."

"Then those parts should have come home sooner," I snapped.

"Believe me," he replied with sincerity in his voice, "they tried."

I pressed my fingertips to my temples and shut my eyes. I was going to go mad.

"Where are we going?" Alex asked me after a moment, as the rain beat a tattoo on the roof of the motorcar.

"Shopping. I told you."

He seemed to think this over. "No," he said. "I don't think we are. It's raining, and you've always hated shopping. There's something else going on. What exactly are you doing, Jo? What has you hurrying out of Wych Elm House so quickly, besides my presence?"

I couldn't do it. I wasn't built for subterfuge, not like he was. I checked that the pane of glass between us and the driver was up, and then I blurted, "Did you kill your cousin?"

That quieted him. There was no sound but the hum of the motor.

"There's nothing I can do if you did," I continued. "It was years ago, and no one would believe me. *I* wouldn't believe me. The inquest is long over, and it would be your word against mine."

When Alex spoke, his voice was soft, with a chill in it like a descending fog. "How very extraordinary."

"It isn't," I protested. "It isn't extraordinary that I would at least wonder. You were here in the house that day. You specifically requested leave. You were seen talking to her the day before she died. There's so much you haven't explained to me. And don't tell me it wasn't murder, because it was."

"No," Alex said. "It isn't extraordinary that you would wonder, though I don't deny it stings. What's extraordinary is that you and I seem to be on the same mission after all this time."

I stared at him. "What do you mean?"

"You asked me," Alex said slowly, "last night what other reason I had to come to Wych Elm House. Well, now you've found it. I've come here, Jo, because I want to find my cousin's murderer. Just like you do."

CHAPTER THIRTY-ONE

The rain was coming down in cold spatters, blown by gusts of wind. I held the brim of my hat as Alex helped me from the car, and I waited as he unfurled his umbrella and held it over our heads. We were at the end of Anningley's High Street, facing downhill toward the church, but Alex touched my arm and steered me down a side lane. "Let's walk a while," he said.

I followed, my handbag under my arm. Though it was dark and chill, I was still glad to be out of the close confines of the motorcar, and the fresh air on my cheeks was welcome. "I don't suppose you could possibly explain," I said to my husband.

"It's a very long story."

I sighed. "You seem to be full of long stories. Please tell me this one as well."

Alex walked quietly beside me for a moment. We were strolling down a lane lined with small cottages, their front yards thick with hedges and browning rosebushes, the dead heads of rhododendrons bowing over the fences. The ground was wet and dotted with puddles, and but for a single farmer's cart on the road in the distance, no one was about. I leaned in close to him, taking up as much space under the umbrella as I could. He was lost in thought and did not seem to notice.

"I told you," he said finally, "that I turned down Colonel Mabry's offers for most of the war. But in 1917, while I was at the Front, he contacted me about something he said affected me very closely. Something he thought I'd want to know."

"What was it?" I asked.

"Military Intelligence had intercepted a set of plans that were on their way to the enemy. Specifically, it was a map of the Sussex coast near Wych Elm House, along with a detailed drawing of the base there. The Ministry of Fisheries installation had been repurposed for military use in 1915, for the repair and supplying of warships." He glanced at me. "The drawings were skillfully rendered, I can say with authority, since I saw them myself."

"So the gunboats weren't there by accident all those years ago," I said.

"As I said, I'm not told much. The place was taken up for the war effort, since it's in a useful spot on our shipping routes. When Mabry intercepted the drawings on their way to the Germans, of course he knew what it was. The obvious conclusion was that someone either in or around Wych Elm House made the drawings for the enemy."

I was getting wet on one shoulder, so I looped my arm through his and leaned closer to him under the umbrella, frowning. "Why would the Germans want these drawings?"

"To plan an attack on our ships. The inlet is perfectly wide and deep enough for U-boats to get in, if the Germans knew where to send them. The drawings were made from the vantage point I'd used as a boy."

I paused, digesting this in shock. "They were made on Forsyth property? You're saying that the Germans could have used the drawings to attack the base? And someone from Wych Elm House supplied them?"

"It certainly looked that way," Alex replied. His hat was pulled down on his forehead, and he was staring ahead at the road, his long stride adjusted to my shorter one. The wool of his sleeve was warm through my glove. "It's also possible the drawings were made by a visitor to the house, or someone passing through the area."

"The man in the woods," I said immediately. "The stranger who died. You're saying he was a—a spy?" Even as the word came out of my mouth, I could not believe I was walking in the calm, damp, peaceful English countryside, talking about spies.

"I don't know who that man was," Alex admitted. "To this day, I have no idea. The drawings were intercepted long before that day. Intelligence had to send someone, and Colonel Mabry told me that if I did not go to Wych Elm House to investigate, he'd send another agent. I didn't like the idea of some stranger bumbling through my family. So I accepted the assignment and came to my aunt's house in Sussex for a visit."

I was quiet for a moment. "And because it was a secret assignment, you couldn't tell me," I said.

"No," Alex said softly. "I couldn't."

I found myself blinking away tears. He seemed not to notice, but continued to speak. "Aunt Dottie was agreeable to a visit. I was here for a week. I walked the woods and confirmed the vantage point of the drawings. Martin was in France, but I made conversation with Aunt Dottie and Uncle Robert, getting an idea of who had been in the area lately. I watched and I learned. I took a walk through the gardens with Frances and questioned her the best I could, but she was in one of her confused moods and couldn't help. On the second day, I came to the village and talked to some of the locals. When I came back to the house that afternoon, I found that Franny had killed herself, a stranger was dead in the woods, and everything was in chaos."

I bit my lip. If Alex had been in town when Franny died, it would be an easy story to verify. I couldn't see how he could get away with a lie.

"None of it made any sense," Alex continued. "If the man in the woods was the spy, why was he still in Sussex weeks after the drawings were sent? Why would Franny choose that day of all days to commit suicide? And what kind of animal lives in the Sussex woods that would tear a man apart in daylight? They were pieces of a puzzle, but they didn't seem like pieces of the *same* puzzle. And I didn't have much time to put them together before I had to go back to the Front."

"The police didn't pressure you to stay?"

"I was an enlisted man in the middle of war. I had my orders, Franny was a suicide, and I'd been in town, four miles from the woods when the man was killed. No, I was not pressured to stay. I tried to ask my own questions, but it was hopeless—all I got were wild rumors and sinister stories, tales of Dottie covering up Frances's crimes with the help of David Wilde." Bitterness crept into his voice. "I left no wiser than I was the day I came. Whoever had tried to send the sketches to the Germans was still free. I had failed my country."

"You did not fail your country," I said quietly. I realized something vital: Alex was good at everything because he was so very hard on himself. *Striving for the highest thing*, Martin had said of him, *making the rest of us run to keep up with him*. He had only shown me his carefree side. It had taken the war to make me see.

He continued talking. "After I'd left and thought it through, I began to see the sequence of things," he said. "Franny liked to sketch, you see, and it's possible she might have made sketches of the base and the coast. I'd thought of that already, before I arrived. So on that first evening I asked one of the servants whether Franny was still fond of sketching and what kinds of things she drew. And the next day, Frances was dead. It's a loose end that doesn't tie up. I couldn't tell Mabry about my suspicions—what was there to tell? That I thought a mad fifteen-year-old girl was somehow the traitor? Without evidence, I couldn't pursue it. I had to let it go, at least until I was free to take it up again."

We had reached the end of the lane now, and we turned, heading back to High Street. I leaned on Alex's arm, thinking, and said, "There is simply no way it was Frances who sent off the drawings, even if she was the one who drew them."

"No. But someone could have taken them from her sketchbook and sent them off."

I stopped on the street and looked at him, shocked. "Someone did."

"What do you mean?" Alex looked down at me. "Are you saying you found the sketchbook? I never found it—I ran out of time."

"I have it," I said. "Frances gave it to me."

Alex's tone carried a hint of warning. "Jo."

"She did," I persisted. I was starting to feel excited as the pieces came together. "I found it under the covers of my bed. I've been staring at it and staring at it. I thought she wanted to show it to me because of—because of the sketches that were inside. But that wasn't it at all. She wanted to show it to me because of the pages that had been *torn out*. That was what I was supposed to see."

"Jo, anyone could have put the book in your bed. A living human, I mean."

"I was sleeping in the bed at the time."

Alex's gaze darkened. "That's unsettling, and I don't much like the sound of it. But it still could have been a living person."

"Are you denying what you experienced last night?" I asked, stung that he still disbelieved me. "What you heard?"

"I don't quite know what I heard last night," he said, "and I'm not sure I have the courage to explore it."

He put his hand on my elbow, prompting me to walk again, but I stood still, which forced him to stay where he was, holding the umbrella over me. "Tell me one thing," I said.

He looked wary. "What is it?"

"The fact that you failed to find the sketch artist," I said. "That you felt you failed your country. That's why you gave in to Colonel Mabry's idea that you become a spy—why you became Hans Faber. Isn't it?"

The look he gave me, pained with deep exhaustion, was all the answer I needed.

"Come," he said, and touched my arm again. This time I let him lead me as we approached High Street.

The rain had thinned, but still it came down in cold drops that dripped from the trees and pelted the umbrella. There were a few people about in Anningley, and Alex made a stir—shopkeepers idling on their front steps nodded to him, women doing their shopping craned their necks, curtains in upper windows twitched. Alex ignored all of it. Instead, he leaned close so no one could hear him and spoke to me.

"I told you Mabry plays a dirty game," he said. "I couldn't fight anymore, anyway—I'd pressed my luck as a pilot for too long. I applied to be sent back to England as an instructor, since the RAF was short on men who had lived long enough to gain the experience to teach. I was perfectly qualified to do it, but my request was stonewalled. I didn't have to spend much time wondering why."

I closed my eyes briefly. Alex could have come home, could have instructed other pilots from the safety of England? "Go on," I managed.

"It was a death march," Alex said softly as the rain pattered the umbrella. "Most pilots lived for two months—I had managed to live for two *years*. I could come home in a box and leave you a widow, or I could become Hans Faber. Those were my choices."

"So you agreed."

"In the original plan," Alex said, "Hans Faber was to be a well-to-do traveling businessman with a heart condition that kept him from fighting. He would travel the country, ostensibly in the business of supplying cameras and film to the German army for use in reconnaissance and surveillance. He would carry a full set of identity papers, an authentic set of documentation for his heart condition, and a camera kit that was his sales sample. A German citizen, going about his business while quietly taking photographs for England."

"The camera," I said, "and its expensive case."

"Yes. But by the time I agreed to the assignment, things were more difficult inside Germany, and the plan had to change. You were right, Jo. When I left you that last time, I went to Reims again, for more advanced training in undercover work. They gave me Hans Faber's papers, though this time I didn't have the heart condition. I went back into Germany in 1918 as an enlisted man."

I felt like every set of eyes in Anningley was watching us, starting with the people we passed. I began to wonder how many of them could hear us. We were passing the lending library, and I pulled his arm. "Inside," I said. "Let's go."

There was no one else here but the librarian at her desk. Alex folded the umbrella closed. "At least it's out of the rain," he whispered. "Do you actually want a book?"

"This way," I said, whispering myself. I led him to the back, to my favorite set of shelves—containing mostly lowbrow novels and melodramas—and pretended to browse.

"Do you read these?" Alex asked curiously, looking over my shoulder.

"None of your business," I replied. "Keep talking."

He glanced at the librarian, who was napping soundly in her chair, and continued, pretending to look at books over my shoulder. "When we finally did the operation," he said, "it went off without a hitch. I flew over enemy lines and parachuted from the plane with my papers and my German uniform in my pack. As the plane crashed, I landed and quickly changed sides. I walked out of the woods as Faber and hailed the first man I saw in flawless German, telling him I'd seen a plane go down while on the way to join my regiment. No one questioned me for a second."

I shuddered. "Alex, that was bloody dangerous," I said. "You could have been killed."

He was silent for a moment, behind my shoulder, and then he placed a fingertip behind my ear, drawing it along the edge of my hairline. "I've made you use terrible language," he said.

Flustered, I grabbed a book called *Molly of the Plains* from the shelf. It seemed to be about a young girl kidnapped by Indians. "Hans Faber wasn't in a real regiment," I said. "How did you do it?"

"There is chaos on the ground in war," Alex said in my ear. "There are giant masses of men being moved this way and that. My cover was as a messenger, so I was always on the move. I pretended I always had to be on my way to one place or another, urgently. With enough plausible details, I made it work. And when I had the chance, I radioed information back to England about who was moving where, using which supply lines and which routes."

I couldn't imagine it, living like that from day to day. "Was it better than being in the RAF?" I asked. "Or worse?"

He was quiet so long that I didn't think he'd answer. Then he said, "It was both better and worse, I suppose. Worse, because I had to keep the story straight and sleep rough most of the time—I barely slept for months. Because I knew you were home thinking I was missing in action. Better, because instead of being blown into bloody pieces, I had a shadow of a chance to come home."

I bowed my head and stared blindly at the book in my hands. "It worked too well, didn't it?" I said. "That's why you didn't come home."

Ever so gently, he put his palm on the back of my neck, touching my hair almost with reverence. "Yes," he admitted. "After the war, they wouldn't let me go. Hans Faber became a traveling businessman again. He traveled Germany, Austria, Serbia, Belgium. They needed information to pass to the diplomats at the Treaty of Versailles. They needed to know what was happening to the Kaiser in Berlin. They needed to know what was happening in Italy. They always needed something, one thing after another. It was important work, they said. Work that influenced the lives of thousands of people, instead of the life of one man who wanted to go home to his wife."

I could have kissed him then. I had done it a million times, as easily as breathing. I could have turned and pressed my lips to his, felt everything he was thinking, understood everything in his soul. Right there in the Anningley library, with the librarian asleep in her chair. But when I turned around and looked up at him, his expression was marked with pain.

"I thought it would be easier, coming back," he said. "But I can see now that I was naive. I have to find the traitor—I cannot stop until I find him. And I have to find Franny's killer."

Yes, of course. He hadn't come home for me, not completely. I folded my book under my arm and turned away.

CHAPTER THIRTY-TWO

We left the lending library and Alex unfolded the umbrella again. "I knew Franny all of her life," he said. "Aside from your mother, Jo, she was the most tormented person I've ever met. Her grasp on reality was tenuous, and she saw hallucinations. But there was a sort of vitality about her—it's hard to explain. She was very intelligent, very alive, and sometimes very determined. She was not suicidal."

"That's why you believe it was murder?" I asked.

"That, and the timing of it." He shook his head. "Something was not right about that day. I knew it from the minute I came home to find her dead." He glanced at me. "If I believed in such things, I would say that it doesn't surprise me that she haunts the house."

"She wears a dark gray dress and a string of pearls," I said. "Her hair is tied back and held with pins."

He was silent, and I knew that I'd just described what Frances had been wearing the day she died.

"I'm not hallucinating, Alex," I said. "I found photographs in her room—one of them was of me. The one of me as an artist's model. It was in my trunk when I arrived, but I found it folded with two others, with a message on the back. One of the other pictures showed Wych Elm House, and there is a shadow in the window—"

"Enough." He sighed quietly, still unwilling to believe. "We agree that Frances was murdered at least," he said. "Let us agree on our list of suspects."

"Very well," I said. "It must begin with the people in the house that day. So the list starts with Dottie."

"Add the servants, though I'm not sure what the motive would be."

Something about those words triggered a thought in the back of my mind, a memory like an itch, but I could not recall it. "The man in the woods," I added.

"He wasn't in the house," Alex reminded me.

"We don't know that. It isn't impossible, especially if he had an accomplice in either the family or the servants. Was Robert home that day?"

"Yes," Alex replied. "He wasn't in the house when it happened, but he arrived home soon after. He'd been at a neighbor's."

"Did he take the motorcar?"

"No, he walked. He was visiting the Astleys, half a mile away."

"Does he usually walk to the Astleys'?" Robert had taken the motorcar every time he'd visited friends since we'd been home.

"I have no idea what Robert usually does."

"Did anyone ask the Astleys about it?"

"As a matter of fact, I did," Alex said. "I thought it rather convenient that he came walking up the back lane from the trees barely twenty minutes after his daughter died. So I visited the Astleys myself. Robert was there. You're not the only one with a basely suspicious line of thinking."

I ignored that. "Did the Astleys recall exactly what time he left?"

"No, not exactly."

"So he could have done it, left the house, and come back twenty minutes later as if innocent."

"Yes. I don't like to think it, but without a firm timeline, it's possible."

"And you?" I asked. "Where were you exactly when it happened?"

"In the motorcar, on my way home from this very village," Alex replied. "I arrived only minutes after it happened. One of the maids saw her fall, and was screaming." He glanced away, his jaw hard. "It was me who took charge of the body."

He would have had to look at her, dead on the flagstones, and cover her up until the police came. It did not bear thinking of, but I had to be hard-hearted. "That's our list of suspects, then," I said. "Dottie, Robert, the servants, the man in the woods, you. The only person we can rule out safely is Martin, because he was in France."

"No," Alex said. "We cannot rule out Martin." He glanced at me. "If you can be cold, then so can I. If Martin wished his sister dead from his hospital bed in France, then he could have hired someone. He certainly had the means."

"That makes no sense," I said. "He loved her." But I remembered Cora telling me that Martin had burned all of the letters Frances sent to him at the Front during the war. Why would he do that?

"Love and murder go together more often than you think," Alex replied. "And you have left out one other person. By coincidence, here he comes now."

I looked ahead. Approaching us through the rain was a familiar figure, his shriveled arm pinned into the sleeve of his mackintosh. "That's Mr. Wilde."

"Yes, it is."

I had no chance to ask Alex what he meant, as Mr. Wilde was close enough to hear. "Mrs. Manders," he greeted me. He turned to Alex. "Mr. Manders. What a pleasure to see you home from the war. Mrs. Forsyth telephoned me this morning with the news."

"That was quick of her," said Alex.

"I am closely concerned with the Forsyths' business." I wondered at the distinct coolness between them as Mr. Wilde turned to me.

"Mrs. Manders, you look well this morning. I quite enjoyed our dance last night. You dance elegantly."

David Wilde was shorter than Alex, darker of complexion, and older—though the gray in his hair exaggerated the effect, and I had felt for myself his strength when I'd danced with him. With his deformed hand clad, as before, in its gray glove at the end of his sleeve, he looked distinguished, though I noticed that the villagers around us did not look at him as they passed. I recalled how tipsy I'd been in his grasp the night before, his one hand on my waist.

"Thank you," I said. "You were very kind."

"You seem to be having a leisurely morning," Alex said to Mr. Wilde. "Not particularly busy today?"

"I find taking walks refreshing," Mr. Wilde replied. "My days are very quiet, as I have explained to Mrs. Manders." He bowed slightly, the tilt of his head almost sarcastic. "It's good to see a true, honest-to-goodness war hero come home, Mr. Manders. I wish you good day."

"What in the world did I just witness?" I asked Alex when he was out of earshot again.

"How much do you know of David Wilde?" he asked in return, his expression blankly grim.

"Hardly anything."

"Then you know about as much as the rest of us. He's only been Aunt Dottie's solicitor for five years, since her last one died and he took over the practice. There are conflicting stories of where he came from, and he seems to have no other clients." He glanced at me. "He's a womanizer."

I looked at him openmouthed. "You can't possibly know that. And he has a wife."

"I'm a man, so yes I do. And marriage has nothing to do with womanizing, though few people have ever seen the elusive Mrs. Wilde."

"Dottie trusts him," I said.

"Perhaps she does, but I don't, and he knows it. He was at Wych Elm House that day, meeting with Aunt Dottie about business matters."

I frowned. "But Dottie said she was on the terrace when it happened. She thought she heard a sound."

"And Wilde was sitting in the library, waiting for her to return, or so he says. There was no one in the room with him when Franny died."

I pressed a damp, gloved hand to my forehead, under the brim of my hat. "This is terrible," I said. "I thought there would be too few suspects to make a convincing case for murder. Now I find there are too many. I think I am the only person we can safely say could not possibly have murdered your cousin."

"I still haven't convinced you that I didn't do it, have I?" Alex said. "Do you trust me so little?" He shook his head. "Don't answer that. I've known this would happen since I saw your face that day in Victoria Station, when I left you alone, sick with influenza."

I recoiled away from him, moving out from under the umbrella and into the rain. I'd never told him about the influenza. "I had a cold," I said.

"No," Alex said, his voice going dark and bleak. "You didn't. You had influenza. I knew it when I looked at your face, when I felt the fever burning you up." We had stopped walking, and he stepped closer to me, looked down at me with his features hard and unforgiving. "Do you understand? That is the sort of husband you chose. A man who could walk away and leave you in a crowded train station, suffering from a deadly illness, so he could return to the Front as a German. A man who did not defy his orders to send you a single telegram or make a single phone call to end your misery. No wonder you aren't happier to see me."

"Stop it," I said. He was in the grip of that icy anger again, the unfamiliar despair that I had seen last night. "You said yourself you'd have been shot for treason."

He took my arm, his grip solid, though even in his rage he did not hurt me. "Our business is done here," he said. "I think we've put on enough of a display for the village of Anningley, don't you? Let's go."

CHAPTER THIRTY-THREE

After a quick supper, bolted in the kitchen to avoid Alex and the family in the dining room, I was on my way to the stairs when I heard low, whispered voices. I detoured down the corridor and looked through the open door of the morning room.

Martin stood framed in the doorway to the terrace, his back to me. The French door was open, and he was leaning out, speaking in harsh undertones to someone outside. I could not hear the words, but the hostility in his voice made me stop, surprised. From the darkness outside, a woman's voice answered, low and angry.

"Go," Martin said.

I saw a shape through the window—a woman in a dark skirt and coat, retreating. Martin straightened and moved to close the door. I took a step back to turn and leave.

"Cousin Jo," he said.

I stopped still.

He latched the French door shut and turned to me. The rising moonlight was behind him, casting shadows, but I could see that he gave me an apologetic smile. "Well," he said, "here we are. I assumed you'd be at supper with all the others tonight, now that Alex is home. But it looks like you avoided it, like me."

"I'm sorry," I stammered. "I didn't mean—"

"It's quite all right." He came toward me. "I'm on my way back upstairs, and I'm not feeling well. Do you think you could accompany me?"

"Yes, of course." I took his arm, which felt like a matchstick inside the sleeve of the loose sweater he wore. "You should eat something."

"Not possible," he said as we moved out the doorway and down the hall. "I'm not improving, Cousin. That's the truth of it." He was quiet for a long moment as we began to ascend the stairs. "I suppose you're wondering who she was."

"It's none of my business," I replied.

"Still, it looks very bad." He gripped the stair railing with one thin hand and pulled himself up the steps. "The fact is, she's the wife of a man who used to work here."

"I see," I said, though I didn't see much of anything.

"He wasn't here long," Martin said, keeping his gaze on the stairs in front of him. His jaw was set tight, either in pain or in reluctance to tell the story. "He was one of the gardeners. He was a drunk, unreliable, given to fits of anger. Mother sacked him after a few weeks."

"This must have been some time ago," I said. The gardens were overgrown now, though Dottie had hired someone to try to tame them since her return.

"Near the beginning of the war, yes. The fellow didn't take it well, but like most of us, he enlisted. He must have heard that I had enlisted as well, because while I was in the hospital he had the audacity to write me a letter, complaining about Mother's treatment of him and asking for money." He took a deep breath. "There," he said as we crossed the landing and started upward again. "I've just told you something I've never told another soul. I think I might confess all of my crimes before I die."

"Stop talking like that," I said.

"Come now, Cousin," he replied. "We both know if I make it to the wedding it will be a miracle. I feel bad for Mother, because she's putting so much energy into planning the thing. And Cora, of course. But she and I have come to an understanding."

"I don't know what that means," I said. "The doctors—"

"I don't want to talk about doctors," he interrupted. "Wouldn't you like to hear the story about the gardener?"

"All right. Go on."

He sighed. "He sent me a letter. He said he'd been injured in the war and been sent home. He could no longer work. Ours was the last job he'd had, and he'd been sacked unfairly, he said, with no references. He appealed to me as a fellow soldier for money. I thought the entire plea was absurd, and I was in my own hell. I wrote him back and said no."

"I see," I said. This was going somewhere, and I thought I could begin to glimpse where. We reached the top of the stairs and started down the corridor to Martin's room. "And does the story end there?"

"I thought it did. I certainly never heard from him again. But I just learned tonight that the story didn't stop there at all." His breath was rasping from exertion on the stairs; he was in much worse shape than he'd been the day he came home, his features lined with pain. "The man's wife just paid me a visit, as you see. She says he disappeared after coming home in August of 1917 and she hasn't seen him since. She believes him dead."

I stopped in front of his bedroom door. "The man in the woods," I said. "The man who died the day Frances did."

"Exactly, Cousin Jo," Martin replied. "Just maneuver me to the bed over there, if you would. I'll fix the pillows. Yes, she believes her husband died in the woods that day. She's been waiting for our family to come home so she can make her claim."

"Claim?"

"Money, of course." Martin eased back on the bed against the large stack of pillows he'd piled against the headboard. "She believes that Franny's hellhound dog, Princer, tore her husband to pieces, and she blames our cursed family—as she called it—for his death. She wants compensation. She's starting with me, but if I don't pay, she's threatening to go public."

I pulled up a chair and sat next to him. He had relaxed onto the bed, fully clothed, his hands on his stomach. "It's a bluff," I said. "If she truly wanted to go public, she could have done it any time in the past four years."

"I agree. So much simpler to extract money privately from the family, isn't it? Less publicity and more profit. No risk of ridicule over claiming a fictional demon dog killed your husband."

"You'll have to go to the police, the magistrate," I said. "Now that you know the man's identity. The authorities need to be told."

"Except I don't actually know it," he replied. "I only know his disappearance coincided with the unidentified man's death. And even for that, I have only his wife's word."

"Then what are you going to do?"

"Let me take care of it," came a voice from the doorway.

We both turned. Alex stood leaning against the doorjamb, listening, his hands jammed casually into his pockets.

"Alex!" Martin cried happily.

Alex turned his gaze on me. "You weren't at supper," he said.

"Did you enjoy it?" I asked innocently.

"God, no. You should have warned me. I had no idea it would be so excruciating." His voice lowered. "Aunt Dottie told me that your mother died last week. You didn't tell me."

I looked away. "It doesn't matter."

"It does. She also told me you never come to supper."

I turned to Martin, and we exchanged a glance. "Martin is ill," I explained to Alex, "and I'm just the help. We try not to go to supper if we can avoid it."

Alex's voice was quietly angry. "Another fact that you helpfully did not explain to me."

"I say," Martin broke in. "Is everything quite all right between you two?"

Alex pushed off the doorjamb and came into the room. "Oh, yes," he said. "Just keen, as your fiancée would say."

Martin put a hand to his forehead, like a fainting lady in a film. "Please don't make fun of Cora," he said. "She's a good girl. It turns out I rather like her."

"Then you should be happy she went home with her parents. What has gotten into Aunt Dottie and Uncle Robert, by the way? They're practically at each other's throats."

"They're worse than ever, I agree," Martin said. "They've never thought much of each other, but Franny's death seems to have done them in."

Alex stood next to my chair, took his hands from his pockets, and looked down at Martin on the bed. "Matty," he said, "you look like hell."

To my surprise, Martin's chest shook with quiet laughter. "You haven't called me that since we were boys," he said, looking up at Alex with the strange, complex adoration I'd seen on his face in that first moment I'd come into the parlor, a mix of love and a bitter sort of pain. "I take it you overheard what I told Cousin Jo?"

"Enough of it." I could feel the tension vibrating from both of them. "Leave it to me, Matty. What was the man's name?"

Martin seemed to hesitate, looking up into Alex's face, but finally he spoke the words. "George Sanders," he said. "That was the fellow. His wife's name is Alice. She lives in Torbram."

"And how much money did she want?" Alex asked.

"A thousand pounds. I told her I'd think about it. I didn't know what else to say."

"I'll handle it," Alex said softly. "Just get some rest." He studied Martin closely. "You're not on anything for the pain," he observed.

Martin glanced at me, then looked back up at Alex. This time his laugh was bitter. "I'm afraid not, old chap."

Alex rocked back on his heels in comprehension. "Is there nothing that can be done?" he asked.

"It doesn't matter," Martin said. "I don't care anymore, not for myself, anyway. I just want to stay around for the wedding, for Cora's sake. She'll be part of the family then, a married woman, and at least as a proper widow she'll have some options." He looked at Alex thoughtfully. "It's the only reason I don't ask you to get your pistol and put me out of my misery, Coz."

I sat in shocked silence, my stomach turning, as Alex actually seemed to consider the idea.

"No," he said at last.

"You could," Martin said to him, the words a whisper in the quiet room.

"I could," my husband agreed. "But I won't."

They locked gazes for a long moment, and then Martin relaxed back into the pillows and closed his eyes. "Hell," he said, the word coming out on a sigh.

He didn't speak again, and after a moment I felt Alex's hand close over my wrist. His touch was warm on my cold skin. I let him pull me unresisting from my chair and lead me from the room, closing Martin's bedroom door softly behind us.

CHAPTER THIRTY-FOUR

"I can't believe you," I said to Alex as he led me downstairs and along the corridor to my bedroom. "That was barbaric."

"I said no to him," he argued.

"But you thought about it. You actually thought about—about killing him to make the pain stop. Your own cousin."

Alex pulled me into my room and shut the door. "I repeat—I said no," he said. "But I'd do it cleanly, and quicker than whatever is killing him."

"What is the matter with you?" I cried.

He still held my wrist. He leaned in, and I could smell his scent as I felt my own pulse in my throat. "Go to war, Jo," he said. "Go to war, and watch a man die in agony, screaming for his mother, and tell me then that death can't be merciful."

I went still in his grip. "Did you kill people?" I asked him. "When you were—a German? Did you fight? Did you kill English soldiers as part of your cover?"

His grip flinched on my wrist, his fingers flexing without thinking. "No," he said. "My cover was as a messenger, remember? No, I didn't

251

fight. Not then. But I can't speak to what I did before I became Hans Faber, Jo. Don't ask me. I don't much like to remember."

I looked into his blue eyes and held his gaze. He had always been so good at everything—he'd be good at killing, too, even if he didn't want to be. "I did go to war," I said. "Maybe I didn't shoot guns or parachute out of planes, but I *did* go to war. I rolled bandages and I bought liberty bonds and I lined up for rationed food. And I read the casualty lists, and I waited, and I wrote the War Office and the Red Cross after the Armistice, and—and I packed your things; I put them in boxes. I—"

"Sweetheart," he said.

I jerked my wrist from his grip. "You can't understand," I said, tears burning my eyes. "I did everything wrong, don't you see? Mother shouldn't have been in that place. They told me it was best, but I should have fought them. She died among strangers, alone in the middle of the night. And you . . ." I pressed my hands to my eyes as the tears fought their way down my cheeks, desperate and hot. I sat on the edge of the bed, the strength gone from my legs. "I took all of your things—your clothes, your belongings—and I got rid of them. Dottie was—she was taking me to the Continent, and I couldn't afford the rent on the flat for the three months I would be gone, and I . . ." I heard him sigh, and I took a gasping breath as the words fought their way from my throat. "I should have known," I said, shame burning me, "you were alive. They never found a body. I should have believed. I should have *known*. All of your things, I—the shirts you liked so much, the cuff links you got at Oxford, the coat you wore the day we met."

I heard him kneel in front of me. "Look at me," he said softly.

But I kept my eyes closed. "I couldn't do it anymore," I confessed. "Any of it. I could have begged Dottie to store it, but the truth is I couldn't. I just couldn't. I kept the camera, but everything else, I— even my lavender wool dress. I couldn't look at it anymore. And I'm so *sorry*."

His hands came over mine, lifted them gently from my face. I blinked at him, his face fragmenting as I still fought my tears. He did not speak. Instead, he put his hands gently on my neck, his fingers pressing up into my hair, his thumbs along my jawline. He leaned in, and for a moment I felt his breath on the skin of my neck, just below my ear. Then he kissed me there.

My reaction was so immediate, and so overwhelming, that I gasped. I could not move. He held me still, and he pressed kisses down the side of my neck, slowly, savoring me. Everything in me burned—the blood in my veins, the tears in my eyes, the breath in my lungs, the surface of my skin. Everything burned for him, and when he kissed my lips at last, I stopped thinking.

He pressed me back on the bed, his weight on me, warm and familiar. I arched beneath him as he bit me gently on the tender flesh where my neck met my collarbone and his hands pushed up the hem of my skirt. Then his fingers were tracing my inner thighs, deft and clever, and my hands fisted in the folds of his shirt as I moaned against his neck.

It took only minutes. When I was finished, I helped him undo his trousers, push down my underthings, and then he took his turn. We did not speak. I wrapped my legs around him and arched again, and he met me wave for wave, one hand hard on my hip through the cloth of my skirt, his breath harsh in my ear. It was not slow or graceful, perhaps, but it was *us*, every languorous rainy afternoon or adventurous night or sleepy morning we'd ever had. Afterward he lay on top of me as both of us caught our breath on the rumpled coverlet.

He pushed himself up on his elbows and looked down at me. "Was there anyone else?" he asked.

I blinked at him, stunned. "Is that a serious question?"

"Yes," said Alex. "It bloody well is."

I pressed my hands against his chest and pushed him off me. Then I stood and walked to the washstand against the wall.

"It's a question that's kept me awake at night for three years," Alex said to my back. "Colonel Mabry said you didn't seem to have anyone else, but—"

"Colonel *Mabry*?" I was holding the pitcher of water, and I paused in outrage before I poured water into the basin. "You had Colonel Mabry *watching* me for you?"

"Not precisely," Alex replied. "He gave me updates, but they were very vague. And I never know when Mabry is lying."

I remembered what he'd said when he'd suggested we marry in Crete. *It isn't anyone's damned business what I do.* I had thought he wanted to escape Dottie's prying, but now I knew better. It was Colonel Mabry's observation he'd wanted to escape. I wrung out the cloth and dabbed the insides of my thighs quickly, my back to him. I was too enraged to speak.

"Don't you wonder the same thing?" he asked me.

"No," I said, the word coming out sharply. I could not bear to think about pretty blond German girls following Alex around like puppies. He would have had to fight them off. "I don't want to know." I rinsed the cloth and wrung it out again. My hands were shaking.

I heard him get off the bed, right his clothes. "Damn it, Jo. I can't seem to say the right thing to you anymore."

I let my skirt drop, picked up my underthings from the floor. "We shouldn't do this again."

"I very much disagree."

"I could have a child."

He paused, and I knew I'd wounded him. "You used to want a child," he said.

"I did." I straightened and finally faced him again. "I do. But not here. Not in this place." The thought of a baby in Wych Elm House was flatly horrifying.

"Then we'll leave." Alex strode toward me. "I have money now, Jo. They gave me plenty for the work I did. We don't have to stay here. We can go anywhere."

"We can't leave," I protested. "Not now. Martin is deathly sick, and Dottie and Robert's marriage is a disaster, and someone murdered your cousin. We can't walk away."

He ran a hand through his hair, frustrated. "Very well. But I'm going to Torbram tomorrow to see this Alice Sanders woman. Are you coming with me?"

I paused. Dottie was expecting me to work for her tomorrow, promptly at eight o'clock as usual. "Yes," I said. "I'll come. And there's a woman in the village we should visit as well. A servant who worked here until Frances died." I searched my memory of my encounter with the Bainses at the post office. "Petra Jennings is her name. The postmistress mentioned her to me. She says the girl was dismissed after Franny died, and she never speaks about it. She thinks the family threatened her with something."

"We'll talk to her, too, then," Alex said. "Torbram is several hours' drive, and the weather tomorrow will not be good. We'll have to stay overnight." He watched me, his expression under control now, impassive.

It would mean yet another day off from my duties. "I'll come."

That night, I showed him the sketchbook. He leafed through it, taking careful note of the pages torn from the spine. I showed him the photographs, the handwriting on them, the shadow in the sketchbook that matched the shadow in the picture of Martin and Frances. He looked all of it over, missing nothing, and told me gently that anyone could have taken the picture from my trunk and written the notes to scare me. He thought the shadow in the window was a trick of the light.

I made him sleep on top of the covers again. And I dreamed of a door in a thick, overgrown wall, the lock black with mold. I tried to pry the lock open, my fingers slipping on the metal, my knuckles beginning to bleed. *I've changed my mind*, Alex said from behind me. *Give me the gun. I've changed my mind.* Then the door was gone and I stood on the top turret of Wych Elm House, watching dead leaves swirling before me, the wind cold on my face. And when the hands pushed me and the cobblestones rushed up to meet me, I did not have time to scream.

CHAPTER THIRTY-FIVE

I meant to ask Dottie for leave the next morning, but when I came downstairs she was not in the morning room as usual. Instead, I found her in the large parlor, sitting with Colonel Mabry.

I stopped in the doorway. My horror may have shown in my expression, but Dottie did not notice. She wore one of her supremely sour looks, which said that something had displeased her.

"Manders," she said, "Colonel Mabry has come to see you."

I forced myself to look at him. He sat upright in his place on the sofa, his hat on his lap, his bright, relentless eyes on me.

"I beg your pardon?" I asked.

Dottie's tone was almost disgusted. "He wishes to tour the works in the upstairs gallery, and he has asked for you to be his guide. Please take him and show him the pieces he is interested in."

Again I looked at the colonel. He knew that Alex had come home. Yet here he was, asking to see me, not my husband. I set my shoulders. Perhaps the colonel wouldn't like everything I had to say.

"Certainly," I managed to get out between gritted teeth. "Colonel, please follow me."

"Mrs. Manders," he said softly as we ascended the stairs, "please excuse my intrusion. The small deception was necessary. I wish to speak to you most urgently about a certain matter."

"Is that so?" I asked, my hand on the railing and my gaze trained at the top of the stairs. "I can't imagine what that might be."

"Actually, I believe you know very well."

One of the maids passed us, and we were quiet until I led him into the gallery. The staff had been busy yesterday, tearing down the decorations from the engagement party, and the gallery was restored to rights, the strings of lights and the raised dais gone. Dottie's art lined the high walls. I could not quite believe that the engagement party had been a mere two nights ago.

"I have nothing to say to you," I told the colonel as we stood unseeing before the paintings on the first wall. "You lied to me, Colonel. Repeatedly. Did you think I would just forget about it?"

He was not in the least disturbed. "Some mistruths are essential, Mrs. Manders."

"Pretending you never knew my husband? Showing me his file as if you didn't know he was alive?"

He stood tall and straight beside me, his hat in his hand. "I would very much like to know," he said, "how much Alex has told you."

"Is that why you came here today and performed this silly subterfuge?" I strolled to the next wall of paintings. My anger was steady, like a small jet of water leaking from a massive dam. "To ask me that?"

"Not exactly."

"Then why?" I turned to face him, though even as I did it I knew that to ask him anything was futile. He would tell me only what he wanted me to hear, for reasons I would never know. "Why come at all, even at first, to meet me? Why sit with Mrs. Forsyth, pretending to be interested in her paintings and observing me? Why agree to meet me and go through the entire fiction of my husband's War Office file? Why do any of it?"

Colonel Mabry turned away from me and strolled slowly along the gallery wall. "Very well," he said. "I came because I wanted to see you for myself, Mrs. Manders. I wanted to see what kind of woman you are. In short, I was curious."

"About me?" I followed him, my clicking heels echoing on the empty tile floor. "That's ridiculous. You already knew everything there is to know about me—and anything you didn't know, you had the power to find out. You knew I believed him dead. You knew where I lived. You knew I was working as Mrs. Forsyth's paid companion." He stopped walking and stood again, looking at the paintings, and I wanted to shake him. "Alex came home to finish your assignment. I don't know what that has to do with me."

He looked at me for the first time, the expression in his eyes almost recognizable as surprise. "You don't think he came home for you?"

"I think he came home for several reasons, only some of which had to do with me."

He regarded me for another long moment, then looked back at the paintings with an audible sigh. "Mrs. Manders," he said, his voice calm, businesslike. "Perhaps I should explain something to you. You have been, quite honestly, the bane of my existence since 1914."

I stared at him, openmouthed. "I beg your pardon?"

"If I know Alex at all," Colonel Mabry said, "he's told you everything, even though he isn't supposed to. So I'm going to assume that it won't shock you when I say I have dealt with a great many undercover agents in my career, Mrs. Manders. What you likely don't understand is that most of them are incompetent."

"I'm not following."

He sighed again in disappointment. "They are clumsy, to be frank. They don't go where they're told to go. They ignore pertinent details and give us irrelevant information. They leave their suitcases on the train and lose vital documents. They write things down in letters to their sweethearts. They ask for raises. They drink too much and begin to brag. They leak things to the enemy. They disappear." He shook his head. "It is most difficult to recruit anyone remotely trustworthy. I waste a great deal of time. But not with your husband, Mrs. Manders. Despite his failure here in 1917, Alex is the best recruit I've ever had." He glanced at me again. "Do you understand? I deal with incompetence every day, but Alex worked for me for years with only a single unfinished mission. He remembers every instruction by rote in his brain. He solves problems. His instincts are unmatched. He blames himself for not finding the traitor, but your husband lived with the enemy, side by side, for *three years* without a single slip. Do you begin to see how extraordinary that is?"

I was beginning to. "And now he's resigned, and you blame me for it."

"I blame you because you are the reason. He has been kicking at his traces because he's been miserable. He came to me in 1914 and quit because he wanted to marry you. We were on the verge of war, but still he walked away. Then he enlisted in the RAF—a guarantee he'd end up as butcher's meat—instead of working for me, because he wanted to *impress* you."

"He did not want to impress me," I argued.

"Oh, yes, he did. He wanted to serve honorably, he said. He managed to survive for two years before I convinced him to save his own life and get out."

"You could have saved him!" I was heated now, all pretense at politeness gone. My voice rang off the high walls of the gallery. "He tried to come back to England to be an instructor, but you stopped it!"

"Because it isn't enough to survive the war," Mabry explained. The flush high on his aristocratic cheekbones was his only display of emotion. "You have to *win* it. I couldn't let my best operative train more men for certain death while the enemy *won*. That was unacceptable to my superiors, and it was unacceptable to me."

"Fine," I said. "You got your way. He worked for you. But the war has been over for three years. We *did* win. Let him come home. There is nothing left for him to do."

"There is," he said coldly, as if I were a child, "*plenty* left for him to do, as you put it. There is always work needed to keep England safe. You may think the world has become a garden party now that the war is over, but you would be entirely wrong."

"I don't think that," I snapped. "But Germany is quiet. And Germany is where Alex's expertise lies. You can't use him in Moscow or Japan."

"Where I wish to assign my operative is government business, Mrs. Manders, not yours." He turned to me. "And so we come down to the meat of it. I am asking you to give him back to me. Give him back to his country."

"No," I said instantly. "I won't."

"There is great need in the fight against communism. In Russia. Spain."

"England can fight communism without him," I shot back. "Recruit someone else and train him. If you want a Russian, use Casparov. He wasn't doing much business as a solicitor, anyway."

There was the briefest beat of surprise, and then Mabry said, "I see Alex has indeed told you more than he should have. Casparov was one of the clumsy ones, Mrs. Manders. And in any case, I can't use him because Casparov is dead. We found him shot at his desk in 1918."

I swallowed my shock. "And you'd like my husband to replace him?" I said. "No. He's tired, Colonel." I knew it was true—it came through in Alex's new bitterness, the dreary anger that sometimes crept into his voice. "He's exhausted. He's come to this house to finish the assignment you gave him, to put his cousin's death to rest, and that is all."

"Do you think he's going to be happy?" I could hear exasperation in Colonel Mabry's voice, another unprecedented show of emotion. "Do you think a man like that will be content reading the news and listening to the wireless at night with his children for the next forty years?"

"If he wants to be," I said. "You've just implied that my husband can do almost anything he sets his mind to. If he sets his mind to listening to the wireless with his children, then I'm sure he can do it. If he'd be happier working for you, then Alex will tell me. Until that happens, you're to leave us alone."

They were bold words, but as the colonel took his leave and we descended the stairs, I was unsteady. Outside, the weak late-autumn sun was vanishing behind an ominous bank of clouds as Colonel Mabry walked with a swift, formal gait toward his motorcar, putting his hat briskly back on his head.

Dottie was not in the large parlor, so I walked on watery legs to the morning room, where I found Alex reading the newspaper. He was half sitting on the table, one long leg hitched up, his tall body framed against the French doors behind him. "There you are," he said. "Have you spoken to Aunt Dottie? Pack an overnight bag. We should get going." He glanced up. "Something's upset you. What is it?"

For a moment I couldn't speak. I paced to the French doors and looked out at the terrace, pressing my palms together, trying to make my hands stop shaking. I took a breath.

Behind me, I heard a rustle as Alex put the paper down and stood. "Jo?"

I turned and came toward him. I put my hands on the back of his neck and he let me pull him down and kiss him, but it had a hard, desperate edge to it, and when we parted, his gaze was dark and wary.

"Care to explain?" he asked.

I dropped my hands. "Thank you for coming home," I said.

"I told you I would."

"I know you did." My gaze dropped to the newspaper. *Do you think he'll be happy reading the newspaper and listening to the wireless with his children for the next forty years?* If we didn't have children, he wouldn't even have that. I had not wished to discuss my lack of conception over the years with Colonel Mabry.

The sound of Dottie's oxfords clunking toward us down the hall interrupted the depressing turn of my thoughts. She stood in the doorway and stared at us, her eyes narrowing.

"Alex," she said, "stop looking at your wife like that. I prefer decorum in this house. Manders, pay attention."

"Yes, Dottie," I said.

"A servant tells me that Colonel Mabry has abruptly taken his leave. I am left to assume he did not purchase a painting."

I felt Alex startle in surprise beside me, but I said, "No, he didn't. I'm sorry."

"I see. I certainly hope that his decision had nothing to do with your behavior."

"No, Dottie."

"Then his intentions were not as sincere as he led me to believe, which is something I disapprove of. I dislike having my time wasted, as you know. Please come to the library and begin work, as I have a wedding to plan. Alex, go away and amuse yourself."

As she turned away and clipped back down the corridor, Alex turned to me. "What the hell was she talking about?"

"I'll explain," I said. "Let me talk to Dottie." I followed her down the corridor to the library.

CHAPTER THIRTY-SIX

I came into the library rehearsing what I would say in my head, but Dottie spoke before I had the chance. "You needn't say it, Manders," she said. "I already know."

I should have known she'd anticipate me. "I just need today off, Dottie, and then tomorrow—"

"Don't be a fool," she said. She had circled behind her desk and was sorting through her papers. "I certainly don't intend to be. You're resigning."

"I didn't think I was," I said.

"Didn't you?" Dottie found her cigarette holder beneath her papers—her desk was uncharacteristically messy—and opened her silver cigarette case. "Then I don't think you've been paying attention to what's happened the past few days. Your husband has come home. Your resigning was only a matter of time."

I pulled up the chair at my typewriter desk and sat. "Dottie," I said, "you don't need a paid companion. I'm not sure you ever have."

She screwed a cigarette into the holder and looked at me shrewdly.

"I have a wedding to plan," she said again. "The engagement party was a success, despite my nephew's terrible sense of timing. But the wedding will be something else entirely. It's going to be the event of the season, and I want it to happen before Christmas. Perhaps I don't need a paid companion, but an assistant would have been useful."

"Then I'll help you," I said, surprising myself even as the words left my lips, "but I won't work for you. I won't take your money for it. How does that sound?"

The chair behind her desk creaked as she briskly dropped into it. She lit her cigarette and leaned back, regarding me. "You're being rather charitable," she said, her voice gruff with some emotion I could not read. "I know there's something that's bothering you besides Alex's return. You're a terrible liar, Manders. Just tell me."

I swallowed. Of course Dottie would know—she could always see through me. I couldn't tell her about someone pushing Frances from the roof, or the man in the woods, or the trip to Torbram, not yet. Not until there was something concrete to tell. But I owed her something. "It's Frances," I said.

Her face sagged for a brief moment, but then she snapped to again. "I told you I don't wish to speak of Frances."

"You think I don't understand her, what you went through, what she suffered. But I do."

"Is that what you think?" Dottie said. "It is not as easy as that. There is no maudlin connection between you and me because of your mother. The cases were entirely different. The fact that you lived those years with your mother does not mean you understand."

I watched her prop the cigarette into its ashtray, her movements deliberate. I realized she was shaken. "It isn't just that," I said. "I understand Frances because I've seen her. Here in the house. In the woods. Her dog, Princer . . . I've seen them both. She wears a gray dress and a string of pearls."

"Is that so?" Her voice was brittle. "You think you've seen my daughter's ghost?"

"I have seen it," I said.

"Well." She was reflective for a long moment, her gaze far away. "You know, part of me thought—I thought she might . . ." She shook her head. "She saw the dead so many times. After she died, I started to wonder—it's why I couldn't come back to the house until now. How long have you been seeing her?"

"Since the first day," I said. "Though not constantly."

"I gave her those pearls for her birthday," Dottie said. "I buried her in them. Where is she? Where in the house?"

"She appeared in the small parlor," I said. "As clear as you're sitting before me right now."

"I see. Does she look . . . ?" She could not finish the words.

"She looks the same as I'm sure she did that last day."

That gave her pain, but she swallowed it. "Does she ask for me? I'm her mother. I would know—I would be able to tell what it is she wants."

She was murdered. Your daughter was murdered, and you're one of the few people who could have done it. But I only shook my head. "She doesn't speak."

"I see." She seemed to regain herself, piece by piece. "Well, it's something, I suppose, as mad as it sounds." She glanced at me. "Go find Alex, and do whatever it is the two of you aren't telling me about. We'll discuss the rest of it tomorrow."

"Thank you," I said to her. "You've been very good to me."

"Manders, go away."

I did, but as I left the room, I couldn't help the feeling that it was for the last time. I glanced around at the desk, the shelves of unread books, my little desk with the typewriter under its cover. Whatever came next, my days as a paid companion were over.

"I don't like the way she talks to you," Alex said when we were on the road to Anningley. He had his own motorcar—on loan from the British government, I assumed—and he was driving as I rode in the passenger seat. "Aunt Dottie. She keeps calling you Manders."

I was watching the landscape, the leaves blowing from the trees in the chill wind that was rising from the sea. "It's a habit," I said.

"I'll speak to her about it."

"There's no need. I'm used to it." I leaned back in the comfortable seat. The motorcar was nice, the seats rich leather. "I rather like it, in fact."

"Are you going to tell me what the hell Mabry was doing at the house this morning?"

I glanced at him. His gaze was on the road before him, his jaw set in an angry line. "I told you he pretended to be interested in Dottie's art. Today he pretended he wanted to look at paintings in order to talk to me."

The idea quietly enraged him, I could tell, from that tired anger he had begun to show. "To you alone? What about?" he said.

"He wanted me to encourage you to go work for him again and fight communism."

Alex swore. "That's a fine decision for the two of you to make. What did you tell him?"

"I told him to go away and leave us alone." I watched him for a moment. "Do you want to go fight communism?"

"I don't see how I could," Alex replied. "I know just enough Russian to ask the way to the loo." He paused. "But to answer the question, what I want is to be my own man. I don't even know if that's possible, or for how long, but that's what I want. Does that make sense?"

"Yes," I said, miserable. "If you'd rather go fight communism in order to be happy, please just tell me first, won't you? Please don't disappear again."

He glanced at me, then back at the road before him. "I don't think you've been listening."

"I had to say it. What will you do, then? Have you thought about it?"

"A little. I have some contacts in government, and I believe I could get a decent sort of job. Would you mind moving back to London?"

For the first time it truly sank in that he was home, that we were going to build a life together again. "London would be fine," I said. I hadn't wanted to go back there without him, but with him, I could manage.

"Then I'll see what I can do. What arrangements were made for your mother?"

We talked of practical matters the rest of the way—my mother's burial, my letting go of the Chalcot Road apartment, Mother's final hospital bills. Alex had always been good at solving problems, and two years in RAF airplanes and three years in a double life as Hans Faber hadn't changed that. In this strange, unreal world I could not have imagined three days ago, we tentatively began to speak of our future. But as I looked out the windshield at the foggy road before us, I couldn't see very far.

P etra Jennings lived in a small, tidy cottage on the outskirts of Anningley. The garden was well kept, the walk clear of leaves, the windows scrubbed clean. When Alex knocked on the front door, a woman of about thirty appeared, wearing an everyday housedress, her long thin blond hair woven into a braid down her back. From the house behind her came a damp, soapy smell, steaming the air.

"We're sorry to bother you, Miss Jennings," Alex said to her, removing his hat. "I believe you recognize me?"

From the expression on her face—vague panic laced with unhappiness—she did. "Yes, sir," she said, never taking her eyes from him to look at me. "You're Mrs. Forsyth's nephew. I saw you last on the day Miss Frances died."

"That's right. Alex Manders," said Alex. I could tell he recognized her as well. "This is my wife, Jo. I'd like to ask you a few questions, if you can spare the time."

Petra Jennings stood for a moment, plainly torn. Mrs. Baines had said she never spoke about the family—but Alex *was* the family.

Besides, I could tell she was busy doing some kind of washing. But she finally stood back and swung the door open. "If you please," she said, not kindly.

We stepped inside and found the inner rooms as neat and tidy as the outside, though the steamy smell was pervasive. "I'm sorry," Miss Jennings said, leading us down the corridor past a cozily furnished sitting room. "I'll have to talk to you in the kitchen. I take in washing for a living, and I have the iron on."

The kitchen was piled with clean clothes—shirts, trousers, dresses, shirtwaists, underthings. An ironing board was set up at one end of the room, and a steam iron was resting on it. We took a seat, and Petra Jennings promptly turned her back to us and went back to work.

"You worked for my aunt and her family for a time," Alex said.

Miss Jennings's narrow shoulder blades worked busily beneath the fabric of her day dress. "A year or so, yes. I never talk about the family, if that's what you're asking. I'm the type to keep to myself. I don't know where all the awful rumors come from, but it isn't from me."

"Which rumors would those be?"

"Miss Frances being locked in a room. Her having some kind of dog that roams the woods and eats bad children. I just did my job, that was all, until Mrs. Forsyth dismissed all of us and shut down the house."

"And you've taken in washing since?"

"It's a way to make a living."

I looked around the kitchen. Washing must be rather a good living, by the looks of it—Petra Jennings had a cottage to herself that was above what most servants could afford, and her iron was one of the new electric ones. "How well did you know Frances Forsyth?" I asked.

She deftly flipped a man's shirt onto the ironing board and continued working without looking at me. "Miss Frances never gave me any trouble," she said, her voice cautious. "She had terrors and spells, but she was always sorry about it afterward. She could be moody—angry or weeping. Some days she'd sleep straight through the day without getting out of bed. She wasn't normal, but she never gave me any trouble. Mrs. Forsyth wasn't pleasant to work for, I don't mind saying, but the wages were good enough."

"Miss Jennings," Alex said. Something in his tone made her put down the iron and turn to look at him again. "You were there the day Frances died."

She stared at him like a snake stares at a charmer. "Yes," she said.

"Can you tell me where you were that day? Exactly what happened?"

"It wasn't me that found her," Miss Jennings said. "I was in the kitchen. It was Helen—oh, I don't remember her last name. She was a maid. She was the one that found her."

Alex nodded. "Go on."

She blinked, but still she looked at him, something in her expression beginning to chill me. "Helen was screaming and screaming. I came running up the stairs from the kitchen. I went to the front door, but it was already open, and Mrs. Forsyth was standing on the front step, looking. She didn't say anything. She was a cold woman, and a mean mistress, but I wouldn't wish that on anyone."

"What else?" Alex asked, his voice quiet.

"I looked past her. You were there, sir. You had taken off your overcoat and put it over Miss Frances so no one could see. Helen was being sick in the bushes. One of the gardeners came around the corner, and you shouted at him to call a doctor."

The kitchen was quiet for a moment. I could not imagine the horror of it. I could not.

"What else do you remember?" Alex asked at last.

"Nothing, sir. I went back into the house. The servants were all talking in the kitchen. I didn't want to be out front anymore, didn't want to see. Eventually the doctor came, and the police. They asked us questions, and then they went away."

"Did you see anyone else when it happened?"

"No, sir."

"Did you see Mr. Forsyth?"

"No, sir. I don't believe he was home."

"What about Mr. Wilde?"

She shook her head. "He wasn't there, sir."

"Yes, he was," Alex coaxed. "Do you not recall?"

She paused, then shook her head again. "I'm sorry, sir. I didn't see him. If he was there, I don't recall it."

It went on like this for a few more minutes, with Alex prodding her memory, but Miss Jennings had nothing more to say. Finally, we rose to take our leave.

"You won't tell anyone you talked to me, will you?" she asked as she walked us to the door. "I told you, I don't talk about the family. I don't want a reputation as a gossip."

"It's quite all right," Alex said. He turned to her on the step and put on his hat. "You have my discretion."

"Yes, sir," she said.

He walked down the step toward the motorcar, but when I moved to follow, Petra Jennings gripped my arm. "I know you won't listen to me, but I'll say it anyway," she said.

I paused and looked at her. "What is it?"

"Your husband." Her face was washed of color in the overcast light, her eyes large in her narrow face, her grip cold on my arm. "Everyone said he was dead."

"He was a prisoner," I explained. "He's home now."

"Is that so?" Her gaze was hard. "He came to the house out of nowhere, all the way from France. He asked me questions about Miss Frances, about her sketchbook. He asked me where it was, what kind of things were in it. And the next day, Miss Frances was dead. What do you think that means?"

"He was in his motorcar when it happened, pulling up the drive," I said.

"I didn't see that," she said. "I only know what I saw. He had put his coat over her when I came outside. That's all." She let me go, and I followed Alex into the motorcar. I did not look back at her when we pulled away.

"What was that about?" Alex asked me.

I unfolded the road map and looked for the route to Torbram. "Someone overheard you," I replied.

"Overheard what?"

"You asked Petra Jennings about Frances's sketchbook the day before she died. Someone overheard you and got to it first. Got to Frances first and killed her. Miss Jennings thinks that because you were the one asking questions, the killer is you."

"That explains the fact that she was terrified of me," Alex said. From the corner of my eye, I saw him glance at me. "It's a theory you yourself held not too long ago. I take it my manly charms have made you change your mind?"

I turned the map over. "There is that," I admitted. "However, there is also the fact that Miss Jennings lives in a cottage I see no way she could have paid for. And the fact that the man's shirt she was ironing had pin marks in the left sleeve."

"So you noticed that, too," Alex said. "David Wilde. Whom she has no recollection of seeing that day."

"Yes," I said. "Let's go to Torbram and see what Alice Sanders has to say."

CHAPTER THIRTY-SEVEN

B y the time we drove into Torbram, it was late afternoon and the sky was lowering, the clouds threatening a downpour. We had been spattered with intermittent rain throughout the drive, which had slowed us down. Now we faced the prospect of finding Alice Sanders as early night fell and brought a storm with it from the sea.

We started at an inn, where Alex parked the motorcar, hired us a room for the night, and asked the innkeeper if he was familiar with the Sanderses. As a Londoner, I thought this method of finding someone absurd, but Alex assured me that in a place as small as Torbram, it would work.

He was correct. Torbram was larger than Anningley, with a snappier High Street and a lovely seaside walk along the south coast overlooking the ocean, as well as winding neighborhoods of pretty homes, but it was still a small town. The innkeeper did not know the Sanderses, but his wife had heard of them, and the girl working in the kitchen knew that Alice Sanders served tables at one of the local pubs. Alex and I followed a network of local hearsay, and eventually we made the journey along the seaside under the threatening sky to the place where we'd heard Alice Sanders was waiting tables.

The pub was called The Red-Haired Queen, and it was nestled on the end of the seaside strip, its battered old beams looking out over the cold, dark, rocky beach and the tossing surf beyond. Around the curve of the shoreline, I could faintly see the outline of a lighthouse through the clouds, and I imagined on a clear day I'd be able to see all the way to Cornwall.

The taproom was doing brisk business, many of the men from town huddled over their drinks, happy to get out of the windy cold and sit by the fireplace, where a blaze had been lit. I pulled off my gloves as Alex took my arm and led me to the large, scarred bar and helped me onto a stool.

He ordered us each a beer, making sure to request the dark bitter I liked, then turned and gave me a shrug. "It's been a long day, and I think we'll need it."

"I agree," I said.

He did not take a seat, but leaned on the bar next to me, gracefully propped on one elbow. He removed his hat and ran a hand quickly through his hair. "I'm not entirely sure how to go about this," he said. "I don't want to be too obvious."

"I don't think she's in the room," I told him, sipping the beer that the bartender had slid in front of me. "There's only one serving woman here, and she's past forty. Too old to be the wife of a man of army age."

"Perhaps George Sanders married an older woman," Alex said, though I could tell he agreed with me.

"Unlikely," I replied calmly. "Did you find it strange that the innkeeper's wife knew who the Sanderses were but not that George Sanders has disappeared?"

Alex sipped his own beer, his gaze seeming to rest on me, though I knew there was no detail of the room around us that he'd missed. "Either she hasn't told anyone, or George Sanders was the kind of man no one cares to ask after."

I ran a thumb up the side of my glass. "Or a combination of both. It's possible she hasn't been very vocal about it," I said. "People may think he left her."

He gave me a long look. "Would that also be why she hasn't reported his disappearance to the police?"

"Perhaps she has," I replied. "But the police would assume a man like that simply walked away by choice, that she must have done something to provoke him. Women don't have a great many choices in such situations."

He looked uncomfortable and a little sad. "I tried to leave you taken care of until I got back, you know. Instead I left you in a hell of a mess."

I looked up at him. "It's over," I said. "And I think Alice Sanders just came into the room."

A woman had just entered through the door from the kitchen, carrying two bowls of soup. She was thirtyish, rounded and ruddy, her brown hair tied up under a scarf. She could have been any woman in England, except for the bruised pouches of skin beneath her eyes that betrayed sleeplessness. She set down the soup bowls at a table with barely a glance at her customers, then turned away. I thought I might recognize her figure as the one I'd seen leaving our terrace, but I couldn't be sure.

The woman walked past us, and Alex said softly, "Madam, I beg your pardon."

She stopped and turned, as everyone did when Alex used that particular quiet tone of voice. "I'll serve you in a moment," she said. "Or call the other girl."

"I believe it's you I'm here to see," Alex said, still leaning casually on the bar. "I've been sent here on a certain private matter by Mr. Martin Forsyth."

The woman's eyes widened, and I knew instantly she was truly Alice Sanders. "I have nothing to say to you."

Alex shook his head. "I'm not the police," he said, his voice so low no one could overhear. "I'm Mr. Forsyth's cousin, Alex Manders, and this is my wife. Mr. Forsyth has authorized me to act on his behalf."

Alice looked from Alex to me and back again, her features going hard. "Martin Forsyth's cousin is dead, or so I heard."

"It's a common misunderstanding," Alex said easily. "I'm not dead. Is there somewhere we can talk privately?"

Alice glanced at the other serving woman, then at the bartender behind the bar, and quickly brushed her palms over her apron. "Meet me out back," she said. "I don't have long."

She disappeared into the kitchen. Alex and I sipped our pints for a few more minutes—I was disappointed to let mine go, as it was bitter and delicious—and left by the front door before walking around the building to the back of the pub. The wind was blowing cold and angry now, sweeping mercilessly off the water, and Alice was huddled next to the kitchen door, her arms crossed over her ample chest, the scarf in her hair flattened to her head, her features set in a hard scowl.

"I said everything I have to say to that man," she said as we came in range. "I'm owed money, and that's all. If you're here to negotiate a lower price, I'll not listen."

Alex had put his hat back on, and he maneuvered closer to the wall to avoid the gusts that would blow it off again. "I'm not here to negotiate," he said in a flat tone he had not used inside. "I'm here to ask how you know it was your husband who died in those woods."

"It was him. He left that morning, and he wouldn't say where he was going, and then that girl died and they found a body. He never came home again. It was him."

"Not good enough, Mrs. Sanders. Not for a thousand pounds."

She hesitated. "He was mixed up with the Forsyths. That's all I know."

"How could he be mixed up with the Forsyths?" Alex asked. "He hadn't worked for them for years, and Martin Forsyth was at the Front."

"He told me," she snapped. "The Forsyths owed us. That horrible old woman dismissed him, and he had no references. When he came home from the war, there were no jobs, and no one would take him. He wrote Martin for money as a fellow soldier, but Martin said no. They could have given us something. We have a little boy."

"And how, exactly, was he mixed up with the family?" Alex asked again.

She paused. "He wouldn't tell me all of it. He was very down after Martin wrote that letter—it got bad. He drank too much, stayed out all night. I didn't want him around our son. Then one night he came home with a smile on his face, though he was still drunk. Said that he'd won, that the Forsyths would be the making of us yet."

"The making of you? What does that mean?"

"I guessed it meant money, but George was cagey about it. He said he had one task to do, and then we'd have more money than we'd ever thought possible."

"What was the task?" I asked.

Alice Sanders looked at me, taking in my decent clothes and my new hat and gloves, and looked away again. "He never said."

"But you know." I stepped closer to her.

"I told you, he never said."

I stepped closer again. A queer sort of anger was rising at the back of my throat at the thoughts that were crossing my mind. "You *know*," I said, the wind carrying my words away, over the ocean. "Someone paid him to kill Frances Forsyth, isn't that it? Someone offered him a lot of money for it. You knew it then, and you know now. You even condone it."

"I didn't know then," Alice shot back at me. "I only knew when she died. That was when I figured it out. You can look down your nose at me all you like, but at least I don't belong to a family that would pay someone to kill one of its own."

"No," I said, fighting anger. "You belong to a family that would do the killing for money."

"It was a mercy." Alice Sanders's voice was cold as ice. "She was mad anyway. What kind of life was she ever going to have? She couldn't marry, have children. She'd just end up in an asylum, like the rest of them do. What kind of life is that? My George would have done it quick and painless, and she'd never know a thing. A mercy, like putting a dog down, and we'd have money for our son."

"Except it didn't quite go as planned, did it?" Alex asked. The restrained anger in his eyes reflected my own. "He went to the woods to do the job, but something killed him instead. The dog didn't get put down."

"It's unnatural, that's what it is," said Alice. Her cheeks were flushed despite the cold wind. "That girl was not only mad, but she was some kind of witch. She summoned a beast to kill my husband. When I read about what had been done to the man they found—what kind of wounds he had—" She stopped, swallowed. "He was in pieces. Something ripped him open from head to toe. They never identified him, but I knew it was him. He got a telephone call early that morning, and then he left without a word, and he didn't come home. At first I didn't realize what had happened, but when I saw the article in the newspaper, I knew. The Forsyths killed my husband." She looked at my shocked, outraged expression, her eyes tired and hostile as the wind tried to tear the scarf from her hair. "That girl jumped. Maybe she felt guilty about George. I don't know, and I don't care. All I know is that George is gone, and the money never came. I can tell by the look of you that you don't have a child. If you did, you'd think differently of me."

"Enough," Alex said calmly. "We don't have more time to waste. Mrs. Sanders, we need to know exactly who hired your husband. Who contacted him and promised him the money? Who made the telephone call that morning?"

But she shook her head. "I don't know."

It was the truth. If Alice Sanders had known who to blackmail, she wouldn't have contacted Martin. She'd likely tried him because of

George's letter, and she thought he'd be the easiest touch now that he was home.

Alex must have known the hopelessness of it, but still he pressed her. "George gave you no clue?" he asked. "There's nothing you can remember?"

"There's nothing," she replied coldly. "It was you yourself, for all I know. Everyone in that family is the same to me. I have to go back inside now. What are you going to do about my money?"

"I will speak to the Forsyths about it," Alex told her. "I'm their representative in this matter. You'll be hearing from me very soon."

We made the miserable walk back to the inn in silence, clamping our hats down in the wind, hunching beneath our coats. Rain had begun, but our lack of an umbrella made no difference—any umbrella would have been turned into useless metal and cloth within minutes. There was no way we could talk easily in such weather, and in any case, neither of us wanted to discuss what we'd just heard. What Alice Sanders had told us was too upsetting to speak of.

We arrived cold and wet back at the inn, and found that we were the only patrons. The innkeeper had built up a hearth fire in the main room, and we took off our coats and hats and pulled up two chairs, soaking up the dry warmth. My hands were chilled through despite my gloves, as were my knees and my feet. We refused food, but the innkeeper brought us each a brandy, which he set on the small table between us before leaving us alone.

We sat contemplating the flames for a while as the wind howled in the windowpanes. I patted my hair, which was coming disastrously loose from its pins, then gave up hope and put my hands back in my lap.

"He could have done it," I said at last. "George Sanders could have come into the house and killed her, then been killed while he was escaping. Dottie heard a sound at the back of the house. It could have been him, entering or leaving."

"It's possible," Alex said. "His body wasn't found until hours later. There's no way to pinpoint exactly when he died."

"It could have been after Frances died, then," I said.

"Or we're both wrong, and she jumped," he replied.

"No," I said. I thought of the things rearranged in my room, the photographs, Fran walking to the door to the roof, the sketchbook in my bed. It had been terrifying at the time, but now I saw that it was desperate and sad. "She didn't jump."

Alex turned to me. "We have to face it, Jo. If she didn't jump, someone close pushed her from the roof. Her mother, her father, David Wilde. Someone she knew well enough, trusted well enough, to follow all the way to the roof without screaming for help."

"She may not have followed willingly," I said. "She could have been threatened, drugged, or knocked unconscious."

"It was all so bloody *fast*," Alex said. He leaned forward, his elbows on his knees, and put his head in his hands, scrubbing his hands through his hair. "What a mess," he said. He rubbed his hands over his eyes, and I saw that he was more tired than even I'd realized. "I'll find a way to solve this."

I looked at him for a long time. Even tired and ragged as he was, even after everything that had happened, it was a pleasure to contemplate Alex. He had removed his jacket, and I watched the curve of his back as it flickered in the firelight, the line of his shoulders, and once again I knew what I had first understood that day in 1914: I was horribly, irrevocably in love with him. This time, the thought did not bring the same pain.

I stood from my chair and, without regard to anyone who might come into the room, I sat in his lap. I hooked my legs over his long, strong ones and put my arms around his neck, leaning my shoulder in to him and letting my cheek drop against his collar.

His hand touched my back, but I felt his body tense beneath me. "Jo," he said, "do not tease me."

I raised my head and spoke into his ear, holding him tighter and turning my body to press more snugly against his. "Fine," I said. "I won't. Just tell me whether Hans Faber had any girlfriends."

He sighed in surrender. "No, you idiot," he replied, pulling pins from my tangled hair. "He lived like a monk."

"I know you," I said. "That sounds difficult."

"It was easy."

I paused at that as my heart skipped a beat. Then I gave him a succession of soft kisses along his jaw. "I think we should go and make proper use of our room," I told him, the taste of his skin on my lips. "That is, if you remember what to do?"

He turned my face to his and kissed me, slowly and thoroughly, until my blood was singing. I knew all of Alex's kisses, and this one was full of very serious intent.

We went upstairs. It turned out that neither of us had forgotten a thing. And for all the hours afterward, as the storm blew in from the sea, we pretended we were the only two people in the world.

CHAPTER THIRTY-EIGHT

We set out for Wych Elm House the next morning, over roads strewn with branches and ruts puddled with rain. The sky was sleek gray, the wind nasty and chill, and even in Alex's modern motor-car we could not get entirely warm, the winter cold creeping into our hands and feet.

We were silent during the drive. It was one of those long-married stretches of quiet during which there was no need for us to speak. Alex kept his gaze on the road, watching for the next obstacle through the gloom. I sat with the map unfolded and unread in my lap, my hair tucked under my cloche cap, my gloved hands idle as I watched the landscape out the window.

I was happy—of course I was happy—but I couldn't help the dread that settled on me the longer we drove. It was like the feeling I'd had at the engagement party when I'd noticed that all of the family was gone from the room. As we followed the winding road bringing us closer and closer to Wych Elm House, I couldn't shake the instinct that something was terribly awry. Alex seemed to feel the same way, and as we traveled, his expression grew more grim and he pressed the accelerator, pushing the car to go faster.

We arrived in Anningley around time for luncheon, but neither of us wanted to stop and eat. "Let's press on," I said.

"I'd like to make one stop," Alex replied.

He drove us to the little cottage that belonged to Petra Jennings. Anningley was strangely quiet, and we saw only a handful of people, as if everyone had decided to stay inside out of the cold. The effect was eerie, and only added to my alarm. Perhaps Alex had additional questions for Petra Jennings. Whatever his aim, I hoped he would do it quickly so we could continue up the road.

But he did not get to perform his plan at all. When we approached Miss Jennings's cottage, we found it shut and dark, the curtains drawn over the windows. Alex got out of the car and I watched him knock at the door, then make a quick circuit of the building, looking through the cracks between the curtains.

"She's gone," he said to me when he got back into the motorcar, bringing a breath of icy air with him. "The place is packed up. The clothes are gone from the kitchen, the iron and board, everything. It looks like she plans to be away for a while."

I stared at the dark cottage, my dread increasing. What had made Petra Jennings pack up over the course of a single night and leave her home? Where had she gone? Had something frightened her? Had she even left by her own choice? I glanced up her quiet street and saw a curtain twitch in one of the neighbors' windows.

"Please, Alex," I said. "Let's go."

He only nodded and started the motorcar again.

The road to Wych Elm House had lost the last of its autumn luster and turned from the final red-brown tints of fall to the defeated gray, drained of color, that signaled the waning half of November. The storm had blown through here, too, stripping the trees of their last leaves and exposing branches stark to the bleached sky. As I watched the landscape, my heart started a slow acceleration in my chest, a mix of horrid anticipation and fear. I half expected to see Frances Forsyth appear from a swirl of leaves, her massive dog following at her heels. These were her woods.

"You told me that first night," Alex said, reading my mind, "that you've seen the dog."

I blinked and saw the beast's horrid underside as it leaped over me, reeking of blood. "His name is Princer," I said. "He protects her."

He was quiet for a moment. "Martin spoke of it," he said. "That first night I was back, after I left you. Frances wrote to him about Princer, how he came through the door to protect her. He burned the letters."

"Why?" I asked.

"Because he is not sure how long he will live, and he didn't want anyone to find the letters in his belongings after he's gone. He felt that the things Frances told him in her madness were private."

So that was why he had burned them, then. I wondered if he would tell Cora. "Everyone believes Frances imagined Princer," I said, "that she conjured him to make herself feel safe, especially after her experience at school. But she summoned him when I was taking pictures in the woods. I saw—something. Him." I blinked and turned away from him, staring hard out the window. "It felt very real," I said. "Perhaps I'm as mad as Frances was. But I saw it. I *smelled* it."

Alex did not argue with me this time. "Why?" he asked. "Why did she call him that day? Was she trying to hurt you?"

I shook my head. "I thought so, but no. Princer—he was faster than me. He could have caught me. But he didn't."

"That's a mercy, then," he said, and I knew he was thinking of what Alice Sanders had said. *Something split him open from head to toe.* "If he protected Frances from George Sanders, Jo, perhaps he was protecting you as well."

"From what?"

He shook his head. "I wish I knew."

The family motorcar was not parked in front of the house, and when we came through the front door, we found it dim and quiet, echoing with the emptiness of an unused place. The air was chill, and neither of us removed our coats. I followed Alex down the hall, past one empty room after another. We did not encounter a servant or hear any sounds of people. There was no sign of Martin or Dottie anywhere downstairs. Like the village, the house echoed as if everyone had left.

I paused at the door to the library, then stepped inside. The air in here held a faint fug of cigarette smoke, as if Dottie and her cigarette holder had been here, but it had a stale feel to it. Dottie usually smoked one cigarette at a time. By the smell of the library, something had made her sit in here and smoke one after the other.

The desk was the same mess it had been when I'd left the day before, but lying on top of the pile was a letter, unfolded, the edges dented and crumpled as if it had been well handled. I picked it up.

Mother,

> *This letter is going to distress you, and I beg to apol-*
> *ogize for it, but please read it through and consider*
> *before you pass judgment on me.*
>
> *I have gone to Cora. I have taken the train, and I*
> *will be in London by the time you awake and receive*
> *this. We will also be married, because we plan to do it*
> *by the first arrangement when I get to the city.*
>
> *Mother, I have told Cora everything. I have told her*
> *of all that happened to me in the war—things I never*
> *told even you or Father—and of the addiction that has*
> *dogged me since I was first treated for my injury. It turns*
> *out, Mother, that she is the best sort of girl. The strongest*
> *sort. The kind who can help me, the kind who will help*

me. And, Mother, I need help. Without it, I'm going to leave Cora without a husband and you without a son. I thought I didn't care overmuch about this. But when I read Cora's letters, when I hear her tell me over the telephone that it isn't over yet, it turns out I do care.

She is taking me to her cousin, the doctor on Harley Street, who says he has new ideas for how to treat my pain. He is also an up-and-coming success and knows a great many of London's best surgeons. It's possible, Mother, that the surgeons in Switzerland after the war did a hurried and inexact job, and with testing and treatment a new surgery could remove the last of the shrapnel inside me and repair the damage over time. I could be well and whole. Cora and I have the money, and now we have the will. I have decided for her sake that I am going to do my damnedest to live to a hundred.

Please don't follow us. I am in the very best hands. I know we've cheated you of a grand wedding, but I think when your temper cools and your unassailable logic returns, you'll see this is for the best. Cora is my wife, her children will be your grandchildren, and if God and the doctors of London will it, I will be your son for a while longer.

This is all your doing, Mother. Thank you.

Martin

Alex gave a low whistle as he stood next to me, reading over my shoulder. "That's a shock," he said. "Aunt Dottie must be livid."

She would be, I knew. She would also be hurt, though it would come out as her usual brisk anger. "She followed him," I said. "That's why the house is so quiet, and that's why the motorcar is gone. She followed him to London."

"The house is too quiet," Alex said. "Where are the servants?"

"I dismissed them."

We turned. Robert Forsyth stood at the entrance to the library, watching us. He was dressed in an expensive suit of thick wool, as cleanly put together as ever, his hair combed back, a smirk on his face. He walked toward us, his hands in his pockets.

"Why?" Alex asked him.

"Because I don't want them here," Robert said. "Because I don't want anyone here. Once Martin left and my wife took off after him like a bloodhound, I saw my chance. I was always good at that."

Alex turned to him. My hands went cold. "Your chance at what, Uncle?" Alex asked.

Robert gave him a curious look. "My chance to get rid of both of you," he said, and pulled his hand from his pocket. I had time to see that he held a pistol before he pulled the trigger and shot Alex once in the chest, the sound deafening in the still air of the library, except for the echoing sounds of my screams as my husband fell.

CHAPTER THIRTY-NINE

A hand gripped the hair at the back of my head, knocking my hat off, jerking me backward so I almost overbalanced. "Shut up and stop screaming," Robert said in my ear.

I stared at the ceiling as he bent my head back, the sound choking in my throat. From the floor at my feet came a sound, a hideous liquid gurgle.

"Do you hear that?" Robert said to me. "No, don't look. That's the sound of the life bleeding out of my dear nephew, your husband. The fine fellow who has tried twice now to ruin everything I've done." His grip in my hair squeezed. "And you know all about it, don't you? What a sight he is now, my dear. We'll have to move before the blood soaking into the carpet gets on our shoes."

"Please," I begged.

"*Please,*" he mimicked. "I can't look at him anymore, but I'm not quite done with you yet. Come with me."

"A doctor," I begged him as he dragged me from the room, his hand still gripping my hair, his other holding the gun with his arm around my waist. "Just call a doctor—please—I won't tell—" There was a gasping sound from behind us as we left the library, softer now, and I felt the scream in my throat. *"Alex!"*

Robert threw me forcefully to the ground. I hit the floor of the corridor, my knee cracking, and screamed again. He swung one leather-clad foot and kicked me hard in the ribs, then stood over me, the pistol dangling at his side. His face was mottled red, his slicked-back hair mussed, his gaze angry as he stared down at me.

"You have no idea," he said, "what I've had to suffer."

Pain throbbed in my knee, but I pushed myself along the polished wood of the corridor, away from him. I had to think of something—had to do something. The telephone was in the library, where Alex was, but Robert would never let me use it. "Why?" I asked him, my voice raw, buying time. "Why did you take the sketches?"

"Why do you think?" Robert said. He took a casual step forward, following me as I tried to move away from him. "Money. You of all people should understand that. I am so very tired of living off my termagant wife. Of letting her control me." He took another step, and the pistol swung by his side. Behind him, I heard no more sound from the library, and I choked back a sob. "Franny, my sweet girl, liked to sketch. I found her book one day with the drawings of the military base. The navy was using it during the war. The drawings were very detailed, and it was all perfectly innocent. She was oblivious. I had some connections through friends of mine, and I made inquiries. It seemed my daughter's pictures might be worth an excellent sum. So I arranged to send them." He shook his head. "You see? It was so simple. I'd make my money, and no one would get hurt."

"You aided the enemy," I said.

He swung his foot and kicked me again, painfully, on the sternum. "There is no enemy except poverty," he growled. "No enemy but disappointment and lack of pride. Hasn't my wife taught you the value of money during all those months you spent as her lapdog?"

I tried to get up, gasping in pain, but he put his beefy hands on my shoulders and shoved me down. "I like you better down there," he said. "Listen to me. I'm not going to save your husband. He's a liar. He didn't spend the last three years in any prison camp. He didn't come back here in 1917 for a visit to his dear old aunt and uncle. I'm not stupid. He came here looking for me." I tried to move again, but he only stood more closely over me, aiming the gun down. "I sent off the sketches, and what happened? I heard that Alex was suddenly coming for a visit. I had my suspicions, but I couldn't be sure. There was no way he'd learn anything from me, of course, and Dottie knew nothing. The only one who could innocently let on to dear Alex that her daddy took her drawings was Franny."

"So you found George Sanders," I said.

"No. He found me. He wrote Martin first, begging for money. When Martin said no, he wrote to me. A private letter. He was desperate, he said. So I drove to Torbram." Robert smiled, his teeth glowing white in the dim light of the corridor. "I went at night—Dottie and the servants are used to my being out all night, and they never asked questions. I drove to Torbram, I found George Sanders, and I told him that if he was looking for money from the Forsyth family, I knew just how he could get it."

"You had to kill her?" I shouted at him. "You couldn't quiet her some other way, send her away?"

"We'd sent her away already, and she came back," Robert said. "Her mother would never agree to send her anywhere again. As for silencing her some other way, no one would ever believe the ramblings of a mad girl like Frances. No one except someone who knew her well and was willing to listen to her ravings. Like Alex."

"How could you possibly know he was coming because of the sketches?" I said.

"I tell you, I didn't. I merely ascertained George Sanders's interest and told him that if I needed him to act, I would telephone him. I told him to be ready in case I needed him, and he agreed."

My mind was racing. There was no one within screaming distance to hear me. If I could get my hands on a weapon, I could disable him and get to the telephone—get to Alex. Dottie had a pair of scissors, but they were too small to do any damage, and they were back in the library. I pushed my way down the corridor toward the staircase that led to the kitchen. If I could make it to the kitchen, I could possibly arm myself with a knife before he caught me.

"Alex asked questions," Robert said, following me. "I threatened Frances, told her to stay in her room and plead a stomachache. She complied, but she was always difficult to control. I knew she wouldn't stay afraid of me for very long, and when she talked to her beloved cousin Alex, she'd tell him. Still, it bought me some time. Then I overheard Alex asking a servant about the sketchbook, and I knew he'd been sent here to ferret me out. I also knew my sketches had been intercepted and I'd never get my money for them. I was out of time, and the punishment for treason is execution. So I made the telephone call."

I could see the door to the stairwell now. I'd have to get my feet under me quickly and make a dash for it, shut the door behind me. "Your own daughter," I said to him. "She loved you. Worshipped you."

"Oh, yes, I know," Robert said. "It's easy to sit in judgment when you're not her father. You don't know what it was like, to raise a child like Frances. To listen to her screaming, to hear her delusions. To lie awake at night wondering. To know that she was never going to be well, would never marry, would be a burden for the rest of my life. I don't think you *understand.*" He was breathing heavily now. "I couldn't do it myself. George was a stranger; he had no connection to the house or the woods. He was to do it quickly, without causing her pain, and then disappear again. No one would ever know. It would be assumed she was killed by a vagrant, perhaps, or had an accident. She'd be at rest and my secret would be safe."

I had the doorway in my sights, but I turned and looked up at him. "And what happened?"

Robert blinked, remembering, and for a moment his focus was so distracted that I thought I might be able to make a grab for the pistol. I kept very still.

"I don't know," he said. "I made sure to be out of the house, visiting friends, so no suspicion could fall on me. I walked—I used to walk then, but I hate the woods now, and I never do anymore. I approached the house from the back, expecting to see that the place was in turmoil. Instead, Frances came around the house from the front, running toward me. She was crying. She flung herself into my arms and told me that a man had attacked her in the woods, but Princer had saved her, had killed the man. It was awful, and she'd run and run, and she didn't know what to do."

"Oh, my God," I said softly.

"Can you imagine it?" Robert gave a small smile. "She flung herself at me and called me *Papa*. She was so shaken—she wanted me to save her, to fix things, as if she were a little girl. I held her tight and said everything would be all right, and she should come into the house with me."

I could feel tears on my face now, though my cheeks were numb with fear. "She trusted you," I said, my voice a croak.

"Of course she did. I was her father. I took her up to the roof and asked her to point out the direction in the woods where she'd encountered the strange man. I told her I wanted to see where it was without her having to lead me there. She stood on the edge and pointed, and I pushed her. Then I crept back down the stairs and out the doors of the morning room, and pretended I had just walked home through the trees."

"You're vile," I said. Then I kicked his knee as hard as I could, turned, got my feet under me, and made a dash down the corridor toward the staircase to the kitchen.

Robert shouted behind me. My knee was a knot of pain, and it barely held me, but I pushed it, expecting the pistol to go off, expecting to feel the bullet hit between my shoulder blades. Instead, he launched at me and landed on my back and I fell to the floor again.

I screamed, trying to pull myself from under him, but he held me fast in his grip, his thick, sweaty body on top of mine. Then I felt his focus shift, his weight move off me, and he scrambled for the pistol.

I looked up. Standing in the doorway to the staircase, the doorway I'd just tried to run for, was Dottie. She had had the same thought I had. In one hand, she held a kitchen knife. The look on her face as she stared at her husband was thick with hatred and fury, her lips drawn back, her cheekbones hot and red.

"You killed her!" she cried. "My daughter!"

Robert swung the pistol. I kicked his forearm and the shot went wild, lodging in the corridor wall. Robert wrenched himself from me, stood, and sent his heavy arm out in a long arc, the grip of the pistol connecting with Dottie's temple with a sickening sound. She barely had time to raise her hands before she crumpled to the floor.

I got my feet under me again, sobbing. I ran for the morning room door this time, thinking to get out to the terrace, to run. But again Robert caught me, and again he wrestled me to the floor. He pinned down my hands, pressed a knee hard into my lower back, sending arcs of pain up my spine and down my legs.

"Poor, unbalanced Alex," Robert panted in my ear when I went still, gasping with agony. "The war unbalanced him, I think. I came home to find he'd killed his aunt and was violating his lovely wife, so I shot him. A veteran losing his reason is all too common a story these days, I'm afraid." He bent closer. "I always did like you, Mrs. Manders."

I screamed. I couldn't move, couldn't get away from him, and no one would come—but I screamed, screamed for the death of Frances, for Dottie, for Alex. I screamed in terror and an echoing, horrible despair. I would die here, on the floor halfway through the doorway of the morning room of Wych Elm House, staring at the flowered wallpaper.

Then, on the terrace outside, I saw Frances.

She was watching us. Her expression was impassive and almost sad, her blue eyes beneath the slashes of her brows intelligent. She wore the familiar gray dress and pearls. She was not looking at me. She was looking at her father.

I felt Robert go still on my back. It was cold, I realized, my nose and lips chilled. Outside, I heard the wind.

"Frances," I said.

"No," Robert said. "It can't be."

There was a crash behind us, and I turned, my cheek pressed against the floor. Alex had come out of the library and up the corridor. He was on his knees, his face ashen, his eyes on me. Blood soaked the front of his shirt and the waist of his trousers, soaked his sleeves and the palms of his hands.

"Jo," he said. He leaned forward, swung his arm, and something skidded along the floor toward me, sliding across the carpet. A knife. The knife Dottie had been holding.

"It can't be," Robert said again, still frozen in surprise, and I wrenched my wrist from his grip, grabbed the knife, and jammed it into his thigh.

He roared and lost his balance. I squirmed beneath him, heaved him from my back, and crawled across the floor toward Alex, who had crumpled to the ground. Behind me, I heard the soft click of the French doors unlatching, the quiet creak of the doors opening. A chill wind blew into the room. Carried on it, over the sound of Robert's screams of pain, came a high, shrill whistle.

Alex was ghastly pale, but I could see his chest rise and fall. He was breathing. His eyes were half open, watching me come toward him. When I was close enough, I grasped his icy hand and glanced behind me.

Robert had staggered to his feet. I had hit him on the outside of his thigh, and the blade was still lodged there, the handle of the knife protruding grotesquely, slicked with blood. He could barely stand, but still he pawed at the knife handle, trying to pull the weapon from his body, his hands too slippery to gain purchase. Blood spurted down his leg and onto the floor, soaking his expensive wool trousers. Past him, through the French doors, his daughter still stood at the edge of the terrace. Dead leaves were kicking up around the hem of her skirt, blowing upward, swirling around her in a blur. Behind her, a massive shape emerged from the edge of the trees, hulking and muscled, its long fur wet with filth. It trotted up behind Frances, twice her size, and I glimpsed a pair of hideous eyes before she raised a hand and I looked away.

Perhaps he is protecting you, I heard Alex say.

I crawled to Alex and cradled his head. "Don't look," I whispered, my breath pluming in the icy air. Behind me, there was a smell of blood, the heavy scrabble of something on the terrace tiles, the sound of breath that I knew was hot and rancid, and very soon Robert stopped screaming.

I curled up against Alex in the silence that followed, pressing my body heat to his. He had begun to shiver.

"I have to go to the telephone," I told him, not wanting to let him go. My own hands were shaking, and my stomach churned. I tried not to think of the dragging sounds I'd heard on the terrace. Robert was gone.

Alex found the strength to grip my waist with one bloodied hand. "I already did," he said. "They're coming."

I stroked his temple and pressed my cheek to his. Alex, who solved problems even after he'd been shot. Alex, who had taken every risk in order to come home to me. Alex, who had done everything only because he loved me.

"Don't leave me," I said to him.

He gripped me harder, winding his hand in the fabric of my blouse as if holding on, and then he closed his eyes.

CHAPTER FORTY

In the end, my husband refused to die.

It was a close thing, so close that at my lowest moment I sagged against the wall of the hospital bathroom, where I had just dry-heaved the contents of my empty stomach, and sobbed without restraint. My stomach and chest were dark with bruises from where Robert had kicked me, and my knee was twisted in pain. I had worn the same dress for days. I stared at the bleach-scented tiles through burning eyes and told myself I simply couldn't survive his death again. But afterward, I got up and went back to his bedside and held his hand through another night.

The world became disjointed, as if I were watching it from afar through broken glass. I no longer knew the timeline of my life. Men spoke to me—men I didn't know, one after the other in a long line. Men in suits and uniforms and policemen's caps, men with mustaches and beards. There was a doctor, telling me that the bullet had gone high, angled upward into Alex's shoulder, and had missed his vital organs, but he had bled so much the situation was still grave. *You must be strong, Mrs. Manders, for his sake.* I thought, *I am already strong. I*

was strong yesterday, and the day before that. But I did not know whether
I spoke aloud.

Moments—or hours, or days—later, there were faces of policemen,
asking me questions. *What, exactly, did you see? Where is Robert Forsyth?
Did he strike Mrs. Forsyth before or after he fired the gun at your husband?
Are you sure? Are you certain the knife pierced his leg? What exactly did he
say? Let us go through it again, Mrs. Manders. Are you quite certain?* I
answered them with a voice that seemed to come from someone else's
throat, the words forced and difficult, as if they had been swallowed
inside me and would not come up again. The thought of Frances moved
through my scattered mind, and I remembered that it was very important I not speak of her, that I not tell what her father had done to her,
though I could not quite remember why.

I had memories of moving like a ghost through the corridors of
the hospital, finding my way from the men's ward to the women's
ward. Of Dottie lying in a hospital bed, bandages swathed around her
head, her eyes sunk into dark pools of skin. *Concussion,* they had said.
I sat by her bedside when I could tear myself from Alex's, though I did
not hold her hand. The first time she opened her eyes, she stared at me
blearily without speaking, and we sat in silence, looking at each other
like strangers.

"Where is he?" she asked me finally, her voice a rasp.

I searched my memory. "Gone," I replied.

"Escaped?"

No. Wherever Robert Forsyth was, he had not escaped. "It was
Princer," I said.

Her face relaxed, and she looked away. "Good girl," she said, and
I knew she was not speaking of me.

I did not tell the police about Princer. I told them that Robert
Forsyth had shot my husband, pistol-whipped his wife, and assaulted
me. When I had stuck a knife in his leg, he had run through the doors
to the terrace and vanished into the woods. I saw the rest of it every

time I closed my eyes—the leaves, the thing coming from the woods, Frances raising one pale hand, the sound of the thing coming through the French doors behind me—but I didn't speak it aloud. I sat by Alex's bedside and watched the waxy pallor of his face and tried not to remember any of it at all.

I sat across from David Wilde, who was coaxing me to eat a bowl of soup. He was dressed in a suit of navy wool, with a gray necktie that set off the strands of silver in his hair. He held a cup of tea in his good hand. He, too, spoke to me, and as the soup revived me, I began to comprehend his meaning.

"Newspapers?" I said.

"I have fended them off," Mr. Wilde replied. "No reporter will be bothering either you or Mrs. Forsyth. They're still running stories, of course—what happened at Wych Elm House is prominent news. I'm hoping that with no statement from the family, the interest will eventually die down." He set his teacup in its saucer and pushed my untouched cup across the table toward me with unmistakable meaning. "I have also seen to the servants' wages and arranged to have the house cleaned. It should not be distressing for you and Mrs. Forsyth to return to Wych Elm House."

With the tea, the fog cleared from my brain and it started to work again. "What about Martin?" I asked him.

"He is under a doctor's care in London," Mr. Wilde replied. "I have spoken to both him and Mrs. Forsyth—Mrs. Cora Forsyth, that is. He is not well enough to travel here. He goes under surgery in two days. I have kept the reporters away from them as well."

I thought you might have murdered Frances, I nearly said aloud. What a fool I had been. "Mr. Wilde, I am so sorry," I said.

He thought I was apologizing for the trouble he'd gone to. "It's my job, Mrs. Manders," he said in his calm, competent voice. "The family is going through an exceptionally difficult time." He spoke more gently. "How is he?"

"They tell me he'll live."

"Then you must get back to him."

I returned to the hospital room to find Alex awake in his bed. A nurse had propped a pillow behind him and given him a sip of water. I stood in the doorway for a moment, feeling a wild beat of disappointment because a nurse had been here instead of me. And then I was at his bedside, taking his hand in my shaking one and most certainly not crying.

"Come here," he said after a moment, and I leaned onto the bed, my arms around his neck, as he put his arm around me and let me sob quietly.

"Sorry about that," he said, his voice choking a little. "He took me by surprise. Stupid of me."

"I hate you," I said into his neck.

"Yes, I know." He rubbed my shoulder and my upper arm through my cardigan, his grip weak but determined. "How long have I been out?"

"Four days."

Alex swore softly.

"I'm sorry. Does this hurt?" I asked, trying not to grip him quite so tightly.

"Stay where you are, if you please. I have you exactly where I want you."

"It's been horrible. I am a blotchy, overwrought dishrag," I said, turning my head on the pillow next to him and running my fingers over his four days' beard. It looked handsome on him, of course.

"You are gorgeous," Alex replied, his thumb weakly rubbing the back of my neck beneath my hair. "Now tell me everything that's going on."

"You just woke up."

"Yes, and the police have probably been informed already. They'll be by for a chat anytime. So tell me everything, Jo."

I did, surprised at how much I could recall through the haze of my panic. He stayed awake long enough to say it was all a bloody mess, and he would make everything right, and that he'd be out of bed in no time; it was just one bullet. Then he drifted off to sleep again. I disentangled myself from him and went to the women's ward to see Dottie.

"Alex is awake," I told her.

Her head was still bandaged, but she was sitting up, her hands folded on top of the coverlet. Her gaze was alert, but there was something different about it, something not quite Dottie. There was no sign of her usual sharpness. Instead, she looked at me from her dark-ringed eyes with an expression tinged with confusion.

"I have just spoken with David Wilde," she said.

I nodded. He had visited her after his conversation with me, then. "He told you about Martin?"

"Yes." Her hands twitched on the covers. "Manders," she said, though the word was spoken softly, with none of its old sting. "I have been thinking."

I sat and waited. Her thinking seemed to have slowed.

"I have told David everything," Dottie said, ignoring my surprise at her use of his Christian name. "Everything that I heard . . . Robert say to you. Though I did not repeat what he said about Alex."

She meant the part in which Robert had spoken of Alex coming home to investigate treason. "Dottie, there is an explanation—"

"Stop," she said weakly. "I don't wish to know more than I already heard. Alex's doings for the past three years, whatever they were, are his business. It's David I want to talk about. He has apologized to me."

"Apologized?"

"There is a woman living in the village," Dottie said. "A former servant of the family. Over the time we've been gone, David and this woman have formed a personal attachment." A flash of her old sharpness crossed her glance. "I hope I do not shock you, Manders."

"No," I replied. "Though I wonder about Mrs. Wilde."

She pursed her lips just a little. "David's troubles are of his own making and are not for me to repeat. I'm too tired to even attempt it. However, this woman—"

"Petra Jennings," I supplied.

"Yes." She showed no surprise that I knew the name. "She came to David and told her Robert had threatened her."

"Threatened?"

"Yes. When you and Alex left me that morning, you apparently went to this woman's home and spoke to her. Robert knew of it somehow. He thought that Alex had told her his secret—what he did to Frances and why. He believed she was going to be used against him as a witness to the day Frances died and to the sketches Frances had made in her book. He told her that if she agreed to testify, he would kill her."

I sat back in my chair and stared at her, my tired mind putting it together. "That's why she left her home. That's why she was gone."

"David thought it best to get her to safety, so he accompanied her to her home and helped her pack her things. Then he moved her to a hotel in a nearby town under an assumed name. When he had finished, he fully intended to warn me."

"But he was too late," I said. Alex and I must have come to Petra's house only shortly after they had left.

"Yes." Dottie raised a hand and lightly touched her bandage, then dropped it again. "He wished to apologize to me, not only for his failure but for the embarrassment of his situation. I had no idea about the woman, of course. I would have taken him to task if I'd known."

I thought about it. What if Alex and I had been earlier arriving at Petra's house? What if we'd met her and David Wilde, if we'd been warned? Everything could have been different.

"What I've been thinking," Dottie said, "is that you must have known about Robert. That's why you went to that woman's house. You and Alex must have known, and you did not tell me."

"No," I said. "We didn't know. But we believed it wasn't suicide, that someone had killed her. We thought Petra Jennings might hold the key."

Dottie leaned back against her pillows. "You believed she'd been murdered because of Frances's ghost," she said, her voice tinged with confusion again. "Is that the way of it?"

"Yes. I wanted to tell you, that day in the library, but it already sounded mad. And I had no proof."

Dottie waved a hand at me, and I noticed how the bones were almost visible beneath her pale skin. "I am not interested in more apologies. My daughter, whatever her reasons, chose you to appear to. She chose you to tell."

She also chose me to protect, I thought but did not say. "Yes."

"What I want . . . The *only* thing I want, Manders, is to know whether she is still in Wych Elm House."

I would have to go back to the house to see. The thought of going back there froze me to my seat. "I can't."

"I think you can," Dottie said.

I felt sweat break out on my back, my palms. "And if she's there?"

"Then find out why." Dottie's voice was drifting into exhaustion now. "Find out what keeps her from being at peace."

"Dottie—"

"Please."

She had never said that to me before. She had lost her daughter, her husband, and possibly her son, while I had Alex back. I understood how loss like that can rob you. It made no matter that I never wanted to see Wych Elm House again.

"All right, Dottie. I'll go," I said. I stood, but at the door I turned to her again. "May I ask you one question?"

Her eyes had drifted closed, but she waved a hand in agreement.

"Why did you come back?" I asked. "You left the house to follow Martin to London. Why did you turn around?"

She opened her eyes and gave me that confused look again, and seemed to have to search for the words. "He asked me," she said finally, the words lacking her usual force. "In the letter he left. Martin asked me not to follow him. I disregarded that at first—I was furious. But as

I drove I realized that following him would only make things worse. Martin is grown now, and married, and he did not need his mother chasing him around the country."

"So you turned around and came home," I said, "and overheard everything."

"I was on the front step when I heard the gunshot," she said. "I thought we were being robbed. I told the driver to go for the police, and then I walked around to the kitchen door to get a knife." She closed her eyes again. "The servants were gone. I could hear Robert's voice. You were screaming, screaming." She paused. "I never wish to hear that sound again. But I got a knife and crept up the stairs to see if I could stop it."

I thought of her, small and narrow, walking to the kitchen door in her oxfords to fend off whoever was robbing her precious home. How utterly indomitable she was. "Dottie," I said, "we should have used you to win the war."

But she had already drifted off, and she didn't hear me.

CHAPTER FORTY-ONE

It was nearly ten o'clock the next morning when I stood on the front steps of Wych Elm House, getting up my courage to go in. I felt outside myself, like a strange skin had been pulled over the old Jo, the events of the past few days changing me in ways I did not yet recognize or begin to understand. All I knew was that I wore the same dress as the old Jo, the same shoes, the same hat and gloves. There was an ache behind my eyes that I knew came from exhaustion, my bruises hurt, and my legs felt weak, but still I made myself open the door and go through it.

The house smelled of lemon polish and wood underlaid with a harsh, clean smell that I didn't recognize. Here was the familiar umbrella stand, the worn rug. I stood for a moment, as if Frances would show herself to me as I stood there by the front door, waiting for her to appear. When nothing happened, I walked into the corridor.

I passed rooms left as I remembered them. The large parlor, where I had first met Martin, where I had first seen Alex the night of the party. The small parlor, where I had seen Frances sitting in a chair, her head turned to look at me. She was not there now; nor was there any trace of her. I felt as if I were touring a house I had not seen in years, or perhaps only touring it in the depths of my memory, an old woman thinking back to a place I had been.

In the library, I stopped in the doorway, jolted back to the present. Dottie's desk was tidy, her papers stacked, the telephone in its cradle, her ashtray clean and set perfectly on the front corner. My typewriter under its cover sat at the little table by the window, my chair pulled up beneath it. The shelves of untouched books, the small sofa—all was just as it was supposed to be, yet it had the quality of a museum piece, of strangers putting together a room as they guessed it should look.

I glanced down and noticed that the carpet was different. It had been changed—the old one must have been too soaked with Alex's blood to be saved. I tried to picture a team of servants in here, rearranging the furniture and rolling up the bloodied carpet, but my mind's eye failed me. Alex had been shot here, had staggered to the desk and used the telephone. Someone had dutifully wiped his blood from the receiver.

I backed out of the library and continued down the corridor. My temples were throbbing. Here, on this clean and polished section of floor, was the place where I had fallen, where Robert had kicked me. The skin of my ribs and stomach was still an ugly purple and yellow mix. Here was the place I had lain screaming. I made myself blink and look away.

I passed the doorway to the back stairs, where Dottie had crumpled to the floor, and walked into the morning room. This room, too, was clean, everything put away by strangers. The carpet was new—again, Alex's blood must have ruined the original. Especially in the spot where he had lain, holding on to me, his head in my lap as I waited and waited for the ambulance to come.

I made a choked sound, as if it were all happening again. *It's over,* I tried to remind myself. *It's over. Alex is alive. I just left him at the hospital.* He had woken again that morning, and though he was in pain, we'd sat and talked softly until he'd fallen asleep again. It would take time, but my husband would recover. He had not died, not the first time and not the second. I took a breath and inhaled the scent of cleaner again.

"Mrs. Manders?"

I jumped. It was Mrs. Bennett, the housekeeper, standing in the doorway, watching me. Her expression was sympathetic and wary.

"I'm sorry," I said. "I didn't see you there."

She glanced around the room. "Mr. Wilde had everything cleaned," she said politely. "There was a team of servants. I supervised putting the rooms back together myself. I hope it's acceptable."

"Yes," I stammered. "Yes, of course."

"How are Mr. Manders and Mrs. Forsyth? Is there any news?"

"They are both recovering," I replied. "Mrs. Forsyth was out of bed this morning, and her bandages come off this afternoon."

"That's very good to hear. We're all concerned about her in the servants' quarters. We are anxious for Mrs. Forsyth to come home."

"I'll let her know you asked." I did not tell her I suspected that Dottie would not come back here. There was nothing for her here.

Mrs. Bennett said something else, but I didn't hear her. My gaze had caught on a glassed-in cabinet on the wall, displaying some of the house's ubiquitous figurines and objects of art. In the case was a figure of Salome, holding John the Baptist's head in her lap. The figure that Frances had put on my bedside table the day she'd rearranged my bedroom. I had never replaced it, but had kept it in my room.

"Mrs. Bennett," I said, interrupting whatever she was saying, "how did that figure get into that case?"

She paused, puzzled. "Which figure, Mrs. Manders?"

"The figure of Salome."

Her gaze followed mine, and she frowned. "That figure has always been there," she replied.

"Has my room been cleaned?"

She blinked, and I realized I'd spoken almost sharply. "We have changed the sheets as usual, Mrs. Manders, but—"

"Thank you." I left the morning room—I did not care ever to see it again—and strode to the main staircase, which I climbed briskly, heading for my bedroom.

It was tidy, my clothes placed neatly in the wardrobe. The bed, where I'd sat in my peacock dress talking to Alex, where he'd taken me hurriedly a few days later, where I'd had so many strange dreams and nightmares, was made up like a stranger's. The figurine was gone from the bedside table. I hurried to the table and opened its only drawer, looking for the sketchbook Frances had left under my pillow, which had the photographs folded inside. The drawer was empty. The sketchbook and the photographs were gone.

I pulled open the wardrobe and found the camera tucked inside, on the lowest shelf. I pulled it out and set it on the floor. It had been placed in its leather case; I could not remember putting it away that day after I'd seen Princer in the woods; nor did I know who had put it away for me. I opened the latches and pulled the camera out, expecting to find the inside of the case soaked with water. *There's water running out of it and everything,* Cora had said to me as she'd sat on the floor outside the bathroom door. But there was no water running from the camera now, no water inside the case. I unlatched the camera itself and swung it open, revealing the spools inside, but all of it was dry, unused. There was no film in it.

"Frances?" I said into the still air. There was no answer.

It was all being erased, I thought in a panic as I climbed the stairs to the upper floor. Everything that had happened in this place—it was all being erased as if it had never been. The servants had cleaned; it was their job. But no servant had cleaned the inside of my camera, or put back the figurine Frances had moved. I reached the top of the stairs and went directly into Frances's room.

It was the same as before. The bed with its pretty canopy, the window seat, the patterned rug on the floor—the bedroom of a fifteen-year-old girl, disused because she was away at school perhaps, or was spending a few weeks with friends. I made a beeline for the bookcases, crouching in front of them, reading the spines of the books in the bright, cold, midmorning sunlight that came through the windows. Well-used children's books, books of Christmas stories, *Girl's Own Annual*—all of these were here. But there was no sketchbook, and next to the *World Atlas for Girls* there was no packet of photographs. I looked in the wardrobe, filled with Frances's short lifetime of dresses, and under the bed, but they were not there.

I sat in the rocking chair, staring out the window at the stark branches of the trees. The sketchbook was gone. Robert was gone. Perhaps I truly was as mad as Mother; perhaps I'd wake up one morning, expecting the viscount to come and take me to Budapest or New York. But I found I no longer cared. My mother had loved me the best she could, as much as she could manage. Madness had never stopped that. I understood her better now. I understood what it was like to live in a haze of confusion and fear, and the courage it took to get out of bed every day to face a world that was baffling and sometimes terrifying. I had seen the sketchbook, had awoken with it in my bed. I had touched its pages. I had seen the shadow in the photograph. I had seen Frances in the parlor that day, and watched her pass her bedroom door, and I had seen her in the woods, behind her father's shoulder, warning me—though I had not listened. I had smelled the coppery stench of Princer as he'd leaped over me, as he'd come through the French doors behind me into the morning room.

Perversely, the thought comforted me.

I thought of a face at the window, begging to come in. I thought of a door, and I wondered whether an exceptional fifteen-year-old girl could go through it, back and forth again.

I would tell Dottie that Frances was gone. If it was a lie, she would never know.

Eventually I rose, letting the chair rock on its own behind me, and went back downstairs to pack my things.

CHAPTER FORTY-TWO

Three weeks, later, Robert Forsyth's body washed up on an outcrop of rocks on the shore some seven miles from Wych Elm House. He was identified almost immediately, not only from the scraps of clothes the body was wearing that bore his monogram, but from the fact that his was the most high-profile disappearance in the area in thirty years. Everyone, from the police to the villagers, assumed that Robert Forsyth was dead, but no one knew what exactly had happened.

The body was not a surprise, but it did not solve the mystery. It was in such a degraded condition that the newspapers could not describe it outright, and no cause of death could be precisely determined. The corpse's neck was broken, its limbs torn, though the coroner could not say whether these injuries had happened before or after death. At Dottie's request, the postmortem was done quickly, and then the body was cremated and given to her for disposal. I never knew what she did with the ashes; she certainly did not bury them in the family plot in the Anningley graveyard. I sometimes suspected she dumped them in a trash can, or perhaps down a toilet, though of course she would never tell.

The newspapers reported the finding, of course. The public could not get enough of the tragic story of Wych Elm House's mad patriarch, who had grown so debauched through his wayward ways that he had finally snapped and tried to kill his wife, his nephew, and his niece-in-law. There was no suspicion in the papers about Frances's death; she remained a suicide. Only Dottie, Alex, David Wilde, and I knew the truth, and we did not care to share it with the police or the public. There was no point now that Robert was dead, and to claim he had killed his daughter would bring attention dangerously close to the matter of the sketches and the attempted treason. I assumed Colonel Mabry, wherever he was, approved of our silence.

As I'd thought, Dottie did not go back to Wych Elm House. When she was released from the hospital, a bare five days after the tragedy, she had servants bring her a packed bag, and she went directly to London. There, she installed herself in a hotel and helped Cora and her parents nurse Martin through the two surgeries that they all hoped would repair him and bring him back to life. The surgeries were a success, but Martin's recovery was slow, and her weeks in London stretched to months. Eventually, through the offices of David Wilde, she dismissed the servants and closed the house.

Alex and I did not go back, either. I'd packed all of our belongings that day I visited and had them transported to a hotel room I took a few blocks from the hospital, where Alex was still under care. He was there for nearly three weeks, much longer than Dottie, and I made the trip several times a day between my room and the hospital. The nurses doted on him, of course—he was obviously a ward favorite—and through his own natural strength he recovered quickly, though the wound had been serious.

The day they discharged him, I walked him the few blocks to our hotel and finally had my husband to myself again. I fed him strong tea and roast beef ordered from the kitchen downstairs, then helped him bathe, wash his hair, and shave, both of us in the steamy bathroom for nearly an hour. When that was finished, we did other things. I was worried that it would aggravate his injury, but Alex assured me it was, in fact, the best possible medical therapy, and so I really had no choice at all but to comply.

When he was well enough to travel, we journeyed to London. Christmas had passed with the two of us lazy and cozy in our hotel room, and it was nearly New Year's, the trees lined with frost and the wind icy and damp. Alex drove the motorcar and I sat in the passenger seat as usual, the map in my lap. We stopped frequently for hot tea to warm our blood. We felt rather bohemian, like gypsies living a traveling life, and we did not discuss the fact that we had no permanent home and no certain plans. We talked of politics, the situation on the Continent, and the plays we wanted to see in London. After three years apart, we had an inexhaustible stream of conversation.

Only once did Alex talk to me of what he'd seen that day as he lay on the floor of the morning room in Wych Elm House, looking past my shoulder as I crawled toward him. It was near dawn one morning just before we left for London, and I rolled over in bed to find him propped up on his pillows, wide-awake and thinking.

"What is it?" I asked him.

"I can almost remember it," Alex said. His arm was angled behind his head, the angry scar of the bullet wound visible on his left shoulder above his heart. He had lost weight in the hospital, and in the dawn light his cheeks were slightly hollowed. "It comes to the edges of my memory, and then it goes away again."

I pushed myself up on one elbow; I knew immediately what he was talking about. "What did you see?"

He thought about it, and then he shook his head. "It's so unclear, like I saw it from the corner of my eye. And for some reason it gets mixed up with the war."

"The war?"

"What I saw there." His gaze took on a distant look that was hard and cold. "I thought I'd seen everything that could happen to a man, the things he could suffer. But that—that *thing* came through the doors . . ." He rubbed his forehead, as if the memory gave him pain. "It makes my head hurt," he said finally. "I never really believed you. But you were right about all of it."

"Stop," I said to him. "It doesn't matter. It's done."

It was. But I still felt its shadow even as we sat in the motorcar on the way to London, in the lines on my husband's face, in the way I woke sometimes with cold sweat on my body, my neck aching. The bruises on my body faded, but I remembered how Robert had kicked me, how he'd pushed me that day in the woods, with a rawness that stayed vivid. When we arrived in London, I saw in Dottie an echo of the same rawness in the shadows under her eyes, in the new softness that had entered her manner.

The one who was doing better than all of us, it turned out, was Martin. The surgeries had improved his health dramatically, and though he was still weak in his recovery, he glowed with new life that I hadn't seen in him before. He was shocked and grieving for his father, but in the helpless way of the chronically ill, his own health was topmost in his mind. Marriage agreed with him, as did London. By tacit understanding, none of us told him the truth of Frances's death. That was a conversation, we all believed, for a later time. As for Frances's ghost and Princer, I would never tell him about them at all.

We met with Dottie, Martin, and Cora for supper at the Savoy, where Dottie was staying. Dottie was fully recovered from her injury, sprightly and as tireless as before, wearing her usual severe suit, but I was shocked to see that she'd cut her hair—instead of the usual tightly wound hairstyle, she now wore it cropped and marcelled within an inch of its life, each curl tidy and placed exactly against her head.

"Dottie," I teased her as we took our seats around the table. "You told me that bobbed hair was fast."

"On you it would be," she replied with the conviction of a woman who has talked herself into being right at all costs. "On me it's merely practical."

"It looks very modern on you, Mother," Martin said. He was dressed in his best suit and tie, his hair slicked to a shine. Though he was pale, he had finally managed to gain weight. "I told you that when you got it done."

"Don't be silly, Martin," she admonished him, though she dressed down her son in much milder tones than she'd ever used with me. "Tying my hair back while I was recovering caused pain. I couldn't leave it down, so I simply had to cut it."

"Am I fast?" Cora asked from her seat beside Martin. She was wearing a dress of forest green silk that shimmered in the light. She, too, looked different—happier, perhaps, more confident. "I didn't know, and now that I do, I can't say that I mind." She cast Martin a look from under her lashes. "Darling, you'll have to remind me which fork to use! You know I'll simply pick the wrong one."

"Of course," Martin said, pleased. He turned to Alex. "You look as good as new, Cousin."

"So do you," Alex replied. He'd put on his best winter suit, of rich wool in deep blue-gray that matched his eyes. He'd visited the barbershop when we'd arrived in town, and his hair was as short as he'd worn it before the war, his jaw clean-shaven. Even with the faint lines of weariness at the corners of his eyes, I had to force myself not to stare at him.

There was something about Martin's and Cora's happiness, despite all that had happened, that buoyed the mood. Dottie's strained, faraway look relaxed somewhat, and though she was much changed, I recognized the lightness of her mood as the same one she'd had when we'd traveled Europe. There was something about being in London, about sitting in the Savoy with a pleased pair of newlyweds, ordering champagne, that let us all forget for a little while, that kept the shadows and the memories at bay.

"I suppose this is as good a time as any," Dottie said as dessert was served. "I'm selling the house."

There was a moment of silence around the table. Cora's eyes went as wide as Clara Bow's.

"That's a bit of a shock," Martin said at last.

"Nonsense." Dottie tried for her old tone, though she missed the mark. She patted her pockets for her cigarette holder, then changed her mind, perhaps not wishing to disturb the other diners at the Savoy. "Everyone is gone now, and I'd be there alone. I'll take a flat in London. The house will be packed and empty by Easter, and I'll travel the Continent again." She darted a glance at me. "Perhaps I'll find myself a new companion."

"What about the art?" I asked her.

"Don't worry, Manders. I'll find buyers. And I may acquire more when I travel again. I have an excellent eye."

"I don't know, Mother." Martin sounded doubtful.

"Oh, no, darling," Cora said. "It will be an adventure for her."

Surprisingly, Dottie looked at me. "What do you think?"

There was just the faintest quaver in her voice. Alex was quiet next to me, but I already knew he agreed with what I was about to say. "I think it sounds wonderful," I told her softly.

"You were always a maudlin girl," Dottie said, looking away.

"Yes, Dottie," I said, and we turned back to the others and did not speak of it again.

CHAPTER FORTY-THREE

Two months later — February 1922
Crete

The sun was still rising when I woke. It was early, seven o'clock perhaps, and the light was clear and yellow coming through the thin curtains. Somewhere in the near distance a rooster crowed, loudly greeting the morning.

Alex was already gone from the bed. He usually was; he had always been an early riser, restless and full of thoughts as the dawn came, and now he was even more so. I slid out of bed, washing quickly, twisting my hair back, and pulling on a robe before I left the bedroom to go find him.

He was on the front terrace, sitting on a wicker chair. The morning was chilled, and steam rose from the hot cup of coffee at his elbow. As I approached the doorway I could see he was sitting with one ankle crossed over the other knee, utterly still, his drink untouched, his head bent as he looked at something he held that I couldn't see. He wore a shirt that he'd hastily pulled over his head and a loose pair of trousers, and his feet were bare.

My own bare feet flinched on the cold floorboards, but still I came outside and sat in the chair next to him, pulling my wrap closed over my chest.

"Good morning," I said to him.

Alex looked at me, and for a moment his extraordinary blue eyes with their black-ringed irises flickered over me without recognition before focusing, as they always did, on my face. He was startled, I realized; he'd been engrossed in something.

"Mrs. Manders," he said. "The mail has arrived."

I glanced at the small pile of letters in his lap. "It's early."

"It comes when it comes," he said.

I gave him the ghost of a smile at that, and he returned it. This was how we'd learned to handle everything during the month we'd been in this place—buses, meals, guides, the post. *It comes when it comes.* It was a different sort of life, and not a bad one, though I found myself longing for England, something I hadn't screwed up the courage to mention to him yet.

I turned and looked out past the terrace. The cottage we'd rented was on the shore, and though it was rocky, and February here was cool, the sight and sound of the waves was an unceasing hypnotism—a cure, it turned out, for anything that ailed you. I had grown stronger in four weeks, and so had he. Far off in the water, fishing boats bobbed, moving busily about, and seagulls spun in the air overhead.

"Do you want to know what the mail has brought?" I heard Alex say.

I looked down at my feet and curled my toes. My body was alive with perfect satisfaction, every blood vessel and nerve. I felt no need to fidget or twitch, only to occasionally stretch and flex myself. There was no denying I was pleased as a cat, and the man sitting next to me was quite certainly the cause of it. I thought perhaps that his own pose, barely dressed in the cold and so still that he was hardly breathing, mirrored my own feeling. Here, in private and far from the world, we had no need to hide how in love we obviously were. The mail would change all of that. I could tell from the sound of his voice.

"I suppose," I replied.

"I have received a letter from a man named Chalmers," Alex said. "He works for the Home Office. He says he has a post for me that I am perfectly qualified for, but as it is of a confidential nature, he'll have to speak to me about it in person."

My stomach dropped. I had not thought, in this peaceful place, that a few words from his lips could inspire such sudden fear. "Another assignment?" I made myself ask.

"No," he replied. "At home, in England. I made it clear in my last letter that my terms are not negotiable."

I swallowed and made myself look out at the water again. "I see."

"He encloses another letter, this one from an agent in London. There is a house that can be had for very good terms, in a desirable location. Due to my recommendation from Chalmers, he's willing to hold it until I can make a decision."

"So that's it, then," I said, as the wind blew off the water and lifted my hair, bringing its salty smell. "We have to go back."

"You knew it would happen sooner or later, Jo," he said gently. "It's time."

"I know. It's just—I don't know what's next."

"I know."

I turned and looked at him. He was watching me; I didn't know how long he'd been watching me as I'd stared at the water. "Do you want to do it?" I asked him.

His gaze did not leave me, and his expression did not flinch. "I want to talk to him, yes," he said. "I want to see what he has to say."

"You said you want to be your own man."

"And I have been. But perhaps I can serve my country and be my own man at the same time."

I bit my lip. "And what about me?"

"What do you want to do?"

I opened my mouth and closed it again. He waited patiently, knowing I would speak. "I enjoyed the photography," I said, wondering why the words felt slightly embarrassing. "I found it freeing. I'd like to take it up again."

Not a single second of derision crossed his expression. "You'd like to be a photographer?"

"No," I replied, surprised at how easy the answer came. "I want to learn it and get a studio, and then I want to teach it."

Alex blinked, and his expression relaxed in that way that meant he was looking at something he liked. "You would be very good at that."

I did not mention that every thought, every plan I had for the future, was suffused with the hope for a child as if colored by a lens; he already knew. "I suppose London would be the best place to try it," I said. "But that isn't the only letter you received. There's something else, isn't there?"

His jaw hardened, and the bitter exhaustion I'd seen in him came back into his eyes. *No,* I thought, feeling a beat of panic. *Whatever it is, no, no, no.*

"There is another offer," Alex said.

"Don't say it," I said. "Don't."

But he picked up the letter, a single sheet of unfolded paper. "Colonel Mabry has written me."

"And what does he want?"

"Moscow," Alex said, looking at the black ink of the letter, his gaze going cold and far away. "The terms are very generous."

"You've already explained to him that you can't speak Russian," I said.

"Hans Faber, the German businessman, doesn't need to speak fluent Russian," Alex replied. "He only needs enough to get by on his business travels, which Mabry says I can easily learn."

"No," I said.

"Six weeks only, though of course there will be training beforehand and debriefing afterward."

"No."

"It's been difficult to get true information about Lenin's government. And there are rumors he has health problems. It's important that we know the truth."

"No," I said again.

"I could do a great deal of good, Mabry says."

"You've already done a great deal of good. And you can do more of it in London."

He was quiet for a moment, and then he put the letter down on the small table next to him, placing his untouched cup of coffee over it so it would not blow away. "You're right," he said. "Whatever I do, it won't be for Mabry, and it won't be in the field." He stood and held out his hand. I took it, and when I stood, he dropped my hand and stood back. "Let's get dressed and go for a walk."

I followed him inside. When we emerged again a few minutes later, we crossed the terrace without looking at the letter on the table. We descended the steps and started over the rocky beach toward the water.

When I stumbled, he took my hand again, and he did not let me go this time. Behind us, the wind tugged at the letter on the table. And I didn't think of it again, as we rounded the curve of the shore, with the wind above us, the beach beneath our feet, and nothing else to do but to see where the world might take us.

LOST AMONG *the* LIVING

SIMONE
ST. JAMES

QUESTIONS FOR DISCUSSION

1. What do you think draws Frances's ghost to Jo? In what ways do you feel that Jo and Frances are similar characters? How do you think they are different?

2. Do you believe in ghosts (or do you just enjoy reading about them)? Have you ever felt the presence of a ghost? How did it make you feel?

3. Jo's feelings for her mother are a mix of love and resentment. Do you think she treated her mother properly, or was there more she could have done?

4. Jo had limited choices in her life when she met Alex. Do you think those limits were true to the time period? How are women's choices different today?

5. How did you feel about the scenes in which Jo and Alex met and married? Did you find them romantic, or did you think they were making a hasty mistake?

6. Why do you think Alex made the choices he did? Do you think they were right or wrong? If wrong, what do you think he should have done? Are people's priorities different in a time of war?

7. Did you think Alex acted suspiciously when he came home? Was Jo right to be wary of him? What would you have done in Jo's place in that situation?

8. Did you have sympathy for the Forsyth family? Why or why not? Did your sympathies change over the course of the novel?

9. Martin Forsyth marries because it is his duty to his family. Was this believable for the times? Would this happen now?

10. Were Jo's visions of the mist and the leaves real, or did she imagine them?

11. What do you see happening to Jo and Alex after the end of the book? Do you think they will be happy together? Did you find the ending satisfying?

Don't miss Simone St. James's novel of suspense. . . .

Four lonely teenage girls become friends at a boarding school in Vermont in the 1950s. . . . In the present day, a journalist covering the restoration of the school uncovers a crime—and a haunting—that has long been buried and has disturbing echoes of the tragedy in her own life.

THE BROKEN GIRLS

Now available from Berkley!

PROLOGUE

The sun vanished below the horizon as the girl crested the rise of Old Barrons Road. Night, and she still had three miles to go.

The air here went blue at dusk, purplish and cold, a light that blurred details as if looking through smoke. The girl cast a glance back at the road where it climbed the rise behind her. She squinted, with the breeze tousling her hair and creeping through the thin fabric of her collar, but no one that she could see was following.

Still: *Faster,* she thought.

She hurried down the slope, her thick schoolgirl's shoes pelting stones onto the broken road, her long legs moving like a foal's as she kept her balance. She'd outgrown the gray wool skirt she wore—it hung above her knees now—but there was nothing to be done about it. She carried her uniform skirt in the suitcase that banged against her legs, and she'd be putting it back on soon enough.

If I'm lucky.

Stop it, stupid. Stupid.

325

Faster.

Her palms were sweaty against the suitcase handle. She'd nearly dropped the case as she'd wrestled it off the bus in haste, perspiration stinging her back and armpits as she glanced up at the bus's black windows.

Everything all right? the driver had asked, something about the panic in a teenage girl's face penetrating his disinterest.

Yes, yes— She'd given him a ghastly smile and a wave and turned away, the case banging her knees, as if she were bustling off down a busy city street and not making slow progress across a cracked stretch of pavement known only as the North Road. The shadows had grown long, and she'd glanced back as the door closed and again as the bus drew away.

No one else had gotten off the bus. The scrape of her shoes and the far-off call of a crow were the only sounds. She was alone.

No one had followed.

Not yet.

She reached the bottom of the slope of Old Barrons Road, panting in her haste. She made herself keep her gaze forward. To look back would be to tempt it. If she only looked forward, it would stay away.

The cold wind blew up again, freezing her sweat to ice. She bent, pushed her body faster. If she cut through the trees, she'd travel an exact diagonal that would land her in the sports field, where at least she had a chance she'd meet someone on the way to her dorm. A shorter route than this one, which circled around the woods to the front gates of Idlewild Hall. But that meant leaving the road, walking through the trees in the dark. She could lose direction. She couldn't decide.

Her heart gave a quick stutter behind her rib cage, then returned to its pounding. Exertion always did this to her, as did fear. The toxic mix of both made her light-headed for a minute, unable to think. Her body still wasn't quite right. Though she was fifteen, her breasts were small, and she'd only started bleeding last year. The doctor had warned her there would be a delay, perfectly normal, a biological aftereffect of malnutrition. *You're young and you'll recover,* he'd said, *but it's hell on the body.* The phrase had echoed with her for a while, sifting past the jumble of her thoughts. *Hell on the body.* It was darkly funny, even. When her distant relatives had peered at her afterward and asked what the doctor had said, she'd found herself replying: *He said it's hell on the body.* At the bemused looks that followed, she'd tried to say something comforting: *At least I still have all my teeth.* They'd looked away then, these Americans who didn't understand what an achievement it was to keep all your teeth. She'd been quiet after that.

Closer now to the front gates of Idlewild Hall. Her memories worked in unruly ways; she'd forget the names of half of the classmates she lived with, but she could remember the illustration on the frontispiece of the old copy of *Blackie's Girls' Annual* she'd found on a shelf in the dorm: a girl in a 1920s low-waisted dress, walking a romping dog over a hillside, shading her eyes with her hand as the wind blew her hair. She had stared at that illustration so many times she'd had dreams about it, and she could recall every line of it, even now. Part of her fascination had come from its innocence, the clean milkiness of the girl in the drawing, who could walk her dog without thinking about doctors or teeth or sores or scabs or any of the other things she had buried in her brain, things that bobbed up to the surface before vanishing into the darkness again.

She heard no sound behind her, but just like that, she knew. Even with the wind in her ears and the sound of her own feet, there was a murmur of something, a whisper she must have been attuned to, because when she turned her head this time, her neck creaking in protest, she saw the figure. Cresting the rise she'd just come over herself, it started the descent down the road toward her.

No. I was the only one to get off the bus. There was no one else.

But she'd known, hadn't she? She had. It was why she was already in a near run, her knuckles and her chin going numb with cold. Now she pushed into a jog, her grip nearly slipping on the suitcase handle as the case banged against her leg. She blinked hard in the descending darkness, trying to make out shapes, landmarks. How far away was she? Could she make it?

She glanced back again. Through the fog of darkness, she could see a long black skirt, the narrow waist and shoulders, the gauzy sway of a black veil over the figure's face moving in the wind. Boots that flashed beneath the skirt's hem. The details were visible now because the figure was closer—only moving at a walk, but already somehow closing in, closer every time she looked. The face behind the veil wasn't visible, but the girl knew she was being watched, the unseen gaze fixed on her.

Panicked, she made an abrupt change of direction, leaving the road and plunging into the trees. There was no path, and she made her way slowly through thick tangles of brush, the dead stalks of weeds stinging her legs through her stockings. In seconds the view of the road behind her disappeared, and she guessed at her direction, hoping she was heading in a straight line toward the sports field. The terrain slowed her down, and sweat trickled between her shoulder blades, soaking into the cheap cotton of her blouse, which stuck to her skin. The suitcase was clumsy and heavy, and soon she dropped it in order to move more quickly through the woods. There was no sound but the harsh rasp of her own breathing.

Her ankle twisted, sending sharp pain up her leg, but still she ran. Her hair came out of its pins, and branches scraped her palms as she pushed them from her face, but still she ran. There was no sound from behind her. And then there was.

Mary Hand, Mary Hand, dead and buried under land . . .

Faster, faster. Don't let her catch you.

She'll say she wants to be your friend . . .

Ahead, the trees were thinning, the pearly light of the half-moon illuminating the clearing of the sports field.

Do not let her in again!

The girl's lungs burned, and a sob burst from her throat. She wasn't ready. She *wasn't*. Despite everything that had happened—or perhaps because of it. Her blood still pumped; her broken body still ran for its life. And in a moment of pure, dark clarity, she understood that all of it was for nothing.

She'd always known the monsters were real.

And they were here.

The girl looked into the darkness and screamed.

CHAPTER ONE

BARRONS, VERMONT — NOVEMBER 2014

The shrill of the cell phone jerked Fiona awake in the driver's seat.
She lurched forward, bracing her palms on the wheel, staring
into the blackness of the windshield.

She blinked, focused. Had she fallen asleep? She'd parked on the
gravel shoulder of Old Barrons Road, she remembered, so she could sit
in the unbroken silence and think. She must have drifted off.

The phone rang again. She swiped quickly at her eyes and glanced
at it, sitting on the passenger seat where she'd tossed it. The display
glowed in the darkness. Jamie's name and the time: three o'clock in
the morning. It was the day Deb would have turned forty if she'd still
been alive.

Fiona picked up the phone and answered it. "Jamie," she said.

His voice was a low rumble, half-asleep and accusing, on the other
end of the line. "I woke up and you were gone."

"I couldn't sleep."

"So you left? For God's sake, Fee. Where are you?"

She opened her door and swung her legs out into the chilly air. He'd be angry, but there was nothing she could do about that. "I'm on Old Barrons Road. I'm parked on the shoulder, at the bottom of the hill."

Jamie was quiet for a second, and she knew he was calculating the date. Deb's birthday. "Fee."

"I was going to just go home. I was." She got out of the car and stood, her cramped legs protesting, the cold air slapping her awake and tousling her hair. She walked to the edge of the road and looked up and down, shoving her free hand into the pocket of her windproof jacket. Back the way she'd come, she could see the road sign indicating thirty miles to Burlington and the washed-out lights of the twenty-four-hour gas station at the top of the hill. Past the hill, out of her sight, she knew there was the intersection with the North Road, with its jumble of fast-food restaurants, yet more gas stations, and a couple of hopeful big-box stores. In the other direction, ahead of the car's hood, there was only darkness, as if Old Barrons Road dropped off the face of the earth.

"You didn't have to go home," Jamie was saying.

"I know," Fiona replied. "But I was restless, and I didn't want to wake you up. So I left, and I started driving, but then I started thinking."

He sighed. She could picture him leaning back on the pillows, wearing an old T-shirt and boxer shorts, the sleek muscles of his forearm flexing as he scrubbed a hand over his eyes. He was due on shift at six thirty; she really had been trying not to wake him. "Thinking what?"

"I started wondering how much traffic there is on Old Barrons Road in the middle of the night. You know, if someone parked their car here and left it, how long would it be before someone drove by and noticed? The cops always said it wasn't possible that Christopher could have left his car here for so long, unseen. But they never really tested that, did they?"

And there it was: the ugly thing, the demon, coming to the surface, spoken aloud. The idea had been niggling at her for days as Deb's birthday approached. She'd tried to be quiet about it, but tonight, as she'd lain sleepless, her thoughts couldn't be contained.

"This isn't healthy," Jamie said. "You know it isn't."

"I know," Fiona said. "I know we've been over this. I know what my therapist says. I know it's been twenty years." She tried to keep the pleading from her voice, but it came out anyway. "Just listen to me, okay?"

"Okay," he replied. "Shoot."

She swallowed. "I came here and I parked by the side of the road. I sat here for"—she checked her watch—"thirty minutes. Thirty *minutes*, Jamie. Not a single car passed by. Not one." By her calculations, she'd been here for forty-five minutes, but she'd been asleep for fifteen, so she didn't count those. "This is the same time of night that Deb's body was dumped. He could have parked here and done it. The field at Idlewild Hall is only ten minutes through the trees. He would have had plenty of time."

On the other end of the line, she heard Jamie breathe. They'd been together for a year now—a fact that still surprised her sometimes—and he knew better than to say the usual empty words. *It doesn't matter. This won't bring her back. He's already in prison. It was twenty years ago. You need to move on.* Instead, he said, "Old Barrons Road wasn't the same in 1994. The old drive-in was still open on the east side of the road. It didn't do much business by the nineties, but kids used to party there, especially around Halloween."

Fiona bit back the protest she could feel rising in her throat. Jamie was right. She swiveled and looked into the darkness across the road, where the old drive-in used to be, now an abandoned lot. The big screen had been taken down long ago, the greasy popcorn stand razed, and now there was only a dirt clearing overgrown with weeds behind the trees. She remembered begging her parents to take her and Deb to the drive-in as a kid, thinking with a kid's logic that it would be an exciting experience, a sensory wonder. She'd soon learned it was a fool's quest. Her intellectual parents would no sooner take them to the drive-in to see *Beverly Hills Cop II* than they would take a walk on the moon. Deb, three years older and wiser, had just shaken her head and shrugged at Fiona's disappointment. *What did you expect?* "There wouldn't have been many kids at the drive-in on a Thursday in November," she said.

"But there *were* kids there," Jamie said with the easy logic of someone whose life hadn't been ripped apart. "None of them remembered seeing Christopher's car. This was all covered in the investigation."

Fiona felt a pulse of exhaustion behind her eyes, countered by a spurt of jagged energy that wouldn't let her stay still. She turned and paced away from the hill and the lights of the gas station, toward the darkness past the hood of her car at the other end of Old Barrons Road. "Of course you think they covered everything," she said to Jamie, her voice coming out sharper than she had intended. "You're a cop. You have to believe it. In your world, a girl gets murdered, and Vermont's greatest minds come together to solve the case and put the bad guys away." Her boots scuffed the gravel on the side of the road, and the wind pierced through the legs of her jeans. She pulled up the collar of her coat as a cold shudder moved through her, an icy draft blasting through the layers of her clothes.

Jamie wasn't rising to her bait, which was one of the things that drove her crazy about him. "Fiona, I *know* they covered everything because I've been through the file. More than once. As have you, against all the rules and regulations of my job. It's all there in the murder file. In black and white."

"She wasn't your sister," Fiona said.

He was quiet for a second, acknowledging that. "Christopher was charged," he said. "He was tried and convicted of Deb's murder. He's spent the past twenty years in maximum-security prison. And, Fee, you're still out there on Old Barrons Road at three o'clock in the morning."

The farther she walked, the darker it got. It was colder here, a strange pocket of air that made her hunch further into her coat as her nose grew numb. "I need to know how he did it," she said. Her sister, age twenty, had been strangled and dumped in the middle of the former sports field on the abandoned grounds of Idlewild Hall, lying on one side, her knees drawn up, her eyes open. Her shirt and bra had been ripped open, the fabric and elastic torn straight through. She'd last been seen in her college dorm thirty miles away. Her boyfriend, Tim Christopher, had spent twenty years in prison for the crime. He'd claimed he was innocent, and he still did.

Fiona had been seventeen. She didn't much like to think about how the murder had torn her family apart, how it had affected her life. It was easier to stand on the side of the road and obsess over how Christopher had dumped her sister's body, something that had never been fully understood, since no footprints had been found in the field or the woods, no tire tracks on the side of the road.

Jamie was right. Damn him and his cop brain, which her journalist brain was constantly at odds with. This was a detail that was rubbing her raw, keeping her wound bleeding, long after everyone else had tied their bandages and hobbled away. She should grab a crutch—alcohol or drugs were the convenient ones—and start hobbling with the rest of them. Still, she shivered and stared into the trees, thinking, *How the hell did he carry her through there without leaving footprints?*

The phone was still to her ear. She could hear Jamie breathing, waiting. Always waiting for her. Waiting for her to get over Deb's death; waiting for her to change her mind and move in with him; waiting for her to become a great journalist like her father. She wondered if he would ever get tired of it. She decided not to ask.

She heard the scuff of a footstep behind her, and froze.

"Fiona?" Jamie asked, as though he'd heard it through the phone.

"Ssshh," she said, the sound coming instinctively from her lips. She stopped still and cocked her head. She was in almost complete darkness now. Idlewild Hall, the former girls' boarding school, had been closed and abandoned since before Deb died, the gates locked, the grounds overgrown. There were no lights here at the end of the road, at the gates of the old school. Nothing but the wind in the trees.

She stiffly turned on her heel. It had been distinct, a footstep against the gravel. If it was some creep coming from the woods, she had no weapon to defend herself. She'd have to scream through the phone at Jamie and hope for the best.

She stared into the dark silence behind her, watched the last dying leaves shimmer on the inky trees.

"What the fuck?" Jamie barked. He never swore unless he was alarmed.

"Ssshh," she said to him again. "It's no one. It's nothing. I thought I heard something, that's all."

"Do I have to tell you," he said, "to get off of a dark, abandoned road in the middle of the night?"

"Have you ever thought that there's something creepy about Old Barrons Road?" she asked. "I mean, have you ever been *out* here? It's sort of uncanny. It's like there's something—"

"I can't take much more of this," Jamie said. "Get back in your car and drive home, or I'm coming to get you."

"I'll go, I'll go." Her hands were tingling, even the hand that was frozen to her phone, and she still had a jittery blast of adrenaline blowing down her spine. *That was a footstep. A real one.* The hill was hidden through the trees from here, and she suddenly longed for the comforting sight of the fluorescent gas station lights. She took a step, then realized something. She stopped and turned around again, heading quickly for the gates of Idlewild Hall.

"I hope that sound is you walking toward your car," Jamie said darkly.

"There was a sign," Fiona said. "I saw it. It's posted on the gates. It wasn't there before." She got close enough to read the lettering in the dark: ANOTHER PROJECT BY MACMILLAN CONSTRUCTION, LTD. "Jamie, why is there a sign saying that Idlewild Hall is under construction?"

"Because it is," he replied. "As of next week. The property was sold two years ago, and the new owner is taking it over. It's going to be restored, from what I hear."

"Restored?" Fiona blinked at the sign, trying to take it in. "Restoring it into what?"

"Into a new school," he replied. "They're fixing it up and making it a boarding school again."

"They're *what*?"

"I thought you knew. I thought everybody knew."

Fiona took a step back, still staring at the sign. *Restored.* Girls were going to be playing in the field where Deb's body had lain. The construction company would build new buildings, tear down old ones, add a parking lot, maybe widen the road. All of this landscape that had been here for twenty years, the landscape she knew so well—the landscape of Deb's death—would be gone.

"Damn it," she said to Jamie as she turned and walked back toward her car. "I'll call you tomorrow. I'm going home."

Simone St. James is the *New York Times* bestselling and award-winning author of *The Sun Down Motel*, *The Broken Girls*, *Lost Among the Living*, and *The Haunting of Maddy Clare*. She wrote her first ghost story, about a haunted library, when she was in high school, and spent twenty years behind the scenes in the television business before leaving to write full-time.

CONNECT ONLINE

SimoneStJames.com

 SimoneStJames

 Simone_StJames